"*Luck has no part in this.*"

I nearly dropped the phone. It was the booming voice again—but now that I was a little more awake, I recognized it. It was Frank's voice: the same slight lisp from a broken tooth, the same timbre, only pushed down to the bottom of his range—but somehow I knew it was no longer Frank speaking.

"*He speaks to you to say farewell. I speak to you to warn you, for I may have damned you with my words.*" The phone felt unnaturally warm, warmer than my hands could make it. For a second I smelled a trace of something like dust and dry stone, there and gone so fast it left only the memory of recognition.

Impossible. Even I couldn't catch a scent over the tenuous connection a phone provided. But the hairs on the back of my neck tingled, and my breath quickened, as it did when I got the scent before a hunt.

The speaker took a deep, ragged breath. "*But even if I have, I own no shame, for you are needed and by one greater than I.*"

"Frank?" I said.

"*Hound,*" said the voice, and ice ran down my back. Frank had never known I was called that. "*Hound, watch for a collar. The hunt comes . . .*"

Nothing more. I held on to the phone long after the dial tone of a broken connection crooned in my ear.

"Frank, you son of a bitch," I said at last. "Couldn't you have stayed dead?"

By Margaret Ronald

The Evie Scelan Novels

SPIRAL HUNT

SPIRAL HUNT

An Evie Scelan Novel

MARGARET
RONALD

An Imprint of HarperCollinsPublishers

This is a work of fiction. Names, characters, places, and incidents are drawn from the author's imagination or are used fictitiously and are not to be construed as real. Any resemblance to actual events, locales, organizations, or persons, living or dead, is entirely coincidental.

EOS
An Imprint of HarperCollins*Publishers*
10 East 53rd Street
New York, New York 10022-5299

Copyright © 2009 by Margaret Ronald
Cover art by Don Sipley
ISBN 978-0-06-166241-6
www.eosbooks.com

First Eos paperback printing: February 2009
First Harper special printing: September 2008

HarperCollins® and Eos® are registered trademarks of HarperCollins Publishers.

Printed in the U.S.A.

10 9 8 7 6 5 4 3 2 1

For Josh, Em, and Al—my three better halves, and never mind the math.

SPIRAL HUNT

One

No one ever calls in the middle of the night if they have good news. You'd think I'd remember that and not answer the phone after, say, midnight. But I'm as trained as any of Pavlov's dogs, and so when the phone shrilled I picked it up before coming fully awake. "This is Scelan," I mumbled into the receiver.

"Evie?" That woke me up. Since high school, only close friends have called me Evie. The man on the other end of the phone cleared his throat. "This is— Okay, you remember Castle Island? I kept branches in my car. Green ones, still living. Organic matter. Right?"

"I don't know what you're—" I stopped, memories of an ill-spent summer in South Boston flooding back around me like smoke from a bonfire. "Jesus. *Frank?*"

"Don't say it! Christ, I forgot how stupid you could be about some things."

Definitely Frank. Jerk. "Thanks very much. What the hell happened to you, Frank? I thought you were—" *Not dead*, I thought; *but as good as, when it came to this town.*

He didn't even hear the question. "I haven't— I'm pretty sure this line is okay, but I can't say the same for yours, and I know they'll be watching; they didn't expect me to get away."

"Frank. Slow down." I reached for the light, flailed a moment, then sat up. My legs had gotten tangled up in a big knot of sheets. "Why are you calling me?" I asked.

"I've got good reason—" The phone line squealed as a booming voice interrupted him, laughing and shouting guttural words that definitely weren't English. I held the phone away from my ear until Frank's voice returned. "Shut up! Look, Evie, I know we didn't part on the best of terms—"

"You called me a stupid bitch and said I deserved whatever *they* had for me. And then you disappeared."

"Yeah, well, I know what I did wrong last time. I'm not staying around here—it's gone too far for that, and I can't . . ." He paused, and the booming voice muttered again, incomprehensibly. "Shut up! I'm getting out. Really getting out this time."

"Yeah. Sure." When half of your business contacts are addicts, it gives you a certain perspective on anyone who says he's quit. Frank had quit before, sure, but he'd been a lot younger and less steeped in the undercurrent of Boston. And I'd helped to bring that crashing down, naive as I was. "Look, Frank, if you're calling me in hopes of a quick screw for old time's sake, forget it. I can't help you get out of the city other than the mundane ways, and you know those are watched."

"I know. Danu's tits, I know." He fell silent, and memory dredged forth an image so strong I could see what he must be doing: rubbing one hand over his face as if to clear the slate of his emotions. Of course, he'd be older now, but the gesture was one I unwillingly knew well. "Look, Evie, I know you probably hate me."

"I don't hate you, Frank." It was more complicated than that, and everything had happened so long ago that it didn't matter now. Which made me wonder why I still mattered to *him*. "I just didn't expect to hear from you again."

He hesitated. "Yeah. Well. I don't need help or anything, but I had to let you know that I was going. I can make it out this time."

"Don't boast about it. Just get out." I tugged the sheets back into some semblance of order, then sighed, remembering bonfires and the smell of crushed greenery. "Good luck."

"Luck has no part in this."

I nearly dropped the phone. It was the booming voice again—but now that I was a little more awake, I recognized it. It was Frank's voice: the same slight lisp from a broken tooth, the same timbre, only pushed down to the bottom of his range—but somehow I knew it was no longer Frank speaking.

"He speaks to you to say farewell. I speak to you to warn you, for I may have damned you with my words." The phone felt unnaturally warm, warmer than my hands could make it. For a second I smelled a trace of something like dust and dry stone, there and gone so fast it left only the memory of recognition.

Impossible. Even I couldn't catch a scent over the tenuous connection a phone provided. But the hairs on the back of my neck tingled, and my breath quickened, as it did when I got the scent before a hunt.

The speaker took a deep, ragged breath. *"But even if I have, I own no shame, for you are needed and by one greater than I."*

"Frank?" I said.

"Hound," said the voice, and ice ran down my back. Frank had never known I was called that. *"Hound, watch for a collar. The hunt comes . . ."*

Nothing more. I held on to the phone long after the dial tone of a broken connection crooned in my ear.

"Frank, you son of a bitch," I said at last. "Couldn't you have stayed dead?"

Two

One of my clients called just as I was on my way out the door the next morning: the little old lady who'd asked me to find her aunt's old recipe book. It had been in a junk store in Jamaica Plain, at the bottom of three cases of similar books, most of which were meant for the Dumpster. I'd taken on the job thinking it could be some quick work to go toward my rent, and forgotten the first rule of bargaining: don't argue with a nice little old lady.

"Yes, I understand your point of view," I said as I unlocked my bike, cell phone jammed between chin and shoulder. "But the fact remains that you did sign the contract for expert retrieval and recovery systems—"

A spate of squawking on the other end managed to convey that I charged too much, was a heartless monster for taking advantage of a senior citizen, and must have had some kickback deal with the junk-store owner in order to find her book so quickly. I rubbed at my temples, thinking that I should have taken my time finding the damn thing after all. "Ma'am, I'm sorry, but I'll have to call you back. I have another client on the line."

It wasn't quite a lie, I told myself as I dialed Mercury Courier; it just left out several major facts, the first being that my business relationship with Mercury was completely unrelated to my other work. "Hi, Tania? This is Genevieve. Where do you need me to go?"

I could hear Tania rustling through the mountain of papers on her desk. I'd only seen it once, but the image had burned itself into my mind. "Genevieve? Honey, you're not on shift just yet."

"I always work the Tuesday morning—"

"Schedule changes. The new system has you for the eleven-to-eight shift today."

"Is this the same new system that wanted me to run a package out to Worcester?"

"There's still a few bugs to work out, honey. Call me at eleven and I'll send you out."

I clicked the phone shut and stuffed it away. So much for getting work done early. On the other hand, that meant I had some time to work for my other job . . . or at least to see what the hell had been up with Frank last night.

There wasn't any address listing for him, which was small surprise. Of the other F. McDermots in the phone book, though, one had an address in Southie that I recognized from way back. I got my courier bag, in case Tania called with yet another schedule change, and headed out.

Rush hour was well under way, with the coffee-propelled masses of commuters already filling the streets. I slid out into traffic, darting between two SUVs and a truck to make it into the far lane. Cars honked, but mostly out of jealousy.

I wasn't the only one zipping through the lanes this morning. The bright weather had brought other cyclists out, and there'd be more as June wore on, until the hot spells descended and commuters could no longer ride to work without arriving soaked in sweat. Today, though, the air was crisp and cool. Perfect hunting weather.

I paused at a light near an orange-fenced yard of cement monoliths: the remnants of the Central Artery highway, now demolished as the Big Dig brought the highways underground. Two high school kids and a woman walking a pair of enthusiastic Labradors stopped at the light as well, next to an old professor-looking guy in a tweed jacket that'd seen better days. One of the Labs lurched toward me, tail whipping back and forth, and the woman hauled on its leash to keep from falling over. The man next to her chuckled, seemingly content to just enjoy the sunlight. He didn't even bother to cross as the light changed, just stood there in the sun, waving what looked like a wide-mouthed pipe made of dull metal.

I'd gotten about twenty yards down the road before I realized he'd been holding a silver sieve.

I yanked the bike into a U-turn, bumping up onto the sidewalk and veering around a stroller full of kids. The man didn't notice me as I hurtled back to his corner, so intent was he on the sharp-edged morning shadows.

The bike stopped at the curb. I didn't; I leaped off, dragged it by its crossbar over the curb, and snatched the sieve from the man's hand. "Did you catch any?" I demanded.

He made a startled, squeaking noise as I took the sieve, like a baby deprived of a toy. "Wha?"

I leaned in close, until the brim of my helmet tapped his forehead. "Did you catch any?" I repeated, waving the sieve under his nose.

A few of the people at the crosswalk gave us baffled looks. He returned them shamefacedly, sinking his hands in his pockets. "No," he whined as the light changed and the tide of pedestrians flowed past us again.

"Good." I smashed the sieve against the handlebars of my bike, tearing the fine mesh. He cried out, as if I'd hit him with it. I glanced up at him, and he fell silent. "This is no good," I said, jamming the broken sieve into a nearby trash bin for emphasis. "Hell, even if it were, this is no way to go about it."

"I needed it," said the shadowcatcher sullenly. "I needed a locus."

"Yeah, well, did you ever happen to think that maybe those people need their shadows too? Maybe more than you need your goddamn locus?" I sniffed the air around him on the off chance that he was lying. There was always a chance that he'd succeeded and some poor bastard had walked away missing part of his shadow, unknowingly fated to go nuts for a while, or be unable to see in color for a few weeks.

The shadowcatcher shoved his hands further into his pockets, hunching over so that his chin disappeared into the folds of his collar. He wasn't that old, I realized; not more than forty. Which meant that he must have fallen very fast.

If it'd been anything else, I'd have tried to send him to detox. But detox is no good when people don't believe what you're addicted to exists.

Still, I couldn't just walk away from him. "Christ. Here." I pulled a scrap of paper from my pocket and scrawled three names on it. "The Buddhist place is downtown. The Carmelites are in Roxbury; even if they can't let you stay in the nunnery they'll have some place for you. Society of St. John is across the river; that's best if you really think you'll relapse. Being across water helps." None of them could cleanse him, not unless he outright asked, but the bindings around each place would keep off the worst of it. There were a few other places that might actively try to wean him off the stuff, but of the people that ran them I only trusted Sarah, and the ambient magic at her shop would be no help to someone still in denial.

"Fuck you," the shadowcatcher said, but he took the paper.

"Get some help. Shadowcatching, man, that's the bottom of the goddamn ladder." I wrangled my bike back into a reasonable position. "This is going to kill you."

The shadowcatcher grinned. He was missing two front teeth, and one had been replaced with wood—not rowan, of course. Probably something he'd been told was mistletoe. "I'm not sure I care anymore."

As I rode off, a faint reek of overturned trash followed me. I didn't turn back, because I knew I'd see him scraping through the refuse, searching for his sieve.

* * *

Aside from when work called me there, I hadn't been back to Southie in years. It had changed, and it was hard to say whether that was for the better. *Different*, I thought, and left it at that.

I made my way to the western end of South Boston and chained my bike to a house railing right in the middle of a changing neighborhood. Across the street, another triple-decker had been torn down, and billboards announced new condos coming to the space in August. August seemed an optimistic date; the house's frame was up but still skeletal, and the carpenters didn't seem in any hurry. A couple of them eyed me warily, but stopped when their boss came over.

Some of the other houses on this side of the street also looked redone; I didn't remember seeing more than a post-age stamp of a front yard throughout most of my child-hood, but these had enough for a little garden. A mutt was chained up in one yard, and I clucked my tongue at him. He perked up and ambled over to lick my hand, then settled down to some serious napping.

The houses across the way probably hadn't been reno-vated in years but kept a dignified facade, like a sick man determined to put a good face on everything. Two of them had little gardens out front, one with roses, the other with tomatoes, but the one I went up to remained bare. I glanced down at the gravel, once raked but now in disarray, and de-cided I'd probably come to the right place.

A woman in her early sixties came to the door when I rang. She gave me a suspicious, pinch-lipped look through the screen door. "Mrs. McDermot?" I said.

"Yes." Her expression didn't change.

"My name's Genevieve Scelan. I used to know your son Frank."

A bewildering range of expressions contorted her face when I said his name: shame, hope, anger, bitterness. She stuck with the last. "He doesn't live here."

"I know that, I—"

"Beth? Who is it?" A tall man emerged into the hall and came to stand beside her. I fought down a wave of déjà vu; the resemblance between Frank and his father was so strong that it could have been an older version of Frank in front of me, minus the junkie hollows. "Who's this, now?"

I steadied myself. "Mr. McDermot, your son called me last night." His eyebrows twitched, and the same mix of emotions raced over his face, settling into uncertain sorrow. "I was a—a friend of his a long time ago. The call I got was—was kind of weird, and so I was wondering if you might know where he is or if he's okay."

"He doesn't live here," Frank's mom repeated angrily, as if that were my fault.

Hell, it might be, I thought.

"We haven't been in contact with him in a long time," Frank's dad said. "You probably know more than we do about whether he's okay."

He isn't okay, I thought. *He's decidedly not okay.*

On a hunch, I sniffed. Most of the smells were plain normal, a sure sign that Frank had not been here: dust, old furniture, sawdust from across the street, and a lingering damp reek. And sweat. Frank's mom glared at me, but she was sweating.

"I'm sorry to bother you," I said over the sound of a car pulling up to the sidewalk behind me, and the nervous scent from her doubled. "Thanks very much."

"Wait," Frank's dad said. Frank's mom glanced from him to the street, then me. She took her husband's arm, but he wasn't paying attention to her. "If you do find anything, please let us know. Please."

"I will," I said, and it wasn't quite a lie. If Frank had gotten further into the undercurrent, it might be kinder not to let them know.

I turned and nearly walked straight into the man coming up the stairs. He stumbled back and caught hold of the railing to keep from losing his balance, and the scent of his cologne hit me like a damp pillow. He was about my height, considerably broader across the shoulders, and bald as an egg, with that prickly look around the edges that suggested he'd shaved it rather than display a changing hairline. It suited him well, though. If he'd looked a little scruffier, I'd have taken him for a bouncer in some high-class club; as it was, it was clear that he was much higher on the social ladder. "Excuse me," he said.

"Excused," I said through the fog of scent. "Sorry."

He gave me a curious look as I slipped past him, but turned back to the McDermots.

I glanced back at their door as I unlocked my bike. The bald man spoke quietly to Frank's parents, who opened the screen door and ushered him in. Frank's mom, no longer smelling nervous (even though the cologne still dulled my nose, I could scent that much) took his arm, and his father closed the door behind them.

Strange. I left my bike where it was for the moment and walked over to the bald man's car. It was expensive, but dirty, and that was the extent of what I could tell about it.

A dog howled nearby as I was writing down the license number. A second later, another followed suit. I looked up to see the mutt in the yard two doors up the street sitting on his haunches and sniffing at the air. He bared his teeth at nothing, then yelped and scrambled away as if he'd been hit, tail between his legs. "What's the matter—" I began, and then it hit me too.

A blast of damp gunpowder scent struck me in the face, and with it came a screeching in my ears like ten subway trains coming to a halt. I threw up my hands in an ineffective guard, but the worst had passed, like a ripple in the air, over me and then gone. As I stood there panting, the howls started up again, this time from behind me as the ripple spread over the city, scaring the hell out of every dog it hit. *Like a dog whistle with a blast radius*, I thought, *or the opposite of a dog whistle*.

The mutt cowered against the closest fence, scraping at it as if to dig his way out. I shushed him and stroked his head, and he calmed down enough to lick my hand a second time.

"Okay," I said, more to myself than the dog, "anyone want to tell me what the hell that was?"

"Jesus Christ. Is that Evie Scelan?"

I froze. The voice had come from behind me, and it was loud enough to carry to the next city block. "Who's asking?" I said, and turned.

The boss from the construction site edged around the fence and grinned at me. "Bet you don't recognize me. Hey, I wouldn'ta recognized you either if it wasn't for that black braid you got."

Involuntarily, one hand went to my braid. I was self-conscious about it, but it kept my hair out of my eyes and out from under the bike helmet. Even if it did make me look like I had an electrical cable stapled to the back of my head.

"Yeah. You still got it, huh? Looks like you made up for all the hair I lost." He rubbed one ruddy hand over his thinning hair. "Hey, remember when I played that trick on you in chemistry?"

I remembered an incident with a Bunsen burner and a lab partner who liked laughing at me. I also remembered the six days' detention I got for banging the culprit's head against the lab table. Half of the reason I'd done it was for the stink of burnt hair. I hadn't been able to smell anything for a week. "You'd be . . . Billy?"

"Will," he said, turning slightly redder under his sunburn. He jerked his head back toward the workmen. "Don't let these guys hear you call me Billy, okay?"

"Got it." He hadn't been affected by the ripple, I realized, nor had the workmen. The mutt, though, still cowered in a ball at the end of his chain, and I'd broken out in a sweat just from that sound.

And the scent. The scent was unmistakable.

Will grinned, apparently relieved that I wasn't going to bang his head against anything this time. "So what are you up to these days?"

"Not much." I glanced over my shoulder at the McDermots' door and bit back a curse. The bald man was already on his way out, escorted by Frank's dad.

"Waiting for somebody? . . . Hey, you know, there's a bunch of us all from school who get together at this bar downtown. Everyone'd be thrilled to see you."

"I'm sure they would, but this isn't really a good time—" Too late. The bald man had seen me, and his eyes narrowed. "Maybe later?"

"Later's good. Tonight's better. Here; I'll write down the name of the place for you." Billy—Will—took a pen from his shirt pocket and patted at his other pockets, frowning.

"Excuse me." The bald man had paused at the edge of the street, his hands clasped behind his back. "I can't shake the feeling that I know you from somewhere. Are you a local?"

"Ha!" Will grinned at him. "Always shows in the face, don't it, Evie? Yeah, she used to be a local, same as me, but she sure as hell isn't around here near as often as you. I know everyone around here, Evie," he added as he handed me a folded receipt with a name scratched on the back. "Even know this guy, great guy. Carson, right?"

"Corrigan," the bald man corrected, but absently.

I sighed. "Genevieve Scelan," I said, and shook his hand. His palm was strangely uncalloused, with the exception of rough flesh around the ring on his middle finger. It was a plain gold band like a wedding ring, with a pattern of crude spirals scratched into it, and it was just slightly warmer than his skin.

"Scelan?" he said, one eyebrow raised. "I think I may have heard of you, then. Are you . . ." He paused and glanced at Will, who was happily oblivious to any subtleties in the conversation. "Are you sometimes called Hound?"

I took my hand out of his, too aware of how cold my fingers had gone. "Sometimes," I said, and dragged my bike upright.

"Hound?" Will grinned. "What kind of a name is that?"

I got on my bike. "Better than 'Bitch,'" I said, and left before they could snare me further.

Three

"I still can't believe you told him your name," Sarah said.

I shrugged and fiddled with the cedarwood totems marked 15% Off. Of all the stinky things in the Goddess Garden, the cedar was the least intrusive. "He asked. Besides, Will was right there. If I'd refused, it would have looked suspicious."

"More suspicious than what you were doing?" She shook her head and looked down at the strip of paper her calculator had disgorged. "I swear, this register is possessed . . . Even so, it's not like you couldn't have wiggled out of it somehow. Nomenclature thaumaturgy is some of the most basic stuff out there."

"I know what you're going to say," I said wearily. "Every magician in the city . . ."

Sarah wasn't listening. "Every magician in—" She frowned and shot an exasperated glare at me. "Okay. But it doesn't make it any less true. You can't be a magician and just give out your real name to anyone who asks."

"I do give out my real name. That's because I'm not a magician."

"That's wordplay and you know it."

I tried to think of a clever reply to that and sneezed instead. Sarah sighed, licked her fingers, and pinched out a smoldering incense stick. "Sorry about that," she said. "My aromatherapy distributor complained last time he visited that I didn't have something out. Marketing issues."

"Did you tell him about the time his Essence of Immortality oils gave me a nosebleed?" I shook my head a few times to clear it, which didn't work. "Erg." I turned away, toward the windows, and realized why I was having much more trouble than usual with Sarah's aromatherapy. "What happened to all the houseplants?"

"Moved them to the back, under a sunlamp. They'd been looking a little yellow."

"Guh." I stifled another sneeze. For some reason, plants or pollen didn't usually set off my nose. In fact, some of them helped; if I'd had a long day chasing some vile scent, nothing reset all my systems like a handful of crushed sage. Without Sarah's usual jungle in the window, the aromas of the store were much heavier. "I liked the look you had with them in the window—it really underscored the whole 'garden' theme. Don't your customers expect a garden?"

"Don't change the subject." Sarah fidgeted with her hair, pulling a long ringlet out straight and letting it spring back into place. "It's not even just the magic. There's identity theft, 'Net stuff, all that jazz. If you're going to make this thing into a paying job, you gotta remember those things too."

"I'm not yet sure how well it'll fly as a job." I scooped up a handful of cedar icons and let them patter through my fingers onto the counter. "I made rent this month and last month, but it's anyone's guess how long that'll last."

"I'd put money on it," Sarah said absently. "Wasn't too long ago you had that waitress job too, and you're as glad as I am that's over."

"Yeah. Well." I had hated being a waitress. I hated the thought of going back to it even more. "So, about the call Frank made."

"Yes, go ahead, change the subject again. Don't mind my warnings about strange bald men and flinging your name to the four winds."

"There was this smell," I tried. "It was like stone that'd

been left in a damp room, had that same kind of . . . Look, I know it was over the phone, but . . ."

Sarah blinked at me with the same bafflement that she always got when I tried to talk about scent. The door chimed, three descending notes, and Sarah gave the entering customer a brilliant smile. "First impression, it sounds like spirit to me," she said in an undertone to me.

"Frank was never a spirit man. He was ritual all the way." With maybe a little blood magic, which was what had gotten him in trouble to begin with.

"And you hadn't seen him for, what, fifteen years?" Her smile stayed fixed in place, but her eyes flicked to the customer meaningfully.

I fell silent. In some sense, it meant nothing to talk about magic this way; the boundaries between kinds of magic are hazy at best, and the distinctions don't mean anything in terms of severity. Spirit magic can cover anything from asking the soul of a rowan tree to keep bad influences away to blood sacrifice and total possession by a wandering god. Ritual magic could be a ward scratched into your doorframe or a twenty-hour antiphonal chant during the dark of the moon. And blood magic could be a touch of extra luck—which about a fifth of the population had already and never noticed—or heavy-duty, incapacitating Sight that would tell you the events of ten years from now but not if a bus were hurtling toward you.

The trouble with separating magic out into those categories is that summoning a spirit usually requires some ritual work, rituals go much more easily if you have a bit of blood magic, and blood magic tends to draw attention from wanderers.

Sarah had managed to talk her customer into buying a Motherpeace tarot deck to go with the Rider-Waite deck "to counteract the underlying patriarchal assumptions of those archetypes." "Spirit, like I said," she continued as the door chimed shut. "Maybe he'd split off part of himself, and that was the part that wanted to call you."

I shook my head. "Makes no sense."

"And how is this different from your usual work?" She glanced at her watch. "Speaking of which, shouldn't you be out there right now?"

"Schedule keeps changing." I tried to flip a cedar totem over my fingers, knocked it to the floor and cursed.

"This is really bugging you, isn't it?"

I sighed and bent to pick up the totem. "Frank was a friend. I don't . . . We didn't part on good terms, but I feel like I owe him something."

"Well," Sarah said, returning to the register and examining it with a frown, "you've tried to reach his parents, you tried to work out who else was talking. What else can you do?"

I grinned.

When I didn't speak, Sarah looked up and paled at my expression. "You're not going to hunt him, are you?"

"Why not? I remember his scent well enough."

"Are you sure that's what he wants?"

"No. But I stopped giving a shit about what he wanted when we broke up."

Sarah's eyes narrowed. "Broke up? So there is more to this story. Will I ever hear it?" I shrugged, and she bent over the register again. "You know," she said after a moment, "there's another possibility. I didn't think of it at first, because you said he'd been a friend and you and I swore to stay out of the bad stuff."

I went very still.

"Anyway, there's a possibility that I don't like, but I've heard a few rumors . . . I'd hate to think any friend of yours, or any ex for that matter, was tangled up in the Bright Brotherhood. I wouldn't wish it on any of *my* exes."

"Sarah, that's not something to joke about—"

The door chimed again, and Sarah turned to face it, prepared to smile. Instead she scowled and threw down the register tape. "You! You and I need to have a talk."

I turned to see yet another face out of high school—one I knew and liked a little better. "Hey, Nate."

Nate Hunter grinned down at me. He was on Roller-blades, which lent him an extra two inches he didn't need. "Hi, Evie. What's the problem, Sarah?"

"First of all, take those blasted things off before you come in. You'll roll over Mulligatawny's tail."

Mulligatawny, Sarah's orange thug of a cat, regarded Nate with disdain from his place on the Lovecraft shelf. Mulligatawny didn't like me—few cats did—but either he'd decided I wasn't worth his time or he'd recognized that I was ten times his size and could probably tie him in a knot if I had to. Our current situation of unfriendly détente was harmless enough to satisfy me.

Nate knelt to unfasten his skates, and Sarah pulled three books from a close shelf. "Second of all," she said, waving the books at the top of his head, "you can tell me what the hell you were thinking when you posted all those proofs."

"Proofs?" I glanced at Nate.

Sarah shook her head. "Stay out of this, Evie."

Nate got to his feet and pushed his curly brown hair out of his eyes. I'd never seen the man not in need of a haircut. "Mathematical proofs. How'd you find out that was me?"

She tossed a copy of *The Aleph Code* at him. "This is not a lucrative business, Hunter. I have enough trouble with prices going up and second-rate Goth kids shoplifting my stock"—*and distracted adepts forgetting to pay for their shipment of apple wands,* I mentally added—"without you deconstructing one of my best-sellers on the 'Net for every-one to see."

"So you don't know for sure that it *was* me, then," Nate tried.

"You just admitted to it!" Sarah slammed the books down on the counter. "These are by a local author, you know. He's convinced that I'm the one behind your re-views."

Nate shrugged. "He based an entire chapter on a flawed geometrical assumption, and he keeps forgetting to carry the two in his examples of name numerology."

"Nate, why did you even bother?" I asked. "Did they run out of math for you at MIT?"

He smiled at me, but it had an edge to it. "With my advisor? That'll never happen. This was different . . ." His shoulders slumped, and for the first time I saw the beginning strands of gray in his hair. "I just needed something that I didn't have to think about very hard. Something inessential."

"Like a master chef making macaroni and cheese," I said.

The smile softened a little. "Something like that."

"More like a baker dissecting Twinkies." Sarah retreated behind the counter. "Look, I don't ask anyone who comes into the Goddess Garden to believe everything in every book I sell. That'd take more faith than a church bus full of evangelicals. But it does sting a little to know you were buying them only to mock them."

Nate put *The Aleph Code* back on its shelf. "All right. I'm sorry. I'll even apologize to the author, if you want."

"Don't," Sarah said, tugging a strip of adding paper free from the depths of the register. "He's a pretentious little blister, and he's had it coming for some time. But you didn't hear that from me."

Nate nodded. He still looked a bit crestfallen, so I tried to change the subject. "Nate, have you heard anything from Will Chandler—Billy—from our graduating class?"

Nate raised an eyebrow. "I think so. He keeps trying to get everyone together for a reunion dinner. I think he misses high school."

"I don't," Sarah muttered. "I had enough gossip and backstabbing to last me a lifetime; I don't need more."

"Yeah, well, I usually just found whoever was gossiping and beat the snot out of them." I grinned at Sarah when she shot me a dirty look. "Good thing you didn't come to our school. Nate, you ever been to the Tuesday-night things he's holding?"

"Once or twice. It's not bad. Will just talks at people for a while. He pays for the drinks, which is a plus."

I took out the paper Will had given me and turned it over between my fingers. *8:30, The Adeline*, it read, plus an address in the South End. Just talking for a while, and with people who wouldn't be tainted by magic. Not to mention Will might have some information on the man who visited the McDermots. "I might go," I said aloud.

Sarah raised an eyebrow. "You sure that's a good idea?"

"Can't hurt," I said, without looking at her this time. "Maybe I'll see you there, Nate. How's Katie, by the way?"

He'd moved behind a bookcase, so I couldn't see him well. "She's all right," he said after a moment. "Day camp wasn't easy to arrange, but I think she likes it."

Katie was Nate's sister. I'd only met her once, but you couldn't know Nate without knowing about Katie. The man had reshaped his life around his role as surrogate parent to her.

Nate leaned out from behind the bookcase, next to the shelf of icons and brass images Sarah kept out of Mulligatawny's reach. "You think she'd like this?" he asked, holding up a battered Ganesha.

"Eh. I'd wait till she starts her next year of school."

"I'll keep it till then." He handed Sarah a handful of bills and waited till she gave him his change, shuffling his feet a bit. "So you'll be at the Adeline?" he said.

"Maybe." I crumpled the paper and checked my watch.

"Maybe I'll see you then." Nodding to Sarah, who shook her head at him, Nate opened the door and stepped outside.

Sarah got up as the door closed and glanced down the street after him. "Not my usual sort of customer," she murmured.

"I thought he came by pretty often."

"Only when you're here. This shop has plate glass windows, Evie, and you're pretty visible from the street."

"What's that supposed to mean?"

"Nothing." She looked enigmatic, something she did well. "Any chance you can go get me a coffee before Liz

shows up? I spent last night talking someone through an in-
vocation of the triple goddess, and I'm beat."

"Which goddess is that? Someone I should pray to when
the Sox have a man on second?"

"Is everything baseball with you, Evie? Don't answer
that; I don't think I can take the disillusionment." Sarah
pointed to a plaster icon on the shelf above the counter
showing three robed women. "She's the maiden-mother-
crone, the female principle. Or at least that's what she is
to the woman I was talking to last night; that twit doesn't
know the difference between Kali and Eris. I had to use
small words the whole way through, and can you believe
she was conducting the ritual at the same time as she was
talking to me?"

I glanced at the icon she'd indicated. The women all
looked the same. "That's not good. Trioditis magic is pretty
heavy stuff. Get a maiden, a mother, and a crone together
and you don't even need a locus." I'd never been comfortable with the stuff, and not just because I didn't fit in any of
the roles.

"Like there are a lot of maidens in the undercurrent. No,
Evie, this was just worship, not undercurrent stuff. There's
a difference, and I'm careful to stay on this side of the line.
About that coffee?"

"Nope." I tapped my watch. "Gotta take care of some
stuff before work."

Sarah unlocked the back of a display case and brought
out a rack of cheap silver rings, each with a Lucky Stone
set in it, or so the front of the rack proclaimed. They didn't
smell particularly lucky to me. "And of course you just had
to spend the morning with me, telling me stories guaran-
teed to mess with my head for the rest of the day. Not to
mention interrupt me in mid-rant just because my target
happens to be a friend of yours. I love you too."

I paused in the middle of pulling my gloves back on.
"You really mind?"

"I wouldn't have you here if I minded. Oh . . ." She

paused, one hand extended, just as I put my helmet on. "There is one thing."

"One more damn thing?"

"Okay, two. Or three. Are you sure about this pub thing?"

"I can handle it. I've handled it this far, right?"

"Yeah. Sorry." She bit her lip and ran a hand through her curls, letting them spring every which way. "Can I ask you to do a job for me?"

I looked down at my hands. "Not as a favor."

"Decidedly not as a favor. I've still got a copy of your usual contract; I'll fill it out and send it, and you can give me an invoice. All aboveboard, no obligations."

"It'll have to take second place to Frank."

"Of course. There's no real hurry on this, after all." She began picking up racks across the counter, looking for something. "It's not like I didn't try other avenues, but those all petered out right off. That's what I get for trying to go that way, I guess . . ."

From under the rack of rings, she produced a wad of suede and unwrapped it. Inside was another layer, this one of silk: handwoven, to make the masking even stronger. Organic matter could muffle a magical aura, and matter that's been handled a lot—that's interacted with people and the static they produce—was even better. If Sarah really wanted to keep this thing hidden, I considered, as she unwrapped a chip of stone about the size of my thumbnail, she could always swallow it, and then even I might have trouble locating it. "What is it?"

"It's a rock. They grow them around here." I gave her a sour look, and she grinned. "Really. It's a bit of what's called a chain stone."

"Send seven little rocks on and you get good luck for a year?"

"Break it and your dick falls off. In which case we're both safe. No, not that kind of chain. The originals—there are several of them, probably three at least—should be of the same stone, with carvings on each side. Maybe as big as your fist, maybe smaller. My sources aren't very clear on the details."

I took the silk and spread it out over my hand. The stone tingled a little, not unpleasantly. "Is it dangerous?"

She was silent long enough that I looked up at her. "I don't know," she said. "I don't think so. But in any case, don't go trying to retrieve it. Just find out where one is and let me know. If you find more than one, so much the better."

"Make a note of that in the contract." I brought the silk up to my face as if it were a handkerchief, holding the chip of stone just below my nose.

Old blood. Stone, black stone, and age. Iron too, shading into a different scent from the blood, though they were related. Mildew, as if it'd been kept in a damp room for too long. And something else, something that I could only describe as the olfactory equivalent of a heat haze: a wavering distortion, blurring everything beyond it.

I raised my head, eyes still closed, and inhaled. Sarah's incense still blocked a lot of my senses, but the trail was there. Sarah too, smelling of the incense in which she immersed herself at work and in worship; Mulligatawny, peppery and simmering; and even a trace of Nate, smooth like polished wood. The stone's scent led away from here, to the south and east, tangling with a thousand other scents as it went.

There was a trace of that stone-and-iron lingering in the air, leading further into the city. I smiled, opened my eyes, and rolled the chip back up in its silk. As an afterthought, I bundled the suede around it as well; no point in leaving it out if I didn't have to. "I can follow it. Anything else?"

"Maybe. Yes." She came out from behind the counter and studied my face. I've never figured out how someone eight inches shorter than me could loom over me, but somehow she managed to. "Are you feeling okay, Evie?"

I sighed. Better to tell her part of the truth than to keep

it all back—and while Sarah would believe me if I said that someone was magically harassing Boston's canine population, I didn't want to deal with her theories right now. "Ran into a shadowcatcher on the way to Frank's parents."

"Jesus. People still do that?"

"People still drink Listerine if they can't get real booze."

"What'd you do?"

"Broke his net. Gave him the names of a few places where he could dry out. Not like it's gonna help."

Sarah reached up and squeezed my shoulder gently. "Sorry, Evie."

"Yeah, well." I gave her a tight smile. "I'll see you later on."

Frank's parents weren't picking up their phone. I leaned my bike against the wall of the Goddess Garden, just down the alley from Sarah's back door, and waited through three rings before their answering machine clicked over.

It was a good thing, I thought, as Frank's dad droned through the message, that Frank and his father didn't sound much alike. Otherwise, I'd be having serious qualms about even talking to him. "This is Genevieve Scelan," I said after the beep. "I spoke to you earlier today, and while I know you said that Frank—"

Something clicked on the other end, and a whine of feedback nearly deafened me. "Get away from us, you little bitch," a woman's voice said, so ragged and harsh that I barely recognized Frank's mother. "Get away from my family. It's your fault this happened. Leave us alone."

The last word ended in a sob, and she hung up before I could speak.

Four

Three hours of dodging Boston traffic did much to scour the morning's events from my mind. Seemed like every lawyer in Boston needed material delivered to the other side of the city, and needed it delivered now. I narrowly missed a semi that'd gotten stuck in the North End, carried replies between the State House and Fan Pier for a full hour, and escaped being doored three times.

Sometimes I figured half the reason I'd taken this job was so that I'd have an excuse not to think of undercurrent matters. Usually, it worked pretty well, and on days like this when every driver seemed to have dropped acid before leaving home, I had enough to worry about without adding my other job to the heap.

Still, I couldn't help thinking of Frank. His mom wasn't entirely wrong, as much as I wished she were. I'd helped to wreck his hopes of getting out of Boston, and even if I did so out of ignorance, I still owed him something. And I owed it to him to do it right—not this half-assed detective work, but using what I knew best.

I called in for a lunch break and headed down to the Common. While it's not the geographical center of Boston, it passes for one. The four lines of the subway meet nearby, the commercial center of the city is right next door, and the ley lines that the Freedom Trail runs along are strong enough that in many senses they make it the center of the city. Most of all, it's on real ground, not fill. Boston Common may have been a swampy mess when the colonists came over from England, but it was actual land, which is more than can be said of much of Boston these days, and it always helped to start off grounded.

Dust spun up from the baseball field across the way, where half a Little League team made an attempt at practicing. The usual complement of businessmen, nannies, and tourists milled over the paths and grass alike. I wound my way through them, dodging the children-on-a-string headed for the duckling statues. One of their teachers had overdone her morning perfume, and I had to hold my breath as she passed. Although the worst perfume can do to me physically is give me a headache, it'll always distract me from the hunt.

Once away from the teacher, I turned and stood with my face to the wind, eyes closed against the warm June sun. I inhaled, discarding remainders of last night's concert: half a bottle of cheap white wine spilled into the ground not far away, citronella candles long burnt out, the bones from an order of buffalo wings. And more recent trails near and far: lemon freeze from the vendors by the gates, incense from the Falun Gong practitioners on the other side of the hill, someone's sausage sandwich. With onions.

Then there were the other scents, the ones that didn't correspond to anything in the real world. Burning iron and lavender. Chlorine frost. Graveyard earth. Undercurrent scents. Like the moment on a teetering board when one's weight tips it from one side to the other, my senses shifted, following the trails that weren't quite scent but something else.

My shoulders unknotted, and the heat of today's new sunburn dimmed to a distant pulse. This was better than any drink, as good as skillful foreplay, relaxing and invigorating all at once. I sighed and cast my mind out further, following the trails.

The trouble with this approach is that everything—absolutely everything—becomes fascinating. I kept getting distracted—now by someone who smelled like a ghost but seemed otherwise healthy, now by a pool of water that reeked of smoke, now by a group of protesters with some other, greater scent laid over them like a benediction. Some people smelled of fire, even if they'd never been burned, and some things of stale sweat even though no one had touched them for decades.

Think of one of the pages from an illuminated manuscript, the ones like the *Book of Kells,* where the scribe really went nuts. Concentrate on one line and you'll see it spreads out further and becomes a river, or a horse's tail, or a cat and a mouse sharing a communion wafer. From a distance the whole thing just looks like a snarl of red and gold, but each level has a pattern all its own.

Now imagine that image with uncountable levels, each line becoming a page, and each page of that becoming another. It's similar to fractals, but fractals have some kind of order to them, even if it's just an incomprehensible formula. The only order in this world is what humans give it, and that's not much.

In this tangle, I had to trace one particular scent. I could find anything—lost property, evidence, people not even the police could track down. Cards scattered from the same deck all had the same smell. Someone who'd been at the computer all day still carried a trace of phosphor dots as he hurried past. It wasn't even quite a scent—it was some kind of signature that goes beyond smell—but smell was the closest analogue as well as the trigger for it.

I tried describing this to Sarah once, and she said it must be like a three-year-old with attention deficit disorder surfing the Web while chugging espresso. I told her she was being an idiot, but she was more right than I cared to admit. Even though I had one particular trail in mind, the lure of the other scents was intoxicating.

If all had gone well, I reasoned, if Frank's new plan had

worked where his old one failed, then he'd be out of the city by now. I could at least track him that far, see if he was gone. And if he wasn't—well. If he wasn't, maybe I could help now, where I hadn't before.

And yet . . . There was something odd about the patterns of scent. Nothing I could place, but I had the distinct sense I was being watched. There's nothing of the undercurrent about that; it's something you notice on the subway a lot, when someone will look up just as you glance at them. I frowned, questing back and forth.

"Excuse me?" A strong scent of clean starch and aftershave swamped me, overwhelming any traces I might have found. "I'm sorry to bother you—"

I sneezed. The patterns collapsed in on themselves, winking out like a light extinguished and leaving me with a mental bruise as big as my head. "Not nearly as sorry as I am," I growled, turning to glare at whoever had spoken.

The bald man who'd visited Frank's parents smiled at me, and my words froze in my mouth. He'd donned sunglasses, smoky ovals that hid his eyes as the aftershave hid his true scent. "I'm sorry to bother you," he repeated as I stared at him. "But are you—well, are you practicing?"

"Practicing?" Doubletalk again. Sarah calls it part of a culture of secrecy; I call it a glorified secret club, complete with passwords. "Say what you mean straight out," I said, trying to decide whether to get closer to my bike or just run for it now. "Tell me what I'm practicing."

The man's smile faded, and he glanced over his shoulder. "You really are blatant about it, aren't you . . . okay. Magic," he replied, muttering the last word out of the corner of his mouth. It might have been cute if I hadn't been so unnerved.

"Yeah. Maybe." I sidestepped past him and headed toward the gate.

"Out *here*?"

"Where else would I be?" I snapped. "Cooped up inside a lunarium, muttering to myself? Go away."

He didn't. "I'd heard of finders," he said, hurrying to catch up with me, "but most of them use more esoteric methods, tied closely to their loci. Like scryers, you see, but with a tighter focus—"

"Go away."

"I can't. I think I need to talk to you." He moved to block my path and took off his sunglasses, squinting much more than the June sun necessitated. He had nice eyes, I noticed without wanting to. "You know Frank McDermot."

"I know a lot of people," I shot back, clasping my hands to keep them from shaking. "And I have enough respect for them not to be flinging their names around like—like bird-seed."

He bit his lip. "You won't talk to me, then?"

I hesitated. This man was the first solid lead I had. "Maybe," I allowed. "But not now. Not out here. You have my name; you can find me again." The headache I'd gotten from the interrupted hunt swelled again, and I leaned in close to him, ignoring his heavy, clean scent. "And don't ever interrupt me when I'm hunting. Ever."

His jaw tightened, and he looked down his nose at me. "Understood," he said, and turned to go. I waited until he was out of sight—and until I could no longer easily smell his scent—before turning my back.

Glancing down at my watch, I exhaled. Between this interruption and the time I'd wasted getting caught in the pattern of scents, I didn't have much time left. If I tried another hunt, I'd probably be no less than half an hour late—and there was always the chance that Tania would change my schedule again to make up for it.

Still, there were other methods of finding out information, and other ways to go. If you wanted undercurrent gossip, there was always one sure source for it—assuming you could put up with a certain level of scumminess.

I headed back toward the gates of the Public Garden. Instead of crossing the street and unlocking my bike from where I'd left it, though, I backtracked along the fence until

I reached the ramped entrance to the parking garage below the Common. It wasn't the safest way to get down there, but Leon would be on the lower floors somewhere, and I'd never had any luck finding him when I went via the elevator.

The garage was about ten degrees cooler than the Common, and a thin wind soughed past me. I shivered and bounced on my toes. There were plenty of cars on this level, fewer as I made my way further down, though no people that I could see. Scents, though . . . many of them were familiar from the trance I'd just been in, and I had to fight down the temptation to just pick a trail and follow it.

The smell of damp cement curled around me, now blended with a reek of unwashed skin. Underneath everything, a thin, hot scent ran, tingeing everything like an aftertaste.

It's difficult to describe scents by anything other than analogy, and the only analogy I could come up with for this one didn't make any sense in context: fireworks and rain. The smoky, powdery scent that hangs in the air over the Charles after the Fourth of July, twined inseparably with the steamy scent of rain on hot asphalt. I grimaced; I'd never liked the stink of worked magic, and while I could deal with it in small doses, Leon wasn't a small-dose kind of man. And after this morning's exposure—which I still didn't understand—I'd gotten oversensitive to that particular scent.

I counted concrete columns, turned left and right and left again, and followed the smell farther in, toward a low, insistent noise at the end of the garage. Underneath the constant rumble of traffic above and subway cars below, a man's voice muttered in the talk-pause-talk cadence of a phone call. "Yeah . . . no, I got the other stone okay . . . never noticed a thing . . . Yeah, you better hope they didn't."

I rapped on one of the columns, and when that didn't produce much of a noise, banged on the hood of a nearby SUV. "Leon, you're the only man I know who can get cell phone reception down here," I called.

The man up against the far wall of the garage jumped, snapping his phone shut. "Fucking Christ, Hound, you scared me."

I shook my head. "You could use some scaring, Leon." Leon Fisher had probably been an attractive man once. There were the remnants of an athletic body in the way he moved, like a high school track star who had gone to seed, and I guessed that he'd once had the boyish good looks of wholesome young stars on Christian TV. But it wasn't the years or lack of exercise that had spoiled him. Some of it was the way he tried too hard; his hair was currently a mash of several different dyes, including one sideburn that might have been his natural color. Leon'd still be trying to look like a young punk when he was sixty.

But what was enough to keep me away from him was the wasted, haggard look that I knew too well. I saw it on many of my undercurrent contacts, the drained look that working with magic gives you. Some day I'd see it in my own face, and then I'd know it was time to give up on this job and try accounting instead.

I crossed the concrete floor to Leon, the slap of my sneakers echoing between the cars, as within, I pushed away the riot of undercurrent scents that surrounded me. "Can we talk?"

Leon grinned, and just looking at that grin was like having a slug crawl over my forehead. "What about?"

"Nothing big," I said. "I'd heard some news of an old friend of mine, and wondered if you might have some gossip on him."

"Feh. Shoulda come to me in the first place. Not like I'm not reliable, right, Hound? I can give you a good deal on whatever you want, information, loci, whatever." He started rummaging in his ankle-length black overcoat, worn no matter what season it was. He probably slept in the damn thing.

"You don't give anyone a deal, Leon." I shivered again and tucked my hands into my armpits. "Christ, did they put air conditioners down here or something?"

"Gotta keep it cold down here. Keep it warm, stuff wakes up, you know how it is." He extracted several small muslin bags from his pockets, crouched, then looked up at me with reptilian cunning. "Well, *you* don't, Hound. Not like you don't have eyes, but things aren't the same as they was, and a big fucking thank God for that."

"Yeah, well, you can give me the history lesson later. I'm so cold I might grow a fur coat standing here. Just tell me what you can— Goddammit, I don't need any loci."

He belched laughter and spread a balding square of velvet on the floor. "Show 'em what you got and take 'em for what they're worth, lay it all down and do it again. Story of my fucking life."

He upended the bags and dumped out three vials, two of which glowed against the velvet, a chunk of low-quality amethyst, a charred Hello Kitty barrette, and a twisted root deformed into a screaming face. "So you're looking for a friend. Anything ring any bells? Or maybe you might want a little something for yourself . . ." He tapped one of the glowing vials with a grimy fingernail. It rang softly, a purer sound than he had any right to make. "Made not more than a year ago, still good— Little locus for the lady, mm?"

"I'm no lady," I said. "And the day I need a locus is the day the sky falls in."

Leon seesawed a hand back and forth. "You never know, Hound. You never know when you might need a little something more than your own hoodoo. Always gotta look out for that extra edge, right?"

"Your extra edge tends to cut people up, Leon. I just need to find out what you know."

He spread his hands. "You got a few hours to spare? I could cover half of what I know in that time. Who's this for anyway?"

"You know I don't pass that on." When half of your customer base learns of you through word of mouth, it's better to have a reputation for discretion. No one wants to trust a blabbermouth.

"Go ahead, be a bitch about it. Not like I don't take care

of my customers—you, the seer enclave, that pagan twat in Allston, not like I'm not doing enough for her already—" He closed his mouth with a snap and gave me a guilty look.

I sighed. So he and Sarah were on the outs. No big surprise there; after all, Sarah had standards. "Let's both cut the crap. Have you heard anything about a guy by the name of Frank McDermot?"

Leon shook his head and started scooping up the loci, treating them as if they were Happy Meal toys rather than scraps of people's souls. "No bells. Any chance I could interest you in one of them blasts they got in Nova Scotia? Got a few shipped down, cut straight outta the victim's leg—"

"No. You might not have known him by that name; he went underground a while ago."

He paused, one hand in the depths of his overcoat. "Underground?"

"Not literally," I said, then hesitated. "Well. Maybe. He might have something to do—"

Leon's phone rang, a tinny blast of "Sabre Dance" echoing through the garage. He cursed and fumbled at his pockets, then yelped as all of the vials flared up at once, white light bright enough to leave afterimages. A rotted seam in his coat tore under the pressure, and the contents of one of his many pockets cascaded out onto the floor.

I chuckled. "Leon, you know better than that," I said, and knelt beside the heap. "That's why you don't keep loci and heavy stuff together . . . here, I'll help." I picked up the spilled contents: lint, his still-ringing phone, twenty cents, a crumpled Charlie ticket, and a lump of black rock about the size of a golf ball. Steam rose off it in the chill air.

With it came a scent I recognized: stone and iron, like low-quality ore, with the same bloody scent that bad iron has. The chain-stone scent that Sarah had wanted me to look for. It figured that Leon would have one. "Thanks," I said, crouching to pick up the rock. "This means I can kill two birds with one stone . . . Oof. This thing's heavier than it looks." Locus? No, it wasn't . . . but there was something like a locus in it.

It was carved on three sides, but damned if I could make out what the images were. The carvings didn't want to hold still; every time I blinked, they changed a little, like oil trapped under glass. "Unpleasant little thing, isn't it. Now, about Frank—"

I glanced up at just the wrong time. Leon's eyes were wide with fright, and his right hand reached into the side of his jacket. My nose twitched with recognition of what the undercurrent scents had hidden from me, the stink of fear and the lingering smell of cordite—

I didn't have time to move. I almost didn't have time to let go of the chain stone. I opened my hand, tipping it onto the floor so I could back away, only Leon wasn't going to give me a chance to back away. He pulled the gun free just as I let go of the stone, still thinking, *Since when has Leon carried a gun*—

A man's voice close by shouted three words, words that made my teeth chatter, and the ripping noise of the gunshot tore through the garage. The stone disintegrated, and something stung my forearm. I waited for the pain that would tell me I'd been shot.

It didn't come. I stared at Leon, who was as frozen as I—but for a different reason. His face twitched like a stroke victim's, and the barrel of his gun still pointed at the spot just above my hand where the stone had been. Judging from the twitching tension in his arm, it wasn't where he'd meant to aim.

"That was close." Corrigan stepped out from behind a column, flexing the fingers of his right hand against his left palm.

The fireworks-and-rain smell of power surrounding him struck me like a physical blow. I stumbled to my feet. "You? What the hell did—"

He smiled apologetically. The lenses of his sunglasses were a lot lighter than they had been outside. "I had a feeling I ought to follow you." He glanced at Leon. "Lucky I did."

"What did you do to him?" *And how the hell did you do it*, I thought but didn't say. Among adepts, there are some things you learn not to say out loud.

"Earthfasted him." He pried Leon's fingers from the gun and examined it, grimacing. "Silencer. This must have cost him something; wonder what got into him. Are you hurt?"

"What—no." Except for my ears, which were ringing and would be for the next half hour. Even with a silencer, a gunshot in an enclosed space is damn loud. "But earthfasting—"

"I think you should get out of here." Corrigan nudged one of the loci with his foot, and it rolled a few inches, chiming. "Someone's bound to have heard that, and I'll have to let him go eventually."

He had a point—this was Boston, not New York, and gunshots under the Common weren't the normal state of affairs. Unwilling to leave, I poked at a fragment of the shattered stone. Leon had only winged it, or so it had seemed, and yet it'd blown apart, as if despite its density it had been under pressure from within.

Leon made an urgent, unhappy noise through his locked jaws. I got to my feet. "Look, don't think I'm not grateful, but what are you—I mean, Leon here—"

"Scelan," he said. The way he said my name sounded like he'd mashed extra vowels into it somehow, triggering something in me that I hadn't known existed, some instinct that wanted to twitch to life and run, run forever . . . "Your questions can wait. Trust me on this."

"Who are you?"

"A friend."

I shook my head. "Not mine. I don't even know you."

"No. Frank's."

I stared at him, then jumped as a pair of voices called to each other from one level up in the garage. They didn't sound like police—they lacked cops' curt urgency—but I didn't want to take the chance. But there was Leon. "You won't hurt him?" I asked, never mind that in my place Leon wouldn't have wasted the thought on me.

Corrigan held up three fingers in the old Boy Scout pledge. The ring on his middle finger glinted. "I won't touch him."

"Right." I glanced back at Leon and wiped my hands on my jeans. The stone had left an unpleasant greasy feeling. "Right."

I made my way up to the Public Garden without breaking into a run, then grabbed my bike and rode hell for leather away from there. I couldn't believe what I'd just seen. Not just Leon, though the thought of Leon with a gun was enough to send part of my brain into permanent denial. Even for someone who knew as much about undercurrent and the logistics of magic as I did—perhaps especially for someone who knew it—I didn't believe what I'd just seen.

What that man had done had saved my life.

What that man had done was impossible.

Five

The driver behind me leaned on his horn, and I kicked away from the curb, flipping him off as I turned the corner. *Not like he has room to complain*, I thought. *I bet he hasn't been shot at today.*

Tania had sent three jobs my way, and only the still-wonky schedule meant that I was on time for any of them. And even the distraction of work couldn't make my hands stop shaking.

Impossible. I was no magician—thank God and my mother for small favors—but in my line of work, there were some things I couldn't help learning. And one of those was just how limited magic was. The further a magician gets from his locus, the more difficult magic becomes, and the bigger the magic, the more chance it'll go awry. I'd seen an adept earthfast a man before, only the spell had taken twenty minutes—and that was in the adept's home, where all his loci were close to hand. To just speak a command like that (and speech was the frailest of vehicles for magic) and have it work was damn near unthinkable. And for someone to actually have the confidence to do so meant that he'd be sure it would work, which meant . . .

Meant bad shit for me. Corrigan was either the most powerful or the most careless adept I'd ever seen, and either way that was trouble.

But he'd said he was Frank's friend—

"No," I said out loud. "Frank didn't have friends." That was half of what made him Frank. That was why we'd met.

I hadn't grown up in Southie proper, but a number of my friends from school had, and the summer of my junior year I spent more time in South Boston than in any other part of the city, including my home. Mom didn't make a fuss about it, other than the usual promise extracted every month or so and the big sex lecture she hit me with when school got out. At the time, the sex was what got my attention, but by the end of the summer I found myself wishing I'd taken her other request seriously.

Southie was beginning to fray around the edges that year. The Irish mob's hegemony had more than a few fractures, and it wouldn't be too long before its leader, Whitey Bulger, went on the run, but for those of us who hung out in the park every night, all of it was immaterial. We didn't give a shit who ran what, and if it meant that we sometimes had to settle for two-dollar bottles of Mad Dog rather than weed, that wasn't so bad. Except for the taste of Mad Dog, but I got used to it.

On most nights, despite the occasional cop, we had a bonfire in the park. At least that's what they called it; most Boy Scouts would have called it a campfire and a lousy one at that. But a few nights it got big enough to merit the name, and on one of those nights, in early summer, this kid came by with an armful of branches. He asked permission to use our fire—later, I'd remember that; this thuggish-looking kid, with hair like a flattened porcupine, using such careful, stilted language—and when all he got was a grunt and a wave, dumped them on the fire.

The flames guttered and spat, sending up billows of black smoke that left most of us coughing and choking. I was sober enough to roll out of its path, and so wasn't left a shuddering heap on the ground. Two of the guys rounded on the new kid, asking him what the fuck he was doing, and

I came over to join in. This kind of crap could put me out of commission for a week, though I was still bound enough by my mom's promise that no one knew why I stayed out of the smoke.

The new kid just shrugged. "I couldn't use them anymore," he said. "They're all dried up."

"Dried up my ass!" I yelled. "Those were still green. You don't put green branches on a fire."

He just shrugged again, and by now I was close enough that I could catch his scent. Something about it shocked a memory free: pebbles sliding over one another, moving of their own accord. "They weren't any good," he said, turning away. "Thanks for the fire."

"Wait—" I stumbled after him. "I know you—Frank, right?"

He spun around and grabbed the front of my shirt. "Don't say my fucking name!"

I almost decked him—he wouldn't have been the first kid I'd blunted my knuckles on; I'd been suspended twice already for that reason alone—but the sudden acrid change in his scent stopped me. I hadn't ever smelled fear that strong. He was terrified, and hitting him wouldn't help that.

"I knew you in grade school," I said, holding my hands out where he could see them. "I remember when you left school. I'm Evie Scelan; I sat in the back row, remember?"

The fear-scent eased, and his grip on my shirt relaxed. He abruptly realized where his hand was and let go, turning a deeper shade of scarlet in the firelight. "You remember that, do you," he said.

"Yeah." I tugged my shirt back into place. "Mrs. McIlhinney had us all make up a homework packet for you. She was really ticked off when she found out you wouldn't be back." Those were the only real truths I had then about Frank's absence: the reactions of our class and the knowledge that he'd never received the homework.

Frank shook his head and turned away again, heading off into the scrub trees. I glanced back at the rest of my friends by the fire. Someone had dragged out a broken stereo and was trying to pick up a radio station in the misguided hope that it'd help him get laid. I knew what would happen for the rest of the night: music, someone's stash passed around, maybe a fight if things got exciting. Frank was a mystery, though, and I couldn't turn that down. So I followed him.

He stopped about thirty feet away from the fire, so suddenly that I almost ran into him. "What was it like?" he asked, a weird, pleading note in his voice.

"What was what like?"

"The packet thing. From Mrs. McIlhinney."

"Oh." I racked my brains, trying to remember. "It wasn't much. Just some stuff. What was the school you went to like?"

He laughed, short and painful. "It sucked. I don't want to talk about it. Tell me—" He turned to face me. His eyes had dark smudges under them, exhaustion, or so I thought at the time. "Tell me everything about it. About what it was like without me."

So I did. We walked all night, getting lost more than once, Frank wandering in front and me stumbling along behind, trying my best to reconstruct grade school and middle school. He was hungry for every word, demanding more every time I paused.

Finally we found a bench that was still mostly intact and sat together on it, watching dawn try to pierce the murk over the harbor. I kept talking for a while, but eventually fell silent, my words dropping into his great listening vacuum until they were swallowed up.

Just as I was deciding it was probably time to start back home, Frank turned and kissed me, hard. It wasn't the first time I'd been kissed, but it was the first time I didn't want to hit the perpetrator. He pulled back and looked at me, studying my face with an intent gaze, and then said the first thing that would confuse the hell out of me and later haunt me. "You're the first free woman I've ever kissed."

I didn't know what to say to that. "You wouldn't have done it if the sun was all the way up," I said at last. I'd been deemed "unfuckable" a while back, and had seen nothing to contest that assessment.

"I would," he said, then stood up. "I'm going. See you."

"See you," I echoed. He wandered down the hill, breaking off branches as he went until he had an armful of green, leafy stuff. It wasn't a house he was headed to, I saw, but a broken-down hulk of a car, parked in a little clearing. There weren't any tire tracks leading to it.

He's living in a car, I realized. *He's living in a car, and he wants to hear about grade school.*

I'd like to see him again.

I got my wish. The next night, he was at the bonfire before me, though he hadn't brought any green branches that time. Without saying much, we both walked off together, following the same route as the night before. This time there was more kissing and less talking, though he still had questions about everything I could remember from the last ten years.

This isn't to say I was the only one talking. On the contrary, whenever we got stoned (usually on something from my meager stash; Frank had a few contacts, but little money), it was hard to get him to shut up. He'd talk about things like how everything had gone downhill in the last century, how it used to be that anyone wanting in (to what, he never said) had to fight a dozen warriors while up to his waist in a sandpit. Or long conspiracy theories about Northern Ireland and who was really instigating the Troubles there, killing off some poor kid any time it looked like a cease-fire was even possible.

Most of all, though, he talked about his plans for getting out. "I'm saving up to get passage on a ship," he confided into my ear one night, just as I was trying to convince the last ashes in his pipe to relight. "Rest of it's no good, gotta be a ship. Gotta get *out* of this town."

"Greyhound," I mumbled at him around the pipe stem.

"Get a bus to New York. You can get anywhere from New York. Fucking Yankees," I added, just for the hell of it. They'd been stomping the Sox that year, the bastards.

"Uh-uh. No way. No goddamn way. You ever heard of Taranis' Wheel?" He took the pipe out of my hands—to my lazy protests—knocked the ash out, and drew a funny shape in the dirt: a man's head, or a lump like it, and behind it a wheel, so that almost half of the wheel was occluded. "What's that remind you of?"

"Geometry," I said lazily, and laughed at his glare. "Trig class."

"Fuck you. No." He drew some of the spokes out past the wheel, wiggly and straggling, then erased half of the man's head. "Now?"

I squinted at it, trying to figure why it looked vaguely familiar, then realized it: if the man's head wasn't a head, but negative space instead—if it represented an ocean, and the spokes roads . . . "Boston?" I said.

"And Interstate 95." He traced the rim of the "wheel." "Taranis' fucking wheel. They've got markers all along it; they know if anyone of interest, any talents, crosses that barrier. Great goddamn highway, better than a perimeter guard; it keeps us all in. But you can't magic the sea." He stumbled on the last sentence, stuttering out the word *magic*, and kicked the drawing, missing by six inches.

"Must screw over the commuters something awful," I said.

After a moment Frank laughed too. He looked at me for a long moment, then tossed the pipe back to me. "I should just go to Belfast," he muttered, half under his breath. "Just go there and sabotage it all, show everyone what they're all fighting about, who's been egging them on . . . It can't last forever, you know; sooner or later they'll catch on and reconsecrate the ground, or even just call a real cease-fire. That'd mean the—the old woman under the curse would be no good to them, they'd have to find something else, and I'd be free . . ."

I shook my head and sat down next to him. "Frank, sometimes I wonder what the hell you're talking about."

He smiled, but his eyes were still on the scratched pattern on the ground. "Maybe I should just stay here."

"Screw that," I said, and pulled his arm around my shoulders. "The one thing I know you're talking about is that you want to get out of this shithole. You are gonna get out, right?"

"Right," he said, and like an idiot I believed him. So did he.

Frank's car was the only property he owned, aside from the intellectual property of knowing who to talk to (and even then, he'd said, he couldn't use all of his contacts without *them* catching on). It was an old silver Chrysler painted up like a demolition derby car, but with weirder symbols, like the result of a ghetto graffiti-fest organized by the Rosicrucians. The tires were all intact, but he kept it up on blocks of rotting wood with moss growing out of them, and the back—where he slept—was always full of green branches. I wouldn't realize why until years later, when I learned about the concealing properties of living organic matter, but at the time I did notice that his car's scent did seem to sneak up on me. I wasn't able to scent it until I was up close, and that didn't yet bother me. But I did like the way Frank always smelled a little of crushed greenery.

The first time we had sex, my blood got on the leaves, and Frank noticed it. The next night he brought all of the branches to the bonfire, even though it was several days before they'd lose their protective vitality. He came over to my side after he tossed them in, and we stood there together, watching the smoke rise. If I'd been the poetry-writing sort, I'd have gone home and composed some crappy free verse about my innocence on the pyre, but as it was I just held tight to his hand, dimly glad that I'd proved not to be unfuckable.

It was a good summer. If I kept my blinders on, it was a good summer.

Frank never got any closer to leaving, no matter how big he talked. And as the weeks went by, he got more and more jittery, snappish even. I wasn't in the crowd that was starting to experiment with the hard stuff, so I didn't recognize it for what it was: the shakes of an addict going cold turkey. I got worried about him, and so I did the stupidest thing possible: I tried to distract him.

We were lying together on the ground beside his car. Frank stared into the sky as if it might tell him something, and I was more than a little stoned already. And for the first time since he'd kissed me I thought about grade school again, about how I'd wanted to show off to match his own showing off in the playground at recess, how much it had meant to me then.

"Frank," I said, rolling onto my side. "Watch this. I've got a trick to show you."

He shook himself and grunted, as if coming back to life. "Yeah. Trick?"

"Wake up, jerk." I searched the ground around us for something suitable and came up with a smooth gray rock about the size of a half-dollar and with white streak across it like a gull's silhouette. "Hold on to this."

"Great fucking trick, Evie."

"Shut up. Just keep holding on to it—breathe onto it, if you want. Yeah, that'll work." I closed my eyes and pressed my face against his shoulder. "Now throw it. Throw it anywhere."

I could almost hear him roll his eyes, but the muscles of his arm flexed and a thump sounded not far away. "Now what?"

"Now," I said, getting to my feet, "I'll find it for you." I closed my eyes and inhaled. Frank's car had a touch of that oppressive, hot scent I would later learn was the scent of magic, but Frank had none of it: he smelled of greenery, sweat, and me. I smiled at that and turned my senses further outward. Somewhere here was a stone that carried a trace of Frank, a scent I could track . . .

I walked six steps and picked up the stone. "Found it!"

I'd expected an argument from him, something along the lines of "how can you tell it's the same one?" But Frank just stared at me, his face growing whiter and whiter. "How did you do that?" he finally croaked.

"I've always been able to," I said, tossing the stone from hand to hand and trying to sound nonchalant. "It's just a trick I can—"

"Christ. You're a blood-worker. You've got your own."

"My own what? Frank, it's just a little magic trick—"

"Little?" He rolled to his feet. "You flaunt blood-magic right in front of me—in front of me, when you goddamn well know I can't do it or they'll see me—you call that *little?"*

"Frank, I don't have the slightest idea what you're talking—"

"You don't?" He stomped up to me and leaned in close to my face. Whatever he saw there made some of the fear go out of him, though he was no less angry. "Jesus. You really don't. I thought you could be one of them, you could be a trap of theirs, and instead you're just some stupid little—"

"I am not stupid!" I yelled.

Frank didn't even hear me. "—some stupid bitch who's got God's own luck to stay out of it all—Jesus, how did you escape them? They track magic, they knew when I started—I can't believe you did that, do you know how hard it's been? *Do you know how fucking hard it's been to keep from working my magic?"*

He grabbed me by my arms and shook me hard, as if to emphasize his point. I was still holding the rock, and without thinking I hit him in the face with it. "I don't know what you're talking about," I said as he staggered back, one hand to his bleeding cheekbone. "I don't know anything about magic."

"Yeah, well, that's obvious by now," he muttered. "Get out of here, you stupid bitch. I don't know how you've stayed away from them so long, but as far as I'm concerned, you deserve whatever they've got for you."

"Asshole." I chucked the rock at his car. It didn't break a window—it's hard to aim when you're crying—but it made a satisfactory dent in the hood. "You go to hell."

I heard him laughing as I walked away. "I'm already there," he called after me. "I'm already there."

I sulked for a whole week. Mom was busy—she'd been working two jobs at the time, trying to save for college, though we'd end up using most of the money for her hospital bills. So she didn't get to see most of my mood up close, but she did get the side effects of unwashed dishes, loud music through the wall, and a general pall over the apartment. She didn't go out of her way to make things better for me, but she did give me an extra hug before leaving for work each morning, letting me know that she was there if I needed her.

Finally I decided to go back, if for no other reason than to tell Frank in detail just how much of a jerk he was. I showed up with a six-pack a little after dusk and waited for Frank. It was a heavy, damp night, the electric smell of an oncoming storm promising rain before midnight. The bonfire was only a smudge of a blaze, but the scent of smoke was heavy in the air, crossed with some kind of greasy reek.

Frank didn't show up. I asked around and got no answers. No, he hadn't shown up with his usual contribution to the bonfire. No, no one had seen him. I went looking for him, forgetting for the moment how I always had trouble finding his car. After a while, I gave in and used my talent, never mind that it'd give us something more to argue about when I did find him.

Eventually I found the one trail I hadn't been expecting: not Frank or his car, but the stone I'd had him put his scent on two nights ago. I'd been so busy following the scent, so caught up in the hunt, that I didn't realize what I'd found until a gust of greasy black smoke hit me in the face.

Frank's car was a blackened shell. Greenery, clothing, his cracked CDs and all: everything had burned to the ground, and the remaining smoke was all that was left of his one-time home. There was no sign of Frank, no scent or trace beyond the stone I held.

I gaped like an idiot, then coughed as another gust caught me. My sense of smell had been so hyperactive that coming upon this was like getting socked between the eyes. And now a new scent began to tingle at the back of my nose, one I would only learn to recognize later, one that began to blend in with the burning car's reek as the thunderstorm finally swept in, rain shredding the dark clouds of smoke.

Fireworks and rain.

It was funny, I thought as I coasted over the Charles River again, this time with a packet full of refereed journal articles for some cranky guy down by Longwood, but the first thing I'd thought at the time was *Mom's going to kill me.* Not because I'd had a boyfriend and never told her, or had sex, or been off with the kind of kids she primly referred to as "hooligans," but because I'd been careless. And because I'd been careless, because it would be so hard to face her about it, I'd gone to her first.

She'd taken it all in silence, then put me in her car and drove around the city, stopping at damn near every Catholic church. Since we lived in Boston, this took the better part of the day. "Not here," she muttered, passing another brick church with its saint out front, "the deacon here made a bargain with them years ago; not here, the priest might turn you over to the exorcists; not here, this one's unaffiliated but I wouldn't trust him near my daughter . . ." On and on. At first I listened, trying to make sense of it, but after a while I got bored, though after I noticed that we'd crossed the Charles, the Mystic, and the Fort Point Channel at least three times each, I thought there might be more to her route than just her choice of church.

Finally, after a trip through the North End that involved at least two one-way streets driven backward, she brought me into a little church and ordered me to make confession. "Tell the priest everything you told me," she said, then, a little of her usual reticence returning, "but don't tell him *everything*."

Cryptic as always. I made confession, got a stiff penance and a lecture on both premarital sex and condoms, both of which I'd enjoyed, and met Mom outside. She drove us out to the harbor, and there, by the ocean that can never be enchanted, told me everything she knew about them. The Bright Brotherhood.

Christ, I couldn't even speak their name in my head without flinching. I took a detour into the Fens and paused my bike at the top of a bridge. *Fiana*. There. I'd named them. Done.

And now, now that Frank had crashed back into my mind if not into my life, all I could think of was, again, that Mom would kill me if she knew how careless I had been. Not about my real name—that sort of stuff was for magicians, and I was no magician—but about using my talent, being circumspect, not drawing attention. Not putting myself forward.

I rubbed the back of my neck, leaving a smear of road grime along my hairline, and got off my bike. The cranky doctor could wait an extra ten minutes for his journals, especially after the day I'd had.

Though come to think of it . . . I smiled at the surface of the river. Much of what I'd done today had retraced Mom's route. Crossing water, keeping the tricky spirits of rivers between me and Leon or Corrigan or whoever else might be following me. I took a deep breath, savoring even this murky smell of river and mud, traffic and cut grass and—

and *fireworks*—

Something stirred by the side of the bridge. Without thinking, I shoved my bike against the railing and ran to the stream. "What do you think you're—"

The figure stood up, and I realized my mistake. This was no magician—she didn't look older than eight, and the only thing in her hands was a handful of grass stems. The smell of fireworks was already gone, if indeed it had been there in the first place. "Ah. Sorry, kid. I thought I saw . . . never mind."

"'s okay." The spindly little girl gave me a curiously intent look, as if she were trying to remember something.

I must have had the same expression on my face, because something about this kid looked familiar. Her eyes were a peculiar shade of gray, startlingly light in her tan face, very much like someone else's . . . "Are you Katie Hunter?" I asked.

"Yes." She cocked her head to the side, and a smile broke over her face like the sun coming out from behind clouds. "You're Nate's friend."

"One of them." It'd only been a year or so since I'd seen her last—I'd run into her and Nate while I was doing courier work for the Aquarium—but she looked a lot older. Though, come to think of it, the difference between seven and eight is a lot greater than the difference between thirty-three and thirty-four, in maturity as well as looks. "Aren't you supposed to be in day camp?"

The smile disappeared, and she looked down, a fringe of light brown hair hiding her face. "Day camp sucks," she muttered.

I shouldn't have laughed, but it caught me off guard, and anyway I'm no good at remembering how you're supposed to act around kids. Besides, she reminded me too much of myself—heck, of how I'd acted that summer in Southie, booze and Frank aside. "Lot of lame organized activities, right?" I said, settling down in the grass beside her.

"Sometimes." She crouched, hugging her knees and staring at the river. "The other kids don't like me. Sometimes. If I'm not careful they don't like me."

"Not careful?"

She shrugged. She didn't look much like Nate: round-

faced where he was angular, a Renaissance cherub where
he was more of an elongate Romanesque saint. But the clear
gray eyes were the same: unmistakable Hunter eyes. "So I
came over here. Look."

She pointed under the bridge. I squinted, and after a
moment my eyes adjusted enough to see six blobs of yellow
fluff, followed by a mother duck. "Huh. Cute."

"She's here all the time. She's got a whole family. I come
see her a lot." She was silent a moment. I glanced at her
and changed my opinion: she wasn't much like I had been.
Too quiet, too self-possessed. Maybe it was just because
I'd been thinking about Frank that I'd seen my reflection
in her. And right now I was just another big clumsy adult
intruding on her world.

"I'll let you alone, then." I got to my feet, brushing bits
of grass from my ass.

Katie glanced up at me, biting her lip. "I came here to
see you, too."

I paused in the act of reaching for my bike. "Say what—"

I got no further before the powdery, humid stink of
magic wrapped around me. Katie squawked and scuttled
backward, staring at something behind me. I turned, following her frightened gaze to the apex of the bridge, where
I had been standing not five minutes ago.

A man, naked to the waist and barefoot, stood at the
peak of the bridge, looking down at us with an unreadable
expression. His hair was a shock of iron gray, and he held
one hand to his mouth, as if he were sucking or chewing
on his thumb. The other hand didn't quite touch the handlebars of my bike, but in a way that showed he was de-
liberately not touching it. A shifting haze surrounded him,
like the shimmering air over hot roads. But all that was
secondary; what I saw right away were the blue marks,
blurry spirals and angular designs, that marked him from
head to foot. The marks seemed to writhe as he shifted to
face me, rewriting themselves with each twitch of his skin.
A thin scent reached me, the dry reek of old parchment or

stretched skin, ink and hot iron, overlaid with a tickling texture like grass blades, like leaves, and over all that the reek of power.

"Katie," I said quietly, "get back and stay by the river." She didn't respond, and I didn't turn to see that she'd obeyed. I started for the bridge, but just then the blue man turned and vaulted over the far side of the bridge. There was no splash.

I ran to the bridge and looked around, but the river—and its banks—were empty. The only trace of the man was the lingering scent he'd left behind, a scent I somehow knew, never mind that I'd smelled it for the first time today—

"Katie Hunter!"

I jumped and spun around. A matronly woman in an Allston-Brighton Summer Camp shirt was marching down to the river. She took Katie's unresisting hand, said something low and admonitory, and Katie hung her head, not looking at either of us, though she did steal one last glance at the ducks.

I put a hand to my throat and tried to calm my breathing. The camp leader led Katie past me, but Katie tugged her hand free and ran up to me. "It's okay," she said. "I saw him too."

Six

Only two of my close friends knew anything about how I earned my living; Sarah was one, and the other was a cop. Lt. Llerena Santesteban had drilled into me the proper way to respond to trouble: report it and get backup before you do anything stupid. She said she was sick of people watching too many cop shows and thinking they know how to handle a situation, and I bore the brunt of that frustration. Rena's advice for a day in which I'd received a bizarre phone call, gotten hit with the effects of an anti-dog whistle, been shot at, and seen a half-naked crazy man jump off a bridge would be to call her and get an informal report down. That way I'd at least have some documentation.

It should be no surprise that my actual response differed. I didn't need documentation right now; all it could do was trip me up if someone got too close a look at it. What I needed now was normality, something to counteract the tug of the undercurrent.

I headed home for a shower after work, then looked up the address Will had given me. *It's just a bar*, I thought. *You can talk to Will, see if he's got anything on the McDermots or on Corrigan*—not that I wanted to think about Corrigan just now—*you can talk to some people you used to know, and it'll be one step back from the edge. One step closer to shore . . . even if you'll be closer to a different edge.*

So I pulled on a shirt that wasn't too rumpled, stuffed the flyaway bits of my braid back into place, and walked over to the South End. It had gotten humid, muggy with that staticky scent that promises a thunderstorm, and by the time I reached the address, my shirt was sticky again. Still, I enjoyed the warmth. Spring had come late, and after a very bitter winter; I hadn't been able to breathe outside without having my lungs shrink from the cold. That sort of thing is rough on a finder who uses her nose.

The Adeline Pub looked like it had started off as just another hole-in-the-wall, the kind that might have become the center for some serious nostalgia in other circumstances. Inside, though, someone had gotten decorating ideas, and I groaned inwardly the moment I opened the door. Wicker structures that looked like skeletal kites hung from the ceiling, as did tiny light fixtures in the shape of swans. A bank of TV screens above the bar alternated with lumpy landscape paintings, and it took me a moment to realize that the sound emerging from the screens didn't match the visuals.

The bartender saw my baffled look and, with an ease that must have come from years of getting such a reaction, nodded to the tiny television behind him, where the Sox game was just getting started. I grinned and decided to tip him extra if I could.

"Evie! Evie Scelan, howya doin'?" Will rose from out of one of the peach-painted booths. "Let me buy you a drink."

I gave him a wan smile and met him at the bar. "Ginger ale, please."

"Two Sam Adamses— What? Oh, come on, have a drink on me."

"Thanks, but a ginger ale will be fine."

He caught the slight stress I put on the last words. "Since when have you stopped drinking?"

I sighed. Of course he'd remember what I was like in high school. "Since I woke up with my head sticking to something too many times." True as far as it went, but it glossed over the other reason: when I started using my talent regularly, I stopped drinking. There were other reasons, but they weren't the important ones. "Anyone else here?"

"Come and see." He handed me my drink and led the way to the table, which might have been one of the few relics of the old pub. "Rob Jankin, you remember Rob, there's Laurie Taylor—"

"Used to be Laurie Mienkowicz," the woman Will had gestured to said with a grin, scooting her chair over to make room.

"Yeah, you remember her, and tonight old Nate decided to show up too."

Nate gave me an embarrassed little wave. "Nate and I have kept in touch," I said, sitting down.

"Really? How's that?"

I regarded Nate for a moment. "We ran into each other at a party, when was it? Last year?"

"Halloween. Year before last." He cleared his throat. "It turned out that we had some friends in common."

"Let's see, how did it go?" I tipped my chair back and took a sip of the ginger ale. It bit back; the bartender apparently stocked the good stuff. "Sarah's girlfriend was your ex's boyfriend's ex. Or something like that, with a few more degrees of separation."

Nate nodded. "And it's probably gotten only more complicated since then."

"Good for you, good for you." Will took out a handkerchief and mopped at his face. He had a weird, hyperactive look about him, entirely different from his attitude this morning. If I hadn't known what he was drinking, I'd have said it was a triple espresso. Though maybe he just found this sort of informal reunion energizing. "So anyway, guys, I ran into Evie earlier today, and guess what."

"You talked her into coming here," Rob said with a yawn. "Doesn't take much to guess that."

"You're one hundred percent wrong, you know that? No, Evie, see, I got you figured out. I found out about you." He winked and nodded at me and raised his glass in a complimentary, if baffling, toast. Condensation trickled down the glass and soaked into a lumpy bandage on his hand.

I checked the distance to the door, realized what I was doing, and forced myself to calm down. "What do you mean, you found out about me?"

He winked again, this time at everybody but me. "See, when I saw you today, I had you pegged as some kind of messenger thing, what with the bike and all. Courier, that's the word."

"That's her job," Nate said, his brows furrowing.

Will wagged his finger at him, and I remembered again why I'd tried to beat him up in science class. "Oh-no-no-no. Our Evie's been fooling us all. I looked you up, see. You're a PI."

Nate looked skeptical, but Rob perked up a little. "PI? You mean like a private investigator?"

"Exactly," Will said. "Exactly. 'Expert retrieval and recovery services' is what it says in the Yellow Pages."

I raised my voice over Will's. "It's not quite the same. It's part-time, I only take on certain jobs, and it's nothing like what you see on TV."

"That's gotta be kind of precarious, though," Laurie said. "I mean, financially speaking."

"Laurie's an accountant these days," Rob added by way of explanation.

"It is precarious," I admitted. *In more ways than one.* "That's why I have the other job."

"Still, I can't imagine it." She shook her head. "How do you handle things like . . . oh, I don't know, health insurance?"

I shrugged. "I don't get sick?" That got a laugh from the others, rueful from Nate and too loud from Will. I didn't feel right adding that I had a slight advantage, in that not long ago I'd accepted a well-made charm against disease and accidental injury in payment for an undercurrent job.

It'd hold for a year, and after that, well, I might be back to waitressing.

"Sounds like the plan I'm on," Nate said, tilting his glass so he could see into the bottom of it. "MIT's got bare-bones for me and Katie, but all that means is that we're okay in emergencies."

I glanced at him, a little concerned by the note of hopelessness in his voice. He didn't meet my eyes.

"Katie?" Rob frowned. "Who's Katie?"

"My sister," Nate said absently.

"Hold on. You didn't have a sister when we were back in school—"

Will chuckled into his beer. "No offense, Nate, but your mom must have been quite adventurous. That's twenty years in between kids. What, was she on those hormone things?" Laurie's frantic gesture went unnoticed by Will. *She must know about his mom too*, I thought. "No, wait, I remember," he went on before I could break in, "your mom was pretty young then too, right? I remember Harry Jarvis, you remember him from track, he kept checking her out all through that PTA night—"

Both Laurie and I jumped in, and I got there first. "Will, there was something I wanted to ask you about this morning."

His face brightened up, almost as if someone had switched a second light onto our table. "Yeah? Really?"

Laurie sighed audibly. Nate, though, hadn't reacted—or he had, but by not responding at all. It was as if a lead cloak had suddenly descended around him; his face had become as still as granite. I could even smell the change in him, though no one else could, like a burning fuse shutting down, or sand dumped over a campfire.

Will, though, was off in his own cloak-and-dagger fantasies. "Hey, is that why you were in the neighborhood this morning? Some kind of PI work?"

"Not quite. You know that guy we were talking to? Does he come around often?"

"Who, that guy, whatshisname, Carson? Enough that I

know his face, and besides, he's not the type you see around there usually, so he stands out. Reminds me of the time this one guy came to me for an interview . . ."

He veered off into another anecdote, this time about one of his employees. I glanced at Nate. Finally he drew a long breath and let it out, and the scary locked-down scent faded.

I tried to give him a smile—I remembered his mom, though fuzzily. The two of us had had a mutual unvoiced respect for each other in high school for one major reason: neither of us really had a father to speak of, even if our mothers' marital status differed, and we were both good at evading questions about them. I didn't envy him; the man had had his whole life planned out before this little sister arrived, and then when his mom died, he got stuck with the job of being a substitute father.

What I'd said about meeting at Sarah's party was true. I'd almost forgotten about him. These days I sometimes felt as if he knew a little of what I'd gone through, just because we'd both only had our moms for family, and we'd both lost them. He didn't know about the undercurrent, though. No one who wasn't already in it knew anything about that, for the simple reason that knowing dragged you in.

"But you gotta admit, Evie, it's pretty goddamn glamorous, being a PI. I mean, you get the exciting stuff, like on TV, right?"

"Not in the least," I said, trying to see the score on the Sox game. "No car chases or shoot-outs, and I haven't seen one Maltese Falcon yet."

"Oh, come on. Tell us some story, something good. We won't tell."

Laurie shook her head. "For crying out loud, Will, let her be. She doesn't want to talk about it."

"Yeah," Rob added. "Besides, you haven't once asked me how 'glamorous' it is to be in a band."

"Hey, the kind of music you play . . ."

I tuned Will out. Five-three Sox, in the fifth. That was

something, at least. My eyes unfocused, until I sensed the rest of the Adeline's patrons as only shapes and scents. Rena once told me that sometimes after a bad day she'll look out at the streets and wonder how many people are thieves, how many rapists, how many murderers. Now I had to wonder too, although along a different path: how many here knew about the undercurrent beneath Boston? How many had the sight, or were sensitives and didn't know it? Even those questions didn't begin to cover the sheer depth of strangeness out there. How many of these people were ghosts? How many were eyes and ears for someone else? It was a small number by any estimation, but that the number's even there at all is enough to send some rationalists into twitching fits.

Sometimes, I thought, *it seems like the only reason we think the world's normal is because we make it so.*

Which royally screws over people like me who can't fit into that definition. Maybe the Red Queen could handle six impossible things before breakfast, but I had trouble with two before dinner. I downed more of my ginger ale and wished it was something stronger.

It wasn't just the magic. I'd gotten used to that impossibility long ago. I'd had to learn the rules just to keep myself afloat on the undercurrent, to stand with one foot in the real world and one foot in God knew what. You learn a set of rules in order to stay alive, you tend to think they're immutable.

But Corrigan—what he'd done broke all those rules.

It all came down to loci, I decided. What you needed to do magic, real magic beyond a quick scrying or a warding spell, is a locus—a place that was yours. A locus is a part of your soul (or—usually—someone else's) caught in a bottle or other trap, a source of power that you can draw on to coerce natural law into doing what you want rather than asking it as hedge-magic does. Nothing to it. Except that you couldn't do major magic without your locus close by, and not an adept in a thousand is stupid enough to carry his loci around where they might be endangered, and even if

Corrigan had had a locus it wouldn't have worked because magic takes *time*, dammit, time and—

". . . power. Right, Evie?"

I snapped out of my reverie, my skin prickling with gooseflesh. "Yes. What?"

"I said, it has to do with what kind of power base you got. Now, you take your average Mafia guy—"

"What the hell are we talking about?"

Rob grinned, and Nate muttered, "Six-three Sox." I glanced back; they'd scored a run while I'd been zoned out.

"Irish mob," Laurie said. "Whitey Bulger. Will's favorite topic."

"Oh, Christ. Not that."

"The question," Will said, no longer at rant volume but undeterred, "was about power. When the Irish immigrants—you're Irish, right? You'd know about this."

"Dunno," I said distantly, still gazing at the TV. "Mom never said."

"You've got the coloring for it," Laurie said. "Black hair, blue eyes, pale skin."

"It's pale only because we didn't see the sun for most of the spring." I held up a hand to show the angry red spots on the backs of my hands. "See? Bike gloves don't cover everything. By July half of me will be a nice shade of lobster." I shook myself and looked down at the table. Real wood, real graffiti, real patina from years of use. Real smudge of dried malt vinegar on the cruet. Real fries. When had we ordered appetizers?

"It's the big picture," said Will. "Look, Evie, what I was trying to say was that when the Irish came over here, they were penniless and stranded and away from everything they'd had. So they banded together. Us against the world, right? So they'd rather have a local boy running things than an outsider, no matter if he screws some things up. Even if he's crooked to the bone, he's one of them, and that's what matters." He glared down into his beer. "It ain't pretty, but there's lots of people think that way."

More than you think. I finished my now-watery ginger ale. This was all turning into too much of a reminder of Frank. "Look, I'm sorry, but I gotta get home."

"Hot date?" Laurie asked with a grin.

I blushed before I could stop myself, then damned my fair skin, sunburn and all. "No date," I responded, with a little more snap to my words than I'd intended. "Just no sleep either."

Laurie shrugged. "Not like you couldn't."

"Ha." I have no illusions about my appearance, neither good nor bad. That isn't the problem. The problem is that sooner or later, any man I date finds out what I do for a living and how I do it. The reactions so far have all fallen into two categories: hyper-rational refusal to believe in any of this "creepy shit," or sudden and dangerous interest in said creepy shit. One of my exes got so deep into the lower Dorchester argent cults that he cut off all ties to his family and then sliced off his left ear in some sacrifice. I still had that one on my conscience.

Dating a full-fledged magician was out of the question. I'd learned my lesson with Frank.

At the thought of Frank, I bit my lip and stared at the table. He was still out there somewhere, maybe imprisoned or tortured, and here I was, having drinks with friends. *I shouldn't even be here.*

Will seemed to pick up on my thoughts, or the general direction of them anyway. His expression went from madly jocular to crestfallen in an instant. "Jesus, I'm sorry, Evie. I meant for this to be better—I mean, I didn't want to scare you away."

I spread my hands and smiled. "It's not that. I've just had a tough week so far, and I only had so much time to spare to begin with."

Nate reached across the table and caught my right hand. "You're bleeding."

"What?"

He turned my wrist over to reveal a long scratch on my

forearm. There wasn't much blood, and what there was had mostly dried, but a long dark-brown smudge marred the underside of my arm.

"How the hell did that happen?" *Of course.* Shards of the chain stone had gone everywhere when Leon blew it to smithereens, and one of them must have sliced me. It was a wonder I hadn't been hurt worse.

"It's nothing," I said, and scratched at the mark. It must have broken open again after my shower, but by now it wasn't even bleeding any more.

"I've got a first aid kit in my backpack . . . yes, I know," Nate said to my disbelieving look. "I started carrying one after Katie fell off a swing set last year."

"I don't think I'll need it." I tugged my hand free and got to my feet.

Nate pushed his chair back. "I'll get it for you anyway. I think I want to get on home too, at least before it rains."

We said our goodbyes, and I waited until he'd followed me to the door. "Is that really why you're leaving?" I asked under my breath.

"Mostly. Besides, Katie's sitter charges extra if she has to stay past ten." He handed me a Band-Aid, and I jammed it in my pocket before waving goodbye to the others. "Where you headed?"

"Fens. Home. You?"

"Back Bay Station."

I held the door open for him. It hadn't started to rain yet, but a thin mist clung to everything, soaking into my skin. "See you, then."

He hesitated a moment in the doorway, staring off somewhere to his left. "I'll walk you to the T."

I gave him a skeptical glance. We were going the same way, but something about his manner seemed a little off. "Sure."

"Okay, then." He fell into step beside me. "Katie says she saw you earlier today."

I cursed myself for being so damn forgetful. "That's

right. Down in the Fens. I wandered into the middle of her day camp activities." And had she described a crazy tattooed man as part of those activities? I bit my lip and hoped not.

"I think she's got a mild case of hero worship. She kept asking me to call you, so she could talk to you alone."

"About what?"

"Search me. She may try to invite you to her birthday party."

"Ah . . . no. I'm no good with kids, especially small herds of them."

"You're not alone." He grinned. "*I* could always invite you too. Then you'd have to come."

"Says who?"

Nate laughed.

We walked about half a block in silence, with Nate still looking off to the left every now and then. "Look," I finally said, "if this is a prelude to asking me out, then—"

"It's not," he said, though if the light from the streetlights hadn't already given everything a reddish cast, I'd have sworn he was blushing. "It's just that I think someone's following you."

The ginger ale in my stomach froze over. "You mean someone other than you?" I tried. "Don't tell me you took Will and his 'just like TV' crap seriously."

"No. But that guy back there was waiting in a doorway when we left, and he's been behind us ever since."

"Ah." Crap. My mind raced, trying to think of some way to ditch Nate before anything happened. *It couldn't be the Brotherhood*, I thought; *they don't bother with subtlety . . . or at least they didn't . . .* "Maybe you'd better—"

A gust of wind whirled past us, blowing mist all along the back of my neck. I caught a scent on it: fireworks, but muted, like spent gunpowder; cheap booze; and a familiar, prickly smell that resembled a damp raccoon. "Jesus," I said with a laugh of relief. "It's just Deke."

Nate looked at me sharply. "Deke?"

"Business contact." I turned around and waved to the

crouched figure standing behind a fire hydrant. "He's a bit odd, but he's harmless. You can go on; I'm in no danger from him."

Nate took a breath as if about to say something, then let it out in a long sigh. "If you're sure."

"I am. Get on home."

After a moment, Nate nodded and turned to go, casting one glance back over his shoulder.

I crossed my arms and waited. "Well, Deke? You've freaked out one of my friends already, what have you got to show me?"

Deke edged around the hydrant, keeping one hand on it as if to steady himself. In the same way, he made his way from hydrant to light post to trash can. I sighed and looked up at the sky, trying to judge how long I had before the rain hit. He reached out and steadied himself against the edge of the trash can. "Hound, talk to me," he rasped.

"You talk to me." I joined him at the side of the can. He carried a crisp, dry newspaper and began to methodically shred it, piling the scraps in the middle of the trash. "What's so important that you can't just call? Is every adept in the city going nuts all of a sudden?"

"Only the smart ones." He glanced up at me, or at least his right eye did. The other wandered, staring first at the trash can and then at my hands. "Someone's found you."

"Lots of people find me. Sometimes I find them. You couldn't tell me this on the phone, or just leave a message?"

"No messages. Too vulnerable. If I could leave a message, then the green men could find it just as easily."

"Green men. Uh-huh." I tried to edge into the minimal shelter of an overhanging sign, and got a splat of condensed mist on my neck for my efforts. "I'll take it that we're both talking about the same big nasties there, right?" Deke grunted, and I remembered the man on the bridge. "What about blue men?"

Deke's eyes widened. "Hope not. Not unless the dead are already walking."

I shivered, thinking of how the man hadn't seemed to be entirely real. Deke finished tearing his newspaper, took out a pack of cigarettes, and lit one. I turned my face away from the overpowering clove scent. "Hound, you live here, you grew up here, you came into your power here, but you do not know this city. You think you know what to be wary of, but then you show no care in what you do, who you offend, who you befriend."

Had he talked to me right after my run-in with Leon, I might have listened and might even have been cowed. Just now, though, I didn't have any patience for the undercurrent doubletalk and even less for veiled threats. "Thanks very much for the totally useless warning."

"An adept finds no warning useless."

"I'm not an adept. You know that. I don't hide my name, I don't use a locus, and I don't have any patience with the oracular shit. Now, is there anything else—"

Deke grinned and dropped the lit match onto the paper. I jumped back as flames blazed up, but Deke leaned forward till his face was almost in the fire, blinking back tears from the heat. Figures unlike any fire I'd seen leapt and danced before him, then sank again as the damp air and sodden trash quenched them. A spiral of ash wafted up, then collapsed into a long smudge on the side of the can.

I ducked out of the smoke. "Jesus Christ, Deke, I thought you were going to warn me when you did that!"

He poked at the ashes with his cigarette. "Things look bad, Hound. I was born outside the city, so I don't remember much of how it was when they ruled . . . but things may get bad again. I'm doing what I can to stop it, but there's every chance that'll end up working against you." He shook his head. "And every time I try to look ahead, I see you snared in the middle, with a chain around your throat."

"Shit," I muttered. I'm not fond of pyromancy, but Deke is damned good at it, and if he sees something in the fire it's usually good to believe him. "Any advice?"

He blinked at me. "I just gave you some." He took a drag

on his cigarette, grimaced, then dropped it and ground it out under his foot. "Don't expect to see me for some time. Don't trust anyone, because trust will bite you. And look out for family."

"That's all you have to give me?" I called after his retreating back.

Deke paused a moment. "More and the crows will come for me." He walked on, not looking back.

I stood out in the mist for a few minutes, staring into the smoldering remnants of his magic. I couldn't see a damn thing in it. The ash leapt up in a little circle, then another, and I caught my breath—then swore as the rain started to come down harder, obliterating even the few marks it had made.

The gutters were swirling streams by the time I reached home. I hunched over in a futile attempt to keep some part of me dry and kicked at puddles. As I reached the corner, I blinked rain out of my eyes and tried to focus on my front door.

The shadow by my door shifted, and I saw it for what it was: a person, wrapped in darkness, waiting for me. The scent of fireworks curled around me.

Seven

I stopped in my tracks, the trickle of water down my back forgotten. There are only so many ways for an untalented person to fight an adept, and I'd just lost my chance at most of them by walking this close.

I bent and picked up a handful of mud. It wouldn't do much—if I got the charm wrong, it'd just dry out, and even if I got it right it wouldn't do more than temporarily blind my visitor. "Name yourself," I said, then realized how weird that would sound to anyone outside the undercurrent. "Who's there?"

"It's just me." The figure held out his hands to either side and stepped out of the shadow of the eaves. Streetlights glinted off a rain-slicked pate and glasses beaded with water. "Brendan Corrigan."

"Shit." I dropped my hands to my sides but didn't let go of the mud. "What are you doing here?"

"I looked up your address."

"That's not what I meant." I walked up closer, keeping the flowing gutter between him and me. "I'll try it again and see if you understand. What are *you* doing *here*?"

"I had to talk to you. About—" He glanced down the street, though how he saw anything I had no idea. "About Frank McDermot."

"So talk." He hesitated and looked up at the sky. "I have no trouble keeping you out here for an hour," I added.

"Frank was my friend."

"Frank didn't have friends. Try again."

Brendan shrugged. He was soaked to the skin, and I briefly felt bad about keeping him out here in the rain. "Okay. So maybe 'friend' is too strong a word. I was helping him. Against the Fi—"

"Say that name and you can kiss any chance of talking to me goodbye," I snapped.

"I was trying to help him get out," Brendan insisted. "Out of their organization. He mentioned you a few times, just in passing. And today I saw you at his parents' house, and didn't realize who you were until later. I thought you might know where he is."

"Anyone can claim friendship. Doesn't mean it's true. Prove to me you know Frank."

Brendan closed his eyes. "Okay. Frank told me . . . he told me that he was the first guy you'd ever slept with."

Mud oozed out between my fingers as I squeezed the handful of dirt. Rain washed away the runnels. I didn't speak.

Brendan's face was an interesting shade of pink. "He told me it was also his first time, too."

Ah, God . . . I raised my face to the rain, not trusting my voice to hold steady. "He never mentioned that," I said at last.

"He didn't?"

"No. Goddammit, Frank . . ." I wiped mud from my hands. "I suppose I'd better let you in."

"Wait." He caught at my wrist. I shivered. "My name. It really is Brendan Corrigan."

"Yeah. Tell me another one."

"No, really. It's—well, you can look it up, not that that'll prove anything." He let go of my hand and ran his other hand over his head, swiping the rain off it. "I'm just trying to prove that I'm honest. I don't have to give you my name, and we both know it."

I looked at him in silence. The rain had started to let up, not that it mattered to either of us anymore. He was right, about the names at least. Magicians—or at least the sort I'd known up till now—were so closemouthed about their names that it was like pulling toenails to even get a nickname of reference for them. Names had power; names could be loci under certain circumstances. Names were not given without trust.

"If I could give you any more surety, I would." He grinned. "I'd give you a lock of my hair, except that I'm a bit deficient in that department."

I smiled back. I couldn't help it. "Thanks. And—well, you already know my real name."

Brendan's grin widened. I had to admit that it wasn't bad. And for an adept, he was pretty well dressed. With most of their kind, it's lucky if they get their heads out of the clouds long enough to remember to put on pants. "The Hound."

"Only to some. And I'm not exactly happy about that nickname." I turned my back on him—funny how that was so much easier now that I knew I had his name—and unlocked the door.

The little waterfall in the corner of my office creaked and dried up as I opened the door. Something in it had broken when the former tenant left, and now it worked on its own schedule, which bore no relation to the power switch at its base. I kicked its stand, which usually worked but didn't this time, and dropped my keys into a bowl beside the fountain. "I'll get some napkins or something for you."

"I'll be fine." Brendan took off his jacket and hung it on the hooks beside the door. Even his shirt was soaked through, I noticed, then wished I hadn't noticed.

"Then I'll get them for me." I dug a roll of paper towels out from under the fountain (kept there ever since its last explosion soaked the wallpaper for three feet) and tossed it to him.

Brendan caught the roll, took off his glasses, and dried them first, glancing around my office. His eyes took in the couch by the bay window, the salvaged chairs, the big oak desk with a few scorch marks, the little TV nestled into the bookcases. His gaze didn't linger on the wardrobe or the door to the kitchen, and I relaxed a little. I'd long gotten over any self-consciousness about the setup I had, but didn't feel like discussing my living arrangements just now. "So," I said. "Where's Frank now?"

"I was sort of hoping you could tell me." He squinted at the lenses, replaced them, then took them off again and wiped his face. "I know he contacted you not long before he disappeared, but that's the limit of my knowledge."

"He did." I pulled one of the chairs out from behind my desk and motioned to the couch. "Have a seat." Brendan looked at the couch, then at his dripping trousers. "It'll dry. Have a seat."

He sat, but not before spreading out a few of the towels first. "What did he say to you?"

"Nothing useful. That he was really getting out this time, and that he knew what he did wrong last time. Meaning me, I imagine."

Brendan looked up in the middle of wringing out his cuffs. "How so?"

"He'd stayed away from magic as long as it was just him, but once he found out I could do it the temptation was just too much. That's what I figured anyway. I never got a chance to ask him." I turned the chair around and sat down, resting my head on the back of it. "I'd always figured they killed him for leaving. Turns out they just took him back."

Brendan nodded slowly. "So he was just calling to say goodbye. I thought it might be something like that. Frank had a sort of nostalgia about his time with you. Maybe it was because it was the only time he was ever free of the Fiana."

I held up a hand. "Don't say that name again. Please. I know they're not as strong as they used to be, but I don't want to be the one who finds out the current limits of their power."

"Good point. Sorry."

"Your turn. How'd you know Frank, and how did you get involved in the—the Bright Brotherhood's work?" *And how*, I added mentally, *do you manage to have that much power without going insane? If a taste of it can drive men to scrounging with shadowcatchers, then how can you resist its call with that much at your fingertips?*

Brendan rubbed a hand over his head. It squeaked. "It's a long story."

"So we'll dry out while you tell it."

He grinned again. "Fine. But I'll have to cut out a lot, and some parts aren't really explicable . . . do you know how much of a relief it is just to be able to talk about it at all? Without worrying that you're going to call the mental asylum on me?"

I didn't smile, but he'd hit a nerve. "Yes," I said. "Yes, I know. Go on."

Brendan looked down at his hands. "I grew up in New York. I . . . I don't think I can tell you everything about how I grew up there, because it'd implicate more than just me. Let's just say that I got lucky: by the time I started figuring out magic, I had a mentor, and a very good one. He taught me everything I know. Especially how to remain unsnared."

That would be an impressive trick, if it worked. "What was his epithet?" We don't hear much about other cities' undercurrents in Boston—for the simple reason that we're too busy with our own—but there was always a chance I might have heard of him.

Brendan shook his head. "He didn't have one. He went by his real name, same as you and me. I don't— I'm fine with telling you my name, but his isn't mine to give. Besides," he added, "he's dead now. In any case, what he worked on were big, slow magics, the kind that take decades to complete. Not the stuff that gets gossiped about.

"Before he died, he told me to go to Boston, that I might be needed there. There was something . . . *cancerous* was how he put it, something wrong in the city. Something once good that had corrupted and turned in on itself."

"I'd take issue with that, actually," I said. "I don't know much about the Bright Brotherhood, but I have trouble imagining them ever being altruistic."

Brendan made an equivocal gesture. "Maybe. Hard to say, since neither of us were there when it started. Anyway, he gave me this—" He held up his ring, the one with the crude spirals scratched into it. "It's a glamour of sorts, to keep me hidden from them for a little while. Then he had me come up here and set up shop, quietly of course. Within a week Frank had gotten in touch with me. Maybe my mentor had sent him word; I don't know. All I learned was that Frank was a part of this Fi—Brotherhood, and that he wanted to get out."

"He'd done it once before."

"Yes. A long time ago. He said he knew how to do it right this time, and that if I helped him, he'd tell me everything he'd learned. Including the Brotherhood's weaknesses, and he said there were several."

"That's news to me. News to anyone in Boston, I should think." I pulled my braid over my shoulder and began wringing the water out of it. "If you're going to be in this city, you need to know this stuff. You know how tough it is for magicians to work together?"

Brendan nodded. "My mentor and I used to have month-long shouting matches."

"Well, apparently that's not a hard and fast rule, at least not when it comes to Boston. Most of the time magicians are too afraid someone will steal their precious loci. But when the potato blight hit Ireland hard, the immigrants started coming over here in heaps. It didn't spare anyone: farmers, doctors, poets. Magicians, too."

"They didn't try to stop the blight?"

I raised an eyebrow at him. "This wasn't a regional

problem. Fixing it anywhere would have required fixing it all over the island, and how many magicians do you know who'd go through all that for someone else's benefit? Besides, I've heard that a few did try, but too late—something had sapped all the, the mana from the land. Anyway, dozens of magicians came over here and ended up all in the same place, all without the loci that had been so tied to their homes."

"I see. So they banded together."

"Yeah." What was it Will had said? He'd been talking about the Irish mob, but the principle was the same: under stress, people turned clannish, supporting each other and defending against the outside world. "It was probably for safety at first, but then . . . well, power corrupts, and doubly so when magic is involved. The Bright Brotherhood ruled this town . . ."

It hadn't always been that way. Boston had been a city like any other, with its own skeletons in the closet from the time before the Brotherhood. Sometimes they were literal skeletons, things like why it's not safe to go digging in certain parts of Charlestown. What's in the stones where the Boston Massacre took place. Why Josiah Quincy renamed Dock Square as Odin's Block, and who he put underneath it to seal the deal. Magic had been around as long as the settlers had been here, and longer. This was a city, and like any gathering place, it aggregated its own magic.

And these days, with the Brotherhood lying low, it was easy to forget how muted that magic had been for almost a century. "In the last few decades, they've gone quiet."

"How do you know?"

"You're here, aren't you?" He made a noncommittal noise. "There are other adepts in town now, but no native adepts older than twenty." I waited for him to ask me why I didn't count myself in that tally, and exhaled slowly when he didn't. "No one's really sure why the Brotherhood's receded."

"Maybe they've lost their power."

"Maybe. I doubt it." I shook a handful of water into the fountain's basin. It gurgled in response and siphoned the water away. "So Frank talked to you."

"Yes. A lot. He seemed to miss real conversation." Brendan's gaze grew distant, and he looked down, the tips of his ears turning pink. "He talked a bit about you—about the one time he got free of them. And you were a big part of that."

"If I hadn't been, he might have gotten away."

"I don't think so. There's a sort of, of gravity well in the Brotherhood. It's easy to get used to a bad situation, and Frank had gotten too used to it." He took off his glasses and squinted through them, then looked up at me. "It wasn't your fault."

I stripped another handful of water from my braid and cursed as most of it went onto the floor. "Yeah. Anyway. So you worked out how to get him out."

"Not quite. We were just starting to plan, and somehow they got wind of it. Frank disappeared, and all I could learn was that he'd contacted you beforehand. I haven't heard from him since—for all I know, he might have gotten onto a freighter out of Charlestown and made it to Nova Scotia, or he might be squatting on one of the Harbor Islands and hoping we'll forget about him, or he might be dead."

"Maybe." *Luck has no part in this*, I heard in memory, and shivered. "I still don't understand why Frank would risk that much just to say goodbye to me—we weren't even together for that long—but on the phone, he wasn't the only person talking."

Brendan dropped his glasses. "What do you mean?"

"What I said. There was someone with Frank, someone with a very strange voice." I didn't tell him the feeling that I'd had, that it was still Frank's voice but someone else speaking through him. After all, it'd been the middle of the night, and impressions from that hour tend to be completely incomprehensible in daylight . . . except. Except he'd known my name, the name that I'd gotten saddled with well after

Frank disappeared again. "He called me Hound," I added, getting to my feet.

Hound, watch for a collar.

I see you with a chain around your throat.

The hunt comes . . .

"Hound," Brendan echoed. "That's . . . Did he, I mean the person with Frank, did he say anything else? Anything about where Frank might be going?"

"No." I made a pretense of straightening a picture, one of me and Mom out on Georges Island. Actually, come to think of it, he was the one who talked about goodbyes, not Frank." The picture slid askew again. My fingers felt like sausages, clumsy and too large.

"Nothing—" Brendan raised a hand, grasping for a word that wasn't quite in reach. "Nothing, I don't know, prophetic?"

"Prophetic?" I started to laugh, but the sound caught in my throat, choking me. The pressure on my skin spread, like a weight of water over all of me.

I stepped away from the wall and stumbled, my feet tangling over each other. Brendan leapt up and caught me by the shoulders. "What's—" he began, then gagged as the same constriction hit him. I could almost see the weight bearing down on him, a thousand tiny hands seeking a way in.

Behind him, the light from the bay windows winked out. I looked up to see blank darkness beyond the glass and squawked with what little air I had left. The glass began to bow inwards under the pressure of something huge and insistent, and my nose twitched from the heavy reek sinking through the walls.

I shoved Brendan away and lurched toward the windows, only to halt as he caught me by the arm—the scratched one, which flared up at his touch, burning like a tongue of fire. I croaked in protest and fell back.

Brendan put his hands to his throat, then choked out an obscenity I wouldn't have thought he knew. "Salt," he said. "Do you have salt?"

I tried to answer, then gave up and stumbled past the desk to the kitchen door. A lumpy cylinder at the back of the counter, soft from humidity, provided most of what I used for my meager cooking; I snatched it up and hurried back.

Brendan had already wrung out his jacket onto the floor. Without speaking, he took the salt from me and dumped a pile into the puddle. Scooping up a handful of the resultant mess, he pushed his glasses into place, then dragged the couch to one side and approached the windows until he stood in the niche between them.

Don't, I thought. *Don't. It's out there. It'll see you.*

Muttering words under his breath—words that even at this distance made my bones ache—Brendan smeared the saltwater on his left hand and reached out to touch the center window. A blast of scent struck me, as potent as if someone had set off firecrackers under my nose. The glass surged inward, bubbled, shattered, shards flying everywhere—

And was intact. Brendan's shoulders heaved, but his hand lay flat against the straight pane of glass. Fog spread out from it like breath on cold metal, wiping away the blackness. "Do me a favor," he said, his voice as calm as if nothing had happened, "and bring the rest of that salt over here. I need to draw a few sigils to keep that from happening again, and I'd rather not waste your kitchen supplies."

"What *was* that?"

"Offhand, I'd say a clumsy but powerful attempt to get in, to scry you. Probably the Fia—" He paused, then dipped his finger again in the salty muck and continued drawing a seven-sided sigil in the corner of the glass. "You're right. I shouldn't have been throwing that name around so easily."

"At the moment, I'm not in the mood to say 'I told you so.'" I picked up a coffee mug and scraped the damp salt heap into it. "They know you're here, then?"

"No. At a guess, I'd say they went for you, not me." He glanced back at me, revealing a thin cut over one eye, just the kind that might be made from flying glass, deflected too late. "Frank did talk about you a lot. Maybe they came to the same conclusion I did."

"Shit," I muttered. I hadn't spent years trying to stay out of the Fiana's grasp just so that Frank could drag me back in. "I think . . . If you knew that I'm called Hound, then they probably know too . . . Brendan, while you were at the McDermots' place this morning, something weird happened."

"Weirder than usual?"

"You tell me." I told him about the dogs, how something had been going through the city and startling all of them, how it had skimmed over me as well. "Do you think that might have been them?"

"If so, it was even cruder than this attempt. I suppose when you have that much power, you don't need finesse. Wasteful."

"You don't say." I reached for the cut over his eye, but didn't touch him. "You're bleeding."

He nodded absently, concentrating on the second window and its sigil. The saltwater melted into the glass, leaving a ripple to mark where his complicated work had been, and only orange light and the normal darkness of a Boston night showed beyond. "That's good, in a way; less work . . . With your permission, I'd like to put a few wards down."

"Wards?"

"Alarm systems. Of a sort. I feel . . . well, more than a little responsible for dragging you into this." He glanced down and hissed. "Damn. I thought I kept most of them away from you."

I looked down to see a smudge of red on my forearm. The scratch had split open, probably under the pressure of the intrusion, and was bleeding again.

"Not your fault." Frank's fault, damn him and where was he anyway? I bit my lip and tried to concentrate on the mug of saltwater in my hands.

Brendan dipped two fingers in the mug and kept working. "Well, I did keep saying that name while I was here, so it's not as if I'm guiltless . . . anyway, the wards will hold off things like that clumsy attack. They won't be foolproof, but at the very least they'll let me know if you get any unwanted visitors."

"So you can come bail me out?" I grinned, trying to make a joke of it.

Brendan's smile was slower, more serious. "Something like that."

I glanced at the windows. The darkness behind one—or perhaps it had only been in the glass—was receding, leaving it transparent to match the other two, rain-flecked and warped in places. Wards were skirting close to heavy magic—most adepts had wards up, though given the general state of mind among adepts they almost always had the wards set to keep out anything larger than dust. That was a level of paranoia I couldn't handle. But it wasn't as if I would be the one making the wards, and Brendan was saner than most magicians by an order of magnitude. "If you're sure—"

"I am." He shook the last drops of saltwater from his fingers and straightened up. "After all, I've found one ally in this city, and I don't really want to lose her."

"Small risk of that," I said, uncomfortably aware of how damp my clothes were, how my shirt was still sticking to my skin in places. As his did on him. He smelled like rain, I thought, and something underneath, some trace of the aftershave that had broken my hunt earlier. *It's a lot nicer now,* I thought, and stopped before I could go any further.

I set the mug on the fountain's rim with a thud. "One question. Yankees or Mets?"

"What?"

"You're a New Yorker. Yankees or Mets?"

"Oh. Mets. I don't often pay attention, though—"

"That's fine. As long as you're not a Yankees fan. I can stand many things, but the one thing I can't is a Yankees fan magicking around me." Brendan laughed out loud. "Anything else you need for the wards?"

"Silver, if you have it, just to draw the lines. And some time."

I managed to find the last of Mom's silver forks, wrapped up in flannel in the back of the tool drawer. By that time, Brendan had smudged saltwater over the top and sides of the doorframe. "Here." I handed the fork to him, tines first, then held out a towel. "I thought you might want this too."

"Thanks." He wiped at his forearms, but the towel was an old one and didn't absorb much. "They should be visible to you if you concentrate hard. If they're ever broken or deformed, you'll know someone's been here."

"In which case, we're really screwed." I took the damp towel back and wrung it out over the dry fountain. "You use a locus?"

"Yes. So to speak." He caught the unhappy tone to my voice and shook his head. "Not the usual kind. Those aren't just nastier, they're weaker. I prefer the old ways."

"So I've gathered. Care to elaborate?"

Brendan shook his head. "Not here. Not after what just happened. Maybe tomorrow."

"Maybe tomorrow," I agreed.

He kept working for a while, the complicated marks taking up too much of his attention for conversation. I pulled out a ledger and tried to do some financial house-keeping, but it was difficult with him working magic not ten feet away and with my clothes still clammy. At last he stood up from etching the last ward into the threshold of my kitchen and stretched. "That ought to do it. You might want to be careful at your home too—the phone book just had this address, but even if you're unlisted, there are ways for them to find where you live."

"I'll be fine," I said, not looking up from the ledger. "Thanks."

"Welcome. I—" He glanced out the windows again, brows furrowed, and nodded. "I'll get going, then."

I stood up, one hand over my scraped forearm. "Are you— Will you need an umbrella?"

"Probably not. But then again, I didn't think I'd need one when I came over here." He smiled again, and again I couldn't help smiling back.

I waited about twenty minutes after he'd left to pull the blinds. It was probably better, I told myself as I rooted through the wardrobe for a towel and a change of clothes, that he'd just assumed this was only my office. I pulled out the fold-down couch, switched off the lights, and curled up, damp hair spread out to the side, my back to the windows. If I concentrated, I could still see the glimmering marks of the wards he had put down.

Safe, I thought. That wasn't a word I'd ever expected to associate with magic.

Eight

I had been here before. The walls of the hospital room were gone now, replaced by a milky white glow. We might have been suspended in a cloud—but this was no heaven.

My traitorous feet carried me forward, to the edge of the bed. The dull thrum of a monitor was the only sound; not even a breath disturbed it. Whatever part of me recognized this for a dream found it annoying that while all other features of the room had been stripped away, the damn monitor remained, its lines drawing out my mother's life strand by strand.

The woman curled between the sheets had barely enough substance to keep top and bottom sheets apart. At first I thought she was gray-haired, not the artificial white that my mother's hair had turned under the chemo. This woman was old, much older than my mother had ever been. But I blinked, and she was my mother again.

I stood by the bed, and I watched, and I did not want her to open her eyes. But her face turned to me like a flower to the sun, and her eyes—my eyes, the same shade of blue— opened. "Sweet," she breathed, her voice full of dust, and then she called me the name only my mother used.

I took her hand and willed her not to speak. But she

shook her head as if she'd read my thoughts, and her hand tightened around mine. "You know what I need to ask you," she said.

I jerked upright in bed, gasping for breath, my lungs failing me as hers had at the last. The room was dark and claustrophobic, and not even the dim glow of my alarm clock made an impression on the blackness. I pressed a hand to my throat, feeling the blood jump under my skin again and again, then fumbled for the light.

Gold light filled the room, and I drew a shuddering breath. "It didn't happen that way," I muttered. "It didn't."

It didn't make me feel any better—it was hard to imagine what would—but the thunder in my ears dwindled, and after a moment I could untangle my legs from the sheets with hands that didn't shake. My arm grazed the edge of the couch as I got up, and I winced. The scratch was redder than it had been, though it hadn't bled any more, and the skin around it was hot to the touch. *Should have used the damn first aid kit,* I thought.

I wrapped myself in an old fuzzy robe, stumbled to the bathroom, and dumped Bactine on my forearm until I was pounding the sink with my other fist. It seemed to help, or at least the redness faded a bit. I closed the medicine cabinet and regarded my reflection in the mirror a moment. "Can't be too careful," I muttered, and opened the cabinet again.

There were a few small stoppered vials on the top shelf, next to packets of expired medicine and a jar of Vicks'. Two were holy water; one was a tisane of witch hazel and rowan sap. I gazed at them, sighed, and took them down.

I must be paranoid to do this, I thought, and dabbed the tisane on the scratch. Certainly it pushed me a little further down the way to becoming a crazed adept who never told anyone her name and never stepped outside her door without a hawthorn circle. But this wound had been acquired when some really heavy magic had been destroyed, and it'd gotten worse when Brendan worked his wardmaking. Things could sometimes get in through breaks in the skin—breaches in the integrity of one's self—and I hadn't stayed alive this far by being careless.

The witch hazel was pleasantly soothing after the screaming Bactine, and the holy water didn't fizz, so I figured I was okay for now. "This is what you get for staying up talking magic with a Lex Luthor look-alike," I told my reflection. "Nightmares and bad blood." My reflection didn't answer.

Sleep was out of the question, for now at least. I made a cup of coffee, mainly for the smell, and folded the couch into its functional state.

Hospitals . . . I could almost smell that antiseptic reek from the dream. "It didn't happen that way," I said again, and drew my feet up onto the couch, holding the coffee as if it were a reliquary.

Sweet . . . You know what I need to ask you.

Mom hadn't asked. She hadn't needed to, by then. We'd agreed ahead of time, and by the time she was that far gone, she hadn't been able to speak. Her last request for me hadn't been—hadn't been that. It had been the same promise she wanted from me, the same one as every year. She never asked for something for herself. If she'd asked—

If she'd asked, I would have known that she hadn't changed her mind. I put the coffee down, slopping a little onto the stained end table, and put my hands over my ears as if they'd block out my thoughts. *Don't think of it,* I thought; *you've gone over it enough since. Think of something else.* Frank. No. Leon. No, that was a mess. Brendan. *Think of Brendan, of how his eyes looked without the dark glasses, of the wards.* There was still a trace of his scent on the wards, muted among the old-gunpowder magicky smell. Or maybe that was just the scent he'd left here, the result of his presence. Whatever it was, it was rather nice. I smiled and burrowed a little deeper into the couch.

I woke with sunlight flooding in through the bay windows and the phone ringing in my ear. I blinked at it, then at the now cold and useless coffee. "Goddammit," I mumbled, then shook myself and grabbed the phone. "God*dammit*. Hello?"

"Genevieve? What are you doing at home? You're supposed to be on shift now." Tania sounded far too perky for this early in the morning.

"What? I thought I had this morning off."

"Schedule changes, honey. I've got you working a double shift today."

I covered the mouthpiece and cursed. "Aren't you supposed to give me warning first?"

"I did. Called your cell phone and left a message. Not my fault if you don't check it. Now hurry up and get down to State Street; I've got someone needing a courier in twenty minutes. If you're there I can tell the boss that you were here on time and just forgot to check in."

I hung up, took the world's fastest shower, and got to State Street only ten minutes late. The package had to go all the way out to Newton, and then it was back into town again. Today everyone had messages that needed to be run across the city, and those who didn't were clogging the streets. I barely had time to pee, never mind continuing the interrupted hunt. That last rankled, like an itch in my brain. But I'd wanted mundanity, and this was mundanity with a vengeance.

I finally got off shift at seven, and discovered what else had gone by the wayside this morning. I'd forgotten sunscreen, and the spots on my hands and face where my gloves and helmet let in light were an angry red. I prodded them and hissed.

I rode down to the Esplanade, parked my bike, and went out to one of the docks on the Charles so I could sit with my feet in the water. The Charles these days is clean enough that you can do that without getting ulcerated soles, but more importantly, it kept me near running water. And water is the one thing that magic can't get a reliable hold on. Stone would flow to the right touch, lead would shift itself away from a questing adept, even cold iron could rust away under the constant pressure of a spell, but water has too many individual spirits for anyone to fully bind it.

My cell showed two calls besides the belated warning from Tania: one a missed call from Sarah, no message, and one from a number I didn't recognize. I checked the message and grinned: Brendan, sounding very nervous, asking if we could meet sometime today.

I called him back, and he answered on the first ring. "Brendan? This is Genevieve Scelan. I'm out on the Esplanade. Any chance you could meet me here?"

"Sure. Why there?"

"River. Running water. I'm on the island, at the end near the Hatch Shell. I might be able to do some tracking, but after last night I'd rather have you with me in case something goes wrong."

"You'll be able to find Frank?"

"Maybe. It's worth a try." I didn't mention that I'd been doing that same damn thing when he'd interrupted me on the Common. No sense in bringing that up now. "Can you come out here, or should I head downtown?"

"I'm pretty close by. Be there in ten minutes."

"Good." I clicked my phone shut, then reconsidered and dialed Sarah's number. The line buzzed, then switched over to the Goddess Garden's answering machine, which Sarah interrupted with an ungoddessly curse. "That's hardly the way to greet a potential customer," I said.

"Evie, the day you're a potential customer is the day the sky falls in. What did you want?"

"That's what I was going to ask you. You called and didn't leave a message."

Sarah cursed again. "I always forget you cell phone people can tell that sort of thing . . . Okay. I was calling about the chain stones."

"Yeah." Damn. In the aftermath of Leon's gunshot, I'd forgotten he'd had one of them. "About those."

"I think it might not be necessary to have you hunt them anymore. I've got a few leads on where they might be."

"Don't worry about it. I'll still keep an eye out for them; I just may have a little more on my plate at the moment." I considered telling her about the attack of the night before, then dismissed it. I didn't want to get Sarah drawn any further into this, and if she knew I'd had wards put up, I'd get a lecture about staying out of the hard stuff. "Anyway, I found one of them, but it's no longer available—or even existing in one piece. Leon Fisher had it."

"Leon. Really?"

"I'm surprised he didn't get in touch with you; he knows you better than me, and he'd have tried to flog it to you with the rest of his junk."

"I usually turn him down flat. That's probably why he didn't call." She hesitated, and even over the phone I could hear the tension in her voice. "There's something else, isn't there?"

I glanced over my shoulder. No one within earshot. "Leon pulled a gun on me."

"You're kidding. The same Leon you and I know? Scummy but harmless?"

"Same one, down to the hair dye. Shot the stone off my hand and blew it to pieces. He was aiming for me, and he would have got me, except—" I glanced over my shoulder again; no sign of Brendan. "Except this guy stopped him— and Sarah, he did it with just a word—"

"That's not possible."

"Tell me something I don't know."

"This guy who stopped Leon—what'd he look like?"

"Bald. About my height. Maybe my age, maybe younger. Hard to tell. Dressed nicely, not what I'd guess for a magician. He didn't strike me as predatory, if that's what you're asking."

Sarah let out her breath in a long hiss. "No, that's not it. But I'd be careful around this guy in future."

"He *did* save my life, Sarah."

"This time he did. Besides, that's not all there is to it. There's a reason I pay you for your work, you know."

It took me a moment to realize what she meant. "Ah. Thanks. I'll keep it in mind."

The fact that money was exchanged left both of us without any obligations, and in the undercurrent, favors owed would come back to bite you in the ass. It was possible that Brendan hadn't realized what an obligation he had put on me; possible, but extremely unlikely if he was as good a magician as he seemed. You don't get that good by ignoring some of the basic laws of exchange. There were tides in the undercurrent, and not even the adepts pretended to understand them. It wasn't like there were little Erinyes who would come charging after me if I ditched him, but bargains were still important. So was payment. Think of the tithe to Hell the fairies were said to pay, or the coins set aside for Charon the ferryman, and you'll start to understand how important.

I don't like bindings. I don't like them even in a non-magical sense; I hate owing debts, I hate obligations, and I hate promises. It's probably because I find it very difficult to walk away from them. Sarah would say this is what causes a lot of my relationship troubles. I would say she's full of crap.

"Do that, then," Sarah said, and I started; I'd been quiet so long that I'd forgotten she was there. "But you don't need to worry about the whole chain-stone thing."

"I'll keep an eye out. Or a nose. That could be phrased better, couldn't it?" A shadow crossed my lap, then shrank as the person casting it sat down beside me. "I'll talk to you later, okay?"

Brendan hadn't really taken a seat, I saw as I clicked off my cell; he'd just crouched down, keeping his pants clear of the dust. "That didn't take long," I said.

"I was closer than I thought." He stood up and offered me a hand. "I keep getting confused about distances in this city. Hadn't they invented straight lines yet when they planned it?"

"The Back Bay's not so bad," I said. "It's built on fill over a big tidal, muck pool, like Southie. They didn't have any cow paths in place already, so they laid out the streets at right angles." I dusted off my butt and shook out the cramps in my legs. "Now, don't take this the wrong way, but I should have asked this last night—"

"I told you. Mets, not Yankees."

I grinned, and he did too. Even with the sunglasses, it looked good. "No. Really. You've saved my life, twice if last night was as bad as it looked, and you did me a big favor by setting those wards. What do you want in return?"

He looked down, then took off his glasses and started to polish them with a fold of his jacket. "It wasn't that big a favor."

"It still counts."

Brendan shook his head. "I don't know. I didn't really do it with the intent of putting you in debt to me. Can't we just defer it till later?"

Sarah would have said no. Deke would have said no. Leon would have said no and gotten the hell out of there, and I think it was this that spurred me to the opposite point of view. After all, I wasn't a magician. I made no secret of my name and walked in the sunlight; I could handle the deferment of a debt. "All right. But don't make it something too big when you come to collect."

He winced at my phrasing. "Nothing that's beyond you. I promise. Now, you were going to try to find Frank?"

"I can try. I . . . know his scent. Pretty well, though it's been a while."

Brendan's eyes gleamed. "How— But people's scents change over the years, don't they? Wouldn't it—"

"Yes." I held up a hand to stem the flow of questions. "But I can still do it. The ephemera will have changed, but he won't."

"Right. Right." He visibly restrained himself from asking more. "What do you want me to do?"

"Watch my back. Keep me from getting distracted. If

anyone with too much perfume or B.O. comes by, try to reroute them. I can usually deal with incidental scents, but it'll take me longer if someone's breathing garlic over my shoulder." Brendan wore the same scent today as yesterday, something that curled around me like September sunlight. It was pleasant, and would be a distraction if I let it, but I could adjust for the sake of having someone at my back. "And if I start going glassy-eyed or speaking in tongues, throw me in the river."

He looked from me to the Charles and back. "Are you sure?"

"Well, maybe just splash me." I grinned at him and took a step back, onto the rocks of the shoreline, and closed my eyes.

The air smelled of June, and car exhaust from Storrow Drive, and warm grass, and walkers or joggers passing by, and lunches on the grass, and Brendan. Damn. Not Brendan. "Could you step back just a little bit?" I said.

"Sorry. Have you— Were you always able to do this?"

"Always." I didn't know where my talent came from. Neither Mom nor Dad had it, though according to him, it was all his doing: as a cop in Pennsylvania, he took care of the squad's two tracking bloodhounds from the K–9 unit. One of them, he claimed, must have jumped over my cradle when I was a baby, and he was pretty sure he knew which one, since Old Beau never hunted as well after I was born. He loved telling that story, and probably still tells it.

Mom's only comment on that story was that I never had a cradle. I remember she always used to sit still and silent when Dad had me show off by finding where a guest had hidden his keys or some other trick. When she and I left for Boston, she told me never to do those tricks again. So I didn't—for some time, at least. Not till Frank, first in grade school and then that summer in Southie.

"Frank," I murmured, and heard the crunch of Brendan's feet on dirt as he moved closer. "Where are you, Frank . . ."

It was like trying to locate a bakery in the evening based

on the remaining scent of its early-morning shift. There were traces, some like Frank, some not—a dim echo, as if he were nearby but muffled somehow . . .

"This is what you were doing," Brendan said softly. "When I saw you on the Common."

"Something like this," I said when I remembered to answer. Speech was irrelevant now, unimportant compared to the riot of scents, and yet it was a tether back to the world.

I found Frank's scent more quickly than I expected; he'd been here on the Esplanade, not more than a week ago, but he hadn't stayed around. Was there something new about the scent? Something new, but familiar . . . ink and dry skin, hot iron, something more than the gunpowder scent that was even more ingrained now than it had been when I knew him . . .

For a long time I lost myself in the patterns, untangling his scent from the rest. But it wouldn't untangle fully, wouldn't come clear. I tried to speak, and croaked through a dry throat. "There's . . . I think something's gone wrong. It's like he's blocked from me."

"Maybe he managed to get away."

"Maybe. No. The scent's too close for that; he's definitely somewhere in the Hub . . . a river. There's a strong river scent mixed with his."

"There are islands upriver, aren't there? Could he hide out on one of them?"

I shrugged. "That's going up past Newton, and I'm not sure he'd have had the strength . . . wait . . ." Something more. Something heavy and oppressive, rising up from the ground like a miasma, like the smell of basements flooded and never quite dried, old towels left in a heap at the end of summer, grass clippings left to rot after a rain and a week of hot sun. "Mildew. Damp. Something really bad—"

My cell blared a blast of music, and the entire image in my head, thousands of people scents and trails and everything, abruptly shut down. I lurched to one side and rebounded from Brendan's arms as he caught me. "Dammit. Forgot—*ow*—forgot to turn it off—" I opened my eyes, regretted it as the evening sun knifed into my brain, and groped for my phone. "Christ, I can ignore everything else, but not this, you think I'd know better . . . This is Scelan," I said into the phone.

"Evie! Baby! This is Will, from last night."

"Goddammit, Will." I gave Brendan an apologetic look, and he shrugged, settling down on the closest bench. "What is it?"

"Nothing much. It's just I got to thinking about the kind of stuff you do, and I thought a little about some things that have been bugging me, like this one time . . ."

"Can you save the story for later, Will? I'm a little busy at the moment."

"Busy, yeah. Hey, you out on a case? Huh? Tracking down a perp?"

"Will . . ." I sighed, and Brendan gave me a sympathetic look. "I don't do that sort of stuff, Will. I told you that last night."

"Okay, sorry, so I got carried away. The thing is, I think I might have a job for you."

"No," I said. "I don't work for friends." Especially not friends who knew nothing about the undercurrent, who could only get sucked into it. I had a sudden image of Will on a street corner, silver sieve in hand, and I shuddered. "I have my reasons."

"Oh." I could almost hear his shoulders sagging. "You sure? I mean, I thought it might be kinda fun."

Fun. Yeah. Right. "Maybe another time, Will. But right now, I've got enough on my plate already, and I have real qualms about mixing work and social life." Not that I had much of the latter. "It's just not good for my reputation."

"Reputation. Yeah." Now he sounded drained, as if my refusal had driven all the life out of him, or as if he'd gone from full caffeine high to early-morning me in two seconds. "Okay. If you're sure."

"I am. Sorry, Will." I hesitated, then went on. "When's the next thing at the Adeline? I had a good time."

"Next week, maybe. I don't know. Take care out there, Evie." He hung up before I could respond.

I lowered my phone and gazed at it a moment. "That was weird."

"You don't work for friends?" Brendan asked, getting to his feet.

"It'd take a hell of a lot to get me to work for them. Like a life-or-death matter, that sort of thing. What?—" I looked up to see concern he was trying to hide. "Allies are different. Besides, I'm not working for you, I'm working with you."

"So that was a friend, then?"

"High school friend." I tossed the phone from one hand to the other. "He sounded . . . weird. Come to think of it, he looked kind of weird last night. I think he may have gotten a bee in his bonnet about what I do for a living . . . hell, I might have to sit him down and explain my whole policy. Not right now, though. Not till we find Frank, at least."

"Mm." Brendan frowned, looking out onto the river.

Two kids on Rollerblades passed us, one with a German shepherd on a leash who nearly unbalanced her as he swerved to say hi to me. I gave him a friendly thump and put away my cell.

Brendan seemed to have reached a decision. "Do you think you can find him tonight?"

I rubbed the bridge of my nose. Part of me wanted to say yes, we'll hunt him down and give him a hell of a time for pulling this stunt. "I might," I admitted. "But after a shock like that, it's going to take me even longer to catch his trail, and it'll be getting close to dark by the time I have it. And there are things that it's better to face in the daytime." Adepts were near the top of that particular list.

"I see." He gazed off into the distance, a thin line forming between his brows. "I think I may want to check on a few matters too, myself. There's been a little too much unrest among some of my contacts recently."

"Got that right." Unrest was the right word, given how little sleep I'd gotten the last couple of nights. The thought triggered something else, something about strangenesses in Boston . . . "Brendan, did Frank . . . did he ever tell you whether the . . . Brotherhood had anything to do with tattooed people? People with runes drawn on them?" People who smelled like loci?

He spun around to face me, blotting out the low sun. "Where did you hear of those?"

My fingers dug into my jeans. "I think . . . I think I may have seen one. I don't know if there's any connection to Frank, but it just seemed so strange—" And there had been a strong magic scent on him, potent as the magic Brendan exuded when he was working.

Brendan's eyes were hidden behind his glasses, dark again from the daylight. I couldn't make sense of his expression. Finally he exhaled and bowed his head. "They're . . . As far as I could figure from Frank, they're bad news. Eyes and ears, people taken over by the Brotherhood and turned into little more than vehicles—vessels—for them. Stay away from them, even if you don't think the Brotherhood can see you: they're powerful, and not even close to sane."

"I'll try to." I picked up my helmet from where I'd left it, keeping my face turned away so he wouldn't read my doubt. The blue man I'd seen in the Fens had smelled powerful enough to be what Brendan had described, but there hadn't been any of that heavy, dank smell about him. No mildew. No threat either. And above all that, he'd smelled . . . well, familiar. As if I knew him, even though I'd never seen anyone like him. As if he were family. "Your wards seem to be holding well, by the way."

He grinned a boy's boastful grin. "You've had two visitors today, other than the mailman. Both of them left messages. One had some mud from the Fens under his feet, and the other tried your door several times before waiting for about twenty minutes." I gaped, and he chuckled. "When I make a ward, I make it well."

"Scarily so." I tucked my helmet under my arm and tried to think of some way to go. It didn't help that I wanted to stay, more than a little. "I should go."

Brendan didn't notice my indecision. "Yes. Oh, here's my card, in case you need it." He took out a cream-colored card and handed it to me. "I don't have a cell, but you can reach me any other way."

I glanced at it. It was in green ink, showing an address in the Leather District and three different e-mail addresses. "'Investment banking'?"

He looked sheepish. "Sometimes. It's a day job, sort of a holdover from my New York days."

"Better than my day job." I tucked the card into my pocket and pulled my gloves on. "Call me if you hear anything."

"Take care of yourself, Genevieve. I don't worry about you when you're at the office, but I can't set wards everywhere."

I laughed as I pulled my helmet on. "If you could, I'd be more scared of you than of the Brotherhood."

Nine

Brendan had been right about the visitors. On top of the heap of mail at the foot of my door was a flyer about a neighborhood blood drive (I'd been giving for several years now; if someone tried to perform sympathetic magic against me using my blood, they'd find their target split between three blood banks) and a folded scrap of paper. I scooped the heap onto the end table and unfolded the scrap, smiling as Brendan's ward tingled underfoot.

The paper was a sheet torn out of a notebook with a scrawl in blotted ballpoint pen. My smile fell away as I read it. *Evie, where the hell are you?—Rena.*

She'd been here, looking for me . . . and Rena was on shift today, wasn't she? I glanced at the phone. Its light flashed red: three messages. *This better not be about Leon,* I thought. I didn't know how I'd explain that.

The tape scraped backward and then began to play an accented voice against a background of loud office sounds and the garbled chatter of police scanners. "Evie, this is Rena. I'd like you to come down here as soon as possible. We've run into something, well, something weird, and I need a second opinion on it. Call me."

Click. Next one. "Evie, dammit, pick up your phone. This is not a joke. It's even weirder than it was at first glance, and I need some backup."

Click. "Okay. Okay, so it's not as urgent anymore." Rena, again, and she paused to draw a long breath. "But I still think you ought to come down here. Just to humor me, if nothing else."

I checked the time stamp on that one. She'd left it twenty minutes ago, though—I checked—the others were both from this morning. Tossing the mail on the desk, I dialed Rena's number.

It took me a few interchanges to reach her line, but she picked up immediately. "Evie? What took you so long?"

"I haven't been home. You were calling my home phone, not my cell."

Rena muttered something derogatory in Spanish. "Well, what's done is done. I'd still like your opinion on this."

"What's 'this'?"

"I'd rather not say. Not yet." *It couldn't be about the gunshot in the parking garage,* I thought. If Rena were going to arrest me, she'd have told me straight off. It was one of her quirks; if she was pissed off, she'd say so, but if she was unsure, she'd clam up. "In any case, it's gotten a little easier since I first called; I can do this all mostly off the record, and it'll speed some things up."

"You're being purposely obtuse, aren't you?"

"I'd say more if I could." Something about the tone of her voice told me she wasn't smiling.

I sighed and gave the cold cup of coffee on my desk a mournful look. So much for a nice evening in. "So where do you want to meet?"

Rena rattled off an address, and I copied it down. "I don't think I know the place," I said.

"No reason you should. I'll meet you there in ten minutes."

I first met Rena after a nasty incident in East Boston. I was looking for what turned out to be a murder weapon, she was trying to find the murderer, and we both ran into the wrong thing at the wrong time. When it was over, Rena had three long gouges down the back of her neck and I had a dislocated shoulder, but we were both alive, and we started talking while waiting for the ambulance. She'd seen a little too much for me to pretend that my work was wholly rational, but she didn't want to know any more. I think she felt that way partly because she regarded the whole mess as suspect, and partly because she saw it as a distraction from her work, and that was not to be allowed.

She preferred not to call me in; it hurt her ego to admit she needed my help (or anyone's, for that matter). But Rena was also a pragmatist, and thus unwilling to discard any tool that might be useful. The only cases she'd asked my help on were all strange ones, ones that just skimmed the tide beneath the city, and not the kind that can be dismissed with a mundane explanation. Like the time six homeless people froze to death last August on a 60-degree night, and they put it down to a freak microclimate pattern. I only saw that one from the fringes, and I still got nightmares. If she'd decided I ought to be called in on this, that meant it was something bizarre, and I didn't really want to deal with bizarre right now.

The building she'd sent me to was an ugly concrete lump, the best of sixties architecture. I stifled a sneeze at the mold growing in the ventilation system and waved to the officer on duty. He didn't smile back.

Rena met me at the front desk. "Good to see you, Evie," she said. She wasn't smiling either. "Nguyen, sign her in."

"Wanna tell me what this is about, Rena?"

She glanced at me, then shook her head. "Not just yet. Hoped you could tell me, once you get a look." Frankly, I'm a lot more comfortable in Rena's company when neither of us is working; both of us tend to put on work like a suit of armor. Right now she was so encased in it, it even showed in her scent: metallic traces on her normal scent, which made my nose twitch.

The guard gave me a funny look. "This about the Lechmere thing?"

Rena sighed. "Yeah."

"I thought we'd—"

"We did. I just want a second opinion, okay?"

He shrugged and slid the ledger across for my signature.

Rena led me down through the halls to the elevators. There were some familiar smells here, and not all of them were cops. We passed a row of doors. Behind one someone was sobbing. Rena lowered her eyes as we passed that one.

"What's this about Lechmere?" I asked as the doors opened.

Rena ran her hands through her short black hair. "Look, I'm not trying to spring a surprise on you. But we've got a lot of people who think they know what's going on here, and if I let them prejudice you—"

"No, no, I get it." I waited as we descended two floors, into the basement. "So what kind of surprise is it?"

She held the elevator door open for me. "Not a good one."

That was putting it mildly. I got about as far as the second bend in the hall before spots floated in front of my eyes. The place smelled awful—not corrupt, but viciously clean, the kind of clean that has to be there to stave off worse scents.

It might have worked for most people, but damn my sensitive nose, it didn't work for me. The lingering odor beneath it all was too potent: a sweetish, cloying scent of delayed decay and tissue rotting. The scent of corpses. Once you've smelled it, you never forget it, no matter how hard you try.

Rena took my elbow to steady me. "Sorry to bring you in here, Evie."

"The morgue," I muttered. "Jesus, you brought me down to the morgue."

"I had a good reason for it," she insisted. "I've never— I haven't run into this sort of thing before. It's too much like all that—that crazy *bruja* shit you run around with. I need your help."

I coughed and pinched my nose shut, breathing through

my mouth. Even then I could taste the smell. This scent was like any other, I told myself; I could get used to it if I tried. Somehow that just made it worse; the scent of death shouldn't be something one could get used to. "Right," I said, shaking off Rena's hand. "Show me what you have to."

I waited in a room full of cabinets, shivering, while Rena ran her finger down a list of numbers, chose a drawer at about hip height, and opened it. A lumpy black bag lay within, its plastic smell muted by the cold.

I held my breath. *It's okay*, I told myself, *she didn't ask you in to identify someone*. Still, I couldn't shake the sense that someone I knew might be in there. Sarah. Leon. Will. Anyone.

Rena glanced at me, and I nodded. Without any ceremony, she unzipped the bag, all the way down, leaving the body entirely exposed.

The man lying on the flat of the drawer hadn't been dead long; the scent of decay on him wasn't strong. He was stark naked, with the peculiar vulnerability that comes with being dead. I wanted to look away or drape something over him, give his corpse some semblance of dignity.

His feet were long and bony, fuzzed on top with dark hair, and dirt had worked its way into the seams of his toes. His arms were thick with muscle, the lines of his torso as well developed as any health club addict, and long strands of greasy dark hair twisted well past his shoulders.

My gaze traveled up his body to his face, and I caught my breath. "Good God."

Rena nodded. "That's what I said."

The man had the face of an eighty-year-old, so at odds with the relative health of the rest of his body that I found myself looking for seams, stitches, anything to explain the incongruity in age.

It didn't take a coroner to determine the cause of death. In the center of the corpse's wrinkled forehead gaped a black hole roughly the size of a dime, and I had to fight down a new wave of nausea when I realized that the reason his head was at such a strange angle was that the back of it had been blown off. "Point-blank shot?"

"Execution's my guess," Rena said. "There aren't any marks of a struggle on him, save for some abrasions on his knees. Harry—he's the guy who handled the body—thinks he might have been made to kneel. But take a closer look. Not at his face," she added as I bent over the corpse. "His arms and chest."

I grimaced but did so. "Rena, you're a sick—"

I stopped. Rena nodded. "You see them, right?"

I did. Thin lines marked every inch of his skin, even his face, though there they were faded to a tracery like veins below the skin. Spirals and knots, sigils that I did not know but could guess at, streaked his entire body with patterns more appropriate to a second-rate Celtic brooch than a corpse. He was like a faded version of the blue man on the bridge, all the lines and power bleached from his skin. "Tattoos?" I asked.

"No. Just ink. It's all over him, down to his ankles. He couldn't have drawn them himself, not unless he was double-jointed and capable of dislocating both shoulders. Harry thinks they were drawn before he died, but it's hard to be certain."

I straightened up. "Rena, I think it's time you told me what's going on."

She shrugged. In the harsh light, her skin looked gray— but when I glanced back at the dead man, I realized that "gray" could never accurately describe a living human. "We fished him out of the Charles early this morning. He'd gotten caught in the locks down by Lechmere. My guess is he was dumped not too far away."

This morning. It could be the same man I'd seen in the Fens with Katie, then . . . but it wasn't. "You said you'd already identified him."

She nodded, still gazing down at the corpse. "We matched his prints with an old arrest record, and his parents came down not long ago to ID him. His name's Frank McDermot."

The room tilted around me, as if someone had yanked the earth's axis to one side for a moment. I caught the edge of the drawer to steady myself. "No," I heard myself say. "That's not possible."

Rena glanced up at me, eyes narrowed. "Why not?"

"Frank—I knew a Frank McDermot." I took a deep breath, then regretted it and had to cough the stink from my lungs. "But he was my age. This couldn't be him."

"His parents gave us a positive ID. They . . . they weren't happy about what had happened to his face, but his mother said that the birthmark on his shoulder was unmistakable."

I looked where she pointed. Sure enough, there was a wine-colored splotch of color on his left shoulder, and now that I saw it, I knew it too. I'd seen it above me—in poor light, a long time ago, to be sure, but I had kissed that birthmark and bitten it too, and I knew it. "Can't be," I said, shaking my head as if to rid it of the sight. "How could he—how did he get this old?"

"That's what I was hoping you could tell me." Rena reached out to the corpse's—Frank's—face, her fingertips hovering above his skin. "I've seen men and women younger than either of us who look fifty. But they're old . . . old all over, if you know what I mean. This man was healthy. Healthier than I am. He'd have lived to be a hundred if someone hadn't shot him. But his face is wrong." She drew her hand back and wiped it on her pants leg, as if age might be contagious. "We'd barely pulled him out of the river before someone sent down word that we were to keep this quiet. My supervisor thinks it's part of some meth deals gone bad, some big bunch of ravers turning in on themselves. I don't buy it."

"I wouldn't, in your place." I closed my eyes and inhaled again, this time determined to prove my eyes and Rena's words wrong. But the proof faced the other direction. The last traces of Frank's scent clung to the body. No question about it, it was Frank. Frank the skinny guy in back, the goggle-eyed kid with one moment of grade-school fame. Frank, who'd been swallowed by a world I'd hardly known about back then. Frank, who'd turned up twice since, each time bringing chaos and the undercurrent into my life. Frank, whom I might have loved for a little while.

I opened my eyes again and tried to see some trace of the man I knew or the boy he'd been in that seamed face. So much of what happened had been obscured by later events, and the haze of time, and the endless promises to my mother . . . But was there something familiar about the eyes, perhaps? The hands? A flash of memory returned: a boy's hand, stretched above a heap of playground gravel.

Rena's voice broke my concentration, shunting the memory back to its depths. "That face plus the ink made me think this might be something outside my experience. Maybe something you might be familiar with. Doesn't match any gang we know, but it seems too well organized for something wholly random."

I made a noncommittal noise. "Can't say. But it's got the stink of the undercurrent about it. Not literally," I added, more for my benefit than hers.

She shook her head. "More of that crazy *bruja* shit, right?"

"Something along those lines." Rena snorted and moved to shut the drawer. I caught her hand. "Just a second."

I leaned in close to the body—Frank's body. There was one thick line of ink around his neck, marked with little clumps of lines off it like a barbed-wire collar. I rubbed at my neck, too aware of how my own throat closed up in sympathy, then closed my eyes and inhaled.

"*Jesus*, Evie."

"You asked me to come here, Rena, and you know how I work." I took another deep breath. "Now let me do my job."

She muttered something under her breath. Hell, I was uncomfortable with it too, and I was the one who had to trace the scent. I inhaled again, searching beyond the ammonia reek, into the scent of his body.

Frank's body smelled of the Charles River, not a nice scent under any circumstances. No wonder I'd caught his scent tied to the river earlier that day. Even if he'd already been dead, I'd found him. I just hadn't known it at the time.

I found other traces on him: the mud ground into his nails, a trace of gunpowder from the charred circle in his forehead, the blood spilled from the back of his head. Old blood smells terrible, like rust and unclean things, and even the lingering scent of fireworks couldn't stifle that clotted smell. He smelled a little musty, as if he'd been cooped up awhile. Maybe his apartment had gotten mildew; we'd had a wet spring, and my office had smelled like wet socks for three weeks.

There was more, though; a dry scent clinging to him like a shroud. Dry skin, stretched on a frame . . . bone and ink, something *old*. If it had been a sound, it would have been a cry down a tunnel, endlessly reverberating. If it had been a picture, it would have been drawn in black and drying red.

And the mildew reek, growing more and more intense the longer I sought. *This is it*, I thought. This was what I'd run into when hunting him . . . The Brotherhood's scent.

I straightened up, eyes still closed. Rena exhaled, but I didn't open my eyes just yet. The mildew dissipated as soon as it left his body; if there were trails, they weren't readily apparent. The other trail began and ended with Frank, like poison in a suicide. If there was any clue to his death in it, I was incapable of tracking it.

I opened my eyes and looked down at that old face, shivering. "Sorry, Rena," I said. "Nothing."

"Jesus, Evie, it looked like you were going to *kiss* him."

A smile cracked my lips. "Not any more. Frank lost kissing privileges a long time ago." I sighed, then choked on the aggressively clean air.

Rena waited while I coughed my way through another fit. She tapped her fingers against the drawer, then smacked it with the flat of her hand. "Drug deal my ass, Evie! There's something fishy about this whole situation, and every time I think I'm getting through to my supervisor, he tells me it's being taken care of. Gives me the creeps." She leaned down and started to zip the bag back up, preparing to put Frank back in his anonymous slot. "Any chance you could help me out with this?"

"I can't promise . . ." I paused. Someone was shouting, not far away. A woman's voice, shrill and cracked with pain.

Rena glanced over her shoulder, toward the voice, then hissed through her teeth. "We don't have much time. Evie, I know I don't know the weird stuff you run with, but I can function better if I can go to you for advice on it."

"I don't know," I said wretchedly. Now the commotion was at the door, and I thought I knew the woman's voice. "Can we close this—this drawer thing? Or at least cover Frank up? I don't want—"

"Please, Evie. I'd rather have you with me on this than someone else who hasn't . . . hasn't been through the same sort of thing." She reached up to scratch the scars on the back of her neck.

I started to say no. I wanted to say no. But she was looking at Frank, and I thought about the last time I'd seen him and the first time we'd met at the bonfire. How alone he'd been, distant from everyone except, later, me. And now he had no one to help him, no one to speak for him, no one to do what my mother had done for me. No one but me.

There are some things I can't turn down. I hated it, but there was nothing I could do about it.

"All right," I said, and the doors to the morgue opened.

Two officers followed a small woman in, apparently trying to hold her back. "—just want to see him one more time, just to say goodbye!" Mrs. McDermot shouted at them, then turned and saw me. Her face went white so fast I thought she'd faint, and she grabbed at one of the officers to keep herself upright. "Get out!" she screamed. "Get out, you bitch, get away from him, it's your fault he's here—"

Rena held up her hands. "Mrs. McDermot, I called Ms. Scelan in here on a consultation. I'm very sorry you have to see your son like this, but it was necessary." Mrs. Mc-

Dermot paused to draw breath, and Rena leaned closer to me. "Maybe it's better if you get out of here. I'll call you as soon as I have anything."

"Great." I tried to give her an encouraging smile, but part of me hoped she wouldn't find anything. Safer for her. "Excuse me," I added above Mrs. McDermot's continued litany of my sins, and edged past her. The officers were still too busy with her to do more than give me harried nods of acknowledgment.

I breathed easier as soon as I made it into the elevator, but a hand caught the doors just as they closed. My stomach twisted as Frank's father pushed the doors apart and entered the elevator beside me. I caught my breath, and with it a last dose of the morgue-scent that had followed me here.

"You're the girl," he said without preamble as the doors closed. "The one Frank mentioned. The one who came looking for him."

I nodded as I coughed the last of the morgue away. "I'm sorry. I didn't know."

"Neither did we. Not then." He took a deep breath and ran his hand over his face, the gesture hauntingly familiar. "She didn't mean it, what she said to you. I wanted to let you know . . . Bethie's never forgiven herself, you see. Not since he called, all those years ago, after you left, and she told them where he'd gone . . . She thought it was a great opportunity for him. A way for him to get ahead. She'd always thought so. Until now."

His lower lip trembled as he said this last, and he didn't take his hand from his face. "I'm sorry," I said again, knowing it was inadequate, hating myself for my inability to say more. "I . . . I knew he was trying to get away. The man, the one I met outside your house, he told me Frank was trying to get out."

The doors opened. I stepped out, and Frank's father raised his reddened eyes to mine. "That's what he told us too," he said, and let the door slide shut again.

# Ten

His words followed me all the way downtown. If things had been just a little different, I could easily have been the one lying dead in that drawer.

Instead it was Frank who was dead, and I was out and walking, getting lost in the Leather District and trying to read Brendan's card under the streetlights. Common sense told me that if I was that worried I could just call him. I've never been good at listening to common sense.

I'd expected Brendan's address to lead me to an office building, but it turned out to be one of the new developments, the kind that started out as factories and had a brief stint as studio space before being converted into fancy apartments. The parts of the building that weren't old brick were glass and steel, merging with the older building in a way that suggested a skyscraper trying to eat a warehouse. The doorman wore a suit not nearly as good as Brendan's, and he gave me a look that assessed my net worth and found it several tax brackets too low to come within shouting distance.

"I'm here to see Mr. Corrigan," I said, my voice squeaking just a little. The doorman tried to look down his nose at me—difficult since I was half a foot taller—and held a whispered conversation with the intercom before waving me through.

Brendan was waiting for me outside the door of his apartment. "Genevieve! Sorry about the guy downstairs. I'm kind of in the middle of something—"

"Frank's dead," I said.

Brendan's face went blank, and the hand he'd held out to me dropped back to his side. "How—" he began, then shook his head. "No, I'd—I'd better finish this, end the tele-conference, and then you can tell me everything. Come in. Please."

I let myself be guided into his front room. "Cops pulled him out of the river," I said, and this time my voice was steady. "They got to him. Not the cops. The others. He didn't get away."

"Shh." Brendan pulled a few pillows off a chair and led me to it. "Just hold on. I'll be back in a minute."

He went into the other room—an office, from what I could see through the open door—and after a moment he spoke again, too low for me to make out the words. A scratchy voice with a strong accent answered him, saying something about mutual funds. Maybe the key to being a sane adept was having a day job; we certainly had that in common. Except I wasn't an adept.

Dammit, don't think of that right now. Find a distraction. I ran a hand over my face and glanced around the living room. Much of it was very plain, clean white lines and big comfortable chairs, arranged to face each other rather than a TV. A bundle of dried flowers in a pewter tankard had been placed in the center of the low table, and a forgotten mug beside it still carried the hint of a morning cup of coffee. French Roast, by the scent. I smiled, then paused as the flowers' scent became recognizable. Rue and primrose, the latter bound with red thread. *Aha.*

I sniffed again, and this time caught only the faintest trace of fireworks—old ones, that had been set off a long time ago. The warding magic here was strong, but well masked; if I hadn't been looking for it, I wouldn't have noticed it at all.

I got up and examined a little sculpture on one shelf that, to an untrained eye, was nothing more than a pleasing arrangement of semiprecious stones wrapped in wire. But a moment's concentration revealed that it anchored a good portion of the warding magic, as well as acting as a fail-safe in case of another anchor faltering. Most magicians I knew would have this out in the middle of the floor, where they could tinker with it and fuss over it and check every five minutes to see that it hadn't been disturbed. Here it was a part of the room, as much as the books on the next shelf.

I ran a finger over the books on his shelves. They were a motley lot: *The Art of the Deal*, *Early Irish Myths*, *Secret Agent X–9*, *Training Your Older Dog* . . . I took the last one off the shelf and flipped through it as Brendan entered. "You have a dog?"

He shrugged. "I've been thinking about getting one. You know, maybe a golden retriever or something like that."

I glanced at him, then looked pointedly at the dimensions of the living room, which, while it was a damn sight larger than mine, wouldn't be nearly enough space for an enthusiastic dog.

Brendan laughed. "Okay. Maybe something smaller."

"As long as it's not a Chihuahua. Can't stand those." I turned over another page. *Many older dogs from a shelter will have difficulty trusting a new owner*, it read. *Before establishing yourself as the alpha of its pack, you must first gain its trust.* Not a problem I'd ever had. "I've always liked sheepdogs," I said. "Or they've always liked me; any time I see one on the Common it always wants to play."

"If a golden retriever would be bad for this apartment, I don't think I could handle a sheepdog." He took the book from my hands. "What happened?"

"I don't—" I glanced over his shoulder, into the office. There, at least, no magic scent repelled me. "What was all that about? The conference or whatever."

"Consulting work. I run a small business from home.

You don't think I can afford all this through magic, do you?"

"If anyone could, it'd be you," I murmured, then closed my eyes and rested my forehead against the bookshelf. The spines were cool and nubbly; a few held a fizzy scent that probably came from the warding magic. "Police called me in to identify a body. They do that sometimes, if they think it's weird stuff. This time it was Frank. There was something, something wrong with his face, it had gotten all old, and . . ." I took a deep breath and forced myself to slow down. "He had those lines on him. All over. Like the tattooed man I saw earlier."

Brendan let out a long exhalation and sank into the chair where I'd been sitting. "They got him, then."

I slumped against the side of the chair. "No wonder I smelled his scent twined with the river this afternoon, right? Hah." Brendan shook his head but didn't reply. "But there were other scents on him. One was really old and foreign. Not just from a different country. Different era, different time—different species, maybe. The other . . ."

Heavy, and damp, like the air on a day when it ought to rain but doesn't, like walking through a cloud that smelled awful, mildew and must and dead fishy things and low tide and it was strong, it was *here* . . .

"No—" I opened my eyes. The mildew scent—the Brotherhood's scent. "Christ. They've found you."

"What?" Brendan stared at me. I leaned in close to him, and he pressed back into the cushions as if afraid I would bite him, but I was only trying to catch that smell again. There it was, twining about him the same way it had around Frank's scent, around Frank's body. It wasn't as thick. The warm, sunlight-scent I'd come to associate with him still was there, still reassuring, but I couldn't ignore the other. Brendan cleared his throat. "Genevieve, are you saying—"

"They've found you. I don't know how, I don't think I led them to you, maybe Frank's mother talked . . ." I backed away, turning my face from the malevolent reek that Brendan couldn't sense, gasping for untainted air. Now that I'd noticed it, it seemed to be everywhere. "You need to get out. Go underground, get out of the city somehow—sea travel's best, it won't break Taranis' Wheel—"

"Wheel?" He tried a laugh, but it was shaky. "I know you Boston folks like to think of yourself as the hub of the universe, but that's going a little far."

"I wish to God I were joking, Brendan. I'm not. You need to take your loci and get as far away from this town as you can."

He got to his feet. "I'm not leaving you."

"I'll be fine, Goddammit. I kept my head down before, I can do so now." He looked dubious, and I clenched my hands into fists. "Jesus, if you won't leave town, then at least find a place to hide! Otherwise you're going to end up as just another fucking body in the Charles!"

Brendan looked at me in amazement, and for a moment I was sure he was going to say something stupid like "I can take care of myself" or "Are you absolutely certain?" Instead he went to the other side of the room and reached behind a wine rack. "Emergency bag," he said, hefting a bulging backpack. "I started keeping one after September eleventh, though mine's a little different than the usual kind."

"If it'll keep you alive, all the better." I hurried out the door and held it for him. "I'd tell you to call me, but there's a chance they'll be watching me too, and they might try to tap my phone."

"Not with my wards," he said with a grim smile.

I glanced down the hallway in both directions. It was clear. "Great. Stay over water, if you can, or heavy traffic if you can't; there are hotels above the Mass Pike—"

Brendan caught me by the shoulder. Startled, I looked up just as he cupped the back of my neck and pulled me to him in a hard kiss. He hadn't shaved, and his mouth was rough and scratchy and delicious. "I'll take the stairs," he said against my lips. "You take the elevator. Better if we're not seen together."

Unable to speak, I nodded. He let go of me and turned away, striding down the hall as casually as if he were just going for an evening stroll.

The doorman may have eyeballed me on the way out; I didn't notice. I didn't notice much of anything until I was halfway home, and even then it was only small things like *I'm getting rained on again*.

This was stupid, I told myself. It was only a kiss; it shouldn't affect me this way. Except . . . he was intelligent, and handsome, and took me seriously even about the weird stuff. And he was sane, which was more than I could say for most of the guys I met in my work. And it had been at least a year, a whole goddamn year, since I'd even gotten that far with anyone.

Maybe I should have remained unfuckable, I thought sourly. *Then I wouldn't get my hopes up like this.* But that just brought me back to thoughts of Frank, and the mildew reek on him, and how he shouldn't have died like this.

I paused a moment on one of the bridges that cross the Fens. Fenway was dark now—tonight's was an away game—but its usual static was in place. Even this far away, I could smell its magical field if I tried: the residual magic left by thousands of people over generations of visits. To-night there might be no one in the stands, but the ghosts were there nonetheless, and that alone was enough to comfort me. Frank hadn't been much of a Sox fan, but there might be something of him in that collective ghost, as something of him remained in the city's magic. Something more than just his body. And with any luck, something more of Brendan might remain than a corpse in the river.

I headed home, to my office buried in the aura of Fenway. It wasn't until I was in bed and switching out the light that I realized Brendan hadn't ever asked me how Frank had died.

I had been here before. The white walls were closer now to a hospital than they had been, though the creased corners smoothed out when I looked away, and the edges of the bed tried to fade into the blankness. But the frail form in the bed was unchanged, and the slow, tortured breathing still the same.

I didn't want to look at her. I didn't want to recognize her, even acknowledge her. Instead I looked down at my hands, one of which held a hypodermic syringe. Sleep dripped in a clear bulge from its tip.

My entire body shuddered, and I jerked awake, or tried to. Something heavy and slow lay over my eyes, and what felt like wakefulness only led back to that room. The white walls. The bed. The woman. My hands, holding a syringe—

No.

The walls. The bed. The woman. My hands holding a syringe—

No. Wake up.

The walls. The bed. The woman.

My hands holding a *knife*—

I shuddered awake, flailing at the bedsheets as if they would strangle me. My hands stung from where I'd clawed them together, trying to rid myself of a weapon I'd never had. "No," I croaked aloud. "No."

Only the silvery glow of Brendan's wards answered me, and after a moment I could breathe again. I reached down and unwrapped the sheets from my ankles. My room was reddish with streetlight glow, and white headlights chased themselves across the room as someone drove by, stereo thudding. Normally it would take more than that to wake me up, but right now it served to banish what was left of sleep.

I switched on the light and swung my legs over the side of the bed, shivering a little as they touched the cold wood of the floor. Why a knife, of all things? Why a syringe, for that matter? It hadn't been anything as blatant as that. All it had taken was a quick fudging of medication times on her chart, a few purposefully misunderstood directions, and Mom had rested. She hadn't even been conscious for it, though I still swore I'd heard her sigh as the final dose reached her bloodstream.

I had been determined to feel no guilt for it, and Mom had advised me not to do so. She had decided on this end long ago, and I'd been the one who had balked when the first possibility of a terminal diagnosis had cropped up. I'd been doing what she wanted, or so I told myself every time I thought of her. But the memory of her in that bed would not leave me.

Frank, I thought. *Frank, damn you for dredging all this up.* I couldn't just feel guilty about one thing; I had to feel guilty for all of it.

I stretched, trying to clear my head. Something twinged in my forearm, and I turned it over to look. The scratch was a livid, painful streak, but it had healed over. That was a good sign; magical wounds tended to be more of the never-healing sort. Still, I dragged myself out of bed and over to the corner, where a dry flower arrangement took up space in an old metal milk jug. Among the pussy willow and bundles of everlasting were several whippy rowan branches; dried and no longer good for their value as masking matter, but still a decent bane against external witchcraft. I bent one into a rough helix and wrapped it around my arm, securing the ends with a cracked rubber band.

My hands twitched as I did so, and a momentary flash of memory returned, so strong it almost overruled sight: the knife, black and twisted like an iron thorn, settling into my palm as if it belonged there. I closed my eyes and drew a deep breath.

There was no way I was going back to bed. Not if that was what awaited me. I went back into the kitchen and stared at the tabletop until it began to grow light.

Eleven

I woke to a ringing phone and a crick in my neck. The microwave flashed 00:00 at me—magicians coming and going had messed with its electronics so much that it had given up on keeping proper time—but the pendulum clock next to it read seven thirty. Too damn early.

My mouth tasted like an army of zombies had risen from it, and when I raised my head, I found that I'd been sleeping on my braid, leaving little ciphered marks all over my right cheek. I made my usual promise to chop the damn thing off and rubbed at my face until it stopped tingling.

The phone was still buzzing. I managed to stand, stumbled out of the office, and located it on the second try. "Scelan," I mumbled, retreating into the kitchen.

"Evie? It's Rena. I've got a lead on some older cases, and I want you to come along. There was a series of mutilations—"

"Nngh. No mutilations. Not this early." I wedged the phone between my neck and chin, grimacing as I pulled the same muscle that had gotten cramped, and dragged the coffeemaker forward.

"Early? This isn't early, Evie. Don't tell me I woke you up."

"Had a bad night." I opened one of the top cabinets and

reached up for the coffee. The clumsy rowan helix shifted, and the rubber band gave way with a sullen twang, dropping the whole mess to the counter. I gazed at it for a moment, thoughts coming in and out of focus.

"Evie? You still there?"

"Still here. Just a little woozy." I pulled down a can of cheap coffee, opened the top, and inhaled the scent of the ground beans. "Okay. Talk to me. I can't promise you won't have to recap later, but this is the best you're going to get from me before coffee."

Rena sighed. "One of these days, I'm going to get you in here and have you listen to the whole 'clean living' talk the D.A.R.E. guys give. If nothing else, it'll keep you from getting hung over for a while."

"I am *not* hung over." I banged the can on the counter. "I don't drink, dammit. You know that."

"Easy, Evie. Sorry. I forgot."

"I'm just exhausted this morning." As was evidenced by how I'd almost added the coffee without a filter in place. Not that I hadn't made coffee that way before, and even drank it if I was desperate enough. "Go on. Something about cold cases?"

"Yeah. Well, that's not quite accurate, since these were all listed as solved, though they weren't much more than shelved. Anyway, in the late seventies somebody dumped several bodies down near the Riverway."

"Were they marked up like Frank?"

"Yes. Well, no. See, I went through all the stuff on tattoos and didn't turn up anything that looked related. But these bodies, the ones from the seventies, they were cut up all over. It wasn't exactly the same as the marks on this stiff, but similar enough."

"Similar how?" I checked the filter again, closed the coffeemaker, and listened to it burble. "And, Rena, can you do me a favor and call him Frank? The guy was my friend, after all."

She was silent a moment. "Got it. Sorry."

"No problem." I sniffed at my hair and started unbraiding it. "Go on about the mutilations," I said.

"That's something I never thought I'd hear you say. Anyway, what's important about them is that the patterns and the symbols used resembled those on . . . on Frank. Not a one-one match, but enough that I wanted to follow up on it."

"I see." I unhooked a mug from the rack and considered whether I could get it under the drip without spilling what little had dripped into the coffeepot. "I can find the guys who worked on the case for you; just give me their names and some time."

"No need. I found one already, and he's just the one I want to see. He's at Crofter House these days."

"What's that?" I maneuvered the pot and cup together so that only a few drops hissed onto the hot plate. A sharp burning scent rose up and was gone. I wrinkled my nose and blinked, my vision coming clearer. "One of the new health spas?"

Rena exhaled. The low drone of traffic on her end of the phone only emphasized her silence. "No, Evie. It's an assisted living facility. What they used to call an old folks' home."

"Oh."

"Chances are good that he knows something, but I think he might be more likely to talk if he knows he won't get laughed at, and you're good for that."

"Why? Am I that ridiculous?"

Rena didn't even go for the straight line. Damn. "I'd appreciate it if you could be there at nine so we can talk to him," she said.

I'd started nodding, but balked at "be there at nine." "Nine's not possible. I've got work."

"You sure? I called Mercury Courier to find out if I should try your cell or home, and they said you were off today."

I cursed. "Goddamn schedule changes. Okay. Fine."

"The place is in Jamaica Plain, off Pond Street." She named an address, and I sipped my coffee. I was tempted to just go back to bed for another two hours. If I did that, though, I might dream . . .

"I'll be there," I said to stop that train of thought. "Anything you want me to bring?"

"Not really. I won't be in uniform; today's my day off."

"I can think of better ways to spend a day off."

"So can I. I'll see you there."

I glared at the phone, sighed, and carried it back out to its cradle.

Crofter House was one of those places that clung to the idea of what a proper New England home ought to look like, no matter how the reality of New England changed around it. It was a big brick building, ivy over every surface, with a high and crumbling wall surrounding it. The wall probably helped to muffle the sound of highway traffic not too far away, but to me it just made the place look closed-off and isolated, like a brick fortress against the encroaching cultures on either side, a proper Boston Brahmin in a fish market, holding his nose and his propriety aloft.

The gardens inside the gate mitigated the fortress effect somewhat, as well as explaining why the wall was deteriorating: the ivy was using it as a staging ground for a full-scale attack on the house itself. Rena was waiting for me a little ways away from the door. She wore her idea of plainclothes—jeans and a drab button-down shirt two steps away from her uniform—and finished off a last drag on her cigarette as I walked up. "I thought you'd quit," I said.

"I have. This is just a reward; I allow myself one a week."

I shook my head. "That'll just keep you addicted, you know."

"I know. How many cups of coffee did you suck down this morning?"

"None of your business." I'd left half a cup on my desk

in my hurry to get here, and now regretted the loss. "They let you smoke out here?"

"As long as I stay fifteen feet away from the door." She crushed the cigarette against an ornamental lantern and looked around for an ashtray. "Can we talk about something else?"

"Okay. Why am I here?"

"I told you already. Must have been before you got some coffee." She shook her head and dropped the butt in a pot of azaleas. "Yacoubian had a reputation for being close-mouthed when it came to the weird cases, and that was even before he retired. I have a feeling if I go in there alone, he won't be very forthcoming."

"What makes you think he'll talk to me?"

"You're not me, for one." She opened the door and waved me in. "I'm terrible at talking to people casually. My partner says I'm only good in an interrogation room."

"Shows what he knows. He's never seen you sing karaoke."

"Shut up."

Despite the soft music and potpourri everywhere (or maybe because of the potpourri; I can't stand the stuff), the inside of Crofter House gave me the willies. It wasn't like the harsh cleanliness of the morgue, but the two shared some of the same elements. In the morgue, chemicals and more chemicals peeled away the reek of decay, and here, constant care held death at bay. But despite that attention, the musty scent of death and the accompanying smells of age and illness were equally present.

A small dark-skinned woman smiled at us from the front desk. "Can I help you?" she asked, her accent mildly Caribbean.

"We're here to see Joseph Yacoubian," Rena said.

The receptionist sorted through the papers on her desk. "I don't see . . . ah, here it is. He's on the third floor, room eighteen."

"Thanks." Rena headed for the stairs and I followed in

her wake. Some of the residents who were up and about waved or gave us suspicious glances, though most were too wrapped up in their own pursuits to notice us.

The stairwell door clanged shut below us. I jumped at the sound and stumbled over a warp in the flooring. The air in here tasted flat. "I hate these places."

Rena was halfway up the stairs, but she paused and turned back. "Why is that?"

"It's just—well, the people here. All of them were young and strong once, all of them did things, most were moms or dads, people who made a difference. And here it's just—just old people in little rooms." My dream of the night before came back in a rush, and I gripped the iron railing until it dug into my palm. "They're powerless. These places, they—they leech strength from people. You can go in as CEO of ConHugeCo, but once you're in you're just an old man with bedsores."

Rena was silent a moment. She turned the bend and kept climbing. "My dad's in a nursing home," she said at last. "We put him there two years ago."

"Shit. Rena, I'm sorry."

"Of course you are." She still didn't look at me. "I wasn't any happier about it than you would be. But he's more at ease there than he would be in one of our homes, and we make damn sure he's happy."

I didn't answer, still shamed.

"I know what you mean about power," she said. "Some of the places we looked, the people there might as well have been numbers on a board. But they didn't start out that way, and I'll be damned if I'll treat them that way. You want to make these people less powerless, you start treating them like people. Got it?"

I stared at the step in front of me. Time and many feet had worn the treads on the no-slip guard away, leaving only a tracery of grooves. "Got it."

"Good."

We made it down to room 18, past both open and closed

doors. Through one I could see a slender woman helping a withered grandmother to her feet, talking merrily the whole time. The old woman didn't speak, but she nodded and laughed at the nurse's jokes. I inhaled as I went past: lavender and strawberries.

Rena waited for me at the door. "I'm not mad at you," she said. "I just wanted to make that whole thing clear before we went in. Otherwise, no matter how much of a *bruja* you are, he's not gonna talk to you."

"I know." She laid a hand on the doorknob. "But I'm no *bruja*."

She shrugged. "Close enough."

Not for me, I thought.

Rena knocked, and a cracked voice called from within. "It's open. Come on in."

Yacoubian's rooms were not much bigger than my own apartment, and the low drone of sports scores spilled out into the hall as we entered. A kitchenette took up one corner, complete with last night's dishes, and a door next to it led to a room smelling of socks. Papers covered every available surface and some that weren't; aging sticky notes clung to the walls and even to the undersides of shelves.

A grizzled man in a plaid shirt and a wheelchair muted the TV and waved to us. "I'd have let you in," he said, "but I took a tumble last week and my hip's out again."

"That's too bad," Rena sympathized.

Yacoubian shook his head. "Oh, don't worry about it. I'll be out of this thing in another week." He was short and burly, or had once been, I could tell. Most of his hair was gone; the little left was a dull gray and swept over the top of his head in what might have been a comb-over had it been long enough to reach the other side. He leaned back, gazing at us with bright, knowing eyes. "Now, let's see. You're a cop, aren't you?"

Rena blinked and opened her mouth, obviously preparing some kind of denial. I stepped in to take the hit instead. "Yes, I am," I said, edging around the end table with its inevitable potpourri.

"Not you. Her. Don't look so shocked, Miss Santesteban; it's something about the way you walk. Most cops have it, and if you're around them as long as I was, it's something you never forget." He wheeled around so that he was facing the TV and flipped the remote between his hands. "So, have a seat. What do you want to talk to me about?" He folded his hands over his belly, smiling like a Buddha with a secret.

Rena glanced at me, and the unvoiced sigh passed between us. "In nineteen seventy-eight there were a series of murders in Boston. The victims were all dumped along the Riverway."

The smile didn't disappear, but it did turn a little hard at the corners. "Nothing new there."

"These were a little stranger than the run-of-the-mill murders. All the victims were discovered mutilated, with their flesh cut in spirals and meaningless shapes."

Not quite meaningless, I thought.

"At least one of them appears to have died of blood loss during the mutilation." I must have made some noise, because Yacoubian glanced at me, but Rena continued on, no expression in her voice. "The other two died from gunshot wounds inflicted after mutilation."

Yacoubian shifted in his seat, winced, and returned his gaze to the TV. "It's a sick world. I've heard of worse. I've even seen worse."

"I don't doubt it. But you did see these bodies. You're listed as the coroner on the autopsy report." Rena waited a moment, and when Yacoubian remained silent, continued, "No connection between the victims could ever be made. One was a housewife from South Boston; one was a recent Haitian immigrant, one was—"

"You don't have to recite the facts for me. I remember them well enough." He fumbled for a water glass with an inch still left in it and drank it down. "They weren't the sort of cases you forget easily."

Rena looked relieved. "Then maybe you can tell us a little about it. Off the record, of course."

"All the official statements are where you can get to them easy. Back at the station. That's all I had to say then and all I have to say now." Yacoubian turned the TV up a notch, but didn't ask us to go.

Rena pulled a chair over and sat down in it, elbows resting on her knees. "Mr. Yacoubian, there's more to these murders than what's on the record. The official statements are contradictory. The department stated that the first death was a random act, and the other two were either Satanists who'd gotten an idea or copycat killers. That makes no sense when you consider that every single body was mutilated in the same way, and, according to your report, with the same weapon. It's like someone in the department tried to keep these three from being linked."

"Damn right someone tried." He raised his empty glass to his lips and scowled at it. "Someone succeeded, and well enough that I couldn't get anyone to take a second look at those files. Every time I did, they'd forget about them or stuff them in their desk drawer or just plain ignore me."

"Like the files didn't exist for anyone but you," I said slowly. "Like they'd just fallen off the map."

Yacoubian flicked a glance at me. "Exactly. Not the first time it'd happened, but usually I could bully someone into taking a second look."

I nodded. There were small charms that could be put on certain things—papers, letters, money—that would work on people's subconscious, make the things distasteful and unpleasant, or just not worth the trouble. Such charms usually didn't do much, but if they were strong, they'd take a while to wear off. And they had trouble affecting anyone with blood-magic. It was possible that both Rena and Yacoubian had a little of that, perhaps no more than a flicker of extra luck. That would explain why so many of Rena's "crazy hunches" turned out to be right.

Yacoubian held out his glass to us. "Do an old man a favor and refill that, will you?"

I leaned over Rena to take the glass. "So there *was*

something irregular about these cases, then?" Rena asked.

"Irregular, regular, who cares? The only regular I care about these days is whether my bowels are regular, and I can give you a day-by-day account of that if you want. The cases are cold, the files are shut, the guys in charge have their comforting answers and changing that won't make those poor people any less dead." He wrenched himself around to glare at her, gripping the back of his wheelchair. "Maybe I was wrong about you. Maybe you're not a cop, you're just one of those idiots who've watched too much TV and think you're Perry Mason or Jack Whatever. Think you can get at the truth better than we did. And who are *you* anyway?" he demanded of me as I brought him his water. "Moral support?"

Rena answered before I could. "She was a friend of the dead man."

Yacoubian started, then craned around to stare at me. "No way. You're way too young; you'd have been a kid when these happened."

"Not them," I said as I filled up his glass. "The new one. Frank McDermot."

His eyes flickered. "Don't know any McDermot," he said, but there was a question in his voice, and Rena knew how to answer it.

"He was found in the Charles two days ago. Dead of a gunshot wound, execution-style to the forehead. His body was covered in inked spirals and marks similar to the ones you reported on the bodies found along the Riverway."

"Ink isn't the same as blood, and don't you tell me that it is," Yacoubian snapped. "Are you proposing that someone drew out a . . . a little map for mutilation, a cut-by-numbers, and then said to hell with it and shot him instead? Real god-damn likely."

"There are a number of other similarities, Mr. Yacoubian—"

"I'm sure you think so. But I don't believe this murder has anything to do with those three people from twenty-odd years ago." He twisted his chair around and glared at the television.

Rena sighed, ran her fingers through her hair, and gave me a pleading look. I shrugged. If you asked me, it wasn't so unusual that this man didn't want to dredge up memories of brutal murders from decades ago. It just showed good sense on his part.

Except . . . he wanted to be convinced, I realized abruptly; he was just too scared of spilling everything and then having it come back to bite him. In his place I might be doing the same thing.

I suddenly didn't want to help pull this man's secrets out of him. "Mr. Yacoubian—"

"Joe. If the pair of you are going to badger me, you might as well do it with my first name." The left corner of his mouth twitched into a smile.

"Joe. Can I use your bathroom?"

"You can, but at the moment it's filled with all the contraptions necessary to help me out of this damn thing—" he whacked his wheelchair, "—and onto the pot. If I remember right, there's a restroom down the hall, three doors on the right. Can't remember if it's men's or women's, though."

"I'll deal. Rena, you okay without me?"

"For now. Mr. Yacoubian, Joseph, you're no doubt aware that the second victim, all those years ago, had often been reported missing by his landlady prior to his death. Mr. Mc-Dermot had also had a number of gaps in his history, times when he could not be accounted for. Now, the reason—"

She went on with a list of parallels as I made my way to the door. None were near as strong as the runic patterns on all four bodies, but that didn't matter right now. At this point it was all up to Yacoubian and how much he wanted to tell.

I closed the door behind me. The scratch on my arm twinged, and I rubbed at it, shivering. It was still too cold in here.

As I walked down the hall, counting doors, a weird

feeling descended over me, as if I were being watched. I glanced around; there was no one else in the hall, and most of the doors were shut tight. Even the window showed only clear sky, without even a tree that a watcher could climb.

But someone was there. I knew it, the way you know in dreams. As if that thought had triggered it, the back of my neck prickled, and at the same time the tiles seemed to jump under me, an imperceptible shift to the left that left me staggering. My arm throbbed, and for a moment the air was far too hot, like a sudden blast from a furnace—

I cursed under my breath and braced my hands on my knees, breathing hard. It was exactly like being jerked out of a dream. And after last night, I didn't want to think about dreams any more than I had to.

Someone's dreaming me, I thought, and it didn't feel like my thought. Not the Brotherhood; it didn't have their stink. Something else . . . someone I knew . . .

I pressed the heel of my hand to my forehead. "Go away. I don't know what you're dreaming, but you can stop it right now."

The heavy, feverish feeling receded. I straightened up, and as I did so noticed that the door on my left, which had been closed before, now stood open a crack.

Curiosity killed the cat, I thought.

"Never said anything about what it did to the hound, though," I said aloud, and pushed the door open.

Twelve

This suite was smaller than Yacoubian's, and it didn't take much to see why. Yacoubian, despite his wrenched hip, was still an active man and one who took some pride in his self-sufficiency; the amount of use his kitchenette had seen told me that much. But the inhabitant of this room was anything but self-sufficient.

It was a bright corner room, and light streaming in had discolored the few hotel-quality paintings on the walls. Even the linens on the bed seemed washed to a bleached shade of white. The woman below them, though, remained dark and unfaded, like a blood spot on feathers.

I closed my eyes. This was not the hospital room I had seen last night in my dream, and this was not my mother. Nevertheless, that queer doubled feeling persisted, as if at any moment the room would shift around me. As if reality weren't quite the same; in this room, ice might burn or fire quench.

I opened my eyes and looked down at my hands. Empty.

There was no heavy, dreaming feeling here, no sense of whatever had been watching me a few seconds ago. Whatever that was, it had no power in this room. In fact, the room didn't have much of a smell at all, apart from the chilled-dust scent of an air conditioner on full blast, keeping it at least several degrees cooler than the hallway.

Keep it warm, stuff wakes up, you know how it is? Leon had said, sniggering at my ignorance. Well, no, I didn't know how it was, but in this room you'd think the cold would wake up the old woman. I focused on her, trying to see her for what she truly was. The lines in her face were so deep they looked like fissures in stone, though her hair was still thick and gray, the color of pitted aluminum pans, twisting into elf-locks where it reached her shoulders. Her eyes were closed, the lids twitching in heavy dream sleep. Even the thunk of the door closing hadn't roused her.

I took a few steps closer. *See?* I told myself. *Not Mom. She never made it this far, and you know she wouldn't have wanted it. You wouldn't have let her be put here.*

Like you'd have had the money to "put her here," another part of me sneered.

Without thinking, I looked at my hands again. No morphine. No knife. Not even a pen.

The woman shifted in her sleep, and I halted. One of her hands lay outside the coverlet, gnarled and twisted. For some reason my mind tossed up a memory: a movie I'd seen when I was little, some fantasy movie using puppets, not the one with David Bowie in unfortunate pants. There had been scary beaked monsters, and little elfy people, but what had stayed with me were the old wise beings, the ones who looked like kind, warm-blooded lizards. Their faces had been wrinkled with age, but the wrinkles had twisted into spiral patterns, patterns like the ones they drew in the sand.

This woman's hand was like that. There was a pattern in the lines of it, a pattern I didn't know how to read.

She frowned in her sleep and seemed about to say something, mutter or complain or snore. Instead she sighed, a sigh too deep to come from such a frail body, and settled further into the pillows.

Any minute now she would open her eyes, eyes that would be the same shade as mine, and she would speak and call me the name my mother called me, she would open her eyes—

"Excuse me?"

I spun around. A thin-faced man in a white coat stood at the door. "How did you get in here?"

"The door—" I muttered.

"Speak up." He saw me glance toward the woman and shook his head. "Don't worry about her. It takes more than voices to wake Mrs. Crowe out of her morning nap." He smiled, a wide grin that made me think unaccountably of a shark, and opened the door wider. "She does, however, value her privacy. And therefore Crofter House does as well."

"The door was open," I said stubbornly, knowing it was no excuse. He was right; I was trespassing.

"I'll have a word with our housekeeping staff, then. But just because they're lax doesn't mean you can take advantage of it." He gestured to the woman in the bed. "If she were your mother, would you want strangers wandering in at all hours?"

"She's not my mother," I said without thinking.

The doctor blinked. "I never said she was."

"I—sorry. Sorry." I hurried past him, but just as I did I caught a scent—the first clear scent I'd found in this room. Without thinking I reached out to catch the door as it closed.

"What is it now?" the doctor said coldly.

"I thought I . . ." The scent was gone, but I'd had it long enough to identify it. "Thought I'd left something in there."

He gave me a look that implied it was more likely I'd taken something, but didn't press the issue. "If we find anything that looks out of place, we'll let you know."

"Um. Thanks. Where's the ladies' room?"

"Two doors down." He pointed, and I walked away. Glancing back, I noticed that he'd waited till I was down the hall to close the door and lock it.

Rena was in mid-rant as I returned to Yacoubian's room. "—doesn't matter! Whatever troubles there were in the department, and I'm not saying there were any, have long since passed—"

"Or retired? Like me?" Yacoubian grinned at me. "You find the bathroom?"

"I did. After running into one of the doctors."

"Short man? Supercilious? Bedside manner of a baboon?"

"Well, he was short," I admitted. "Brown hair and kind of a sharp face."

Yacoubian sighed. "That would be our Dr. Connor, God's gift to the medical profession. Little bastard's been here near as long as I have; he came in when one of his patients got transferred over, and the director doesn't like arguing with him." He whacked the chair next to him. "Have a seat, Miss Not-a-Cop. Maybe you can spot your friend as she tries to take me down again."

"Not this time." Rena got to her feet. "Three doors down, you said?"

"Three doors, and make sure it's got a restroom sign outside. I walked in on one of the patients."

"Dammit, Evie—"

"It's okay. Well, she didn't yell at me anyway. She wasn't awake."

Yacoubian snorted laughter. "You walked in on Sleeping Beauty? No wonder Connor got pissy with you; she's his pet patient. I'll wager this chair that half his salary comes from the kickbacks he gets from her family. She's not even supposed to be in this wing; we're assisted living over here, not hospice care."

"What's she doing over here, then?" Rena asked, and I could tell she was thinking of her father's nursing home.

"Says she prefers to be surrounded by active people. Which I can buy, but what about what us active people prefer? I don't think I've seen her awake since I got here." He waved his empty glass at me. "Top that off again, will you? And Miss Santesteban, if you feel like wandering down a floor, there's a coffeemaker in the staff lounge. Get me a cup with two sugars and I might feel better about talking to you."

Rena rolled her eyes and shut the door behind her. Yacoubian maneuvered his wheelchair around to face the TV again. "This is a classic cop tactic," he said. "Don't think I haven't seen it in action. Good cop, bad cop; talky cop, quiet cop, call it what you want."

"I'm not a cop. You said so yourself." I handed him his water and settled into the chair beside him. "Oh, turn it up. I missed this part of the game."

He glanced at me, but did so. "Jesus, I wish I'd seen that play," I said as the catcher tagged his third Devil Ray of the night. "I got distracted and had to head home before the last few innings."

"Ah, you didn't miss anything. Same play he always does, the little punk. He's going free agent at the end of the season; you watch, he'll go straight to Steinbrenner."

"I hope to God you're wrong." We watched the replay a second time, and I shook my head. "You know, I hate to say it, but I miss Nomar sometimes. I know we probably wouldn't have won the Series if we'd kept him, but I miss him anyway."

"I tell my grandson the same thing, and he spews all this crap about spoiled players. Spoiled, my ass. That's tough work." He gave me a sidelong look. "So why are you here, if you're not a cop? Don't tell me it's because of that new stiff. You don't look like a devastated girlfriend."

I shrugged. "I'm not. Rena promised me free beer." Yacoubian chuckled. "Really, it's no big reason," I said, even though it felt like a betrayal of Frank to do so. "I'm a . . . a local expert in some fields, and she wanted my opinion."

"Local expert." He was silent a moment, and neither of us looked away from the replay, though by now it'd moved on to a hatchet-jawed guy speculating on the Patriots' draft picks. "What kind of stuff?"

"Weird stuff. It's not really interesting unless you already know about it. Frank was a friend of mine, but really, I'm doing this because Rena guilted me into it." That was only half true; I'd made the guilt trip my own self.

"Hmph. And here I thought you were pulling this whole girl-power thing on me just so your friend could get a gold star for her work."

I shook my head. "Sisterhood is powerful, and all that? Nah. It makes a cute slogan, but I've never had much to do with sisterhood." I took a deep breath. This was risking a lot on what Yacoubian might or might not know, and Rena could be back any minute, but I had to try. "Or brotherhood, for that matter. Especially in this city."

"Brotherhood." He was silent for a long moment. The TV switched from sports report to commercial to another commercial and back. Finally, Yacoubian cleared his throat. "You, ah, you ever heard of a locus?"

I didn't turn around. "I've heard of them," I admitted without taking my eyes from the TV. "Never used one." Never needed one, though I didn't see any reason to share that with him. I thought again of Leon and wondered what he was doing. Whether he still was going around armed. How Brendan had managed to chase him off. Where Brendan might be now.

Yacoubian sighed, then reached over and shut off the TV. "There are some days I think I dreamed up the whole mess," he said. "Most days I want to have dreamed it."

"I feel the same way most days." I turned to face him. "My name's Genevieve Scelan, by the way."

The offering of a name didn't seem to mean anything to him. Good. "Jesus, it was so long ago . . . but it ate at me, you know?" His face was grayish, and his merry malice in deflecting Rena's questions had passed. "I mean, I thought I had experience with this sort of thing. Time to time, we'd get a body in that had obviously been beaten to death, and all the witnesses would say was that he'd fallen downstairs. Or a guy hanged in his cell, and the word from on high was that we were to ignore it and move on. Most of those times it was Whitey and his boys, his pet feds. But this—" He flapped one hand as if to brush it all away.

"Worse?"

"No. Just inexplicable. You could explain away the rest, even if you hated the explanation." He scratched at the back of his neck as the door opened.

Rena came in, glanced at me and then at him. "Something I should know?"

"Should?" Yacoubian coughed a laugh. "This sort of stuff is nothing anyone should know, far as I'm concerned. But you're gonna hear it anyway. Because of her." He pointed at me as if accusing me of a crime, which for all I know he might have been. "She knows this stuff. She won't laugh at me or tell me I'm a crazy old man."

"Neither would I," said Rena.

"Yeah, but only because you're with her. Course, I am a crazy old man, but that won't make a difference." He set the remote on a table and ran one hand through what was left of his hair. "This case . . . I did some looking into it on my own. Kind of like you're doing now. Found one link. Didn't make any sense." He gazed into his water glass, then put it down so hard it rattled the table. "The black guy, he'd been a big whaddayacallit, a houngan, back home. The woman had just joined this Wicca thing out of BU. The kid, the one from Southie, he had the MIT paranormal researchers begging him to let them study him. Said he'd got a precognitive predisposition, or something like that."

"Magic," I said. "That was the link." Crazy *bruja* shit.

Yacoubian flicked a glance at me. "Call it what you want. I called it weird. I caught some rumors about this gang in town, and I figured, hey, they want what all the other gangs want, right? Little more power, little more territory. Only it wasn't the same kind of territory. Not like neighborhoods. More like . . . I don't know, people's heads, maybe."

He gazed down at his hands. "I still see those marks, you know? All those scratch marks and hash marks all over the bodies, like circles with little thorns sticking up out of them, like a kid keeping track of numbers, only cut in deep around the arms, the legs, the woman had a circle of them on her stomach just below her belly button . . . Bad nights here, when I forget my pills or when my hip gets to me, I feel like there's this big net of them all around me, just waiting to close in like they did on those poor people . . ."

He was silent, and his fingers clutched the remote so hard they began to go white. "What did you find?" Rena asked after a moment.

Yacoubian laughed, a dry sound like the smell of leaves in November. "I found nothing. Scraps. Fragments. Jack shit. Two people wanted to talk to me, but when I went to meet them they were gone, and both times this big spiral was scratched into their front doors, gouged in with some kind of chisel . . ." He took a long, shuddering breath. "After that I stopped asking."

"Maybe if you came downtown and examined Mr. Mc-Dermot—" Rena began.

She stopped as the door opened behind us. "Excuse me, miss," Dr. Connor said, edging past Rena. "You've got some lovely visitors today, Mr. Yacoubian. The guys down the hall are all jealous." He flashed a toothy grin at Rena and a faltering one at me. "It's not every day a pair of beautiful women come to see one of our residents."

"Go to hell, doc," Yacoubian said wearily. "It can't be time for my shot again."

"Look at your watch and tell me it isn't." Dr. Connor took a syringe from his lab coat and held it up against the light. "I'm afraid I'm going to have to ask you both to leave," he said over his shoulder. "As you can see, Mr. Yacoubian isn't well."

"I'm well enough, and I'm telling you again to fuck off. Don't make me say it a third time." Yacoubian's shoulders slumped and he switched the TV on again, gazing dully at it over Dr. Connor's shoulder. "Look, I'll sort through my stuff," he said to Rena. "There's a chance I might find something. No more than a one in a hundred chance, really, but what else am I going to do while I'm in this damn chair?"

Rena managed a smile. "Call us if you find anything, then. Thanks very much for your time."

"You're always welcome to it. And next time remember that coffee. Two sugars."

"Now, Mr. Yacoubian," Dr. Connor said, rolling up the old man's sleeve, "you know you're not allowed caffeine under your current regimen."

"I know you don't allow anyone a decent cup of coffee." Yacoubian sighed. "Take care, both of you. And come to visit even if you give up; it's been nice sparring with you."

Rena let out a long exhalation as she closed the door behind us. "Sparring is the right word. He'd probably get along with my supervisor, come to think of it."

"Maybe you can invite them both to dinner sometime." I waited until we'd reached the bottom of the stairs to speak again. "So what did you get from him while I was out?"

"A little." She waved to the receptionist as we made our way out. "He did take notes during the case. Said he keeps his brain on paper, and judging by the state of his room I'd agree. I don't know if he still has them, though."

"Or if they'll make any sense." I took a deep breath as we got out into the garden; clean air again. Or as clean as you get in Boston. "That stuff about gangs mean anything to you?"

"Not immediately. The pattern makes sense, though; after all, my boss was the one who said this looked like a gang killing. You?"

"I don't know," I said slowly, thinking of a bunch of cops—Rena among them—going up against the Bright Brotherhood. It wasn't a pretty thought. "I was here in seventy-eight but it's not like I noticed anything outside school. And I didn't start getting involved in the . . . in the crazy shit until after I dropped out of college."

She turned to face me. "Evie, answer me straight. Is this a gang?"

I scuffed at the gravel path with the toe of my shoe. "Yes," I said finally. "A really nasty one. *Bruja* shit exclusively. They'd been inactive for a while, but it looks like they're not anymore."

Rena waited for me to say more. "Anything else you can tell me?" she asked after I stayed quiet.

"Not without getting into the bad stuff big time. Rena, I really think you ought to consider backing out of this. It's not safe."

Rena looked at me as if I'd just suggested she cut off her hands so she'd stop biting her nails. "Fuck *safe*, Evie. You know I can't worry about that. If I did, I'd never leave the house."

"Okay. Okay. But at least watch yourself. This could get ugly very fast."

"There's a lot more leeway between staying safe and being stupid than you seem to think, Evie."

"Does it look that way to you? Really?" I tried a smile.

Rena sighed, ran both hands through her hair, and absently reached for her cigarettes. "All right. I'll be careful. I'll give him a call tomorrow. If he's got anything, I'll call you about it; if not, we'll just let him be. I'll go digging again, see what I can find on any occult organizations in the city."

"Ten to one says it's all woo-woo, right up there with the guys who rant about the Freemasons."

"No bet." She started up the street toward her car, then paused. "You still on for Saturday after next? The way things are going, I'm not going to get any time off this weekend, but I could really use a break."

"Yeah. But promise me this: you will only demand to sing 'I Like 'em Big and Stupid' if we're actually at a karaoke place. The DJ at Jillian's is probably still traumatized from last time."

"He'll recover. Call me if you get anything."

"You got it."

I took my cell phone from my pocket as I headed down the hill. Rena honked as she passed, and I flipped her off. That could have gone worse. She hadn't pressed me for more about the Bright Brotherhood, and if what I'd said had made any dent, she might think twice about getting too tied up with it.

At least I could take care of a few small matters first. I dialed Sarah's number, and she picked up on the second ring. "Goddess Garden."

"Sarah, it's Evie. I got a lead on one of those chain stones."

"Evie, I thought I told you I didn't need—"

"It's okay. I didn't go out of my way or anything. I just picked it up while working on something else."

"Okay." She covered the phone for a moment. "Liz, take the counter . . . All right. Since you've already found it."

"Well, I didn't get a chance to go back and verify it, but I think one of the stones may belong to one of the residents at Crofter House."

"Wait a minute; I need to write this down." She muttered to herself for a moment, and I heard the crash and clatter of a jar full of pencils overturning. "Crap. Go ahead."

"One of the residents at Crofter House," I repeated. "I caught the scent as I was leaving her room. A Mrs. Crowe; didn't get her first name. Chances are she's got it among her personal effects."

"Mrs. Crowe." She was silent a moment. "So you sensed one of the chain stones on her?"

"In her room." Come to think of it, there hadn't been much scent to the old woman at all; just age and dryness. Only that hint of the stone had made any impression on me. Hell, with the lousy night I'd had, it was a wonder I wasn't in worse shape. "You may have some trouble with the attendants; there's a doctor who chased me out of her room. If you can talk to her it might be easier, but she seemed out cold. Didn't even wake up while the doctor was bitching at me."

"Asleep. Hm. Thanks. This was where?"

"Crofter House. Big brick thing up on the Jamaica Plain border, near the end of the E line." I glanced over my shoulder, but the curve of the hill had already hidden the building from me. A T train squealed past. "Look, I'll try to go back later and give you a better location—"

"No need. I'll go through someone else, see if I can set something up."

"Well. All right, then. You okay, Sarah?"

She sighed. "I'm dealing with some crap from the coven. Nothing big. Come by sometime so you can distract me from all this."

"I'll try to." I clicked the phone shut and walked on, pausing by a restaurant and pretending to read the menu while I thought.

The lack of most scents in Mrs. Crowe's room bothered me. Granted, I don't always use my nose; if I did, I'd go mad from sensory overload. But it was rare that I didn't sense anything at all. With this it had been as if the scents were screened off, muted somehow, perhaps even warded—

The acrid scent of fear was what warned me. Fear, and magic, and grimy leather. I ducked away from the side alley that served as the restaurant's trash heap just as a skinny hand snatched at my arm. "Don't you touch me, Leon," I spat. "What the hell do you think you're doing?"

Leon's watery eyes glinted in the shadows of the alley. "I could ask the same thing of you, Hound. Get over here."

"In there? With you? You gonna shoot me again?"

"No gun." He rattled his coat and looked over his shoulder, though there wasn't anything but blank wall behind him. "He took it."

"Good for him. You're the last person I want to see packing, Leon."

He hawked a yellow glob by my feet. "I need to talk to you, Hound, and the longer you stand out there talking to me, the bigger the chance someone's gonna come and look. You don't want that. You don't want that, and neither do I." He jammed his hands into his pockets, making his coat clink with the sound of vials rattling against each other. "You ever seen what a dozen loci look like all lit up?"

I caught my breath. "Lit up how?"

"Well, that's the question, right? Some of 'em might catch fire, some of them might start screaming, some might start snaking back to their graves and hitch a ride on anyone they can find. Which'd be you, right now. Nasty." He leaned close. "Now, anyone comes over this way, any car even slows down, and we all go up. You got that?" He grinned, his eyes darting to either side. "How about you come over here, where no one's gonna start getting curious?"

I muttered a curse under my breath. But he was right; the middle-aged women on the other side of the street were already giving me weird looks. They might not come this way, but I didn't want to risk it. "Okay," I said, and sidled around garbage bags into the alley. "Leon, what the hell—"

"I said over here!" He grabbed my arm and yanked me forward, right over the garbage. My foot caught, and the punch I had prepared for his stomach whiffed, bloodying my knuckles against the wall. Leon twisted the arm he'd caught up against my back and jammed something sharp and beery against my throat: a broken bottle. "You wanna ask why? This far along and you wanna ask why?"

I froze, the skin of my throat twitching away from the jagged glass edge. "What are you talking about, Leon?"

"As if you didn't know. As if you didn't fucking know!" He pressed the bottle harder against my neck. "You been in this city a long time, Hound. Long time, and you mostly seem to have sense, but fuck all if I know what kind of sense you've got now. What side you on?"

"I don't know what you're talking about." If he really wanted to keep me pinned, he was holding me all wrong. I still had a free arm, and his knee was close enough to my foot . . . and if I snapped my head back right . . .

"You don't! The fuck you don't! Listen: they got a shadowcatcher the other day. Nothing big, just a pissant shadowcatcher, but they spent *time* on him. I drag him out of the gutter, you know what he tells me? That you talked to him that morning. That's all. Now, you talked to me too, and if they haven't got me yet it's only because I'm not a stupid fucking shadowcatcher."

Christ. "Is he okay?"

"Who? The shadowcatcher? He's fine. Won't hold a locus for weeks, not that it stopped him from buying six of mine. Now you wanna tell me why they went after him?"

"I didn't know they were looking for me." Not then, I didn't. I shifted my weight, readying myself. "Where's your gun, Leon?"

"Bald fucker took it. Took it and looked at me . . ." The glass against my neck shook.

"If all he did is look at you, I say you got off easy." I sniffed. "You smell like shit, Leon." Shit and blood, now that I was this close; a thick layer of both underneath the fear.

He laughed, a hoarse, despairing sound. "Course I smell like shit. Hound's good at smelling shit, except when she's wading in it. You and your fucking *geisa*, gotta help who-ever asks, gonna get you killed someday."

The hairs on the back of my neck started to prickle, and a dull glow of heat enveloped me, rich with the scent of ink and skin. *Oh, no*, I thought, *not now.*

"Now I'm only going to ask this one more time, so you listen and if you can't give me a real answer then for fuck's sake give me a fake one. Which . . . fucking side . . . are you on?"

The trash-slimed cement beneath my feet skidded to one side, slipping like the floor in a dream. For a second an image flashed into my head, an image of a man sleeping below mountains, so huge that when he turned in his sleep the foothills rumbled. It was gone as quickly as the twitch, leaving me outside his dream once more. Leon's grip on me slackened. "What the fuck—"

I twisted away and hammered the heel of my shoe against his kneecap. Leon shrieked, and I took the oppor-tunity to grab his bottle-wielding hand and smash it against the wall until he let go.

"No side," I panted. "No fucking side. Okay? I'm keep-ing my head down. Now leave me the hell alone. I'm sorry I got your stone shattered, but you're the one who shot it, not me. If you need help, I'll give it, but don't you ever threaten me again, you understand?"

Leon slid down against the wall, cradling his hand. "Fuck the stone. The stone is nothing, you hear me? Nothing." He took a shuddering breath. "I'm too old for this shit. I'm too old to be running from them and their old woman."

"What?" I crouched down next to him. "What old woman?"

"Fuck you, Hound. You don't have a side, you don't get to know." He yanked a vial from his coat and smashed it on the ground. White mist rose up from the shattered glass, and the hot reek of fireworks wrapped around me. I fell back onto my butt, coughing and choking, eyes streaming from the stink. When I looked up Leon was already a block away, limping to freedom.

I wearily got to my feet, brushed dried carrot peels off my jeans, and tried to clear my head. No luck. I headed back out of the alley and glanced toward the T station. Nothing.

Except, for a second, what might have been a blue-inked arm waving from behind a T car. It was gone before I could look a second time.

Thirteen

I got back home just in time for Tania to chew me out for ditching my early morning shift even after Rena had checked earlier. Schedule changes again. I made a cursory protest and headed out into the city.

In truth, I'd never been so glad to be on the road. Over the river, over the channel, back and across and back again until my path was as twisted as mangrove roots, and if Leon had marked me he'd have a hell of a time finding me again.

I thought about calling Sarah to ask if she knew what the hell was up with Leon. But given how they felt about each other, the only answer I was likely to get was "what *isn't* up with Leon?"

I must have taken Brendan's card out eight times, trying to decide whether I could risk contacting him, whether tracking him might be easier or safer than calling. That was juvenile, I knew; all I wanted was someone to go to and panic at for a while, and Brendan had a lot on his hands right now. I couldn't interrupt him just because I was nervous.

Still, I yanked out my phone with embarrassing speed as soon as it rang. "This is Scelan," I said, squeaking a little.

"Evie, girl! How are you?"

I slumped. "For Christ's sake, Will. What the hell are you calling me for?"

"Now, I'm sorry to bother you, and I know you're pretty busy, but this is more important than the last time we talked. I'm outside your apartment now, and—"

"You're what?" A passerby gave me a curious glance; I shook my head and got off my bike, dragging it up onto the curb.

"Outside your apartment, and I need you to tell this guy it's all right for me to be here, okay?"

"Wait—dammit, Will—"

His voice faded to an indistinct murmur, and there was the sound of a phone changing hands. "Hello?" an unfamiliar male voice asked.

"Hi. Who is this?"

"This is Officer James Burson of the Boston Police. To whom am I speaking?"

"Um. Genevieve Scelan." I hesitated, heart pounding, and then gave him my address, in case that might do something for Will. Had Rena sent someone to my house? "What's the matter?"

"We got a complaint about a man loitering on the steps here. Sounds like a few of your neighbors are a bit nervous about strange men blocking the entrance for hours at a time."

Will was at my apartment? Will had been at my apartment for *hours*? "You heard from Mrs. Heppelwhite, right?" Third-floor neighbor, and I sometimes believed she had no other occupation beyond watching everyone's windows and overreacting.

"That'd be the one."

"Yes, um, it's okay. I . . ." How could I explain this? "Jesus, I had an appointment with him earlier today and forgot about it. I'll be over there in about ten minutes."

"Thank you. Ordinarily I'd have no trouble with leaving him here, but you have some very vocal neighbors."

"Tell me about it. I can't even play my stereo without getting screamed at."

He chuckled, then paused. "Your friend doesn't look so good," Officer Burson added quietly.

"He's had a rough week," I said, then bit down the questions that threatened to spill out. Doesn't look good how? Spirals on his body? Is he hurt? And what the hell is he doing there? "Ten minutes, officer. I'll be there and I'll take care of him."

"Ten minutes."

He must have handed the phone back to Will, who got back on the line, sounding even more hyper than he had at the Adeline. "Hey, Evie, you got that straightened out, then?"

"Will, stay right there. I'll be there in a moment and then you can tell me what the hell's going on."

"Thanks. Knew you'd come through for me." He lowered the phone, and I heard the muffled start of another high school anecdote before he hung up. I clicked my phone shut and took off down Boylston Street.

The officer had been right: Will didn't look good. In fact, he looked as if he hadn't slept since I saw him at the Adeline. He was hunkered down on the steps, head in his hands, paying no attention to the police car on the other side of the street. I pulled up my bike beside him and began locking it to the rack. "Jesus, Will, what are you doing here?"

He looked up, and his eyes lit up with a manic enthusiasm. "Evie, hey, great to see you! Thanks for getting me out of that—I thought I'd just sit out here and wait till you got home, but apparently some of your neighbors are really uptight about loitering in this neighborhood."

Not loitering, I thought, *so much as people not wanting to find scary people on their doorsteps.* Will looked worse than Leon had. He looked—and I didn't much like the thought of it—strung out. I turned to the police car and waved, trying to look like I was in control of the situation, and the policeman in the driver's seat nodded in return. "Let's get you inside," I said.

"Yeah, that'd be a good idea." He hauled himself up by the railing and stood there, wobbling a little, as I opened the door. A lumpy bandage on his hand caught on a rough spot and trailed cotton fibers as he shook free of it.

"How long have you been here?" I asked as I let him in. The little waterfall in the corner spat and burbled to life.

Will glanced at it. "That's cute."

"Yeah. Guy who lived here before me left it behind. Will, you didn't answer my—"

"About four hours." He plopped into a chair and pinched the bridge of his nose. "Give or take."

"Four hours? Didn't you—don't you have work?"

"Yeah. I mean, I guess I do. I left around lunchtime. I think I told LeFave where I was going, but it's all a little blurry."

I dragged another chair over and turned it around. "Okay. Start at the beginning."

"Beginning. Right. I don't even really know when the beginning is." He looked like a kicked puppy—well, a large, balding puppy. "Right after we talked by the site, I kept getting this feeling . . . no, what's the word. Compulsion. Like I had to come talk to you."

I must have made some noise of disbelief, because Will managed to crack a smile. "Not like that. I'm a married man, and my Jeannie is all I'll ever need. No offense. This was something different. I just . . . it was like I couldn't stop thinking about the work you do, the PI stuff, and I just thought, hey, maybe I could get a job together for you. Send you off on a mission, right?"

His voice faded a little, and he leaned back, eyes closed. "Only I couldn't really think of one right away. I knew I'd come up with one if I could just talk to you again, but then . . . I guess I just up and left work today. They'll . . . they're probably worried about me."

"So's Jeannie, probably," I added. I closed my eyes and sighed—then stopped as the faintest scent of gunpowder reached my nose. Could have been my imagination, but . . . "Will, do me a favor and keep your eyes closed for a moment."

"That's an easy favor. I feel like I could go to sleep right here." He opened his eyes and gave me a pleading look. "Just as long as you take on a job for me first, okay? I just . . . I have this feeling. Like I need to get this done."

"I know. Close your eyes." He did so. I got up, trying to be as quiet as possible, and leaned in close to him. There was the sawdust scent of the construction site, and the gummy film of Boston traffic, and a full, warm smell that was probably Will's natural scent . . . and the slightest residue of gunpowder. "Will, do you use blasting powder or anything like that at the site?"

"Hell no. We had some kids with firecrackers there back in May, but I chased them off good, and Jerry told me he'd talked to their parents." He heaved a sigh and slumped deeper in the chair. "Jeannie's gotta be frantic by now. I'd called home first, when I thought I might just come home, but then I changed my mind and came out here instead."

Four hours ago? Frantic wouldn't be the word. "I'll call her. When did you cut your hand?"

"This?" He waved the bandage at me. "This is nothing. Got it three . . . two days ago. Snagged it on a rough board; got a splinter long as a nail stuck in it. I was gonna bring the stupid thing home to show Jeannie, maybe keep it for the worker's comp claim, but it wasn't in my jacket when I went home. Must have dropped it somewhere."

A missing splinter, with a little of Will's blood on it. I didn't like that. A lot of ritual magic drew on the idea of sympathetic magic: affect something that represents the person, and you affect the person. It's the basis of what most people consider voodoo, and a lot of the popular conception of witchcraft springs from it. That's why so many adepts were skittish about letting anyone touch them or even get too close.

A compulsion, a *geis*, could be created if you had a drop of blood from your target. It'd take a lot of power to get it to work . . . but if there was one thing the Brotherhood had, it was power. "Will, have you ever heard of a *geis*? *Geisa*?"

"Gesso? Jeannie's a painter, she uses that stuff—"

"Never mind." I shook him by the shoulder, and he grunted, coming awake. "The compulsion you had—it was just that you had to get me to take on a job for you, right?"

"Right. I kept thinking that I didn't have anything really good for you—even thought I might have you follow Jeannie for a day, but that's stupid and anyway she'd have my hide for it. But I knew I'd come up with something." His brow creased in thought, as if he was trying to remember someone's name.

"Don't think about it. No, really. Don't." I took one of the magazines from the side table and handed it to him. "I'm going to go in the back for a minute. You hide this somewhere in this room, and I'll find it when I come back. I'll do it for fifty cents. Okay?"

He looked from the magazine to me and back. "You're kidding, right?"

"Nope. Be back in a moment." I picked up the phone and started to head into the kitchen. "Will, did you drive here?"

Will shook his head. "Walked."

Jesus. "Okay. I'll arrange for a ride home." I went into the kitchen, leaving the door open a crack so I could hear if Will decided to go wandering.

This wasn't much of a ruse, but things of the undercurrent weren't usually known to be smart. Just unearthly. You could fool them, if you knew the rules. The little pseudo-hunt I had planned might be close enough to the *geis* placed on Will that it would break the hold on him. I wasn't an expert cursebreaker—Deke was good, though so nervous that he was more likely to run from a curse than break it—but I'd learned a few things just to stay afloat. It was all hedge-magic, minor ritual stuff, the kind that doesn't get addictive unless you start using it regularly. Pot versus heroin, I suppose, though it's neither that clear nor that comforting.

I searched through the phone for Nate's number without luck, turned the kitchen upside down looking for it, and even tried calling Sarah to see if she knew it. She didn't answer, though, and the sounds from the office indicated that Will had finished hiding the magazine.

Finally I found the damned thing at the bottom of my junk drawer, scribbled on the side of a Thai restaurant menu. I listened at the door to make sure Will was still there, then dialed Nate's number. "Nate? This is Evie."

"Evie? What is it—is something the matter?"

"Nothing—okay, that's not true." I dug out the flannel with the last of Mom's silver, then shook my head. Silver wasn't what was needed here; it broke some magics, but wasn't as all-around unfriendly to magic as steel. "Listen, do you have a car?"

"Yes," he said slowly, as if admitting to it would get him a parking ticket. "Why?"

"Will's here, at my office. He's not doing so well. I think he may be sick." I was glad he couldn't see me; the lie felt flat on my tongue and I was sure it was obvious on my face. "Could you take him home? I'd call a taxi for him, but I'd feel better if he was with someone he knows." I pulled out my flatware drawer and took out a double handful of knives and forks.

"Sure. I'll be right there. Where are you again?"

"Fens. Off Park Drive." I gave him quick directions through the one-way maze. "Thanks for doing this, Nate."

"Any time."

Will was slumped in the same chair when I returned, though his hands no longer held the magazine. "Did what you said," he mumbled without opening his eyes. "Hid it well."

"Good. That's good, Will." I sorted the knives out, then shrugged; the blades didn't matter so much as the stainless steel. "I need you to just sit there for a while, okay? Don't get up, and don't think about much of anything." I knelt and began placing the flatware in a circle around his chair, handle touching blade touching tines, unbroken steel.

Will laughed wearily. "That's kinda tough to do, you

know? Like that whole 'don't think of a pink elephant' thing. Jeannie's into the whole yoga bit, yoga and pirates or whatever it is. Meditating, thinking of nothing. Never made any sense to me; it's like if you're thinking of nothing, you're still thinking, right?"

I smiled. "All right, then. Tell me about work. How's the job going?"

"Ah, slower than the Big Dig . . . no, maybe not that bad. MacPherson's always arguing with me about the plans. Thinks he's a big expert on these sort of things." A little more animation had returned to his voice as he talked, and as I completed the circle around him his color began to improve. "Gonna be a great place, the kind I'd like to have. Good neighborhood, too. Even with the cranks across the street."

"Really." I got to my feet and brushed off my knees. The fireworks smell was less, but still present. I traced a similar circle on the palm of my hand and whispered to it the way I'd seen Deke do, and the smell flared once before going out. Now I just had to hope that my false hunt would fool the *geis* enough. Will's scent was strong, but somewhere in this room would be that magazine . . . "Have they given you any trouble?"

"Nah. Just not the nicest of folks. Hey, yeah, you know them; they're the folks you were talking to, the ones that guy you were staking out went to see."

"I wasn't staking him out." Behind the couch, under the storage chest. Bingo.

"Whatever. He's there all the time."

I paused, magazine in hand. *Had Brendan ever told me what he was doing at Frank's parents' place?* "Okay. Give me fifty cents."

Without looking, Will held out two quarters. "Lucky I didn't empty the change outta my pockets last night."

I took the coins from his hand and put the magazine in their place. "There. You've given me a job, and I've completed it for payment. Feel any better?"

Will sat up, blinking. "Yeah. Yeah, I do. That's weird."

I spun one of the quarters between my fingers. "About the house . . . do you remember any other people coming to visit?"

"I got things to do, Evie; I can't spend the whole day watching people that aren't even my neighbors."

"Yeah. Sorry." Silly of me to ask. I pulled over a chair and settled into it.

"No, wait. There was one other thing I heard about them—they had a kid, about our age. All I heard about him was that he was kind of messed up." He shrugged. "Me, I figured the guy who kept visiting was their son, but I guess I was wrong about that."

"Yeah. Well. Messed-up was right." The doorbell chimed, and I got up to open it. "Listen, do you go to church?"

"Not really. Jeannie was part of Our Lady down in Newton, but since the whole priests and kids thing went down she's been staying away. Can't say as I blame her."

"Okay, then. It's just—" The bell rang again, and I hesitated, one hand on the doorknob. "Don't take this the wrong way, but it might be best if you, I don't know, went to Mass next Sunday. Or gave confession."

Will's eyes widened. "When'd you get religion, Evie?"

"That's not it at all. It's just . . ." Okay, how could I frame this? "It's the psychological benefit. This kind of, of disorder can sometimes crop up again. To prevent a relapse, you may need to, I don't know, get back in touch with some of the traditions of your family." That was pretty weak, but fake psychology was better than saying one needed a new binding to override the *geis*. Despite my time spent wading in the undercurrent, I still didn't feel at all qualified to talk about the existence of God or whether he had any particular favorites among religions. But evidence showed that religious ritual could negate some antagonistic magic. I'd known one or two adepts who'd been baptized or, in one case, become a Buddhist nun, in order to get out from under a nasty binding. Mom, at least, had believed it enough that one time.

Will shook his head. "Traditions of my family usually

meant shouting at each other across the table and screaming at the Sox. Hey, I can do the last one, no problem."

"Okay. Just think about it, all right?"

Nate was leaning against the railing when I reached the
door. "How is he?" he asked.

"Better. If you could just get him home—"

There was a crash from my office. "What the hell," Will
called out into the hall, "are all these forks doing on the
floor?"

Nate raised an eyebrow. I sighed, shrugged, and let him
in.

Will tossed the magazine onto the couch as I followed
Nate in. "Did you have a picnic or something when I wasn't
looking?" he asked, nudging the circle of flatware with his
shoe.

"Long story," I said, very aware of Nate's puzzled look.
"You feeling better, Will?"

"A little. Maybe all I needed was to sit down for a bit."
He grinned at Nate and thumped him on the shoulder.
"Good to see you. You my ride?"

"I guess I am." Nate nodded to the forks and looked a
question at me. I played dumb and shrugged. "I can drop
you off at work, if you want."

"No. No, I think I'd better just go home." He looked at
me, then away, swallowing. "Good to see you, Evie."

He held out his hand awkwardly in a stiff formality very
different from his earlier demeanor. I shook his hand and
was glad to see that he didn't flinch. "Think about what I
said, okay?"

"I will." He winked.

I smiled weakly. Nate gave me another "what the hell?"
look as he followed Will out, but didn't say anything.

I waited until the outer door closed, then locked my door
and sank into the closest chair. The message light on my
phone blinked at me. I ignored it for the moment and called
up Tania to tell her I'd be out sick the rest of the afternoon.
She, of course, told me that I shouldn't worry since I wasn't
on shift yet.

I turned the machine up and played the messages while I picked up the forks. One was from a BC professor convinced that his BU counterpart was hoarding manuscript pages, one from a young woman in Dorchester who'd lost an heirloom of some kind while moving last week. Two messages that were blank: probably a telemarketer.

Nothing from anyone in the undercurrent. That shouldn't have been surprising, but it was still unnerving. If what had happened to that shadowcatcher wasn't the norm—if they really were targeting my acquaintances—I could lose all contacts with the undercurrent. And my job.

And your life, of course, I thought. *Priorities, woman.*

The Dorchester woman wasn't in, so I left a message with her sister saying that I'd come by later in the week. The professor didn't mind the delay, though he did want to complain at me for a while about how unprofessional his colleague was being. Under other circumstances, it might have been mildly entertaining.

I took out Brendan's card and lay it flat on the table. *Call him*, I thought. *This has gotten bigger than either of you expected, and he's the only link you have to Frank's death.*

Call Sarah. Brendan's in hiding, and he's obviously keeping something from you. Sarah knows magic, she knows history, and she can tell you at the very least why someone would lay a geis on your friend.

Call them both. Have a party!

"Christ," I muttered. "You really did miss your coffee this morning, girl."

I'd picked up the phone, still not knowing whom I meant to call, when the doorbell rang again. "It's open," I yelled without looking up.

The wards flickered as Nate entered and closed the door behind him. "You saw him home okay?" I asked.

He nodded. "Traffic was light. I'm parked on the street."

"Don't leave it there long; you'll get a ticket." I turned over Brendan's card and dropped the phone back in its cradle. "Thanks for taking Will home."

"Sure."

"How's Katie?" Unscarred by the encounter we'd had the other day, I hoped.

"She's all right. Still wants to see you again. I said I could call you, but she said she wanted to talk to you alone. Kids." He paused a moment, running a finger over the back of the merrily bubbling fountain. "Will was saying some pretty crazy stuff."

Damn. I took a file from my desk and pretended to look through it. "How so?"

"Stuff like how he had to go get some holy water, maybe see if he needed an exorcism. And he mentioned something about a *geis*."

I tried to look blank. "Which is what?"

Nate's lips twitched into a smile. "Something I haven't heard since I stopped playing Dungeons and Dragons. I had a girlfriend back in college who was big into the whole pagan thing, and she talked about it too."

"Would this be the one who's dating Sarah's ex?"

"No, before that." The fountain drizzled water over his hand and creaked to a halt. He shook the drops off, making a face at the fountain. "Crazy stuff, like I said."

No one would ever call me the world's best conversationalist, but I could see where this was headed. "So why didn't you stay and talk to Will about them?"

Nate shrugged. "This is Will we're talking about. How accurate do you want to bet his answers are going to be? Besides, Jeannie came running out as soon as we pulled up to the house. She bundled him inside before I could even say goodbye."

Good for her. "That's too bad, then." I realized I'd been looking at the same page for two minutes without noticing it was upside-down. At least Nate couldn't see it either. "Was there something else?"

Nate hesitated, then let out a long breath and sat down on the couch, in the same place Brendan had sat, his long hands open in his lap as if awaiting a gift. "Evie, I . . . we've both changed a lot since high school, I think."

"Big surprise there."

One of Nate's hands curled closed, then opened again. "I'm only just now realizing that I don't know you all that well."

Oh, God . . . why now, why Nate? I liked the man; he made me feel like there was something real beyond the undercurrent and its tides. But associating with me would hurt him—especially now, when I might at any moment find another dark tide pressing the windows inward again.

I set down the useless file and cleared my throat. "Let me see if I can guess where you're going," I said. "You're worried about me because I'm doing something strange and therefore interesting, and you want to both get a voyeuristic glimpse of my work, same way as Will, and feel all manly and protective. You're going to tell me to be careful out there, because I can't take care of myself in this big scary world, even though you don't know anything about what I'm walking into."

Nate's eyes flashed, and for a second I caught a flicker of that iron-gate scent, the curtain coming over his emotions to hide them from everyone, himself included. Then he seemed to shake himself, and his lips twisted wryly. "Something along those lines. Only with a little more tact."

"And if I told you that I am already careful? More than you can know?"

"You've made your point and driven it home. I concede."

"Concede nothing." I glared at him across my desk, trying to hide how much it scared me that he'd gotten even this close to the undercurrent. Nate was too good to go down that way. "You have no business telling me to be careful, or assuming that this sort of situation is the same for both of us. You'd be dead in a week doing what I do."

Again that momentary shutdown, everything kept in check. "Are you trying to piss me off?" he asked.

"I'm trying to scare you off. There's a difference." He didn't answer, and after a moment my shoulders slumped. How long had it been since I'd had a full night's sleep? "It's not that I don't appreciate your intentions. And yeah, some of your fears may be founded. But as much as this will hurt to hear, there is nothing you can do about them."

Nate's lips twisted into a self-deprecating grin. "And down goes my ego in flames."

"If it's any comfort," I added, "there's very little I can do either."

"No comfort. But it puts things in perspective. I'll try to stop worrying about your situation. About you, though . . ." He looked down at his hands and pressed the knuckles of one against the palm of the other. "It's more than just what you're working on. The last few times I've seen you, you've looked like you're walking a tightrope. Stressed, strained. Like you've got something drawing you out to a breaking point." He looked down at his hands, stained with ink along the fingertips. "I know what that's like. Believe me, I know it. I guess what I'm offering, since I can't do anything to help you, is just to give you what I don't have. Someone who'll listen, if you need it. Even if I don't understand a tenth of it."

I didn't answer right away. The undercurrent was full of temptations, I'd known that since the beginning, but this was more potent than any of them. And more dangerous, now that it wasn't just me. But it sure would be nice to talk to him, especially now Brendan was gone . . .

The phone rang. I jumped, fumbled with it for a moment, then picked it up. "This is Scelan."

"Genevieve. It's me." Brendan's voice, and still his own, no stranger's voices using his mouth. Thank God. "I need to talk to you now."

"Where are you?" I asked. Nate started to get up; I waved him away and turned aside, curling my hands over the phone. "Are you all right?"

"Yes. I've put down a false trail, so I should be okay for another day. Can you come meet me?"

"Yes. Where?"

"There's a statue at the west end of the Commonwealth

Avenue mall, near where the turnpike crosses it. I'll be at the foot of it." He hesitated. "If something looks wrong, just turn around and walk out of there. Don't run. They'll catch on if you start to run."

"I'll be there. Hang on." I switched the phone off and got to my feet. "I've gotta go."

"You'll be okay?" Nate paused. "No, wait, I know. You will be okay, without my worrying. I'll see you, then."

"See you." I opened the lower drawer of my desk, regarded the contents, then shook my head. Better not to bring in that complication.

Nate paused at the door. "The offer still stands, you know."

"I'll think about it," I said, but my gut decision had already been made. I'd lived this long by keeping my head down, and if keeping it down further would make sure Nate stayed out of the undercurrent, then I could do that too. "Get going," I said. "And watch your back."

He opened his mouth as if to ask another question, but stopped himself and only nodded instead. I counted to thirty after hearing his car start up outside, then bolted for the door.

Fourteen

Not running to the rendezvous was one of the hardest things I'd ever had to do. *He's not in danger*, I kept telling myself; *this isn't a distress call. Don't panic. Don't run.*

The end result was that by the time I reached the statue, I thought all my muscles would cramp at once just from the tension. A few people were out on the mall, some businessmen walking home and a few dog walkers with their cadres, but no sign of Brendan yet.

I looked for the statue and found it, a red stone thing that could only have been a Victorian's idea of a Viking. He had the helmet-with-wings-on, the hunting horn, and two very poorly placed breastplates with little spikes that made him look like the Viking inventor of pasties. Even tense as I was, I still couldn't keep from grinning when I saw those.

No Brendan. There was a shadow at the base of the statue that resolved itself into a bum in a hooded sweatshirt and baseball cap, but he didn't quite look right . . . I paused a moment, trying to reconcile what my nose told me with what I saw. What I saw was the guy in the sweatshirt, a duffel bag on his lap, muttering to himself. No one else seemed to pay any attention to him; even the muffin-sized dogs yanking their owners every which way only gave him fleeting looks. What I smelled was the warm, familiar scent of Brendan, plus a persistent fireworks whiff that intensified when I looked straight at him.

Aversion ward. Minor enough, but I didn't want to have to push against it for long. I walked up and leaned against the statue. "You're all right?" I said quietly.

Brendan looked up, and right away I saw why he'd needed the aversion ward. His disguise wasn't much of one; anyone who looked closely would notice that this bum was wearing well-tailored trousers with the grubby sweatshirt, plus the same sunglasses Brendan usually wore. "You're quick."

"It's a lousy disguise. Besides, I'd know your scent anywhere."

He managed to look both flattered and hurt at the same time, and I laughed as he explained, "It was this or a heavy-duty ward, and I'd rather not call on that much magic right now. I don't want to get in the habit."

"You won't get an argument from me." It also was a point in his favor; most adepts would pull out all the stops to make sure they stayed safe, but this kind of restraint only reinforced my impression of him as sane.

Brendan pushed the duffel bag off his lap and got to his feet. "I'm staying in a safe house of sorts, but I didn't want to bring you there—actually, I'm not sure I could, come to think of it. This was the best way I could think of to meet you in the open."

I noticed how stiffly he moved, and took a step closer to him. "Are you all right?"

Brendan hesitated, then sighed and took off his sunglasses. His left eye was bloodshot—no, beyond bloodshot. It looked as if several blood vessels had all burst at once, leaving his eye splattered with red. "I got careless," he said by way of explanation. "One of their servants almost got me."

"Jesus. Will you be okay?" I reached a hand up to touch the side of his face, then paused, sniffing. "Their smell's still on you."

"They're still hunting me. I may have to vacate the safe house soon." He tried a smile. With the eye, it only looked ghoulish.

"Goddammit!" I had to clench my fists to keep from shaking him. "Why the hell are you still in the city? I told you to get out, even if it's only as far as Gloucester—"

"I can't leave. Not just yet." He crouched and began rummaging through the duffel bag.

I hesitated, thinking about what Will had said. "When I first saw you, back in Southie—what were you doing there?"

Brendan glanced up at me. "In South Boston? Running messages, mostly. Frank's parents were worried about their son, and I was able to pass a few letters back and forth." He frowned, his gaze unfocusing and looking far away. "I wonder if that's how the Brotherhood found him . . . I never did vet his parents, and they might have talked."

Okay. That made sense, at least, and something like that had happened before. I thought of Frank's father, how he hadn't seemed surprised by Frank's death, and shivered.

"Funny you should mention it just now," he went on. "Frank left a few things with his parents. I didn't have a chance to collect them before now, but when I saw them I knew why he mentioned you."

"Other than the whole nostalgia thing," I said.

"Other than that, yes." He pulled out a flat wooden box, about the size of my hand. "Some of the things he'd learned in the Brotherhood included its enemies. That's a bit inaccurate . . . 'people in their orbit' was how he put it."

"Sounds like Frank." I helped Brendan to his feet. His hand was warm. "What is it?"

"A key-coffer—sort of a safe-deposit box. Frank gave me some clues as to where it was, but until I knew he was dead I didn't want to go after it." He opened the box and took out a thin handkerchief, plain white muslin so fine, light shone through it. "Apparently there's an old woman who had a run-in with the Brotherhood some years back, and she wounded them somehow before giving in."

" 'The old woman under the curse,' " I murmured.

Brendan looked up, eyes narrowed. "What?"

"Something Frank mentioned, a long time ago." What had he said about her? Nothing about a fight, but something else . . . "I didn't know what it meant."

The line of Brendan's shoulders relaxed. "I doubt he did either, then. Anyway, this was hers, and he left it in the coffer. I might be able to locate her using it, but it'd take time, and we don't have that anymore. But Frank knew what you could do, and he knew I'd go to you . . ."

"You want me to hunt her? Find her and ask her how she managed to wound the Brotherhood?" And if she was under a curse, maybe I could do something about that as well.

Brendan nodded. "That's the gist of it. I know I'm asking a lot of you."

"Screw that. You've saved my life more than once now. I owe you this at least."

"This isn't payment. I can't hold you to that." He held the handkerchief out to me. "I'm asking you only as a friend."

"Either way, you've got a yes." I took the handkerchief and cupped it below my nose. Below the scents of dust and lavender, stale air and dry rot—all surface smells—there was something else. *Iron*, I thought, *and the scent of magic, and blood, and . . . stone?*

Stone. Yes. This scent was similar to that of the chain stone Sarah had asked me to find. Which meant the two were linked . . .

"This may be easier than I thought," I told Brendan without looking at him. "I met a woman in Crofter House today who had a scent very like this. A Mrs. Crowe."

"Crowe," he repeated. "You're sure it was in Crofter House?"

"Yes." I folded the handkerchief and rubbed it between my fingers. Someone had embroidered a Greek-key pattern of three angular spirals in one corner; the thread had faded with age to a pale gold. "There's something odd about this scent, and I didn't get a strong impression of her while I was there. I'll go back tomorrow and see if I can confirm it."

"Tomorrow. Good. Great."

I inhaled again; again that heavy, scorched-blood scent. "It's funny . . . I keep having nightmares about her. Well, not her. Someone who looks like her."

Brendan took the handkerchief from me, letting his fingers rest against mine for a moment before putting it back in the box. "How so?"

"Just . . . nightmares. Nothing real. I thought it might be something wrong with me, but the holy water and rowan I tried didn't do anything, so it's probably just my subconscious throwing a tantrum."

"No. Wait." He leaned forward to look into my eyes. I held his gaze, even though it was a little disconcerting with his bloodied eyeball. "How long have you been having these dreams?"

"Just the last couple nights. Really, it's not too bad."

He closed his eyes. "Since I put the wards up. Damn."

"You think there's some connection?"

"Probably. The magic I use . . . it can have side effects like this. I thought that since you were familiar with magic, it wouldn't affect you too badly, but it looks like I was wrong." He crouched and rummaged through the bag again, stowing the wooden box and coming up with a scrap of paper. "If it happens again, call me and tell me exactly what you dreamed. It might be important."

"I don't see how." I willed away the memory of how my dream had intruded on Mrs. Crowe's room. That was my own neurosis coming to the fore, and it was none of his business. "They're familiar, you see, they're just the usual guilt dreams, and I've been stressed, so that's why they're coming up—"

"Genevieve." He touched my chin and lifted my face. My blood started to roar in my ears. "It is important. Some of the entities the Brotherhood uses—they can get to you in ways that seem natural. They find a chink in your armor and worm their way in, get you used to them before you realize they're even there."

"I don't think they'd be that subtle." I stepped back, out of his reach, and hesitated, running my fingers over the base of the statue. It had the Viking's name—Leif Ericson—as well as futhark runes, and I wondered if that might be why Brendan had chosen this particular spot. Dublin aside, the Vikings and the Irish weren't known for getting along. "My friend Will . . . you remember the guy who called me yesterday while I was hunting for Frank? I think the Brotherhood was trying to use him to get to me."

I told him about the *geis* on Will, and Brendan's face grew grim. "Clumsy," he said at last, "but it's what I've come to expect of them. No finesse."

"Since finesse would probably have gotten me into their trap, I'm quite happy they stayed clumsy."

Brendan didn't seem to hear me. "I've been concerned about that visitor . . . The wards told me that someone had visited you, but since he didn't register as an adept, I didn't think twice. There was another visitor, right? One who came back?"

"That'd be Nate. He's—he's another friend. A little closer than Will; we've kept in touch these last few years." I thought of Nate's offer, sincere and misguided, and forced a smile. "I used to have a huge crush on him back in ninth grade. But tell him that and I'll hunt you down."

Brendan raised his hands in mock surrender, and I laughed. "Sorry," he said. "I just wondered. But still . . . if the Brotherhood knows one of your friends, it's possible they know about others. Be careful. You don't know who's on their payroll."

Funny, I thought, *how I could take offense at Nate's warning and get the chills from Brendan's.* "Will's *geis*—"

"Was comparatively easy to break. They were stupid to bind their *geis* to a transaction like that." He reached up, hesitated, then touched my shoulder. "I don't like leaving you alone like this. Nightmares, ward backfires, your friends turning on you . . . I'm not sure it's safe for you to be alone."

The roar of blood in my ears returned, about twice as loud this time. Ash seeds rose up in a dust devil on the other side of me and subsided. "There's a simple solution," I said. *This is a stupid idea*, I thought. *But I'm going ahead anyway.* "You could stay with me. Tonight."

Brendan's expression froze. After a moment I looked away. "Okay, I get it," I said, shrugging his hand from my shoulder. "Sorry. Forget I said anything."

"I—no, Genevieve—"

"No, it's okay. Stupid of me. I'll be fine, and you can check on the wards sometime when people aren't trying to kill us. So listen, I was thinking maybe if Frank left one safe deposit box, he might have left another; I know his parents aren't too happy with me right now, but I could ask—"

I'd been carefully looking at anything other than Brendan, so I didn't even have a chance to react when he caught me by both shoulders and pulled me to him. I caught my breath, and then his mouth was on mine, as warm and rough as I remembered. This time I could kiss back, and did.

Brendan leaned back after a moment, his bloodshot eye in shadow. "Sex leaves a mark on a person," he said, and his voice was hoarse. "Magically speaking, I mean. If I come home with you, there's every chance our auras would get mixed up, and then you'd be in as much or more danger than I am."

"Understood," I said, or panted; I was still out of breath, and he was still very close to me. "Besides, my, um, partners don't seem to do very well against the Brotherhood."

"That won't happen to me," he said, and let go of me, though his hand trailed down my neck, leaving little electrical shocks in its wake. "When this is done—"

I touched his lips, and he drew in his breath sharply. "When this is done," I agreed.

He nodded, and we each stepped a pace back, acting for all the world like two teenagers trying to hide any evidence of a makeout session. "I'm still worried about those nightmares," he said after a moment, his voice almost back to normal again. "I do have a phone with me, but it's not secure by any means."

"Would it lead them to you?"

"Not unless one of us says something stupid." He unfolded the paper and scrawled on it—green ink again, I noticed. "If it happens again tonight, call me."

"This is silly," I muttered, but took the paper.

"Better silly than compromised. I don't want you scarred by ward blowback." He met my eyes, and a second tremor ran through me. "I'll be all right."

"Don't get killed," I said inanely.

Brendan smiled. "I'll try not to."

I walked home, as blind as I'd been on the way down but for different reasons. I kept oscillating between kicking myself for getting so involved, wondering where this would go, and just being shapelessly happy in that first-date way. I kept touching my lips, thinking of his.

When I got home, I didn't even bother with the stack of paper by my desk, and the foolish little smile didn't leave my face until I went to bed.

I had been here before. There was the hospital bed, there the damn beeping monitor, and there the woman who was not Mrs. Crowe. Not my mother.

I retreated away from the bed, backing up against the white glow of the wall. The woman stirred, and I pressed back against the wall until it yielded and broke, dropping me into darkness—

The spear was heavy in my hand, but lighter than surrender would ever be. Men screamed and died around me, and I laughed to hear their cries.

I pointed skyward, shouting guttural words, calling my host to battle, to slaughter, to feed the crows upon carrion.

And at my instigation men in harsh skins charged forward, their hair bristling with battle rage, rational thought lost in my frenzy. The blue marks on their skin were pale imitations of the spirals running up my arms, curling through my hair, clinging to each finger like the reins that I jerked again to send my gray horses wheeling, my chariot flying behind them.

The spear's haft quivered as I drove its blade into the eye of an enemy. His blood spattered my face, and I laughed, laughed in harmony with the howls of the injured and the death cries of the slain.

I jerked awake, the last of a scream dying in my throat. Dim light filled the room, a few shades paler than moonlight, throwing ghost shadows into the corners. My breath sawed in and out of my throat, and for a long moment I couldn't distinguish the sweat drying on my skin from the blood of the dream. The spirals had drunk that blood, I remembered, and glowed all the more fiercely, as they were glowing now—

I choked out a new scream, this one hoarse and disbelieving. There had been a glow. There hadn't been. My arms—

Books fell to the floor as I fumbled for the light. Its warm light was no comfort, even if it did banish the memory of the faint blue glow, the glow of thin lines like those that had covered Frank's body. Like the ones in my dream.

I held out my arms: nothing. Except that the damn scratch had flared up again, and badly; thin lines of red now streaked up from it, twisting in a way that could almost resemble spirals.

Brendan's note had fallen on my bed, faceup. I stared at it, then grabbed the phone and started dialing, shivering convulsively though the night was warm. I pulled the blankets up around me and rocked back and forth as the phone rang.

At last the other end of the line clicked. "Hello?" Brendan's voice said fuzzily.

"Brendan? It's—it's Genevieve. I'm sorry, I know it's lat—"

"Genevieve? Are you all right?"

"I . . ." It sounded so stupid now in the lamplight. "I had another nightmare. I'm sorry; I shouldn't have woken you up, this is stupid of me—"

"No. Wait." I heard a rustling, and a creak of bedsprings. "Are the . . . the things I left with you still up?"

"I think so." I stared at the windows and concentrated, and the silver lines flickered into view. "They are. No one's been here while I've been asleep, have they?"

"No. Not even a scrying. What happened in the nightmare?"

"I was . . ." I shook my head; I couldn't tell him that I'd woken up to find my arms glowing. Not in lamplight, not with the wards safe around me. And *Don't bother him*, I thought, and it felt like the echo of a thought. *This is just woman's worry. Nothing he needs to know.* "There was the old woman," I said, forcing the words out past the strange reticence that had fallen over me. "And then I was someone else. I was killing people. A lot of them."

Brendan whistled. "Sounds like a doozy."

"It wasn't here, it was somewhere else. Somewhere in the past." I knew I wasn't making any sense.

"Even if it was somewhere else, it was still a dream. You're here, you're talking to me, and you're real. You are Genevieve."

"I am. I am." I drew a deep breath and let it out slowly. "I want my old dreams back. I want to be chasing bunnies again." He laughed, and I couldn't help smiling, if sheepishly. "Really. I chase rabbits all night and wake up with my feet knotted up in the sheets." Or a very unhappy bed partner, on those occasions when someone stayed the night. Probably Brendan was thinking the same thing right now; probably he was relieved things hadn't gone any further. "Jesus, Brendan, I'm sorry. What time is it? Three twenty?"

"Three eighteen by my clock. But you're close." He chuckled. "Don't worry about it. Just try to relax a little."

"I'll try."

"Good." He paused. "Look, I used to have insomnia, back when I was in college. I don't know if this'll help, but I could just talk for a while. Not about . . . anything important, you understand."

"I understand." I reseated the phone under my chin and tried to sit up. "Fire away, then."

"All right. There was this one time, back when I was ten . . ." He went on, his voice soothing and calm, drawing the story out until it was the only sound I heard, weaving a cocoon around me, keeping me safe.

I switched off the light and slid down until my head was back on the pillow. "'s a good story," I mumbled.

"I know. Now go to sleep."

"'kay. Thanks, Nate." I switched off the phone and, smiling, kept it by me all night.

Fifteen

I woke up with the phone under my pillow and a mouthful of blanket. I guess Brendan's fixes to the wards had worked; it was back to the bunnies for me.

I staggered out and managed to get the shower working on the second try. As I stood under the water, wishing I'd had the foresight to start the coffeemaker beforehand, last night's conversation slowly crept back to me. I groaned and banged my head against the tiles. Had I really called him by the wrong name?

Better over the phone than under other circumstances, a mocking little voice in the back of my mind said.

Would he have noticed? Maybe not. It had been three in the morning, after all, and I'd been mumbling. I ducked my head under the hot water until the rest of my skin was as red as my face. It wasn't even as if they were very alike; Brendan was sophisticated and urbane, while Nate gave the impression that he'd never quite grown up, responsibilities and pressures aside.

I shut off the water just as the phone rang. Cursing, I wrapped myself in the closest towel, which was neither the largest nor the driest, and ran out to the office. "Don't hang up!—This is Scelan."

A dry voice laughed on the other end of the line. "I'm

not hanging up. Not yet anyway. This is Joseph Yacoubian. We met yesterday, didn't we?"

"We did." I tucked the phone under my chin and tried to dry off without dislodging it.

"Good. Thought I might have imagined it all. I was going to call your friend, but I didn't get anything resembling a phone number off her, and there was no way I was going to call the station. You, though, were in the phone book—and, hey, I even saw the reference to your listing in the Yellow Pages. Never seen anyone under 'finder.' What is it?"

"What it says. So what did you dig up?"

"Not much, mostly because I didn't have much to begin with. It's been damn near thirty years, you know, and I've moved so many times since I worked on this case that my files have gotten pretty thin. But I did keep a few things, just little mementos. I'd take them out and go over them again, you know, when I wanted to kick myself for a while."

He was obviously going to take his time about this, so I sat down and finished drying off. "Go on."

"Well, in those days you couldn't get anything out of an informant unless you were a Fed or something like that. Big joke on us, the way some of the Feds were on the mob payroll."

You don't know who's on their payroll, Brendan said in my memory. I shook my head and tried to listen.

"Anyway, I did some work on my own, under the table. This case bugged me so much I had to do something, even off the record. I finally managed to convince one poor schmuck to trust me. Guy took forever to convince, and he had the weirdest sense of humor. Big Sox fan too; you'd have liked him. But he didn't even know much, just where it happened—where they killed those people before they dumped them. I figured, hell, that was something; half the trouble we'd had was the lack of physical evidence. A crime scene would be pure gold."

"Uh-huh." A crime scene was good for me too; it was just the sort of thing Rena would latch on to, and she'd no longer need me. She and her battalion of investigators could sweep down on it with fine-tooth combs and plastic gloves. If it was twenty-odd years old, the site might even be safe—and unless it was actually in the river, it wasn't likely that Frank had been killed there too. The river scent had been too strong on him for that. "So where did the murders take place?"

Yacoubian sighed. "Well, that's the problem. See, he wrote the place down for me, but there's no way I can tell it to you."

"Mr. Yacoubian, if you're worried about someone listening—"

"No, no, that's not it," Yacoubian broke in. "Well, yes and no. See, I'm on the front desk phone; the young lady in charge is off getting me a coffee. She's a sweetie. But this thing, you see, this note is in a different language. I can't read it—can't even sound it out—but I can give it to you. So you get down here, all right?"

Christ. "You're kidding, right?"

"Not in the least. If you're worried about someone taking it before you get here, well, stop worrying right now. I'm tough as old boots; I can handle them." He paused. "*Are* you worried?"

"Yes. Look, Mr. Yacoubian, you need to get back to your room and lock the door as soon as possible. Don't let anyone in."

"I know *that*."

"Then do it. And—" In the absence of wards, what could you do? "Get as much cold iron as you can—table knives will do, if they're stainless steel—and put it across the threshold. Across the windowsill too."

"I thought it was garlic that kept them out."

"That's vampires, and you better hope *they're* not after you too." He laughed, and despite the knot in my gut, I smiled too. "You know, Mr. Yacoubian, if I didn't know better, I'd think this was all an elaborate plan to get a cup of joe."

"Ha! I wouldn't say no to one; I used to be an eight-cup-a-day man. Some days I think half the reason I'm tired all the time has nothing to do with my age and everything to do with that damn doctor's restrictions." He covered the mouthpiece and coughed; an old smoker's cough. "I can't say I wouldn't mind a few more visitors, and it may be that I went through all those notes just so I can talk to you. It's been a goddamn relief to know that I wasn't going nuts, that there really is all this—this magic stuff out there. That I wasn't insane about the seventy-eight killings."

"It helps, doesn't it? Just having someone else know what you mean makes it all a lot better." I thought of Brendan again and quashed the memory.

"Yeah. But you know what, Miss Scelan? Now that you know what I knew, I'll be just as happy putting it back on the shelf again."

I smiled, a little sadly. "You and me both. Look, I'll call Rena, and we'll be down there as soon as possible. Keep yourself safe."

"Safe from everything but those damn diets. Oh, and speak of the devil, here comes that bastard Connor. Probably here to tell me I'm not allowed behind the desk. Yes, yes, I see you, Doc—"

He hung up. I did the same, then called Rena's number while I dragged fresh clothes out of the laundry heap. The woman on duty said that Lt. Santesteban was out sick, and did I want to leave a message? I told her no and then had to hunt through my address book to find Rena's home number. I could rattle off her work extension without trouble, but I'd almost never called her at home.

She picked up on the second ring. "I thought you were out sick," I said.

"I am. I've got a migraine like you wouldn't believe."

Migraine. Or just a headache, caused by looking through too many things that had aversion charms on them. Even though she didn't know magic, Rena still caught the side effects.

I heard her yawn down the line, jolting me out of my thoughts. "So what have you got?"

"Yacoubian called me. He's got something; an informant wrote down the name of the place where the killings happened, but he can't read the language. Says we should come and take it off his hands."

"You're kidding me. Is he safe?"

"As safe as Crofter House and some of my advice could make him. Which isn't very."

"Damn. I'll be there as soon as I can. Anything else?"

"I—" *There's this strange tattooed guy*, I almost said; *looked like he had as many spirals on him as Frank did, only he wasn't dead. Oh, and I seem to have been targeted for some nefarious scheme by the Bright Brotherhood.* I went over the words in my head and realized how stupid they'd sound, even to Rena. "Nothing at the moment. I'll see you at Crofter House."

"See you there." I closed up the futon, opened the blinds, and left, Brendan's wards twinkling as I stepped over them.

I got there just as Rena pulled up. "Great timing," I said.

"Count yourself lucky," she said as she climbed out of her car. "I almost had to stay behind and look after my sister's kids. Someone ought to tell her that a sick day for me doesn't mean free day care for her." She ran both hands through her short black hair. "God, my head feels like it's going to pop. And, yes, I already took some painkillers, before you ask. Ready?"

"I'm not allowed to say no, am I?"

We opened the front door just in time to hear Connor yelling at the receptionist. "—so stupid? You checked her documentation, right?"

"I did, Dr. Connor," said the receptionist, blinking away tears. "I swear I did."

"You can't have, or else you'd have noticed that she

wasn't legitimate. I swear to God, it's bad enough that you're letting a patient temp for you while you go for a god-damn coffee break—"

"Excuse me," Rena said in what I recognized as her cop voice, the one that can stop an argument from thirty paces.

Connor turned to face us, and a flicker of a smirk crossed his face. My stomach went cold. "Can I help you?"

"We're here to see Joseph Yacoubian."

The receptionist sniffed and tried to compose herself. "He's expecting you. You can go on up."

"Have a nice visit." Connor turned back to the reception-ist. "You know Crofter House's policy on visits, right?" he said, speaking more quietly now. "You had that all spelled out for you, right? So do you want to tell me how I'm sup-posed to explain—"

"Jerk," Rena muttered as we entered the stairwell. "Just listening to that man makes my head hurt more."

"Yeah." I couldn't stop thinking about that little smirk.

I knew something was wrong the minute Rena opened Yacoubian's door. It was the smell, the kind that can't be hidden no matter how many cleaning solutions you use, and here they hadn't cleaned. Not yet. "Rena—"

"Mr. Yacoubian?" She tapped on the door as we entered. "Mr. Yacoubian, it's Rena Santesteban and Genevieve Scelan."

He was slumped in his wheelchair, chin on his chest, the remote still in his hand. On the TV, a pair of smiling news anchors talked fashion trends. A paper cup of coffee rested on the edge of the table, next to a handful of spoons. No steam rose from the coffee's flat surface. "Rena," I said again.

"Mr. Yacoubian?" She touched his shoulder, then shook it.

I closed the door behind me. "He's dead, Rena. I can smell it." And the scents in this room told me how, as clearly as if I'd had a step-by-step diagram.

All the precautions I'd given him, I thought, and they

weren't worth a damn. Not when he'd been betrayed like this. He hadn't known who was on the Brotherhood's payroll either.

"No," Rena muttered, turning his wrist over to check for a pulse. "No, dammit, no. He's warm, he can't be—"

"Drug overdose. Or interaction. Whatever they call it." I nodded to the open pillbox on the table beside him and the empty water glass. "Helped along by someone."

Rena's head jerked up, and her eyes narrowed. "Who?"

"Go stand by the door. Lock it if you can; I don't want to be disturbed." I knelt by Yacoubian, took his hand, and raised it to my lips like a knight kissing her lord's signet ring. His scent was fresh, as was another's: antiseptic, touched with damp rot. "Connor," I said. "His scent's all over the pills."

"Jesus." Rena flipped her phone open.

"Don't call for backup." I glared at her, and she lowered the phone. "What evidence have we got? A scent? That's bullshit, and unless you want to watch some defense attorney take me apart on the stand—and dismantle your career while he does it—you'll let it go. Find something else if you want a case. And I doubt Connor left any other clues."

"Then why the hell am I guarding the door?" she asked through tight lips.

"Because Yacoubian had something to show us." I rose to my feet and walked over to Yacoubian's bookshelf. He'd organized it in a system that could only be called idiosyncratic; papers and photos stuck out from between books and magazines, the ubiquitous sticky notes laminating everything together. "You know," I said as I bent close to the shelves, "my dad used to have me do this, before Mom and I left Philadelphia. He'd have a guest take one of the books off the shelf, flip through it, then put it back. Then he'd call me in and ask me to tell him which book his guest had looked at, and I always went for the right one."

Yacoubian's scent was all over these books, but fresher on some, and I would be looking for one with a very recent mark. "I found out a while ago that most people can do something similar," I went on. "Seems we've all got a decent sense of smell. Or maybe it's touch; maybe the spines hold some residual warmth from people's hands . . . in any case, it works out to the same thing."

"Will you stop blathering and hurry up?"

I glanced at her. "I am blathering, Rena, because when I am hunting like this I need something to keep me in the real world. You understand? Don't think I'm ignoring Yacoubian's death. Don't ever think that." Rena looked down, and I bit my lip hard. "If I don't do this now," I said, staring at the thousand sticky notes Yacoubian had left, "his death will mean nothing—and if I don't talk while I do it, I'm going to break into a thousand pieces. Understand?"

Rena subsided. "This does not put us in a very good position," she muttered. "The longer we stay here with the door locked, the more it's going to look like we had something to do with his death."

"We did have something to do with his death, if you take the long view." I closed my eyes and ran a hand over the books on the top shelf. One bore Yacoubian's scent more strongly than the others; he must have actually stood up to put this one away. I could only begin to imagine the pain that had caused him. He had touched it recently, within the last hour. Before his death—before the pills, though? Hard to say, but I couldn't rid myself of the image of Yacoubian struggling to the shelf, putting the book back in place, even while the overdose drained his strength. I cleared my throat. "Besides, if I'm right, Connor will have done his damnedest to make this look accidental, which should clear us."

Rena looked dubious, but didn't open her phone. I took down the book—*Celtic Mythology* by B. Austin—and flipped through it. A sheet of yellowed paper fell out, and I caught it as it fluttered down. "I think this is it."

"Let me see."

I unfolded the paper. It showed a wide, straggling spiral, about a hand's width across, with lines slashed off it at different angles, clumping together in clusters like thorns, branching through the spiral or off it.

I shivered, thinking of the coil around Frank's throat, and handed the paper to Rena.

Her brows furrowed. "What the hell is this?" She turned the paper over. "Is it a map?"

"It's Ogham. Prehistoric Irish. I can't read it," I added as she turned to me with wide eyes. "Most of the time it's written in a straight line, not a spiral."

Which was why I hadn't recognized it on Frank. Or in Brendan's wards, come to think of it . . . spirals gouged into doors, spirals cut into skin . . .

"Jesus. Where am I going to find a translator for this?"

I didn't answer right away. I still held the book open to the page where Yacoubian had stashed the Ogham note, and I scanned down the lines of text. A section in italics caught my eye: *Lucian of Samosata relates that a frieze in a sanctuary of the god Oghmios (Oghma in the insular pantheon), patron of strength, prophecy, and eloquence, portrayed the god as a youth with the face of an old man. Oghmios was shown leading a line of men by a chain that ran from his mouth to their ears, symbolizing the beguiling power of his words.*

I may have damned you with my words.

"Evie?"

"What? Translator. Right. Try BU? There's gotta be someone in their ancient languages departments who reads Ogham." There was a good chance Sarah could read it, I thought, but whether she would do it for the police was another matter. I put the book back on the shelf. "I don't think we'll find anything else here. If Yacoubian left anything out, Connor would have taken it. Better call the nurse."

"Put the damn book back first." She ran her fingers through her hair again, then opened the door. "We need some help over here!" she yelled down the hall.

I found the call button across the room—too far for Yacoubian to have reached it, and even then it would only have brought Connor again—and rang it several times.

Yacoubian's body looked sad and vacant. Though he was dressed and home, among his belongings, he still looked as vulnerable as Frank had. His cup of coffee was cold. His last cup of coffee, and it was cold.

I knelt down and touched the back of his hand. "I'm sorry," I said. "I shouldn't have gotten you back into this."

It wasn't enough. It wouldn't ever be enough.

Rena ran back in, followed by the young woman I'd seen helping another resident yesterday. "—just sleeping, but then we couldn't wake him up, and—"

"Oh, no." The nurse took Yacoubian's wrist to check for a pulse, then saw the open pillbox. "Oh, no. I've told him he's not supposed to take them without supervision. Dr. Connor said he'd be up to check later—it's terrible, the drug companies make them all the same shade of green now . . ." The pager at her belt started squawking, and she spoke into it, giving Yacoubian's room number. "Get a stretcher up here, and . . . and call the funeral home." She shook her head as she stood up. "Dr. Connor is not going to be happy about this. Not after what happened to Mrs. Crowe."

"He's not the only one—" Rena began.

"Whoa. Wait." I put my hand on the nurse's arm. "What about Mrs. Crowe?"

The nurse gave me a worried look. "Her daughter came to take her out for a while yesterday afternoon—well, we thought she was her daughter, she had all the right paperwork. But when Dr. Connor came back from break, he just about threw a fit, saying the woman didn't have any living relatives."

"If she didn't have family—" I caught my breath. If she didn't have family, who was paying the kickbacks to Connor?

The same people who'd had him kill Yacoubian. I dropped the bag with the coffee and ran out into the hall.

Connor was at the door to Mrs. Crowe's room, having moved on from humiliating the receptionist to haranguing his other subordinates. He looked up as I approached. "No one's allow—"

"Move!" I shoved him out of the way and ran inside, only to come to a halt two steps past the threshold.

The bed was empty. Not even a hair remained on the sheets to show that anyone had been there; not a trace of her remained, save that lingering scent of blood and iron, the one that had so baffled me. The one that both Brendan and Sarah had asked me to find.

And on the heels of that recognition came another scent, one I didn't want to acknowledge.

"Miss, you'll have to leave—" the subordinate began.

"Hush," said Connor. "Let her finish."

I closed my eyes and followed the patterns of scent. The air conditioner had been turned off, and the stagnant air held the remnants of a trail. The new scent led from the door to the side of the bed, and then back out again, this time with Mrs. Crowe's stony scent. I'd thought that it wasn't Mrs. Crowe's scent, just the scent of the chain stones, but it was the only trace of her in the room. And it had been carried away with her, accompanied by the scent of whoever had kidnapped her.

Incense. Sandalwood incense, and not just that, but a particular brand, the brand whose distributor complained if it wasn't on display.

I cursed the air blue and got to my feet. "When did it happen?"

Connor gave me a measuring look. "Yesterday afternoon," he said grudgingly.

Before Brendan sent me hunting. I swallowed another volley of curses and made myself face Connor. "You have another patient who's having trouble," I said, and the stink of relief off him was nauseating. "Mr. Yacoubian isn't very well."

His expression of surprise was almost convincing. "Really? I'll go take a look—oh."

We both turned in time to see the attendants hurrying

up the stairs and into Yacoubian's room. Connor followed them, a little too slowly. I glared at his retreating back as Rena emerged.

"I've called the station," she said. "I should tell them why I was here in the first place."

"Don't tell them about the scent," I said.

"I'm not stupid." She sighed. "I'm going to catch so much shit over this."

"You're not the only one. Look, Rena, I've gotta get going."

"What? Evie, we just got here—I can't do anything with this scrap of Oggra—"

"Ogham. Try BU, like I said. I've got— My shift's starting, and I've gotta get to work."

She gave me a hard look, and I suddenly understood what her partner meant when he said Rena was good in the interrogation room. "Your job's more urgent than murder?"

"Might be," I said, trying to keep my voice even.

"If this is just some excuse to get out of—"

"It's not. Believe me." If anything, I was about to get even deeper in.

Rena sucked in a breath through her teeth, then shook her head. "Fine. But I want you at the station at seven tomorrow morning. Hell, I'll even bring you the damn coffee."

"I'll be there."

The still-sniffling receptionist waved at me as I left.

I trailed my fingers along the brick wall as I walked away from Crofter House. The mortar was old and crumbling; fragments flaked under my touch to join the rest of the sidewalk detritus.

Incense. Sarah's incense. She'd been there. I'd told her that the damn stone she was looking for was in Mrs. Crowe's possession. If she had been desperate enough—

"No," I muttered, not caring if anyone heard me. "No, Sarah wouldn't have done that." I slumped against the wall where it was thick with overhanging branches from the maples behind it. "Sarah wouldn't have done that," I said again, as if repeating it would make it true.

I closed my eyes and tried to clear my head. My feet twitched with that same dreaming shudder that I'd felt before in this place, but I ignored it. Crazy men with tattoos—even Frank if it came down to that—were secondary to this, this bizarre betrayal.

It made no sense. Just as I found the one woman for whom Frank had left me a lead, she disappeared, kidnapped by the one person I thought I could trust not to get into the heavy side of magic. The one person in the undercurrent I had thought was truly sane.

"I wish . . ." I muttered aloud. "I wish I knew what Sarah is doing, where Mrs. Crowe is now."

"Wonderful for telling," a hoarse voice said in my ear, "but I cannot make it. It is beyond me."

I opened my eyes to see Frank McDermot's blue-lined face hanging upside-down in front of me.

 Sixteen

I screamed. Frank—no, it wasn't Frank, Frank was dead—screamed too. He somersaulted forward and landed before me in a crouch, then spun as he straightened up, moving with the grace of a much younger man. The bastard had been crouched on top of the wall right above my head, I realized; he'd followed me all the way from Crofter House.

He smelled of ink and dry skin—and of greenness, and the gunpowder stink of power. An image recurred in my mind, of the giant sleeping under the turf, and for an irrational moment I couldn't shake the feeling that that was the same person who now stood in front of me.

The eyes and ears of the Brotherhood, Brendan had said, but the mildew scent was only a trace, as if it couldn't get a hold on him. I felt that I recognized him, despite the panic his appearance and the Fiana-stink had given me, though I couldn't put a name to him. Something in me knew this man, knew him as well as I knew Nate or Sarah or—well, better than I knew Brendan.

Didn't mean I wasn't still angry, though. "Who the hell are you?"

He cocked his head to one side, regarding me with youthful eyes that were at odds with his iron-gray hair. "Know you not, cousin's child? Has the world so turned over that a hunter must not only ask his hound's aid, but prove himself as well?"

The word *hound* stopped me in my tracks. "How do you know my na—what I'm called?"

The man brought his hand to his mouth, gnawing on his thumb again. The entire world seemed to flicker around him, as if he threw off heat shimmers, or as if the laws of physics ignored him. "So they have not stolen you too. So much they stole—my strength, even the name of my companions—but you stay unbound, as your line has always been." He reached out as if to caress my forehead, and touched my hair instead, twining a few loose strands around his fingers. "Scelan," he said, his accent mashing vowels into it. "Scelan, Sceolang, cousin's child, long have I been imprisoned."

"By who—" Stupid question. "How? Where were you—Did you know Frank? . . . He got painted up same as you, he might have been with Og—"

Someone shouted from up the hill. I turned to see a figure in white running toward us from Crofter House's gate, mildew and antiseptic on the wind before him. Connor. The spiral-inked man hissed through his teeth and spat a glottal phrase that had to be a curse. "Comes the usurpers' man. Best he not catch you alone."

He grinned at me and jerked his hand away. Pain shot through my head, and I yelped, clutching at the patch on my scalp where he'd yanked hairs out. "And best he not catch me at all," he continued, winding the strands around his palm. "But he will."

"What are you talking—"

He was off and running before I got the second word out, vaulting over cars and ducking under scaffolds, all without breaking stride.

I could take a hint, even from a madman. I ran in the opposite direction, skidding through alleyways, not stopping till I reached running water—which in this case was a scummy stream tailored to ring a condominium tower. I skidded on goose crap as I reached the far bank, flailed for a moment, and just managed to avoid landing on my ass.

I paused, panting, and glanced behind me. There was no sign of Connor. I'd lost him—that is, if he'd followed me instead of the inked man. I drew a shuddering breath and waved frantically at the nearest taxi. "Harvard Ave, in Allston," I told him, and reached for my cell phone.

Rena's number went straight to voice mail. The cabbie raised an eyebrow at me as I cursed, but only shook his head and touched the rosary hanging from his rearview mirror. "Rena, it's Evie," I said. "I just got accosted by this guy—same marks as Frank, only he was up and talking. You might want to put out an APB or whatever it is you do for—" Hell, how did I go about describing him? "On a half-naked man with gray hair and marks like Frank's. Call me."

"You get mugged?" the driver asked as I closed my phone.

"Yes. Well, not quite. Guy came up to me and pulled out some of my hair."

He shook his head. "Crazy people, this city. My sister, she has to get an order against man who watches her every time she goes to grocery. Every day, trying to flip up her skirt. Crazy people."

"Crazy," I agreed absently.

"You get mugged, I take you to police."

"Thanks, but it's not necessary. Just get me to Allston."

He shrugged. "Is your funeral. You get mugged easier in Allston than here. Now, my sister . . ."

He rambled into another story, and I drummed my fingers on the armrest. Crazy people watching me, crazy people murdering old men, crazy people kidnapping old women . . . "Dammit," I muttered, and got an exasperated look from the driver.

I got out in front of the Goddess Garden, though I had to turn down another offer to take me to the police station. The police were the last people I wanted to see just now.

The Goddess Garden reeked of essential oils, enough to give me a headache as soon as I walked in the door. Sarah's assistant was at the counter, playing what looked like Tarot solitaire. Bad idea, I could have told her. "Can I help you?" she droned.

"I'm looking for Sarah."

"She's not available right now."

"I need to see her." I folded my arms and waited, hoping to convey that I was willing to stand there all day if necessary. Mulligatawny woke up and glared at me with his usual lazy hostility.

Sarah's assistant gave me the put-upon expression of bored retail workers everywhere, then sighed and rang the cheap Tibetan gong by the cash register. "Sarah? Someone wants to talk to you."

"All right," said a voice from the back. The door to the back room opened, and Sarah emerged, dressed in the same fluttery robes as the woman on the store's sign. "Evie! How's—" and that was as far as she got before she saw my face.

"We need to talk," I said.

Sarah closed her eyes and squared her shoulders. "It would seem that we do. Liz, the store's yours till I come back. And for crying out loud," she added, "don't use those cards. What are you trying to do, give yourself an aneurysm?"

"What's wrong with these?" the assistant complained, but Sarah and I ignored her. She opened the door for me and followed me into the back room.

I realized just how much I'd been betrayed when I felt the gentle pressure of a gun at the small of my back. Damn.

"There's no need for that, Hawk," Sarah said as she closed the door.

"No need?" The man behind me laughed, an unpleasant, nasal sound. "Fisher is dead. Don't tell me there's no need for this." He punctuated it with a jab, banging the muzzle against my spine.

I raised my hands away from my body. It wasn't easy in the narrow hallway. "You've really stepped up security here, Sarah," I said lightly, then stopped as Hawk's words caught up with me. "Hold on one moment. Leon's not dead, is he?"

Sarah sighed. "Killed sometime last night."

"Killed? That's putting it mildly." Hawk spat on the floor, and Sarah made a wordless noise of protest. "We found him on the steps of the Esplanade, cut all to bits. Spirals and Ogham and the Twice-Nine, all gouged into him with a dull knife. And they'd cut out his eyes and fed them to the crows."

I closed my eyes and took a deep breath. Dead. And it was a lousy epitaph that the first thing I'd felt was sickened relief. Leon had scared me more than I'd realized. "Who did it?"

"Who do you think?"

Damn. "Can I turn around?"

"Not until we know you're unarmed." He pawed at my back, and I tensed.

"Goddess damn you, Hawk, she's not armed. This is Evie. She wouldn't come here armed."

"That's what you think," he sneered, but he stopped fumbling at me and stepped away.

"Thanks," I said to Sarah as I turned.

Sarah shrugged. "That, and I know how you carry a gun. That shirt you're wearing would get stretched way out of shape if you tried to cover the grip."

Trust Sarah to think about clothes at a time like this. I had more things to worry about, though. Hawk still held his little gun with all the assurance of someone who'd been watching too many action movies. His expression suggested that he'd ignored his mother's advice and made a face one too many times, leaving it stuck. "You're sure that's how Leon died?" I said. Had the Brotherhood somehow tracked me to him as he'd feared—but if so, why hadn't they found him sooner?

Unless it had to do with Frank. I'd asked Leon about Frank, just before he tried to shoot me. But I'd left him with Brendan, who had been Frank's friend, and even if Leon had been scared afterward, at least he'd been alive . . .

"It's hard to tell exactly what killed him," Hawk said. "Could have been the cuts, or the disemboweling, or the eyes, or maybe they just stripped him of all his loci. That's sometimes enough to kill." He shook his head. "Lucky we came by and got his body moved before the police found it. Got it properly burned too, so he won't go all hungry ghost on us."

"I'm sorry he's dead," I said, knowing it was inadequate.

"Sorry? *Sorry?* You led the Fiana straight to him!"

"She did no such thing." Sarah rubbed at her temples as if she had a headache coming on. "If she led anyone, it was us, and she did that well. Hawk, give me the gun."

"No way in hell."

"Hawk, remember who I am. If you want to stay in the coven, you won't piss off the only person you haven't alienated." She held out her hand.

He glared at me, then made a show of pointing the gun away from me before handing it to her. I relaxed; idiots with guns are a lot more dangerous than people who know what they're doing.

Sarah sighed. "I'm sorry, Evie. He's a little excitable."

"He's not the problem," I said over Hawk's muttered rejoinder. "Sarah, I didn't have anything to do with Leon's death. At least not as far as I know." Hawk rolled his eyes. I ignored him. "I'm sorry for it. No one deserved that end, not even Leon. But that's not why I'm here."

"No," she said, and raised her eyes to meet mine. "I suspect it isn't."

"You have two minutes to tell me why you kidnapped that old woman and where she is, or by blade and bone and stone I swear I'll walk out that door and sever every tie between us."

"You'll have to get through me," said Hawk.

"Shut up, Hawk." Sarah bowed her head and was silent. "It'll take more than two minutes," she said finally. "To start with, I hired Leon to arrange the theft of the chain stones. That's what got him killed."

I blinked. "Chain stones? Are you sure? He never said

anything about Frank?" I paused, remembering Leon's terrified expression. I'd picked up the stone and asked about Frank, and my arrogant guilt had to assume that Leon was afraid of Frank. "Oh, damn."

Sarah didn't ask what I meant. "I promise you, I didn't go over your head; I tried to call you off after the deal came through."

I folded my arms. "I'll give you that," I said. "Go on."

"The chain stones belonged to the Brotherhood—"

"The Fiana," corrected Hawk. "At least *some* of us are brave enough to call them by their rightful name."

"Rightful, my sweet ass!" Sarah drew another deep breath, started to run her fingers through her hair, stopped, and switched the gun to her other hand. "The name isn't even theirs. It used to mean a roving band of warriors, especially those under the command of Finn Mac Cool, the semi-divine hero of legend."

"Don't tell me the legend," I said. I was willing to give Sarah more than two minutes, but not if she slipped into full lecture mode.

Hawk interrupted me. "How much are you planning to tell her? You don't even know what side she's on!"

"Everything," Sarah said.

"Well, hell, we might as well just turn ourselves in! Want me to go outside and shout our plans on the corner for everyone to hear, while you're at it?"

"Hawk—"

"No. If you're going to let in every unconsecrated idiot off the street, then count me out."

Sarah hesitated, then nodded. "Fine. Go ahead."

Hawk blinked. His lips tightened. "All right, then. On your own head be it." He gave me a last furious glare and stomped back into the store, banging the door behind him.

Sarah sighed. "Funny, he was so committed to this before." She saw the look on my face and shook her head. "He'll be back. He usually is. Where was I?"

"About to tell me everything."

"Ha. Yes." She put the gun down on one of the stacks of

Aquarian Weekly and rubbed at her temples. "About their name, there's nothing to tell. Or rather, there's a lot but it's not relevant because the Brotherhood has perverted the old myths so you can't make heads or tails out of them. The Fenian Cycle alone . . ." I cleared my throat, and Sarah looked up, startled. "Right. Anyway, Evie, think about it. You know as many magicians as I do. How well do they work together?"

I shrugged. "I'd say it's like herding cats, except cats don't slip out of existence or make interdimensional litter boxes or explode."

"Right. Adepts working in concert isn't a normal state; they're all afraid of having their precious loci stolen. But it happened here, and it'd never happened before. Ever. Even if you count Atlantis, which I don't, personally. But, Evie, think about it. Why would adepts band together *here*?"

"Because they had to—they were in a strange city—"

"That only makes sense if you're talking about sane people. Your average magician is more paranoid than a convention of conspiracy theorists. The only thing that can keep a society of adepts together is power."

I shook my head. "It'd never work. You'd need a locus the size of Nebraska—" I paused, a sinking feeling in my chest, remembering Brendan's effortless use of power.

"*Exactly.*" Sarah's eyes gleamed. "Exactly. So they did something horrible. The most recent one, the one they started up in the last few years—I don't know all the details of it, but it's rooted in something like voudoun, calling a god or a pseudo-divine spirit down to possess a human host."

"The houngan in seventy-eight," I murmured.

"What?"

"Nothing. Go on."

"Okay. Okay, so voudoun. Only in this case, once they call the god into a human's body, they make it so that particular human—and the god with him—is sealed to their use alone. They made loci out of people, Evie."

I blinked, then put a hand to my throat as if to shield it. "But—no. No, they couldn't have done that."

"Why not? A locus is just a bit of soul in a jar. But the whole soul, imprisoned in living flesh, with a second spirit in the same body, riding it and bound entirely to the Brotherhood's will . . . It's awful, I'll grant you that straight off, awful and inhumane, and an affront to god and human both. But it's not impossible."

"But it—" It turned my stomach. It made all of us prey.

Sarah raised a hand. "There's worse. The stuff they did back in the nineteen seventies was pretty dreadful, I'll grant you, but that's only the things the police turned up. I've done some reading; the earlier stuff was worse. Back in the Victorian days, the price the Fox sisters alone had to pay just to hold their séances was crippling. In more ways than one."

"How many?"

"How many what?"

"How many like Leon?" How many like Frank, like the three from seventy-eight, like poor Joseph Yacoubian, who'd died without even his last cup of coffee? How many had died because the Fiana needed more power?

Sarah was silent a moment. "We think at least two hundred. Spaced out over the years."

Two hundred, plus Leon. He'd been working for Sarah too, on an entirely different track, and it had just been poor bad chance that we'd ended up doing the same thing. And the Fiana had followed me to him—which meant they might have followed me to Brendan . . .

No. Think. Brendan was there when you asked Leon about Frank. Brendan was there.

You don't know who's on the payroll.

"This still doesn't explain Mrs. Crowe," I said. "She was no locus."

"No. She wasn't. You see, they went back to Ireland and did this ritual, this perversion of a consecration. She—Evie, she's not even a woman. She's the Fiana's next step, beyond the hybrid loci—"

"She's an old, helpless woman who was in a coma, for Christ's sake—"

"She is Brigid," Sarah said. "Brigid the blazing, the goddess of fire, who got turned into St. Bridget when the Christians syncretized all the pagan cults. She's a goddess, brought to earth."

"Don't start with another lecture," I said, but for a moment my vision went white, and I remembered blood splashing over my hands and the feel of a spear sinking into my enemy's flesh. I shivered.

Sarah shook her head, too caught up in her own defense to notice my reaction. "They consecrated the whole of Ireland to her, Evie. They made it her sacred space, and then they siphoned off her power. Just think of how many shrines to St. Bridget there are, and that's just the wells alone. A constant flow of sacrifices, keeping her strong—she's an aspect of the Triple Goddess, so that would magnify their power even further. But they put her in an incarnate body so that she's now only a locus. An incredibly powerful locus, but no more than that. The chain stones are what hold her in corporeal form. A sleeping goddess, betrayed by those who should have worshiped her." Her voice softened, as if she were praying aloud now rather than talking to me.

"I don't give a rat's ass about sleeping goddesses," I said. "I do understand kidnapping. You used me to find her." My voice wobbled, and I bit my lip until I could speak normally. "You *used* me, Sarah. So you did it for a good reason. Hooray for you. But it doesn't change the lies at all."

"I'd do it again." Her lower lip trembled, but she met my gaze without flinching. "I'm sorry, Evie, but I would. I can't just live my life in the shadow of something that wrong. I can't go on pretending it's not there. Sometimes you have to choose a side."

"Choose a side, and you get eaten up," I snapped. "Goddess or not, and I'm not saying I buy any of that, the point is that because of what I did for you, an old woman is missing. I don't want that death on my conscience too. Where is she?"

Sarah shook her head. "I can't tell you that."

I regarded her in silence. "I could find her."

"I know."

We stayed like that for a long moment, neither of us moving. "I'm leaving," I said at last. Sarah opened the door to the shop and waited for me to pass.

Sarah's assistant, Liz, had moved on from her solitaire to playing dominoes with the rune stones, probably foretelling a storm somewhere in the North Sea. Sarah walked me to the door, then paused. "I know you don't trust me," she said.

"Damn right I don't." I didn't—couldn't—look at her. My face felt so hot it was probably the same shade as Sarah's dress.

"But I'll say this: if you need help, and if I'm still alive to give it, you and yours can always come to me. I'll do whatever I can to repay—to try to mend what I've done. It won't be enough, I know—"

"Don't tell me that," I said, my voice breaking. The insides of my eyelids prickled. "For God's sake, don't tell me that. If you say it's not enough, then it won't ever be enough, and—"

I groped for the door with one hand and scraped away tears with the heel of the other. If Sarah tried to say more, I didn't hear it, and in that moment I told myself I didn't care.

The T is a great place to be depressed. There are enough crazies riding the subway in this town that no one likes to look too closely at anything unusual. So one woman sitting in the back pressing her hands to her eyes didn't draw attention.

I walked most of the way from the station to home without looking up, too wrapped up in my own black cloud. Even in my usual state of mind I paid more attention to scent than sight, and so since I didn't smell mildew, or stones, or blood, I didn't think anything about the two pickup trucks parked down at my end of the street until I was too close.

Three men in torn jeans and T-shirts leaned against the

hood of one truck, drinking cans of off-brand soda. "That's her," one said, nudging the other two.

I slowed, turning my senses outward. It was a magician's reflex rather than a sensible person's, but it told me one thing straight off: these didn't smell like the Fiana. But that didn't mean they weren't on the payroll. And they weren't bothering to keep their voices down, so whatever they wanted, it wasn't the kind of thing that needed secrecy.

"You're sure?" asked the second, a big blond guy with a tan several shades past leathery.

"Yeah. She was the one talking to him."

I stopped. No hawthorn down at this side of the street, nothing I could turn into a weapon . . . maybe if Mrs. Heppelwhite was doing her usual snooping, the police would show up quickly. Maybe.

The first two men tossed their drinks into the bed of the truck and walked toward me, one glancing behind him to make sure the third was coming. The third pulled a sledgehammer as long as my arm out of the bed of the truck and followed. All three of them looked vaguely familiar, but no more than that.

The man in front, older and Hispanic with a scar running up from his lip, stopped a few feet away from me. "We'd like to talk to you, miss," he said.

"Funny, I don't feel like talking to anyone," I said.

The second man closed the distance between us and grabbed my arm. "That's too bad," he said, and his voice was a little too high, his eyes showing a little too much white.

I looked down at his hand, then back up, into his eyes. "Let go."

And just like that, he let go—not arguing, not bluffing, but withdrawing as if I'd actually made a threat. He backed up to where the other men waited, a few steps away. "Sorry," he said, and now I could identify the note in his voice: fear. "Sorry, I didn't mean—"

"Easy, Clay." The man with the sledgehammer held it in

front of him like a guard, as if it were a talisman to keep me at bay. "He didn't mean anything, miss. But we do need to talk to you."

They were scared of *me*, I realized, and with it came a little shiver, not entirely of surprise. "Fine," I said. "Talk."

"This way." He turned and walked toward the second truck. The other two waited until I'd passed them to fall into step behind me like a ragged sort of honor guard.

It wasn't until I got close to the truck that I read the imprint on its side: *Chandler Contractors (Construction and Siding).* "Oh, no," I breathed. The man with the sledgehammer heard and nodded. He opened the passenger's side door and stood to one side.

Will was almost unrecognizable. He'd gone from ruddy to ghost-pale, with circles under his eyes that looked as if they'd been drawn on in blue marker. He was slumped in his seat, his head lolling to one side, but when he realized the door was open he tried to sit up. "Hey—hey, did we get there yet? I gotta get down to the Fens, gotta talk to this old friend of mine—"

His voice trailed off, and when he turned to face me, his eyes didn't focus. One pupil was dilated almost all the way, and the other had shrunk to the size of a pinprick. "Evie! Baby! Hey, I got this idea . . ." He trailed off, staring blankly at me, then shook his head. "No, wait, I remember, I'm not supposed to be here. I got work to do, right? Right?"

"You do," said the man with the sledgehammer, as gently as if Will were his own child. "You do. Just relax a moment, okay?"

"I . . . no, there's something I gotta do. Maybe in the Fens . . ." He sagged in his seat again, gazing at nothing. "Or maybe I did it already. Evie'll know. I gotta talk to her."

"Jesus, Will." I stepped forward and took one of his hands. He jumped, stared at my hand as if it were something totally alien, then broke into a sunny, idiotic smile.

His eyes began to water. I moved between him and the sunlight, but it made no difference. "Will, I'm so sorry."

"He's been like this all day," the man with the hammer said, and now I recognized him as the foreman at Will's site. "We told him he shouldn't come in to work, but he wouldn't go home. He keeps saying your name, you know that?" His hands flexed, one after the other. "His Jeannie's my cousin. I don't like to think what it must be like for her, hearing him babbling nonstop about you."

"It's not like that," I said. I bent over Will's hand, trying to tell if the *geis* I'd tried to break was still in place. It wasn't, but the remnants of it were still there, and they hadn't weakened. They were like the remains of a bear trap, closing on anything they could find, like a snare coated with glass shards. "Nothing like that at all," I repeated. Will squeezed my hand, then let go as if it were a snake.

The foreman sighed. "Thought so. Thing is . . ." He paused, glanced down the street, and leaned closer to me. "Thing is, we already paid our dues, right? It's not like we're some kind of new guys into town, we know what's what. We already paid you people not to come down on us. There wasn't any call for you to do this."

"You think *I'm* with them?" No need to say who *they* were, not in these circumstances.

He shrugged. "He keeps saying your name and wanting to come here, so yeah, that's what it looks like. You, the bald guy who's always around, does it matter? But it needs to stop. He's a good guy. He doesn't deserve this, no matter what he did."

"No," I said. "He doesn't." I straightened up, unable to look away from the wreck of Will. "It's my fault—they were using him to get to me, and I tried to fix it. I thought I had fixed it."

One of the men behind me muttered something, and the foreman shook his head. He didn't believe me. He didn't have any reason to.

Will blinked at me, then grinned. "Evie! Funny seeing

you here. Listen, I got this idea . . ." He stopped, his skin going ashen, and before I could do anything the foreman had slid a bucket from the floor in front of Will. He was just in time; Will bent over and vomited into the bucket, the startled expression never leaving his face. The routine ease with which the foreman had moved, not to mention the lack of response behind me, told me that this had happened more than once already.

"You get them to stop this," he said, and handed the bucket to one of the other men, who hurried off to dump its contents. "Or else we'll be here tomorrow, and the next day, and the next, and you get to see just what you've done to a good man."

"What you're doing won't help him," I said. "*I* can't help him." I couldn't help him, even after I'd tried . . . no matter how hard I ever tried, my actions always seemed to break other people. "I didn't do this to him," I said, knowing how weak it was.

"But you know who did." He took the bucket back, slid it between Will's feet, and closed the door. "Get them to stop it."

"I can't."

He gave me another long, contemptuous look. "Then we'll see you tomorrow." He nodded to the other two men, who returned to their truck. I turned back to see Will's face pressed against the window. For a moment he seemed to focus on me, and the mingled terror and hope was something I never wanted to see on a human face again. He started yelling, the words unintelligible through the glass, even as the foreman got in and started the truck.

I could hear him yelling even after they'd driven down the block and away.

Seventeen

My father had been prone to moods like this. It was one of the reasons my mother had left and taken me to Boston. Maybe it hadn't been the moods themselves so much as what he did when he was in them. He got drunk when he got down, and angry when he got drunk, and Mom had left before it got really bad. Maybe because I'd seen him in those moods, I always stayed sober when I was in a lousy mood.

Well, I thought as I stepped out of the station and into the sunlight, *it may have taken a while, but here I am following in his footsteps at last. Like father, like daughter.*

Sarah, using me. Probably Brendan too, no matter how much I wanted to believe otherwise. About the only person who wasn't using me was Rena, and even to her I wasn't much more than a resource for her detective work. Whatever I did, I fell into a new trap, and when I tried to help someone else out, I ended up making it worse.

I made my way over to the Adeline. Maybe it wasn't the best place for a drink, and the surreality of it wouldn't help matters, but it was more familiar than any of the other bars around. And if the Brotherhood had it staked out, then they could come find me and dance a reel on my bones. I didn't care.

Screw you, Sarah, I thought. *Screw you, Brendan; screw you, Rena; screw you, Mom—you and your endless damn promises you knew I couldn't keep. Screw you, Evie. And may God have mercy on poor broken Will.* I started for the door.

As I did, footsteps came up behind me, and the way my heart abruptly shifted into high gear told me that maybe I wasn't as cavalier about the Brotherhood as I liked to think. "Isn't it a little early?" said a familiar voice.

I closed my eyes and sighed. "I don't care how fucking early it is, Nate," I said, turning to face him.

Nate gazed down at me with a strange expression, nothing of which I could identify beyond that it wasn't pity. For that little kindness, at least, I was glad. "Are you going in there for what I think?"

"Yes. And don't you dare tell me it can't be that bad."

"I wasn't going to."

I crossed my arms. "So go ahead. Be the good friend. Tell me I shouldn't go in there."

"All right. You shouldn't go in there." He smiled, and I relented a little. I'd walked into that one. "Come and have a cup of coffee with me first. Okay? Then afterward you can come back and drink yourself into a stupor, if that's what you really want."

Coming from Nate, the blunt words really stung. It didn't help that he kept the same pleasant tone of voice all the way through. "Fine, you son of a bitch," I muttered. "Just for the damn coffee."

Nate led the way to a café with the requisite disaffected youth loitering outside. I gave them a look, and they quickly shifted their general disdain to someone else. Nate staked out a spot in the back, left me to glare at his stack of books, and returned with a pair of tall glasses. "Here. Drink."

"In my own damn time." I pressed my fingers against the base of the glass, savoring the scalding heat. "This isn't coffee."

Nate sighed. "No. I lied."

"Screw you." I took a drink. It was too sweet and tasted like caramel.

"You're welcome." He took a sip of his own and began sorting through his papers, paying no attention to me.

I glared at him for a while, until it became clear that I was being childish. *Not like I don't have a right to be childish,* I thought, making a face at the caramel drink.

A right, maybe, but not the time or the leeway. I couldn't lose it now, not when so many people had been pulled into this.

I pushed my drink to the side and stretched my arms out over the table, then rested my head on them. Nate flicked a glance at me, but was good enough not to say anything.

So maybe Sarah was telling the truth, even if her covenmate was a prick. The Brotherhood wanted Mrs. Crowe back, and they wanted my help. But that couldn't have been the only reason they wanted me, because Mrs. Crowe had still been fine—asleep, but fine—when they roughed up the shadowcatcher.

I pressed my face against my forearms, trying to blot out the image of Leon's panicked face the last time I'd seen him alive. He'd been a two-faced opportunist, and it took an effort of will to miss him, but nobody deserved what had been done to him. He'd died for trying to fence something of theirs; Yacoubian had been murdered for the possibility that he might know something. What about me, who'd gone asking questions about one of their own?

Maybe Brendan was keeping them away from me. Back in the lot under the Common, he hadn't hurt Leon, only taken his gun (for which, under the circumstances, I could hardly blame him). Maybe his protection didn't extend to Will.

But Will's foreman had thought that either Brendan or I worked for the Fiana . . .

I couldn't trust Brendan, I decided. It hurt to admit it—I wanted to trust him, not least to prove to myself that I hadn't been a fool. My instinct said I could trust him, but right now instinct was up against both reason and paranoia. Even if Frank had trusted him, enough to tell him about what we'd had, I couldn't bank on that any longer.

Frank must have been made into a locus, I realized, in the way Sarah described. There had been two voices on the phone, after all; both Frank and Oghmios, riding the same body and trapped by the same bindings. And both had wanted to reach me, Frank to say goodbye and Oghmios for his own reasons. Which I still didn't understand.

There was a slim possibility that Brendan could be outside all of this, as I was, on neither side. If Sarah was right about Mrs. Crowe, then of course everyone would be trying to find her, and not just for altruistic reasons. Except—well, at that point all of my links fell apart. I didn't know much Irish mythology, but it was really hard to connect "Brigid the blazing" with the withered woman in that bed, who was more like a shadow, more of a crone than any maiden saint, more like—

—more like my mother.

I sat up and pressed the heels of my hands to my eyes. My forearm itched; the scratch looked worse, as if it'd gotten inflamed while I was at Crofter House. And no matter what Brendan said, the weird stuff had started happening after Leon blasted the chain stone to pieces.

I ran my fingers over the scratch. "Nate," I began. Without looking at me, he slid a pack of tissues across the table. That little gesture was enough to make my eyes prickle again. I pulled one free, blew my nose, and took a long drink of the steamed milk. It wasn't bad, if you didn't mind the cloying sweetness. Maybe I was just too used to black coffee. "Nate, uh, how come you were walking here?"

"Tutoring job," he said without looking up. "I usually have a cup of coffee here between that and picking Katie up from school or day camp."

"If you can call that coffee," I said with a nod toward his own concoction.

He shrugged, unperturbed. "Okay, a cup of sugar, then. Works out to the same thing."

"Thanks."

"Any time." He nodded to my drink. "You going to finish that?"

I took possessive hold of it. "Yes. Get your own damn seconds."

Nate smiled and folded a page in half. I gazed into my drink a moment, then pulled a napkin from the dispenser. Time to work out what I had, even if it was little enough. "Can I borrow a pen?"

"Sure." He handed me his. I drew a long spiral, like the one Yacoubian had left for us. How had the Ogham letters gone? Three this way, three another, two on a slant . . . not like I could even read it anyway; I just knew it from hanging out with Sarah . . . dammit, even thinking of her still hurt. Then there were the pages Yacoubian had stuck the note between, the paragraph about Oghmios. An old man leading others with the strength of his words . . . a youth with the face of an old man . . .

God of prophecy and eloquence. Well, there hadn't been much eloquence in that last appeal, but perhaps he—Oghmios—had known what was coming.

I turned the napkin over. No point in following that train of thought.

I drew a second spiral, going inward from the edge of the napkin this time. Sarah, following her own path, making her choices and arranging the kidnapping of Mrs. Crowe. And another spiral, this one starting on the opposite side of the page but meeting the first at the center. Rena, chasing her suspicions about Frank's death. Both of them meeting at Crofter House. At the Fiana.

At me.

"You should talk to this guy I know."

I glanced up. "What?"

Nate pointed to my crude drawing with the end of his pencil. "One of the guys in my class has an obsession with spiral mathematics. Says he's got a whole new take on it, inspired by illuminated manuscripts. For a while there we were afraid he'd go all aliens-and-crop-circles on us."

"Sounds like you should put him in touch with Sarah." I flipped the napkin over, realized that this just showed the Ogham underneath, and refolded it so only the blank inside was exposed. My fingers twitched; I shifted my grip on the pen and trailed its point over the paper. "No—forget I said that about Sarah."

Nate gave me an inquisitive look. "Sure, if you say so. That's a good one." He nodded to the napkin again. "I once lost a bar bet to that guy. He said I couldn't draw something like that on the first try."

"What?" I looked down where he pointed. Instead of absently doodling, I'd actually drawn something:

My skin went cold. I'd seen this pattern. Seen it inscribed in blue light on my body, seen it imprinted in the wrinkles of Mrs. Crowe's hands, seen it—

"I think it's from the New Grange. Somewhere in Ireland."

Ireland. I crumpled the napkin and pushed it away from me. Ireland didn't matter. The Fiana wasn't going to push its way into everything. I was here, in a coffee shop that smelled like burned sugar, and here was Nate, Nate goddammit, Nate who studied *math*. That had to be rational. *Get hold of yourself, Evie.*

I took a deep breath and closed my eyes. Okay. Not the wards. Not Brendan's magic. Something else. Time to think about what you need to do.

For a moment I thought about telling Nate why I was scrawling spirals. I didn't want to dump this on him. But I could really use his help; the coffee if nothing else had proved that.

But after what had happened to Will . . .

Nate waited for me to speak, and when I didn't, went back to his work. After a moment I heard the rustle of pages again. "Nate," I said without opening my eyes, "can you do something for me?"

"Name it."

I thought of the truths Sarah had omitted, the things Brendan wasn't saying, how the circle of people I trusted was shrinking rapidly to just me. "Don't lie to me. Just tell me the truth, when I need it."

He was silent for a long moment. I opened my eyes to see him gazing off into space, brows furrowed. "Can't do it. Everyone lies, Evie. Even without meaning to." He looked at his hands, and I thought of how he'd shut himself off completely, how even his scent had changed when he started to get angry. Then he shook himself and gave me a rueful smile. "Besides, I already lied to you about the coffee."

"Nate—" I sighed. "That's not what I mean."

"I know. But I'll try, if you really want." His gray eyes seemed to darken as his expression turned serious. "Do you still want to go to the bar?"

"Want to? Yes." I drained the last of my caramel-sticky milk and made a face. "*Will* I go there? No. Not now. Too many things I gotta do." I pushed my chair back and got to my feet. "Thanks."

"Always." He gave me another of those long, silent looks, the ones that always had something else left to say. "See you later."

"Hope so."

The little fountain in the corner, at odds with my mood, burbled merrily away as I entered, and a few bills had been stuffed in the mail slot. Brendan's wards were still untouched, though he'd probably checked on them several times while I'd been gone. That made me much more nervous now, and I tried not to touch the silvery lines or even get near them.

Wards weren't the problem now. This went deeper than that. If I was going to start fighting back, I'd have to start the battle on my home turf.

I considered making a cup of coffee to compensate for the dreck Nate had given me, but decided against it. Especially not with Yacoubian's memory still fresh. Instead I switched on the radio and found the beginning of the Sox afternoon game. That alone was enough to relax me—probably more than two beers could have done, come to think of it.

Rena's phone was still out. I didn't leave a message this time; she'd just think I was panicking. *Besides*, I thought as I searched through the medicine cabinet for the rubbing alcohol, *right now would not be a good time for her to come by.*

The sharpest knife in the drawer was dull in spots, but it was sharp enough to cut, and it was steel, which mattered more. I cleared off my desk and set the knife to one side, little sticky bandages with gauze and tape to the other side, and the rubbing alcohol in the middle.

In this particular case, I thought as I swabbed the blade with alcohol, *it didn't matter whether Brendan or Sarah was right about the Brotherhood's plans.* What mattered here and now was that Brendan was wrong about one thing: where my nightmares had come from. Sure, they'd started up after the wards were put in place, but they'd also started up after Leon blew up the chain stone on my palm. It was then that I had started dreaming of Mrs. Crowe, even if I didn't know it was she at the time. And it wasn't long after the stone had shattered that the blue man had found me.

I ran my fingers over the healing scratch again. There was definitely something under the skin; no wonder I hadn't scented it. Living organic matter would shield it even from my nose, and it was just bad luck that it had been my own living organic matter.

Bad luck, I thought, *or something else.* I set the tip of the knife against my forearm, took a deep breath, and sliced.

The blade scraped against something hard, and the room went white.

My hands were full, though not with the knife (thank God, I thought), and it took me a moment to recognize that someone was holding them. Withered hands, frail as birds' bones. I blinked, trying to clear the fog from my vision, and focused on the white hospital bed before me.

"Sweet," whispered the old woman, not quite Mrs. Crowe and not quite my mother, and then she spoke the name only my mother called me.

"I'm here," I said, and my voice came back to me thin and muffled, as if I were speaking from several yards away.

Her grip on mine tightened. This wasn't the dream, I realized; this was Mom's hospital room, re-created down to the zigzagging crack in the plaster on the far wall. If I listened, if I turned my attention away from the woman in the bed, I could hear the susurrus of hospital business from the hall, of doctors conferring, learning who would die and who would live, who could be helped and who couldn't.

As if reading my mind, the woman's gaze shifted to over my shoulder, where the door to the hallway had been. "Help me," she whispered. "Please."

"I will," I said without thinking, then caught my breath, remembering how I had helped my mother at the end. If I could have taken it back, I would have—but there were some things I couldn't turn down, and Mom . . .

But instead of asking me to do what would kill us both, the old woman closed her eyes and smiled. She let go of my hand only long enough to grab on to my shoulder, then did the same with her other hand, hauling herself up into a sitting position. Her bones grated against each other, joints frozen into place unwilling to flex once more.

I caught her against me, trying to support her lolling head as one would with a newborn, but she was stronger than I had thought. She put her arms around me and held me close in an embrace of thanks or farewell.

I blinked back tears, remembering Mom, how her body, which had withstood everything else, had given out all at once, and the old woman murmured wordlessly in my ear. I tried to hold her closer, let her know that I was here, but my hands passed through her body as if it were no more than vapor. Her arms dissolved, becoming smoke, smoke that sank into my skin, into my lungs, through my body—

I jerked back from the desk, knocking the chair and myself both to the floor. The knife lay where it had fallen, its blade unbloodied. Everything else was as I'd left it, still arranged as if for surgery or ritual, and the familiar drone of the Sox announcers still offset the noise from the traffic outside.

For a split second, the room seemed to double, as if I were watching it from a slightly different perspective, or as if someone had started filming in 3-D and forgotten to give anyone the special glasses. A blurry image flared between the two exposures: spirals, three that spun out from the air around me, though none touched me. The illusion resolved itself into normal sight, leaving only the goose bumps on my skin. I shivered and looked at my arm to see whether I'd need to call an ambulance.

My forearm was unmarked by either old or new wounds, and the skin was smooth. It didn't even itch. I ran a hand over my face, then realized my cheeks were wet.

I got unsteadily to my feet, went to the bathroom and splashed cold water over my face until I started to feel human again. I didn't look in the mirror.

When I returned, the announcers were shouting about a line drive that went just shy of the foul line—and giving the score for the sixth inning. I picked up the radio and shook it, then realized how useless that was and checked my watch instead. They weren't wrong. Two hours had slipped by while I sat there, dreaming of my mother's deathbed.

"Oh, God," I murmured, and rubbed my forehead. Even the scents in the room smelled somehow off, as if someone had come in and sprinkled aniseed oil over everything when I was out. *Everything feels more alive*, I thought, *more warm, more* awake.

Someone banged on the door. I jumped, forced my breathing to slow down, and went to open it. "Nate? I told you I wasn't going to the bar; you didn't have to check—"

"I need your help," he said, and I saw how his arms were crossed tight against his chest, holding something to him. "I need your help," he said again, and held out what he'd clutched so close: a child's backpack. "Katie's gone."

Eighteen

Gone?" I stepped aside to let him in, then practically had to drag him past the threshold. "Gone where?"

"I don't know. I went to pick her up from her half-day at camp, and the counselor said someone else had picked her up instead. Said the man had a signed release form. No one's supposed to—she wouldn't have gone with anyone else—" He looked down at the backpack, and his long fingers crumpled it, creasing the stickers.

"Christ. Sit down." I pulled out a chair and led him to it, but he stayed standing. "Have you called the police?"

"Not yet. I didn't know what to do, and you—I know you find things . . ."

My stomach slowly turned over. I stepped back, raising my hands as if to shove him back or ward him off. "Nate, don't ask this of me. Please don't."

He shook his head. "It's Katie. I have to ask; I can't just sit around and wait to find out where she . . . Please—you find things for a living, you might be able to at least help the police."

"Nate, you don't know *how* I find things. It's not something that's— It doesn't work that way." If he saw what I did for a living, if he even skirted the edges of the world I worked in, it'd pull him in as well.

"I can't—" He stopped and raised a hand to his eyes. "No. I can't do this. You asked me earlier not to lie to you, and I didn't . . . didn't expect that to be tested so soon."

I reached up and moved his hand so I could look into his face. "Nate, what are you talking about?"

He shook my hand away. "Is anyone else here?"

"No. Why?"

"Can anyone hear us in here?"

"There's no—" I stopped and glanced at the door. The wards were still there, and they'd have registered Nate's presence. Wards could work in a number of ways: they could keep out bad stuff, let Brendan know who did come in . . . but what else could these particular wards do? How much information did they pass on to him?

"Damn," I muttered. "Every day in every way, I am getting more and more paranoid. Wait just a moment." Where had Brendan put the wards? Each window, the front door, the door to the kitchen . . . but there was one other room. "Come on," I said.

The bathroom was cramped even for one person, and the two of us barely fit in it. "Turn on the shower," I told Nate. "And the sink. High as it can go."

Nate gave me a look as if I'd just grown another head. "Hot or cold?" he asked, in the same tone of voice you'd use to ask a street loony if the voices were being broadcast from Saturn or Neptune.

"Doesn't matter." I lifted the lid off the toilet tank. "What's important is that it's running water. It may not work, but it's the best protection I can think of." I unhooked the bulb in the tank so that it wouldn't stop running, then replaced the lid and flushed.

"I don't think I understand," Nate said, but he reached in and turned the shower up full blast.

"Be grateful. Now tell me what happened."

He closed his eyes and took a deep breath. "They left her backpack on the corner. That's where I found it. When I touched it—when I bent down to pick it up, there was this chalk message on the sidewalk underneath." He hugged the backpack closer to him, crinkling it further. "It said that if I didn't go to you, if I went to the police, they'd—they'd send me her hands."

"Jesus."

"And when I looked again, it wasn't even letters, it was just spirals and little squiggles in chalk, like a kid's drawing, like . . ." *Like what you were drawing on that napkin,* he didn't say, but he didn't need to. "Evie, what the hell is going on?"

I sighed, rubbing at my eyes, then looked at him again. All this talk of keeping my head down, not sticking my neck out, not choosing a side, all those metaphors and ways of dancing around the truth, and all they came down to was this: a girl had been stolen.

"Give me the backpack," I said.

He looked at me in disbelief, then held it out to me.

I took it and unzipped the back pocket. Papers and a stuffed panda, none of which had any trace of magic. "What's going on is the same thing that damn near drove me to drink myself under this morning. Someone's been watching me, targeting my friends, and either they saw me with Katie a few days ago or they saw me with you and followed you to her. They're—Jesus, Nate, I don't know how to say this so you won't think I'm crazy."

"I already think *I'm* crazy, Evie." The words came out in a snarl. I looked up, almost expecting to see his teeth bared; instead that inhuman control encased him again. "Tell me who's got my sister and why they want you and what the *fuck* I can do about it."

I had to look away. "Magicians, Nate. A society of magicians, and if you tell me there's no such thing as magic, then nothing I say to you is going to make any sense."

He nodded slowly, the momentary rage fading and his iron self-control going with it. "I'm willing to believe it if it'll bring Katie home."

"Good. Because these are the kind of people I work

with. Half of my job is just dealing with these magicians."
I closed the bag and flipped it over. "This is the real under-
world, Nate. And I'm caught in between."

I hadn't meant to say that. I turned away and pressed
the backpack to my face, inhaling. Katie's scent threaded
all the way through the backpack, which was a plain and
much-mended purple one, papered all over with stickers of
the Powerpuff Girls and Harry Potter and little Japanese
fighting beasts. Her scent was almost as bright as she was
quiet, vibrant as the scent of rosemary on a cloudy day.

And twined with it, clinging obscenely close to her
scent, was the mildew reek of the Fiana.

I raised my head. Even in the closed air here, there was
a trace of that bright scent, in the same way that neighbors
baking two floors down will leave a trace in the hall of even
closed-up apartments. Katie wasn't lost yet. "She's still in
the city," I said. "I'll know more when I get outside."

I opened my eyes and there it was, the expression I
always get from my normal clients when they don't know
how I work. Nate stared at me, confused and concerned
and just a little horrified. "You said you didn't care how I
work," I retorted, and shoved the backpack at him.

He caught it against his chest. "I don't," he said after a
moment. "But— You'll be okay too, right?"

"Oh, it's a trap. There's no question about that." I headed
back to my office, flinging the connecting door open so
hard it banged against the wall. "But if I know, that makes
it less of one." I unlocked the lower right drawer of my desk
and gazed at the contents, then sighed and took out the gun.
"Besides," I said as I checked the magazine—silver and
iron bullets, modified and made by the old man in China-
town who first started calling me Hound, "it's not as if I'm
going in unprotected."

The sound of water from the bathroom shut off, and
Nate closed the door behind him. I waved to the coatrack
by the door. "Hand me that jacket. Someone recently told
me that this shirt wouldn't hide a gun."

Nate's eyes widened, but he fetched my jacket. "I'm coming with you."

"You are *not*," I said, sliding the magazine back into place. "Not unless you want them to know that you told me everything. These people weren't lying about cutting off bits of Katie, Nate. I'm not having you risk that just because you want to be doing something." He crimsoned, and I knew I'd hit a sore spot. "But you need to get somewhere safe," I added. "Where . . . Christ, 'safe' doesn't mean the same thing to me as to you, does it?"

"Not in this context," he said, but there was the slightest edge of a laugh to it, a hint that the Nate I knew was still there.

"I don't think . . ." I pressed my forefinger and thumb against the bridge of my nose, then shook my head. "Idiot, Evie."

I yanked a sheet of paper from my desk and scrawled on it: *Sarah—Nate needs a safe place to stay. You said you'd help me and mine. Evie.* "Take this to Sarah at the Goddess Garden. Don't give it to her assistant, and, hell, if there's a ponytailed guy with an attitude, just steer clear of him. She'll hide you, and I'll know where to find you. Tell her— tell her I'm choosing my side. Okay?"

"I don't like this."

"And I do?" I pressed the paper into his hand. "Stay safe. Don't come looking for me. Not unless you're sure I'm not coming back."

He looked down at his sister's backpack. "Promise me you'll come back," he said softly.

"I'll certainly try. Now get out of here."

Katie's trail led northeast. If I had more time, or if I really were helping the cops, I could follow her path rather than her scent itself, trace which way the kidnappers had taken her. But I didn't have time, and where Katie had been was not as important as where she was now.

I stopped at every corner, pausing to inhale and reorient

myself. Katie's scent was nearby, I could tell that much. But nearby could mean just within the confines of the city, and that meant a lot of ground to cover.

I followed it up Mass Ave, then down Boylston to the library, and had to stop there to get my bearings. Three pedestrians bumped into me at once. I muttered an apology to the most offended of them and shuffled out of his way.

The trail wasn't right. I'd swear she was close, on this side of the river at the very least, but there was still something funny about it. If I'd been tracking by sound rather than scent, I'd say something was muffling it, or perhaps muffling my own senses. The weirdness nagged at me, but the hunt was on, and there was no time to stop.

The Back Bay may be one of the most posh places to live in Boston, but the alleys in back of the town houses aren't nearly as appealing. There are a few decks back here, but not many: who wants to look at a bare alley? And there's the trash, and the rats that go along with it. I had yet to see a complete block of the Back Bay where everyone knew when the trash collectors came and put their stuff out accordingly; usually they let it age a little outside first.

I prowled among the alleys, tracking, tracing, hunting. Victorian architecture loomed up on either side of me: brick and spots where ivy might have been and little bits of scrollwork on stone. I tracked Katie's scent into an alley, down a bunch of little twisty lanes so narrow that the back entrances all had their own lights to keep yuppies from tripping over the rats.

Her scent was strongest here—but she wasn't here, and that same filter kept coming between me and her. I followed her scent to a low gate and opened it onto the backyard of one of the town houses.

Someone had made a little courtyard back here some years ago, but either the money had run out or it'd just gotten too depressing to continue. The sun didn't make it down this far very often, and so the vine remnants on the trellises to either side were sickly and pale. In the middle of the patio were a few lawn chairs with collapsed seats and a round fishpond set into the ground. Whoever had done the landscaping hadn't been very good; the pool leaked tendrils of murky brown water across the cobblestones. Leaves and the detritus of last summer clotted the pool's surface, probably killing any fish that might have lived there.

Katie's scent led to a door at the other end of the yard, a big wood-paneled thing that wouldn't have looked out of place on the front of this building. I glanced down the alley and took out my gun. The smell of foul water was stronger than fireworks or mildew, but I didn't want to take any chances.

I glanced up at what little sky I could see, then edged along the courtyard, picking my way over the rounded cobblestones. The leaves were still wet from the rain of a few days ago, and I slipped, recovering my balance just as my foot sank into one of the puddles.

Black water splashed up onto my ankle, and the pool exploded. I ducked and rolled away from the fell thing that lunged at me. Something huge struck the stones beside me, sending chips flying in every direction. Murk and mist rose up around me, and I clambered to my feet, gun out and aimed.

The thing in the pool looked like a parody of sculpture. When it paused a moment, it seemed to be the front half of a horse, as if it stood deep within the pool and had reared up to strike at me. But when it moved, it did so as a wave, flowing from one place to another along its waterlines, a thing made of stagnation and corrupted water. Its teeth were the color of old blood, and its eyes were completely insane.

It smelled of good water poisoned, and I pressed my hand to my mouth to keep from inhaling the fog that surrounded us. I raised the gun, but hesitated; gunshots in a deserted parking garage were one thing. Gunshots in the Back Bay were another. "Let me pass," I said.

The horse thing made no sound, but it blurred and

crashed again, this time two inches from my ear. I ducked, but too late to avoid the miasma that came with it, a tendril of which snaked into my lungs. My chest filled with leaden air, and I fell to one knee, choking and coughing.

Corroded brown teeth snapped in front of my nose, and pain blasted up my right arm. I made a garbled noise as I dropped the gun and rolled out of the way, clutching my arm.

I wheezed, slowly regaining my breath, not that it would matter in a moment. But the horse paused, turning its head to regard me with one mad eye. A rainbow film of gasoline slid over it, fogging my reflection. *"Free me,"* it whispered in a voice like rivers underground.

My skin began to prickle, as if someone had run a ball of needles all along it. This close I could see the slimy ropes yoking this thing in place, grime and sickness slicking its skin. "How?" I whispered back.

"Die."

The world seemed to double again into two different perspectives. One stared uncomprehending into the horse's eye; the other was closer to the gun, and that was the one that took over. I rolled a second time, grabbed the gun, flattened myself under the horse's belly, and shot up under what would have been its breastbone.

The horse shrieked like a theremin on a bad acid trip, and two streetlights burst, scattering shards of glass and metal across the street. Filthy water surged and roiled above me, a black spot of silver and iron suspended within, and the horse's body turned in upon itself. I sidled out from underneath, hissing as the drops caught my bare skin.

It wasn't dead, I realized, but it was wounded, and badly. It wouldn't attack me right away, but staying around was not a good idea. I turned and ran to the door.

The lights dimmed as my fingers brushed the smooth wood, and I actually looked back to see if there was a brownout before realizing that it wasn't them. My limbs went cold as January, and the building before me warped and blurred. I slumped forward, clawing at the bricks and trying to drag a counterspell out of my sluggish brain. "Damn," I managed.

The last things I saw were the crude lines of Ogham scratched into the stone, two inches from my nose. Knowing hadn't made it any less of a trap after all.

Nineteen

I woke propped up on something stiff and cool, icy metal against my wrists. I raised my hands a fraction of an inch and heard a clink. The tug on my legs told me that they were chained with the same length. Not good—but it wasn't handcuffs, and that was something.

"Good, you're awake."

The voice was so deep it made the soles of my feet shiver. It reminded me of my ninth-grade history teacher, the one who'd tossed half the book out because it "left out the important things." Maybe I'd banged my head on the way down.

"I always get the time on those damn sleep wards wrong, and then I try to overcompensate. I was afraid you wouldn't wake till morning, and I've got other people to talk to."

I opened my eyes and looked up—and up—to see him. The man next to me was nothing like my history teacher. Mr. Stuart had been small and weedy. None of us would have dared try anything if this man had been our teacher. We probably wouldn't have dared to ask questions either.

He was big. That's really the only word for it. For starters, his head was several sizes larger than mine; any hat he could comfortably wear would slide all the way down to rest on my shoulders. The rest of him was built to the same scale. His brilliant red hair curled around his head like a fiery halo.

The room smelled like stagnant water, and the underlying scents were more of the same; mold, mildew, dust, the heavy scent of earth and rot. The tingling smell of fireworks and rain overlaid it, but intensified, like iron heated to cherry red. The stink of profligate power. And another scent, clean and familiar—

Don't think about it. He'll see if you do. I wrenched my attention back to the big man. "Drink?" he asked, holding out an amber glass.

I raised my hands. About three feet of chain linked my wrists and ankles, enough so that I could move a little, but not enough to allow any comfort. And now that I looked closer, the chain wasn't padlocked, just looped in wide knots that should have been a few seconds' work to pick apart. Except they wouldn't budge. I shifted—the leather cushions of the couch squeaked beneath me—and cleared my throat. "That might be a little difficult in this position."

He shrugged. "A creative person would have found a way around it. Still," he added, "I suppose I should put this away, then. I have a bad habit after my second drink of challenging prisoners to drinking contests."

"Really. What's the winner get?"

Another casual shrug as he busied himself at a tiny cabinet made of wood so old it was almost black. "Winner gets to not be the loser. Loser gets to have his head cut off and stuck by our door, to warn other idiots who get the wrong idea about us."

"Ah." Still keeping an eye on him, I tried to get a look at the room I was in. The walls were brick—old brick, from the looks of it—marred every few feet by vertical wooden beams, at least as old as the brick. Whoever had decorated had done the best they could: lights in every corner made up for the lack of any windows, and the ceiling had been arched in an attempt to make it look a little higher. As it was, the redheaded man had to duck when he got near the wall. A big desk that would have been the envy of any CEO took up most of the other side of the room; the couch I'd been propped on took up this side. Between them was a liquor cabinet, a throw rug that looked like it'd gone through several owners, and nothing else. No immediate exits, no windows . . . It smelled like damp rot, like a log that had been soaked in seawater, like tidal flats. Like the way Boston Harbor used to be on a bad day, only worse.

The big man started to speak, then grimaced as a low rumble, followed by a squeal of brakes, interrupted him, dislodging a haze of dust from the ceiling. The sound of a Green Line train, and close by . . . "Noisy neighbors," he said. "My apologies."

Green Line, seawater, oak pilings . . . We were under the Back Bay. Under the houses that the Boston upper class had built to get away from the immigrants flooding downtown . . . but of course they couldn't lower themselves to fill in the tide flats on their own, could they? And suppose their hired help had hollowed out a few spaces for themselves, a place free from the rich folks above . . . and then the Fiana had moved in, like a cancer invading healthy tissue.

Now that I was fully awake, the power in the room weighed down on me like ten feet of water. My skin kept wanting to come loose, and if I turned my head too quickly, afterimages flashed across my vision. Raw magic crawled like beetles over my skin. "I don't suppose," I mumbled, trying to cling to something real, "that I'm going to get out of here in time for the second half of the Sox double-header."

The man shook his head. "I apologize. Like I said, I always get the time wrong, and, well, I'm afraid the game's almost over. We lost the first one, six-two."

Crap. Three, four hours gone just like that. "Well, at least I'm rested," I said, leaning back as far as the chain let me.

He chuckled and pulled a chair from behind the desk, then turned it around so he could sit astride it. It creaked in protest, but held his weight without splintering. "Sorry. No luck there either. Sleep wards don't work like that; they use the intruder's own strength as power. So congratulations, you've just been a locus." He took a sip of his drink and grimaced appreciatively. "Though from what I hear, you tend to stay away from loci."

I twisted the chain between my wrists again. I could even see the knot; it shouldn't have held more than twenty seconds. "Since you seem to know so much about me," I said, "how about you tell me your name? I can't just call you 'big scary dude.'"

The man smiled with one side of his mouth. "You can call me Boru. It's more of a title than a name; I'm not such a trusting fool as to give mine out at the drop of a hat. Or put it in the Yellow Pages under a listing that practically screams for attention from people like us."

"Which, I suppose, makes me a fool."

"Well, you did turn down a good glass of whiskey." Boru took another sip of his and regarded me with his head to one side. "And the fact remains that I'm not the one in chains."

"Point taken." I tugged on the links again. "From the looks of it, though, you don't really need these." Boru guffawed at that, but I kept on. "I know power when I smell it, and you could probably earthfast me with no more than a thought. So how about letting me out of this—this thing, okay?"

He shook his head. "I don't think so. For one thing, I'm trying to make a point here, and that chain's as good a focus as any. I'll explain in a moment. For another, there is a chance you could hurt me. A tiny chance, maybe, but I'm not about to give you even that. After all, you did manage to wound the *each uisce* at our gates. I'll admit we keep it there mostly for show, but it still should have given you more trouble than a few bruises."

"It tried," I said.

Boru smiled. "And then you did bring this."

He reached behind his back and pulled out my gun. His hand was so huge it made the weapon look like a toy. "Do you often bring weapons when you go hunting? I hadn't had that impression . . . or maybe you had a reason this time. Maybe a little bird told you, hm?"

It took a lot to keep from reacting. *He doesn't know*, I told myself; *he can't know for sure that Nate warned you. He's bluffing.* "Do you know how many missing children I've been asked to find?" I demanded, hoping anger would hide my panic. "Do you know how many times I've found the kid—with some sicko who's convinced the kid is fair game for his fantasies, or kidnapped by a noncustodial parent with a gun-show rifle and a grudge?"

"Or how many times," Boru said softly, "all you've found was a heap of earth on the outskirts of the city?"

I lunged for him and succeeded only in cutting off the circulation to my hands and feet. Boru laughed and leaned close to me. He had a rich, mellow laugh, entirely out of place under the ground. "How many times, Scelan? How many times have you hunted, all for nothing? How many times have you been called off the chase halfway through, or had to deal with some petty matter, or given up entirely just because the mundane world wouldn't let you reach your quarry?" Boru's eyes gleamed. "Spinning your wheels, Scelan. Spinning them, grinding the gears, running and running and getting absolutely nowhere."

He set the gun on the desk. "You know, back when I was married my wife bought me a treadmill. Said I needed to get in shape." He looked down at the mountain of his body. "Heh. Anyway, I used it a few times, but there's nothing enjoyable about running in the same damn spot all the time. You do that too long, all you do is wear a hole in the floor. And in your feet."

I shook my head just to keep from staring at him, mesmerized like a raccoon before headlights. He'd hit a nerve—a whole bundle of them. I used my talent to hunt because that was what felt most right, but the number of times that I'd been able to truly hunt, to chase down the quarry and bring it back, were few.

There were times when I'd been tempted to fake a hunt, just so I could come home feeling better. Like how when they use sniffer dogs at a disaster site, they fake a rescue at the end of the day so that the dog won't have had a day of only finding dead people over and over. What he said called to my talent, to the part of me I'd used but had tried to ignore for the last ten years. I was addicted to my own blood-magic, as addicted as any shadowcatcher. Who was I to question Frank, to worry about Sarah? I'd been on the hard stuff since I was six years old.

Boru set down his glass and got up. I shrank back as he bent over me, but it was just to loosen the chains that I'd tightened. "Chains of one kind or another, Scelan. That's all they are. Let me tell you a story," he added as he dragged his chair closer. "Do you know the name Finn Mac Cool?"

"No . . . wait, maybe." Sarah'd mentioned it—but hadn't there been a story, something my mom had read to me, or from school? "He was a giant, right? Dressed up like a baby who bit this other giant's brass finger off."

Boru sighed. "'A Legend of Knockmany.' I hate that story; it makes everything so . . . cartoony. No, the real Finn was no giant. He was a hero, a leader of men. Some say he was a god, or a demigod at least. There are a lot of stories told about him, but the one I'm interested in—and you should be interested too, Scelan—involves his hounds.

"See, Finn had a maiden aunt, and he arranged for her to be married to this lord. Only the lord already had a wife, and a fairy at that. So when Finn's aunt arrived at her husband's home after the honeymoon, his first wife changed her into a hound and chased her out of the house." He took another sip and grinned. "Women. The poor girl wandered as a dog for a while and, because she'd already been pregnant when she was changed, eventually littered a pair of pups. Finn found the three of them and changed her back to human, but he couldn't change her children. So he took his cousins under his wing and gave them primacy at the head of his pack of hunting hounds. Bet the other dogs gave them shit about that. Anyway, Finn's hounds were already known as the best in Ireland, and Bran and Sceolang were the best of the batch, being partly human. We know that Bran died, but Sceolang lived, and—we think—became human again at some point. Human enough to father children, who had children of their own."

I tried a derisive smile, but another voice echoed in memory: *Know you not, cousin's child . . .*

The smug crinkle at the corner of his eyes was enough to tell me the rest of the story. I licked my lips. "Prove it."

"I don't need to." Boru's smile grew wider. "You see, there's another legend about Bran and Sceolang, and in it, Sceolang was a monster who could not be bound—save by the golden chain of Bran." He nodded to my wrists. "Which, I'm happy to say, we have on hand."

I stared at him, then at the chain. He laughed again as I gave it a hopeless tug. "I could have just looped that around your wrists, and you still wouldn't be able to get free, Scelan, Sceolang, Sceolang's child."

"I don't believe you," I muttered, but it was mostly for form's sake. I couldn't get loose. I couldn't get out, couldn't run, couldn't hunt . . . "What do you want?"

Boru leaned back, gesturing to the empty brick walls. "Well, a recliner down here would be nice. I mean, the chairs here aren't too comfortable, and someday I'd like to get a wide-screen TV too. Can you just imagine the irony of it, watching the Celtics play down here?" He raised a hand as I glared at him. "I know, I know. No, what I want—from you at least—is your help. You've been away from us—from your proper heritage, your training, your true ability—for far too long."

"You want me to hunt someone down for you."

"Someone, something, what difference does it make? It's what you do. What you were born to do. Why fight it? We can make it so that all you have to worry about is the hunt itself. No more fussing with pissant little tasks like finding someone's car keys; no more scraping by, no more wasted time. Just the hunt."

Just the hunt. Only the hunt. My feet twitched at the thought of it.

I let out a long breath, closed my eyes, and bowed my head until it rested on my wrists. The chain was cold against my forehead, its links greasy like those of a playground swing set. "Will you let Katie go if I say yes?"

"That had been the original plan," Boru said. The ice in his glass clinked. "However, she's got a little blood-magic in her; not much, but enough to cultivate. I'd like to keep her here maybe a few days, introduce her to a few tricks of the trade. She'll like it here. And you'll have a friend with us."

Bring a child into this? Into the undercurrent? I clenched my fists so hard that my nails scratched raw spots into my palms. And not just any child, but Katie, Katie who deserved a normal life after all the crap that had happened to her, to her and Nate—

My breath was loud in the trapped space between my arms and face.

"If you're worried about your friend, don't be. I assure you we'll have her back to her father as soon as possible."

My eyes snapped open. Her father. I bit the sides of my cheeks to keep from snarling with laughter. They thought Nate was her father. They didn't know everything. They might be magicians and powerful, but human for all that and therefore still fallible.

"So let me get this straight," I said, raising my head. "You want me to work for you because of some myth that tells you I'm a hound."

Boru raised his glass to me. "That's about the gist of it."

"Sounds like you've got a real reverence for those myths." I clasped my hands to keep them from worrying at the chain.

"Oh, yes. They're the heart of what we do, really." He

smiled again, as if I'd blundered into some secret joke of his.

"So how come you can play so loose with them that you'll turn"—what was her name, dammit—"Brigid into a withered old stick?"

It didn't have quite the effect I'd intended. Instead of recoiling from the blaze of truth, Boru just blinked at me. "Brigid?"

"Mrs. Crowe."

"Mrs.— Ha! Brigid!" He threw back his head and roared with laughter, a laughter echoed by the rumble of a train's passing. "Brigid? You think we'd waste all that power to chain some little well-goddess, some bimbo so weak that she got swallowed up into sainthood? You think we'd have this much mana from the—the candles peasants light at her wells?"

"She could be Margaret Thatcher for all I care," I said, but Boru wasn't listening.

"My God," he said, thumping the back of his chair, "this explains everything. If those idiot hippies thought we had Brigid, then it all makes sense . . ."

"It's not right," I said, clinging to that one fact. "She shouldn't be—be forever asleep like that."

Boru's laughter abruptly stopped, and his eyes burned as he gazed at me. "Trust me, little Sceolang, you don't want her to wake."

He produced a rough chunk of rock from the depths of the desk, and my nose recognized it before I did. It was the same kind of stone that Sarah had sent me to find, that Leon had stolen for her. A chain stone, the designs on it writhing away from my sight. "Did you really think that just breaking these things would be enough to tame her? If the Morrigan wakes, then the number of deaths we have caused in this city will be nothing compared to the slaughter that queen of carrion could wreak."

"You're full of shit," I said, but in my head I saw again the spirals on my arms, the blood of my enemies watering the ground, the spear haft shuddering as I sank it into someone's eye. That hadn't been the dream of a saint, even if she'd been a goddess at some point. That had been the dream of a goddess of slaughter . . .

"Suit yourself," Boru said. "After all, we've only had her around for decades; what do we know? If I weren't so busy, I'd stay and convince you a little more strenuously. But I've had at least one plea for mercy, so I'll let you think it over for now. If nothing else, I'm sure some time with the little girl will change your mind."

"Fuck you," I snarled.

Boru just smiled as he put away the stone and got to his feet, then snapped his fingers. "Knew I'd forgotten something. You know, I've tried to get one of those things, those little electronic organizer things, to keep me from forgetting things. They don't function so well down here."

He took another object from his pocket and flourished it between the forefinger and thumb of both hands.

My cell phone.

His hands closed over it, and he wrenched it apart as if he were cracking a lobster. Shards of silicon pattered onto the floor, and the ringer gave one last asthmatic beep. "Crappy reception down here." He brushed his hands off, then rummaged through the desk and came up with a dull brown pair of scissors. "This won't hurt."

"The hell it won't!" I struggled against the chains as he approached. As soon as he bent over me, I lashed out at him with my fists locked together, ignoring the pain lancing through my limbs.

Boru dodged the blow and traced a sign in the air. "Stop that."

My muscles locked up, cramping worse than any charley horse I'd ever had, and I crumpled—first to the couch, then to the floor as my balance deserted me. The flagstones hurt more than they would have if I'd just fallen normally, but the only noise I could make through my teeth was a thin grunt. Boru sighed and took my braid by its end. I heard a snip, then felt the thump of the braid settling against my back again.

"I told you it wouldn't hurt." He held up the snippet of hair he'd cut. "I really hate it when people don't believe me. There's a lesson in that, but since I've got other work to do, I'll let it wait for later." He cocked his head to one side and regarded me with amusement. "You know, a really creative person could find a way to have a drink even like that. Gotta start thinking out of the box, Scelan. Or out of the kennel, in your case."

There was a lot I wanted to say to that, but the spell remained in place and my jaw remained clenched. Boru's footsteps receded, then paused. "Sheila," he said. "Take this."

"*Yes.*" It was a voice like stones ground together, the grind of rock giving birth to sound. Even though I couldn't move, I tried to shrink away from it.

"Do you know it now?"

"*Yes.*"

"Then you know who's here. Keep her from leaving, Sheila. Grab her and hold her here if she tries." He paused a moment, and the different echo to his voice when he spoke next told me he'd turned back to face me. "Gotta love that sympathetic magic, Sceolang. Easiest thing in the world, if you've got a bit of someone. You should try it sometime, if you ever decide to get off your pedestal and join us here in the real world."

His footsteps faded further, until there was only the hum of magic, and the far-off rumble of the T, and the silence of underground. And me, locked and bound and huddled on the floor like a teenager in a fit of despair.

I lay there for several minutes, trying to draw breath with what little freedom I had and hoping I wouldn't choke to death. That'd be a kick in the pants for the Fiana, if Boru went to all this trouble to lure me here and then accidentally killed me just because he couldn't be bothered to remove his own spell.

The shadows in the corners of the room seemed to

darken, as if the lights had flickered. I tried to look, but couldn't turn my head. Something whispered, so quiet it might have been rats in the walls or papers sliding over one another. It went on for a moment, then stopped, and the silence was louder than anything that had come before.

My fingers began to tingle. At first I thought it was from lack of circulation, but the pins-and-needles feeling began to spread, all the way up to my chest, the skin visibly twitching as it advanced. The muscles of my arms spasmed as the paralysis dropped away. I made another wordless protest again, then shrieked through my teeth as the last jolt hit my spine like jumper cables hooked up to a monster truck.

I wiped a smudge of drool from my cheek and rolled to a sitting position. "Thanks," I said. "You can come out. I know you're there."

His glasses appeared first, twin gleams of light in the shadows of the far corner like blank eyes. Then the face surrounding them emerged, pressing through the bricks as if they were no more than a projection. "How long have you known I was here?" Brendan asked, the wall re-forming behind him.

"I smelled you when I opened my eyes." I took a deep breath. It felt good, even in this tainted air. "And since you let me lie there for so long, I'm guessing you're not here to rescue me."

He came forward to kneel by me and, much as Boru had done, loosened the chain. "I couldn't risk coming out sooner. Boru will kill me if he finds I've been in here without his knowledge."

"Skip it," I snapped. "Don't start trying to play the nice guy now. You were working for them all along, weren't you?"

Brendan sighed and pushed his glasses further up his nose. "It's not a matter of 'working for them,' Genevieve. It's a little more complicated than that."

"More complicated, my ass," I yelled. He winced as my

words echoed around the small room. "How much was a lie? The apartment? The whole New York bit? Investment banking? Frank's goddamn safe-deposit box?" My voice broke on the last one, and I glared down at my hands.

He was silent. "A lot of it," he said at last. "Not so much with the I-banking; I still work as a consultant now and then—"

"Jesus H. Christ." I shook my head. "I should have seen from the beginning. You weren't conspiring with Frank's parents; you were paying them off. What was that book? Training your older dog? How much were you going to train me?"

Brendan caught my hands and pressed them between his own, cradling them against his chest even when I tried to jerk away. "It wasn't like that at all."

"Did you kill Leon?"

"No. I only scared him off, told him to stay away from you. I thought that'd be sufficient. Boru, though—" He looked down, his face twisted with pain and disgust. "I wanted to gain your trust, then plead for our cause, convince you we were right rather than forcing you into . . . into this sort of situation. This crude extortion is the only thing Boru knows."

"Yeah, well, it looks like you're profiting off this crude extortion too."

"Genevieve, listen." He leaned close to me, so close I could smell the clean scent of his skin, under the aftershave and Fiana stink. He'd as much as warned me there was a glamour on him, but I'd always thought glamours didn't work on me. It hadn't needed to work for long, though. Just long enough for me to jump to all the wrong conclusions when it finally wore out. "McDermot was one of our vessels," he said. "They're people we use to draw down—"

"I know about the vessels, okay? Jesus, do you even think about how inhumane that is?"

"I do. Believe me, I do." He caressed the backs of my hands with his thumbs, and I looked away. "But even they aren't enough for Boru. McDermot held the spirit of the god Oghma, the strong speaker. Boru had him brought here and demanded a prophecy." He laughed, bitter and harsh. "Demanded it! You don't demand prophecies of these beings! Oghma just laughed, and said that Boru could demand whatever he liked, but that as long as the hound of Finn ran free, the Fiana would never stand as it had. And then he said that Boru would die with a hound's teeth in his throat, and Boru got mad—"

"And killed him." God help you, Frank, wherever you are now.

"Not right away. While Boru was raging, Oghma got Frank away, but only for about an hour. When we found him, Boru ordered him to recant, and, well, they both refused. We did some work—after—and I managed to find out that he'd called you."

"'After,'" I repeated. "Jesus, that's gruesome. That's how you found out about my first time with Frank, wasn't it? Sex does leave a mark on someone, especially the first time. And here I thought he'd just boasted."

"No, Genevieve. Please. When I saw you the next day, I knew—I recognized you for what you were and thought that maybe with you, I could overturn the Fiana, turn it into something constructive instead of this, this racket. Boru was stuck on the idea of a hound; he even did that stupid thing with scaring all the dogs in the city, but I knew. I knew it was you."

I raised my chin. "I won't be your bitch, Brendan. Not in any sense of the word."

"That's not what I wanted." He let go of my hands and rubbed at his temples. "That's never what I wanted."

I thrust my chained fists at him. "Then get this goddamned chain off me!"

"I can't cross Boru right now. I'm not strong enough. Believe me, Genevieve, I want to—"

"Don't say you want to and then leave it undone. Untie me."

He drew a breath, then closed his eyes and let it out. "I wish I could make you believe that I'm not a bad guy."

"I've heard that one before. Leave me the hell alone; I can't breathe with you here."

He bowed his head and didn't answer. I watched the wall as he left, but couldn't stop myself from listening to his footsteps until the T's rumble carried them away.

TWENTY

I must have fallen asleep at some point, because the cramped room receded into endless tunnels, the *each uisce*'s rusted teeth snapping an inch away from my nose, Will's face and then Nate's hidden by a lattice of spirals, incoherent dream-images born of my own fear. The dreams receded into darkness, and again I felt the stone beneath me, the cold links of the chain, the dull pain of bruises. But I couldn't open my eyes. The sound of the T was gone as well, and when I shifted, the links slid against each other with no answering chime. Worse, I couldn't smell *anything*, not even my own background scent. I had no way of knowing that I still existed.

Someone touched my hands, sliding her fingers across my palms. Cold hands, but living, and dry as paper. Her skin was soft from age and disuse, and through it her bones were as frail as straw. I clutched for her, the only moving thing in this silent dream, and she gently squeezed back before letting go. Her fingers moved to my wrists, picking at the chain, and it slid away with an audible *clink*.

I jerked awake, gasping for breath. Blue light filled the room, dimming even the lamp's yellow glow. Spirals and runes twined up my arms, glowing blue, growing and receding like a pulse.

"No—" The glow reached the height of my throat and paused there, like a hand stilling my breath, stealing sound from me. Helpless, I watched as the light solidified, twisted around the chain . . . and undid the heavy knot.

The chain slithered down my legs as I scrambled to my feet. Ghostlight flared and waned, and the lines began to sink into my skin, fading like a blush. "Who are you?" I whispered, not sure I wanted an answer.

It gave none, only receding further. I could feel it riding in me, the same way that I could feel sunlight by its warmth on my back. Warmth in my blood, a breath synchronized with my own, a tingle up my spine like the remnants of Brendan's spell.

And it had just freed me.

I held very still and waited for something horrible to happen. Nothing did. "God in Heaven," I muttered, but stopped. The last exhalation had sounded too much like a laugh.

I searched the desk first. There was precious little, not even any handy incriminating papers; just a few notes, all in illegible handwriting, and in one drawer, a World's Greatest Uncle mug with a film of mold inside. Boru had to keep papers somewhere, I decided, but there was no reason he'd keep them in here. For all I knew, this was the Brotherhood's equivalent of an empty cubicle—nothing to show who had been here or what had been done.

I couldn't find my gun. The aged liquor cabinet still stood open, but it held nothing but bottles. I gave one a cursory slosh and was briefly grateful that Nate had found me in front of the Adeline. Cell phone guts crunched under my feet as I made my way back to the couch I'd been propped on. The pair of bronze scissors that Boru had used to cut my hair were on the end table where he'd left them. I picked them up in lieu of a real weapon and peered down the way Boru had gone.

The arched silhouette of the door seemed off, somehow, and as I got closer I saw why: a crude figure of a woman had been carved into the lintel. She straddled the opening, so that her legs formed either side of the arch, and her hands rested on her thighs as if she were holding them open. Though the stonecutter had given her exaggerated breasts and genitals, he hadn't wasted time on her face, leaving her with only faint outlines of features: two staring eyes and a hopeless, imbecilic smile.

I poked at the figure's legs with the scissors, then jumped back. It didn't move. I touched it with my bare finger, but the stone remained cool and unreactive. There was no scent of tainted water here as there had been around the polluted horse; I listened but heard no sound from outside. Shifting my grip on the scissors, I edged through the doorway—and stumbled back as something yanked hard on my braid.

"Not to leave." The voice was like millstones mating. From this side of the door the same staring woman gazed mournfully down at me, her stone hands gripping my hair so tightly I couldn't even come down off of tiptoe. *"He said not to let this leave,"* she said again, forcing the words out of her gash of a mouth.

"God damn you!" I flailed with the scissors and struck a chip from her fingers. "Let me go!"

"Not to leave. Boru said not to let this leave, Nemhain."

If stone could plead, she was pleading. "Nemhain?" I twisted in place and craned to look up at her. She met my gaze, and her eyes rolled in their sockets. Slowly, like a child playing horsie, she shook my braid once.

Not to let *this* leave. Sympathetic magic, the kind they'd used to put a *geis* on Will—enspell the part and you enspell the whole. Boru used the part to imprint the idea of the whole on this Sheila thing.

But sympathetic magic could work both ways. If a part represents the whole . . .

I put a hand to my braid, below where she gripped it. I'd only trimmed my hair since I was ten, just chopping off split ends when needed, leaving the whole mass in its braid from years of habit. It was foolish—surrounded by Fiana and haunted by something nameless, the last thing I should have been worried about was my hair—but my hand still shook as I raised the scissors to the back of my neck.

The blades had been blunted by my attempt to harm the stone woman, but they had enough of an edge for what I needed. I sawed away, cutting in a ragged line where the braid met my neck. Years of hair fell away into the stone woman's grasp, and I shivered as the ragged ends brushed my neck.

"Keep this here. Boru said." The stone woman raised the braid to her unformed face and cracked the stone with a broad smile. *"Remember sheela-na-gig, Nemhain."*

"I will," I said, and didn't realize I'd said it till the echo faded. My mouth burned as if I'd drunk something caustic. Unwilling to hear myself called Nemhain again, I turned and glanced down the hall. Lamps blazed from the ceiling at intervals; a second look told me that they were no more than bricks themselves, enchanted to glow as brightly as any halogen light. No scent or sweat of humans nearby. No heavy magic beyond the static of power that filled the place to the gills.

Far off, the bright neon of Katie's scent.

I took off down the hall. After a few minutes, I realized that the lights above left me no shadow—or else I'd cut it off too, leaving it in the sheela-na-gig's grip. I kept running.

Some of the rooms I passed were obviously personal, decorated to suit one person's tastes, studies and libraries and lounges for each of the Fiana. Despite those touches of home, the tunnels felt more like a hospital or a courthouse: a place that was not meant for living. People made great decisions here, did their work and received their assignments, but they did not come here to eat or sleep. They had lives for that—lives kept hidden from the Brotherhood even as the Brotherhood was hidden from their aboveground selves.

And then there were the other rooms. One was full of spears lined up along each wall, arcane symbols etched on each blade. Another door had been closed and barred, but the thick smell of blood clung to it, and through it came the sound of a woman's voice mindlessly repeating nursery rhymes. I stopped there, thinking to help her, but the blood couldn't quite mask the corpse scent within, and I knew she was far beyond my help.

I paused at one door that was little more than an archway, and though every bone in my body said I could not have seen it, I will swear that I saw a huge chamber within, higher than a cathedral. It was dark as a dead night, and yet filled with a thousand flickering candle flames, each shedding its light no more than a few inches before succumbing to that heavy blackness. I stood before that door for some minutes, unable to comprehend how such a structure could be down here, what it was for, whether it was some trick of my eyes or whether I had somehow descended through the earth like Dante and now looked upon the stars of the southern hemisphere.

I stood there too long. Voices began to filter down the hall. Unwilling to step into that suspended chamber, I darted across the hall to another door and ducked inside.

Two people walked past me, talking quietly. ". . . doesn't come back," one said as they passed, "we'll have to step up production of the vessels."

The other, a woman, nodded. "All the more reason to stay on the big man's good side. I'd rather not end up bait."

I got a good look at the woman, who passed by the door so closely I could almost touch her. In this light she looked startlingly normal, someone I might enjoy a conversation with, someone who'd had a fine upbringing and a life apart from the Fiana. But her eyes were as cold as Boru's, and her voice hummed with power, and I knew if she saw me she'd cut me down without a second thought.

A whiff of sweat—old sweat and ancient ink—brushed past my nose. I had only just recognized it when a hand clamped onto my wrist. I whirled, the fingernails of my free hand scraping against the wood of the door.

What faced me was as far from human as Frank had

been by the end. She was naked above the waist, her skin scrawled with spirals and sigils that pulsed in the bad light from the door, reeking of age and power. Torn pants caked with mud hid her from the waist to the knees, but below that the spirals continued. Her filthy hair hung in strings over her breasts, so matted that it was impossible to tell what color it had once been. Her face was marred with lines too old for her years and locked in an expression of blind frenzy. She smelled of ink and loci, but unlike the man who'd followed me to Crofter House, she did not smell familiar, not even in the unsettling way that Mrs. Crowe had. I could no more have named her than I could have gotten free.

Her grip on my wrist was stronger than handcuffs. Grimed fingernails dug into my forearm. I groped at the door for splinters, dust, anything to fight back—and met her eyes.

A blur of emotions struck me like a blow—reverence, and awe, and horror that something great had come to this, its power sapped and drained for others' use. Without any conscious recognition, I knew that what stood before me had once been more powerful than even Boru, and now was no more than another tool of the Fiana.

As I would be if I wasn't careful.

My knees buckled, and I sank in an involuntary obeisance. She blinked, that iron gaze flickering for a split second, then let go. "Swift journey, *Badb*," she murmured, and her voice was a young man's, a voice meant for shouting battle cries rather than this rusty good-luck wish.

I nodded, unable to speak, and slid out of the room. The two Fiana were far down the hall. I went the other way.

Must and mildew threatened to drown Katie's scent. The Back Bay was little more than sludge in some places, and these chambers were like tunnels in water, an ant farm chewed out of mud. No wonder the Brotherhood's scent was so much like damp rot. This end of this hall had been neglected, the shadowless glow waning with each yard. A thin sliver of gold light crept out from under the last door, and I stopped and sniffed. Katie.

A pair of sliding bolts at top and bottom held the door shut; probably all that they thought was needed against an eight-year-old. I slid the bolts back, listening for any sound from within.

Katie was curled up on a chair that looked like it had gone through at least three owners. Her overalls were stained and dusty, and one of her barrettes hung askew. My breath caught in my throat for a second—she was so still—but her shoulders stirred, and I relaxed.

I closed the door behind me. "Katie," I whispered. "Katie, it's me. It's Evie Scelan."

She raised her head, frowning from whatever dream she'd been having. Upon seeing me, she shrank back into the chair, shaking her head. I knelt by the chair and took her hands. "Shh, shh, it's all right. Just come with me, okay?"

"No!" She twisted away from me as if I'd burned her. "No! Who are you?"

I caught my breath, unable to speak. "Katie, it's Evie," I said at last, unable to keep my voice from quavering. "It's me—you *know* me, I'm a friend of Nate's."

"I know that!" she snapped, somehow managing to sound both panicked and exasperated at once. "But who are *you*?"

"No one you need fear." The only way I knew I'd said it was the echo of the words and the faint tingling on my tongue.

My grip on Katie's wrists loosened, and for a moment the two of us stared at each other. I took a deep breath. "Is this what you meant," I said, "when you said you wanted to ask me to your party while I was still alone?"

Katie bit her lip, then nodded. "I just had a feeling that if I saw you again, you wouldn't be alone. And I didn't want to invite the one with you."

A dry laugh welled up in me, and I swallowed it back down.

"I didn't know . . . didn't know it would mean this." Her lower lip wobbled.

"That makes two of us, kid." I tried a smile. "But I'm still Evie. Even with a crummy haircut."

She threw her arms around my waist and jammed her head up against my sternum, sniffling. Awkwardly, I patted her hair. "The most important thing right now," I said, "is to get you out of here. No matter how many of us there are." *And once we're out*, I thought, *once things are normal, I'm going to get Nate to take you to the seer enclave in Allston. They may be loons, but they can at least tell you how to keep your head in the present.*

"'Kay," she mumbled into my chest.

I got to my feet and helped her up. "You'll have to be quiet once we're out there. I don't know how we're going to get out just yet, and I'll have to concentrate pretty hard, so don't distract me."

She nodded, her chin tilting up in a way I knew very well. Nate did just the same thing when he had to do something he didn't much care for but knew wouldn't get done otherwise. I took her hand, brandished the scissors in the other, and we snuck out into the hall.

It was deserted, though if I listened hard I could hear distant footsteps. My nose told me that there were more Fiana not too far away, a serious case of damp rot in a nearby room, and something unpleasant a few rooms down from that. And far off, clouded by walls and trails and magic, the sweet clarity of fresh air.

We walked for what seemed like hours, through tunnels used and unused, ducking into corners whenever the smells of humans came too close, like rabbits veering away from the marks of a predator. I itched to be running, hunting once more. Boru's offer came back to me, and I bared my teeth at nothing, forcing the thought away.

Katie stayed quiet, and I was nervous enough to start hearing sounds where there were none. As time went on, though, I kept having the feeling that there was another set of footsteps with us. As if someone else walked beside us, someone always on my other side, never quite in view. Someone with a shuffling, unsteady gait, though her footsteps were barely audible, as if she weighed no more than a bird . . .

Katie shivered and looked over her shoulder for the third time. "Don't look," I whispered, and she clung more tightly to my hand.

But the footsteps weren't all. As we made our way down yet another hall—this one paneled with wood that had warped from the damp brick behind it—my breasts began to grow heavy, and my gut twinged, as if cramps had come on early. I winced and kept walking, forcing the changes away.

I had an idea of what was happening. Regardless of whether Boru or Sarah was right about the Fiana's power, Brigid and the Morrigan had one thing in common. Both were triple goddesses, the maiden and mother and crone together, and when you started working with something as heavy as trioditis magic, you got fallout from it. Magicians might be smart in some ways, but magic itself could be powerfully stupid, and right now the triple-goddess magic was attempting to remake me into the wrong role. Katie was fine, and of course whatever was riding me wasn't affected, but I was the odd woman out. I shook my head as we walked, trying to hold on to my image of myself as Genevieve, not as Mother. *I'm not a mother*, I insisted silently, *Mom was.* I really needed Mom now.

The image of Mrs. Crowe in her hospice bed flickered in my head and was gone.

Katie's energy began to ebb after a while, and I had to fight off a similar weariness. Adrenaline backlash would be hitting me hard sometime soon, and only plain stubbornness kept it at bay now. The walls on either side of us continued unbroken by doors or arches, and the passages curved in on themselves several times until I thought we must be spiraling back to the room where I'd found Katie.

Something silvery gleamed ahead, past the last curve in the hall. I tugged on Katie's hand and quickened my pace. A circular vault door took up the end of the hall, girded with steel bands and incised with markings I recognized as Ogham. A spiral design in what might have been gold shone in the center.

"Is it a way out?" Katie whispered.

"I think so. Smells like it." I put my ear against the door and heard the squeal of brakes. "Subway tunnel. Green Line, if we're lucky. You ever ridden the Green Line, Katie?"

"Lots."

"Good." I handed her the scissors. "Hold these. I think I can get us through this."

"Evie—"

I tugged a strand of hair free and wrapped it around the central bar of the lock. "Deke taught me this charm a while ago, in payment for finding his journal . . . of course, it was easier when I had longer hair," I added with a smile.

"Evie, there's someone—"

I hadn't scented a thing. "What?" I glanced over my shoulder, then spun, slamming my back against the door. The reek of dry skin and ink hit me like a physical blow.

He stood blocking our way back, the marks on his skin like black webbing in the poor light. Vessel. Man made loci. Legend made man. The one who'd chased me, found me in the Fens and at Crofter House, who had named me before I even knew that name.

Cousin. My cousin.

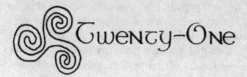

Twenty-One

I pushed Katie behind me and raised the scissors, though they'd probably be as effective as a handful of Pixy Stix. "Get back."

The vessel raised his hands. A few black strands dangled from between his fingers: my hair, yanked away when he'd found me outside Crofter House. "Came the usurper's man, and caught me. Caged me. So I sought you here."

I exhaled. Sympathetic magic again, and of the simplest kind. This was starting to piss me off. "Talk fast, Mac Cool. We've got business outside." I turned back to the door, doing my best to work Deke's lock-breaker charm and keep an eye on Finn at the same time. Katie shrank behind me, clinging to my arm.

"And now you know me," he said softly. "Cousin's child, what wrong has been done us . . ."

"And talk plain English. I don't have time to untangle this cryptic crap."

Finn's eyes narrowed, and he raised his other hand to his mouth to gnaw at his thumb. "Very well. I went hunting you as you hunt others, hunting because of what Oghma the strong one said before they killed him. The prophecy they asked of him was his death."

"You mean Frank's death."

"There was nothing of the summoner in him anymore. This—the servitude the usurpers put us to—breaks both summoned and summoner. Even this man, who called me dreaming from my sleep beside the River Liffey, has worn away beneath my waking dreams. Such is the punishment his fellows put him to, and such was the trap they set for me."

"You're wrong." I yanked too hard on the hair, and it broke. Cursing, I tugged another from my hairline. "Frank was still there—still part of the person, even after Oghma moved into his head."

Katie craned up on tiptoe. "Evie, who's Frank?" she whispered. "And who's *he*?"

"Frank was a friend of mine. Back when I was even younger than you." It wasn't the whole truth, but it would do for now. "I'll tell you the story someday. This guy is, well, I think he's a relative of mine. That's a longer story, and maybe someone will tell it to *me* someday."

Finn shook his head. "Cousin's child—"

"Genevieve," I snapped, then realized I'd done it again, handed out my name as if it were nothing more than a word. Boru would have called me stupid again, and for that alone I didn't regret it.

"Genevieve," he said, tasting the name. "I did not seek you so that we could tell stories while the fire dies. I sought you that you might hear me, and see what the Fiana has wreaked on us."

"I see all right. I saw what it did to Frank. Now go away." I cupped my hands over the lock and whispered Deke's charm. The hair blazed white, then dissolved into dust, and one bar of the lock snapped open. One out of maybe fifteen.

"Cousin's child, you must help us."

"Must?" I whirled and stalked forward. "*Must* nothing. I am not your hound, not anyone's hound. No one tells me what I *must* do. I'm real sorry for all of you—and for your summoners, or whatever—but right now all I want to do is get this girl out of here."

He gazed back at me with equanimity. "Is that all you plan?"

I glared at him, then turned back to the door. "Katie, do me a favor and use these to cut off a little more of my hair. Don't worry about making it look good."

"Okay," she said, then when I gave her the scissors, looked from me to Finn and back. "I can't reach."

I sighed, knelt, and started work on the second bar of the lock. Katie fumbled with the scissors—they were far too large for her hands—and searched for a place to cut.

"Your plans are clear to those who know the ways of the hound," Finn said. "You have a tender heart. Uirne, my mother's sister, did as well, and I count it no shame in either of you. But you bow too easily to those who deserve no pity. You have given your loyalty to one who merits it not." He lowered his voice. "I speak of the woman of the crows."

"She's an old woman," I muttered. Katie glanced at me over my shoulder and tried to get a better grip on the scissors.

"She is not. She is not even summoned into a body, as we were. She is the goddess incarnate, and more dangerous because of it. Our countrymen use her power to bind us, and thus she is the center of the web that holds us all."

My fingers slipped on the lock. I cursed and tried to ignore him.

Finn moved close enough that Katie squeaked and backed up against me. "Sceolang, cousin's child, Genevieve, the Morrigan must not wake. For us to be free, she must die."

"How dare you!" I wheeled on him, and only realized I'd snatched the scissors from Katie when their blades grated against my palm. *"How*—I—"

The scissors clattered to the floor as I choked down the angry words that weren't mine. My head began to pound, and everywhere I looked afterimages flickered like a ghost film. Katie clutched at my arm. "Evie, it's okay. I know you're still there."

Finn crouched next to me, brows furrowed, then nodded slowly. "It seems I was wrong. Your plan is otherwise."

I gritted my teeth and forced down the mad laughter that threatened to break free. "My plan right now is to get out of here."

"So you say. But there are the plans we make for ourselves that we do not see, and *geisa* laid on us that none can break, though they know them not." He reached out and touched my hair, like a priest bestowing a benediction, like a trainer calming a panicky dog. "Remember, though, that no *geis* can hold Sceolang or his descendants, no binding and no spell, save the golden chain of Bran."

I took a deep breath. "At the moment," I said, "the Fiana doesn't need any *geis* to hold me. This door will do just fine."

He took my hand and pulled me to my feet. "Take my strength. Much of it is theirs, but enough suffices to give to you."

I blinked at him stupidly, then backed up a pace. "You want me to use you as a locus?"

Finn nodded.

I shook my head. "That's— I can't, I don't know—I don't do that magic. Especially not with a person; it's like sucking their blood . . ."

"I give you this freely." He bit his thumb again, then smudged the resulting blood and saliva against the notch in his collarbone. The blue lines on his skin writhed in answer, and his entire body seemed to shimmer with heat haze.

"Your gift will be remembered, Mac Cool." I grimaced; I was starting to hate it when that voice used my mouth. "That is, I'll do it this once. But I'd rather cut my thumbs off than use a locus again."

I reached for his hand, pushing my fingers through the thickened air. An intoxicating rush of strength filled me as I touched him, and for a second I realized why Leon had stayed in this business. Even the edges of the undercurrent could be entrancing if they carried the possibility of this kind of magic. "First one's free, kid," I muttered, then braced my shoulders and spoke Deke's lock-breaker.

The lock split open with a resounding clang, and Katie jumped back as the rest of the bars rained onto the floor. I let go of Finn's hand and doubled over, fighting down sudden nausea. "Get out of here," I said. "They'll have heard that, and I don't want you—whoever you once were—ending up like Frank."

He smiled, but for once seemed to lack words. Gravely, he bowed, then turned and ran in long loping strides down the corridor.

I dragged open the door. The squeal of subway brakes far away echoed down this tunnel, and dull fluorescent lights revealed a gravelly floor split by two rails. Fresh air came from the right side of the tunnel. "Great. Let's get out of here, Katie."

Katie eyed the rails. "Don't we have to be careful with those?"

"We're on the Green Line. The electrical stuff's up top. See?" I pointed past the gray stucco walls to the cables running down the ceiling. "We just have to look out for trains, and we'll be able to hear those . . ." I paused. There were voices behind me, too close behind me, and a mildew stink that the clean air threw into relief. "Katie, get into the tunnel. Go to the right, and if you get to a station, find a police officer—"

I shoved her through the door and turned—too late. Two men, reeking of mildew and magic, stood behind me.

"Against the wall," one said. I turned to face the door. *Okay,* I thought, *maybe Katie can make it a little way, maybe I can distract them . . .*

A hand clamped onto my shoulder, and pain radiated out from its grip. I hissed through my teeth, and—

—the spatter of blood on my arms, the spear in my hand and the screams of the dying—

I wrenched the man's hand away so hard that bones

grated beneath my fingers. He made a garbled sound through his teeth, and I twisted his arm further, listening for the inevitable snap. A slow smile spread across my face.

"I have stood fast," the voice of blood and ink rasped from my lips. *"I shall pursue."*

The man's eyes went wide, and I smashed the heel of my hand against his nose. Bone crunched under the blow, and his eyes rolled up in his head as he dropped to the floor.

"I will kill," I howled over the screech of a T passing by. *"I will destroy those who might be subdued."*

The other man had held back from the fray, his hands weaving in a finger-tangling pattern. Remembering Brendan and the swift effect of his magic, I didn't wait for this man to complete his spell. The easiest way for an untalented person to fight a magician is hard and dirty: you get in close and you don't stop hitting them, don't give them a chance to call on whatever allies they might have. In this case, that meant going for the man's throat.

I clamped my hands around his neck and shook him like a puppy with a rag. He choked out a word, but whatever magic he had fizzled and died, leaving only its afterimages. "How—" he gargled as I tightened my grip.

"You should have set me free a long time ago," I said, and drove my fist into his stomach. Only the fraction of me that was still me halted that blow, stopped it from tearing through his flesh as it was meant to. Instead it knocked the air from his lungs, and he went limp in my grasp.

I snarled and flung him to the side, against the wall. Better to kill them. *Better to pull out their hearts and wash in their blood, better to slaughter them without mercy . . .*

"No." I slammed my wounded hand against the wall so hard, pain numbed my fingers. "No, goddammit, get out, stop it . . ."

Better to kill.

"No." I staggered to the door, keeping just enough presence of mind to drag it shut behind me. "No, and never again. Don't ever do that to me again." I sank to my knees and retched, heaving what little I'd had to eat onto the blackened gravel. The screaming rage within me subsided, though reluctantly, sneaking away into the dark corners of my mind.

I almost killed them, I thought. *I almost*—and a new wave of nausea engulfed me.

"Evie?"

I wiped bile from my mouth. "Goddammit, Katie, I thought I told you to run."

"I had to hide." She pointed to one of the niches that lined the tunnel, each the width of a man. "There was a train."

"Jesus. Are you okay?"

She nodded, holding out her arms as if for inspection. "What happened?"

"Nothing." I spat; the taste of blood and vomit lingered. "Nothing. We gotta get moving, Katie."

She was silent a moment, then said, "You're alone now."

"Yes." I wasn't, though. Maybe Katie's talent went only so far, maybe she couldn't see the core of that presence, still inside me like a stone in my gut. But I wasn't going to contradict her just now. "Thanks."

"Is that blood?"

"Probably. Don't worry about it; I'm not hurt bad." I couldn't say the same for the two I'd left in the tunnel, but at least—and the thought made my stomach heave again—at least they wouldn't be telling anyone about us for a while. "Let's see if we can catch the next train."

We made our way down the tunnel, following the smell of fresh air. No trains passed us, and when I checked my watch I discovered why; it was well after midnight. The train that had gone by as I beat the snot out of the Fiana must have been the last of the night. "We're going to have to walk, Katie."

"Is it far?" She wilted a little, clinging to my hand as if it were a life preserver.

"Far enough." After a moment I crouched beside her.

"Come on. I'll carry you part of the way. I'll even tell you a story if you want."

She gave me a skeptical look, but climbed on my back. I got to my feet, swaying a little, and took one sliding step over the gravel. Katie's weight settled onto my back and hips, and I shifted my arms to brace her. "Tell me about the guy you were talking about," she said into my neck.

"What guy?" *Not Finn, please.*

"Frank. You said he was your friend."

I walked in silence for a moment. Her fear scent was fading, but she was still trembling, and her arms locked tight around me. "It doesn't have a happy ending," I said.

"I don't care." Katie buried her face against my shoulder. "Happy endings would be stupid right now."

She had a point. "If you say so, kid." I kicked the ground; chips of blackened stone clattered against the rails. "Okay. My mom and I came to Boston from Philadelphia when I was just six." Another kid might have asked about my dad, but not Katie. Good girl. "I hated leaving," I went on, "but we weren't going back, and I just had to get used to being the new girl. The worst part was that I couldn't show off anymore."

She leaned over my shoulder so she could see my face. "How come?"

I hesitated, but there was little that Katie hadn't already seen. "You know how I found our way out down there? How I found you? Like that. I can smell things out sometimes. I used to show off with it when we lived with my dad, but when we moved out here Mom didn't let me use my talent. Not outside anyway. I wasn't happy—I'd liked being special like that, even if it caused a few problems."

"I—" She curled up close, pressing her cheek against my shoulder blade. "I kinda know what you mean."

The other kids don't like me if I'm not careful, Katie had said. Oh, Boru, you had no idea what you were kidnapping, did you? I gave thanks to whoever might be listening—and I had no doubt that *someone* was—that I'd gotten Katie away from the Fiana.

"Then keep listening. A few months after we moved, I went out for recess and found some kids clustered at the far end of the basketball court. They were all standing around this little heap of gravel off some other part of the playground, and this kid—Frank—was crouching to one side of it, holding his hand over the heap." I held out my hand to demonstrate, then thought better of it as Katie's balance shifted.

"He'd murmur to the gravel, and it would move, making any pattern he wanted. We kept daring him to do more, to draw more, to stand the stones on top of each other and see how tall a tower he could make." One of the things I'd thrown out of my office when I moved in was a little Buddhist stone garden with its own rake for rearranging the sands. I'd hurled it into the Dumpster as hard as I could and only later thought about why I'd done so.

"Was it magic?" She was getting sleepier now; her voice had a drowsy fuzz under the curiosity.

"Yeah. Something like that. So I ran home and told Mom all about it, about how great it was that someone else could do that, and could I please tell Frank about my nose? And she didn't say a word, just got paler and paler. Finally she just knelt down and took me by the shoulders. 'You can tell him,' she said. 'But you wait two weeks first, okay? That way if anything . . . that way you'll know if he's a good enough kid to share your secret with. That's how it is with secrets; you can share them, but you need to know what kind of person shares it with you.'

"That— It makes sense."

"Glad you think so. I didn't at the time." I'd thought about telling Frank anyway, since it wasn't a real secret. It was just a secret for the adults. "But I waited the whole week, while Frank showed off every recess. One time he drew Speed Racer—I remember that, because he couldn't get it right and everyone kept teasing him till the gravel splashed up like he'd hit it."

Mom had been very patient with me that weekend, something she wouldn't repeat till I hit puberty. "On Monday, I'd decided that no matter what Mom said, I was going to show Frank what I could do and prove that he wasn't the only special kid around. And on Monday he was gone."

"Gone?"

"Mrs. McIlhinney told us that Frank would be going to another school from now on, but we had friends at all the other schools in Southie, and he wasn't at any of them. He wasn't even at home, and believe me, we looked. He'd just disappeared. Any time we asked the adults where he'd gone, they just said he was away for a little while. His parents wouldn't talk to anyone, and after a while people stopped asking."

I didn't tell Katie the one thing that had given me nightmares. It'd been my responsibility to deliver the homework packet we'd made to Frank's house. Mrs. McDermot had taken it without a word, closing the door in my face. Two days after delivering it, I'd taken a back-alley shortcut past their house and seen his father burning leaves, and on top of the leaves were the bright construction-paper pages we'd made.

"Was it the same people—the ones who took me?"

"Yeah. Same guys. So I told Mom. She gave me a long hug, and then she made me promise to be careful."

I shouldn't have come back here, she'd said. There are some people who'd like to take you away, like they took Frank. You've got to promise me you'll be careful.

It seemed afterward that every six months she wanted that promise renewed. We'd first come to Boston because she had family there, and then stayed after the family left, and by then Mom had her two jobs, and neither of us wanted to leave, even though it was clear we should. The promise was a substitute for moving, a stopgap solution that in truth stopped nothing.

The only times I lied to her about it were when I was in college and had done "the nose trick" while drunk, and that shamed me too much to confess it. I dropped out to take care of her when she got sick, and eventually money got tight. So I started taking on a few jobs for the people who'd heard about the trick, never anything big, and I never let them see how I did it. Even though I think she knew what I was doing, she didn't complain.

One of the last things she did was to renew that promise once more. That promise—but not the other, the one that still haunted me. She'd had time to ask me to be careful, but not time to reassure me that she still wanted to end on her terms.

"Did you promise?"

I glanced over my shoulder, thinking for a moment that Katie meant the last promise I'd made to Mom. "Yeah. I promised."

Katie was silent for a long moment, long enough that I thought she might have fallen asleep. When she did speak, it was so soft, muffled against my back, that I almost didn't hear it. "Do you want me to promise?"

I stumbled and had to catch myself against the wall. Exhaustion had dried my throat, and my legs felt like cooked noodles. "I'm not your mother, Katie."

"No . . . but . . ."

"It's good to be careful. But I'm not going to make you promise. I hate promises myself, so I'm not about to pile one on you." I shifted her weight so that her legs were no longer digging into my kidneys. "Just rest for now. You've had a long day."

I didn't think she was convinced, but she accepted it, and after a while her breathing evened out. I kept walking, putting one foot in front of the other. I stumbled a few times, but adrenaline and the knowledge of what would happen if the Fiana found us kept me going.

At last we struggled out onto the B Line tracks, where they reached the surface just past Kenmore. The sky was bloodied with sodium light reflecting off the low clouds, and the air was heavy with the promise of rain. Traffic blurred by to either side, and if I looked up at the windows of the buildings around me, I could see the ever-changing lights of the Citgo sign reflected in them, flickering white, receding red, flickering white.

How we made it to the Goddess Garden I'll never know. I had no more cash for a cab, so we must have kept walking. I didn't get any more tired, or didn't let myself feel it if I did. Acknowledging any more weariness would just have meant allowing myself to fall over.

I'd expected to go straight up to Sarah's apartment above the Goddess Garden, but the store light was on, and a lean silhouette paced back and forth in front of the window. I banged on the door, and Nate looked up. He beat Sarah to the door and fumbled with the security lock until she got there. "Evening," I said as the door swung open. A thick reek of too many stinky candles spilled out, and I swayed, grabbing hold of the doorframe to keep from falling over.

"Evie! Thank God." Nate's face looked like painted canvas stretched over sticks. He engulfed me in a hug, then helped Katie down and held her close. "Are you okay?"

She nodded, blinking fast. "I'm real sorry, Nate. I tried to get away from them, but it was like I was asleep, and the teacher didn't even see that they were bad—"

"It's okay. It wasn't your fault." He stroked her hair gently. "It's going to be okay."

I couldn't share his optimism. I worked my hands over the doorframe until I was slightly more upright and looked over at Sarah. "Can I come in?"

Her mouth quirked up. "When couldn't you?" I sighed and closed the door after me. Sarah made a noise like a startled ferret. "What happened to your hair?"

"Had to cut it off. A thing—a sheela-na-gig caught me by my braid." Which I'd left behind, along with the scissors and the chain and anything else that might conceivably be used against the Fiana. It was a miracle I'd remembered to bring Katie out.

"I've heard of them. Threshold guardians, though usually they're on a church."

"They don't usually move either." Or call people by the wrong name, or conspire against their masters.

"I think 'usually' went out the door a while ago," Nate said.

I laughed. My eyes kept trying to focus on two different things at the same time.

Sarah yawned. "How about I get my car and drive the three of you home?"

"Can't," I said. Nate glanced up at me, brows furrowed. "They might be still watching my apartment, and we've got to assume that they know where Nate lives too." My eyes prickled, and I sat down on the ledge of the window display with a thump. "I'm really sorry."

Nate got to his feet, still holding Katie's hands. "Do you want me to repeat what I just told Katie?"

"It'd help if it were true. But it is my fault you're involved in this." I ran a hand through my hair and winced at the short, choppy ends. "I can get myself to a motel for the night. It's not a good idea for me to go straight home. Especially not from here."

"And for us?" Nate picked up Katie; she curled up against him like a kitten.

I closed my eyes. "It might be best if you left town for a little while."

"I agree," said Sarah. "But no one's staying in a motel tonight. I've got room, and we can think this out in the morning."

"Back room again, eh?" I grinned at her; I'd stayed the night in her back room before for camouflage. In a pinch, the amount of magical static from things like sixteen portable altars, dried mandrake, and at least twelve different tarot decks at any given time would foul most scrying attempts. It wasn't Fenway, but it would do.

"No," she said. "Not after the last shipment; you'd be sleeping on boxes. Besides, Liz dropped an aromatherapy rack back there this afternoon."

"Is that what that is?" I could smell lavender and apple

essence and one of those scents that was supposed to be calming but just made me sneeze. And greenery, for some reason . . . that's right, Sarah had moved her houseplants back there. Maybe they'd metabolize some of the stink away, though I wouldn't wish that on most plants. "Where, then?"

"Upstairs. My apartment's big enough to hold all of you, and the residual static from downstairs should help."

"Static?" Nate asked.

"Long story. Have Evie tell you sometime." She sniffed. "I'd also recommend a shower. You smell terrible."

"Think how I feel," I said, and grinned.

Sarah returned the grin, and for a moment the two of us were silent, testing the truce between us. "I see you chose your side," she said.

I shook my head. "There wasn't anything to choose."

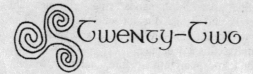# TWENTY-TWO

"Bathroom's on the left." Sarah dragged open the top drawer of a dresser that took up most of the hallway and pulled out a fluffy purple towel. "Don't touch the green towel; it's Alison's, and she has allergies. I don't want her breaking out in hives the next time she sleeps over."

I ducked to fit through the door to her hall; Sarah's apartment hadn't been designed for gangling creatures like me. Nate had already banged his head twice on the way to the living room. "Tell her I sympathize. Your bathroom smells like a turf war between soap factories."

Sarah gave me a sour look. "You're lucky she's out of town. If she were staying the night, I'd kick all of you out and drown my conscience in sex."

"No you wouldn't. You'd let us stay, try to be quiet, and in the morning Katie would have lots of questions about what she heard in the night. I've stayed on your couch before, remember?"

Sarah shrugged. "Point taken. Look, are you sure I can't neaten that up for you? Short hair could look good on you, but not with that cut."

"I can manage. Sarah—" I glanced down the hall to the living room door. It was closed most of the way, and I didn't hear either Katie or Nate. "Where is Mrs. Crowe?"

"She's safe. That's all I can tell you."

Safe, I thought, *is rapidly becoming one of those words with many definitions.* "Sarah, I learned something when I was down there. She's not—"

"Don't." She raised both hands, rings glinting. "I'd be happy to talk about this. But not with them here. The less they know about it, the safer they are, and I won't risk bringing them into this any deeper."

"They didn't know anything before, and they weren't safe then."

"Don't play semantics with me. And don't ask me where she is. I swore an oath, Evie, and I can't break it, not even for you."

"She's not Brigid," I said before she could stop me. "The head guy, the one who had me trapped down there—he said she wasn't Brigid, she was—"

"And you believed him?" Sarah put two fingers over my lips. "I'd consider the source of your information," she whispered, then shoved the towel at me. "Go get a shower. I'll see you in the morning."

I bit my lip, but did as she said.

Sarah was in her room when I emerged. I groped my way along the wall to the living room, where Nate had pulled out Sarah's futon. Katie was out cold and curled around a pillow like a root around a stone, but Nate was awake, sitting beside her.

He looked up as I entered. "She's a heavy sleeper," he said. "She'll be out until noon if we let her."

"She'll probably have the best sleep of any of us tonight." I moved a stack of books off the big frumpy chair that faced the TV.

"How are you holding up?" Nate whispered.

I held up one hand. It didn't shake much. "I'll deal. You?"

He ran a hand over his face, glanced down at Katie, then got up and went to the window. "I fucked up bad, Evie," he said, so quietly I almost didn't hear him.

"Of all of us, I think you're the one who can say that the least." I joined him at the window. The Chinese restaurant across the way was still open, but no customers came by. Even the drunks had gone to sleep.

"I did just what they wanted. I sent you straight to them. I wasn't there—" He fell silent, then looked up into the cloud-covered sky. "Do you know what I thought, after I saw those chalk marks, before I came to see you? I thought, hey, I don't have to deal with this parent crap anymore." He leaned his forehead against the window, eyes closed as if in pain. "It's terrible of me, but it's true."

I glanced over my shoulder. If Katie was awake, she was a very good actor. "We all have moments like that," I tried.

"Doesn't make them any better." He opened his eyes and stared down at nothing. "And then I just dumped it all on you. I didn't even try . . . What kind of a brother am I, if all I can do when my sister's in danger is sit around and eat takeout?"

"A brother who doesn't want his sister's hands cut off," I said. "You know what they'd have done."

He didn't seem to hear me. "If I'd gone down there— do you know, I could have killed that counselor? She just handed Katie over to those creeps without a second thought. She even smiled at me and said she didn't know I had a brother." His hands gripped the windowsill so hard his knuckles went white. "Of course I don't have a god-damn brother! She should have known that—they all get the contact info, they know better than to just give a kid to any creep who says he's her relative."

"Shh," I said, and put an arm around his shoulders, awk-ward and hesitant. "It wasn't the counselor's fault. Chances are he was using a glamour, one that made her think he was trustworthy. Maybe he even changed the contact info, made it look like he was a relative." For the first time, I re-alized that Sarah had probably used similar methods when kidnapping Mrs. Crowe, and shied away from that thought. "You can't blame her."

He shrugged off my arm. "I could have killed her," he said again, and this time I believed him. "I wanted to haul off and hit her so much . . . Sometimes I get so angry, Evie. So mad at my advisor, at the bastard who ran Mom over, at the whole fucking world for doing this to Katie. And to me."

He let go of the sill, but his hands remained curled into fists. "It scares me sometimes. It's like— One of these days it'll all come out. One of these days I'll let go."

An ambulance went by in silence, lights flashing, and receded into the distance. "I know what you mean," I said. "I don't know if you believe me, but I know what you mean." It had been something similar with the Fiana's men tonight; even if something else had been riding me, I recognized that impulse.

Nate laughed, a short, bitter sound. "Yeah, I believe you. When I saw you today . . . Wear the same expression on your face about a hundred times and you learn to recognize it on someone else." He ran both hands over his face again, then stretched till something popped into place in his neck. "Hope you don't mind that I dragged you away from the bar."

"Not now I don't."

We stood there in silence a while longer. "You need sleep," I said at last.

"You're one to talk."

I shrugged. "I'll be okay. Is there some place you can hide out?"

"For how long?"

I started to lie to him, tell him no more than a couple of weeks at the outside, but the look in his eyes stopped me. "I don't know," I said. "Maybe a week. Maybe the rest of your life. I don't think it'll be that bad, but it's hard to say."

"What about you?"

"I don't know, Nate. Things have gone from worse to terrible. Neither of us might be able to come back to Boston, ever. And I hate to say it, but that's one of the best-case scenarios."

A little of the hopelessness I'd been trying to keep down trickled into my voice. Nate heard it, reached across the space between us, and took my hand. "I hope it doesn't come to that."

I looked up at him for a long moment. "Better that than dead." He looked down at Katie but didn't relinquish my hand. "You know, Nate," I said, trying to make a joke of it, "I'm really surprised you haven't just told me I'm insane. I mean, you accepted everything I told you about magic without blinking. If you'd asked me a week ago which of my friends would never believe what I did for a living, I'd have named you straight off. I mean, you're a mathematician. You're, well, rational."

"Rational," he echoed, still gazing away. He let go of my hand, returned to the futon, and was silent long enough that my eyes began to close on their own. "When my mom got pregnant with Katie," he said at last, his words issuing from the shadows, "I got so mad at her. I mean, it had been pretty irresponsible of her to have me in the first place, but she was just a kid then. But now, and again with a guy who wasn't about to help her, that just seemed plain dumb.

"I skipped seminar so I could visit her one day. She was about six months along, and we . . . we just had a shouting match. Well, Mom never shouted, but I did enough to make up for it. I called her irresponsible, and stupid, and asked her if she thought it made sense to go ahead with this."

He shook his head. "And she just looked at me and said, 'Not everything in this world makes sense, Nate.' It shouldn't have affected me like it did—I mean, it's just something you say when a kid's having a tantrum, like 'Life's not fair,' or something like that—but it shut me right up. All my life I'd been trying to build a world out of understandable, quantifiable things, but what she said got me thinking. I must have spent a week coming to terms with it. It sounds so silly now, but at the time it was like my whole world had turned and I was seeing everything from a new direction."

He smiled, so quick I saw it only as a flash of teeth in the dark. "As for math—well, it's not the same as it was in high school. You have to do things like prove the construction of real numbers, and if you go into the higher-level pure math with assumptions that you think are obvious, they'll come right back and bite you . . . I work with impossibilities all day, Evie, and you call me rational? Put it this way: I'll believe anything you tell me to believe."

He drew breath as if to say something more, but Katie mumbled in her sleep and turned over. Nate glanced back at her and smiled.

"I'm sorry," I said. "I underestimated you."

"Yeah, well, I underestimated you. I thought you were just a private investigator with a surly side and some privacy issues."

"You got the surly right."

He chuckled. "I suppose," he added, "we might be able to stay with Katie's Aunt Venice—"

"Don't tell me," I said. "No. Really. There's no better protection against being found than no one knowing where you are."

His lips curled up in that same sad smile. "Your syntax is more convoluted than Yoda's, and you tell me I need sleep?"

"Stuff it. You sound like Sarah." I sank into the chair and closed my eyes, but the memory of my dreams kept intruding. "Nate, can you do me a favor?"

He blinked and looked up, focusing on me for what seemed like the first time. "Go ahead."

"If I start— If I start making noise in my sleep, wake me up. Even if I need the sleep. I can't—" I stopped. "Just wake me up."

He nodded, a shadow against shadows. "You got it."

I'd swear that no more than a minute passed between when I closed my eyes and when Sarah shook my shoulder. Nate was already on his feet, stretching, and Katie was a ball of blankets at the end of the futon. "Did you get any sleep at all?" Sarah asked, exasperated.

"Some." I got to my feet, wobbled, and held on to the

chair for a moment while the world resolved itself. The room was still dark. "What time is it?"

"Six in the morning." Sarah was still in her bathrobe, black curls spilling over her shoulders. Her face was grim.

"That can't be right. It's still pitch—" I turned and stared at the windows. They weren't just dark; they were uniformly black, as if someone had filled the alley with ink. If I looked at them from an angle, the glass seemed to bulge against the frame. *"Shit."*

"You recognize this?" Sarah opened the TV cabinet and dragged down two handfuls of paperbacks from the top shelf.

"They targeted me with something like this a while ago." *Only that time I'd had one of their own to bail me out, and even now it hurt to know that he'd probably set the whole thing up.* "I'm not entirely sure what it was. Back then I thought it was a scrying attempt, but—"

"This isn't scrying." She reached behind the TV and pulled out a soft leather bag.

Katie sat up, rubbing her eyes. "Nate?"

"I'm right here." Nate stroked her hair absently, glancing from one blackened window to the next.

Sarah kicked books out of the way and upended the bag. A heap of polished bone chips spilled out, and she took down the closest candle from its shelf. "You two, get downstairs and be ready to run. I don't think they'll have more than this apartment targeted . . . at least, I hope they won't . . ." She struck a match on the candleholder and murmured over the flame.

Nate helped Katie up off the futon. "Katie, can you run?" She nodded, blinking sleep away. "Good." He paused, then looked at me with an unreadable expression. "You'll be right behind us, right?"

"We'll keep them away from you," I said, knowing it wasn't the answer he wanted.

Nate was silent. "I'll see you again," he said, making a promise of it, then turned and followed Katie down the hall.

Sarah didn't even look up from her work. The bone tiles rattled as she shook them a second time. "Get me the dried sage from the shelf on your left—your other left. There's something funny about this." She took the sage I handed her, crumbled it between her palms as she closed her eyes, and murmured a phrase that made a whiff of fireworks drift past my nose. Her eyes snapped open again. "Whoa. That isn't . . . I didn't expect that."

"Didn't expect what?"

"Windows out front are clear," Nate called from the front hall.

"Good. Get moving." She scooped the tiles back into their bag. "Scare tactics," she said, accepting my help up. "The spell stops at the window. Which means it's not meant as anything other than camouflage; it's a curtain." She tossed the bag of tiles behind the couch. "It would have worked too, if I hadn't forgotten to switch off my alarm . . . today's Saturday, after all, and I'd bet no one else in the building is awake." She eyed a shelf full of crystals and took down a polished gray-green sphere the size of my fist. "I needed these damn things reglazed anyway."

"Wait." I caught her arm. "You're going to break the window?"

"You have a better idea?"

"Yes." I took the rock from her hands. "You throw like a girl." I wound up and hurled the rock at the window before she could stop me.

The glass shattered, and as it did a thin film over it shattered as well, falling away in black rags across the fire escape. A blast of damp, fetid air hit me, and pigeons took off in a burbling chorus. "Get Nate and Katie out of here," I said over my shoulder, and clambered out onto the railing.

Two men stood in the alley by the back door to the Goddess Garden, and as I straightened up one disappeared through that door. The other man looked up, and his shark-wide smile faltered.

"Connor," I breathed. "You murdering son of a bitch!" I

clattered down the stairs. Connor fumbled with something in his jacket, then changed his mind and began drawing symbols in the air.

I didn't wait for him to finish. My hands curled into fists as I flung myself at him. Had I the same strength as the night before, the weird bloody strength that had torn open the skin of the Fiana, the first blow might have been enough to take him down. As it was, he only stumbled back.

I caught his wrists to keep him from completing his magic, and he tried to wrench away. "You stupid, inconvenient bitch," he spat, wrenching away from me. "Always where you're not supposed to be—"

I didn't have anything witty prepared, so I kneed him in the groin. The blood drained from his face, but he didn't drop, and his foot came down hard on my instep.

From above me came the bass rattle of a window opening, then Sarah's voice, declaiming in a language I didn't know. It wouldn't work, I wanted to tell her, not against these guys, but Connor head-butted me, and I had to focus on him. Sparks of gold light began to coalesce in the air above us.

"No!" someone yelled. A child's voice. Katie. I kicked Connor in the gut and turned halfway around.

"Sheepdog slipped her leash," a rumbling voice said by my ear, and my stomach went cold just before something blunt struck the back of my head. I nearly went out the all-natural, no-magic way. I fell to my knees, stars flickering over my vision like the afterimages of magic.

Boru flexed his fist, shaking his head like a disappointed teacher. I groaned and tried to get to my feet—just in time to see Nate fling himself at Boru, snarling fit to beat any hound.

Boru, unfazed, simply swung Nate around, using the momentum of his jump against him, and tossed him at Connor. Connor wasn't much more prepared for this than Nate, but he was only too happy to have someone else to beat up. Above us, Sarah's voice continued to chant, and the flickers in the air began to sharpen, filling the alley with the scent of burning leaves. Boru glanced up. "Seems the sheep want to defend the sheepdog." He stepped over me and regarded Sarah's window with disdain. "Pitiful," he murmured, and held his hands up to his face, framing the window like a movie director blocking out a scene.

I didn't understand what he said then, but even I could feel the effects of it, and the scent was worse than when Leon's loci had exploded in my face. The brick face of the building resonated to Boru's words a moment longer than it should have, holding the sound like the air of a cathedral, and Sarah's chant faltered. The fire she'd called together wavered in the air like a will-o'-the wisp, then splintered and dove toward her window. Her startled shriek cut off in a shatter of glass.

I cursed and dragged myself to one knee. I should kill this bastard, kill them all, tear his throat out and wash in his blood—

"No," I said, gritting my teeth. The tide of fury rose within me, stronger than before. I crossed my arms over my stomach, trying to keep it in, hide it away. If I let it out now, there was no way I'd stop with Boru. What wanted me to kill wouldn't be satisfied with just one death. I'd slaughter everyone I could find and I'd *enjoy* it—"Never again, God damn you, I said *never again*—"

My skin flickered blue, like a guttering gas flame.

Boru gave me a startled look, then grinned. "Wonderful," he said. I spat bile at his boots.

"Evie!"

Katie ran forward from her place behind the corner. "Evie, don't—" She stopped, caught by Boru's gaze.

His smile turned from marveling to predatory. "Well," he said, "so here's where you got to, little one."

"No!" Nate flung Connor aside and leapt between Boru and Katie. "Don't you touch her."

A thin smile crawled over Boru's face. "Not this time," he said, then drew a familiar symbol in the air. Nate barely had time to step back before the magic took him, locking his muscles into immobility. "Not when you'll do."

Connor was on his feet again, and took the opportunity to kick me in the stomach. "That bitch nearly cost me my job," he said as I curled into a ball. He fumbled in his jacket and pulled out a gun—my gun, I recognized; it even had the sigils scratched into the barrel. "Because of her, I've got to go through a inquiry on top of all this."

"You're a murderer," I croaked. "You killed Yacoubian—I'll kill you—"

"Leave her," Boru said. He picked up Nate and slung him over his shoulder. "I have plans for her. Corrigan!"

"Here." Brendan emerged from Sarah's back room, green sap streaking his face like poorly applied camouflage. He carried a thin bundle, folded up like a bolster, wrapped in linen save for one hand—

A hand with strange wrinkles on it, frail as bird bones—

The hand that had held mine last night, and worked to free me.

I made an inarticulate noise and reached for her. Connor kicked me again.

"They had her surrounded by witch's ivy and hellebore," Brendan added, shifting his burden as if Mrs. Crowe were no more than a sack of laundry.

"They could have had her surrounded by monkeys for all I care. Get moving."

Brendan started to move, then halted, staring at me. "Genevieve—how—"

"I said get moving, Corrigan. Question me again and I'll cut off your toes and sew them to your eyelids." Boru flashed a grin back at Katie. "See you later, little one."

She whimpered. So did I.

The three of them walked away with their prizes as the sound of sirens crescendoed. I dragged myself as far as the fire escape and collapsed, shivering, as Katie burst into tears.

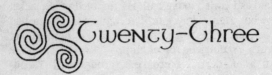

Twenty-Three

Rena found me in one of the waiting rooms at the hospital, slouched in an uncomfortable chair and glaring up at the TV. "Your friend's okay," she said, dragging a chair next to mine.

"Finally, some news. They haven't been telling me anything." I pulled myself upright, wincing as my weight shifted from one set of bruises to another. "Wait. How do you know?"

"Just questioned her." She waited a moment for that to sink in. "So what's your version of events?"

I ran my fingers through my hair. It still smelled like Sarah's stinky shampoo. "I came over to Sarah's last night to talk about some stuff. Girl stuff, nothing big. She was watching Katie for a friend of ours—his name's Nate, he's out of town."

I'll see you again, Nate had said.

"We got to talking, and I ended up staying the night on her couch. In the morning, someone threw a rock through her bedroom window, and I broke the living room window trying to open it. Some guys were trying to break into her back room, and I guess one of them knocked me out. That's all I remember." I waited a moment, returning Rena's gaze with the same bland skepticism, then smiled. "So, how different is the one Sarah told?"

"Different enough. But that wasn't what I was thinking of." Rena sat back in her chair and laced her hands together over her stomach, much the same way that Yacoubian had. "The way you're sitting tells me that you're hurting worse than a whack on the head. Paramedics also said you were conscious when they showed up—stunned, but conscious. And you haven't changed your clothes since yesterday, but at some point since we last talked you've apparently had time to visit a hairdresser. Who was either blind or insane, by the way."

"What, you don't like it?" I rubbed at the back of my neck; I'd cut way too short there, and the hairs were prickly.

Rena chuckled. "You do know," she told me, "that your story's got more holes than a Swiss cheese factory."

"I know." I touched the back of my head again and winced. I had refused treatment as soon as I was able to speak in straight sentences, which was probably stupid. But I didn't want to spend any more time in a hospital than it took to be sure Sarah was okay. "There oughta be some rule about that—you know how the bad guy's alibi is always perfect? On that one show, with the cops. Or maybe it's the other show. Having an alibi with holes should mean that it's real."

"I stopped watching cop shows when I joined the force. Ended up yelling at the screen too many times." Rena continued to regard me with the same calm, official face. "So I wonder, if I went downstairs to pediatrics and asked the kid—"

"Is she okay?"

"Not a scratch on her. Arguing with the nurses, though. So if I asked her what happened, what would she tell me?"

I took a deep breath and exhaled slowly. I couldn't afford to get dragged into a room for questioning right now. "She'd probably tell you to come talk to us."

"Hm. Ha." Rena took a mashed pack of cigarettes from her back pocket, realized what she was doing, and put them back. "You know, this whole mess is starting to make me wish I hadn't given these up."

"You didn't give them up, remember? One a week."

"I've used up my allotment for the next two months on the McDermot case. By the time I've made up for that, I may even have quit for real." She shook her head. "That reminds me: you need any coffee?"

"Depends. Are you gonna do the whole no-drink-until-you-talk thing?"

Rena sighed. "Evie, you're not a suspect. You're not even being officially questioned. I can't even tell if there's been a crime, besides disturbing the peace."

There has been a crime, I thought. Nate. Nate was gone, and who knew how long he'd last in the Brotherhood's hands. I had to get out of here.

I made myself hold on to the arms of the chair until the urge passed. Running out the door in front of Rena would create more problems than it would solve. "So how come you're still here, then?"

"Wanted to be sure you were all right, for one." She glanced at the hospital TV, on which some morning-show host was simpering at her guest. "The EMTs said you had this look like you were going to do something stupid, and I knew exactly what they were talking about."

I shrugged. Stupid had a wide definition.

Rena nudged my shoulder. "You still have that look. Not to mention a really crappy haircut."

"Screw the haircut." I tugged at my hair; the ends kept tickling. "I can't stay here, Rena. I need to get back out there."

"Jesus, Evie, you sound like me that one time I had pneumonia. It was a bad idea then and it's a bad idea now." She reached back for her cigarettes, sighed, and took a mint from another pocket instead. "Besides, you and I were supposed to talk this morning. If nothing else, I was hoping you'd tell me what the hell was up with that phone message you left."

I blinked, and the memory slowly made its way back to me. "Yeah. That. It, um, didn't pan out."

"Didn't pan out? Did you or did you not see the guy painted up like McDermot?"

"I saw him. Or I thought I did. But I lost him, after . . . I lost him. And then I had this to deal with."

"Yeah. This." She sighed, unwrapped the mint, and bit it. "What one neighbor reports as an explosion, another reports as a gunshot, and another didn't hear at all," she said around the mint. "A power outage, someone else claims. Your friend's place broken into, and your friend knocked out by what looks like a rock through the window. And we're back to the 'full of holes' bit." She crunched on the mint for a moment. "These things are terrible. Nothing on the McDermot case?"

"Nothing. At least . . ." I sighed. "All I've got is crazy *bruja* shit. Nothing that will work for you." I could tell her where to find the Fiana, or where the ward trap was at least, but that would be equivalent to handing her an arsenic smoothie. "What about the Ogham thing?"

"Found a guy at BU who could read it." She reached into her breast pocket and pulled out the paper from Yacoubian's room with the Ogham spiral. "He said it meant 'spell-evil-land.' Doesn't mean a thing to me."

It sounded like a junior high student's fantasy country to me. "Nothing here either."

She handed me the paper, and I stared at its chicken-scratched spiral again. I'd seen so much written in this script recently, but I couldn't follow symbols, not without a scent of their own.

"I talked to his doctors," Rena said after a moment. "Not that Connor shit, he got put on probation after I had a word with the director. They said Yacoubian was terminal; it wasn't a broken hip that put him in the wheelchair. But he could have had a few more months, years even, if we hadn't come by." A muscle near her jaw twitched, and she looked back up at the TV, not seeing it. "I've had cases go bad before—I've even lost a couple of friends that way. I've had cases dropped even when we knew who the perp was. But

I've never had someone die just for talking to me. That's not supposed to happen, Evie."

I ran a finger over the spiral, end to end, outside to center and back again. "Everyone's terminal. Us included."

Rena gave me an exasperated look, and just then a nurse came in. "Miss Scelan?" I looked up. "Your friend wants to see you."

"Great." I got to my feet, then helped Rena up. Of the two of us, she was moving more slowly, even with the bruises I'd sustained. "You okay with me going in to talk to her?"

"Not like I can have a problem with it."

I nodded and turned to follow the nurse.

Rena caught my arm. "You know more about this than you're saying," she whispered, her fingers tightening on my jacket. "That's just fine with me; there's a lot you deal with that I can't take. But you do me a favor. You find the guy that ordered Yacoubian's death and you make him pay. I don't care how."

Boru. Who now had Nate, Mrs. Crowe, and my gun, and who knows what other resources of the Fiana behind him. "Just him, or all of them?"

Rena's face went gray. "All of them," she said at last. "All the fuckers."

"I'll try." If I could kick Connor's teeth in while getting Nate out, then hell, it'd be a bonus.

"Good. Good." She let go, then turned on her heel and left.

Sarah waved bandaged hands at me as I came in. "They didn't even have to pack anything in ice!"

"Was it that bad?"

"Not quite, but damn close." She examined the bandage on one hand. "I won't be up to any fine work for a while, but no tendons were cut. Just a lot of little slashes."

"If it hadn't been—" I glanced over my shoulder; no doctors, and the next bed was empty. "If you'd been using anything stronger than hedge-magic, you'd be a smear on the carpet."

"If I'd been using anything stronger than hedge-magic,

I wouldn't have been me." She sat up straighter, grimacing. "Any idea which of these doctors I have to screw to get some of the real painkillers?"

"I don't think that'll help. Besides, if I know you, you have a few small remedies at home." I moved the heap of insurance paperwork to one side and took its place on the edge of the bed. "You had more than just hedge-magic on hand, Sarah."

Her gaze dropped. "Yeah. I wondered when you'd get to that." She drew aimless patterns on the sheets. "They took her, didn't they?"

I caught my breath and nodded. "I'm so goddamn sorry, Sarah. I must have led them to you last night. I led them straight to you." And to Mrs. Crowe. And to Nate. *Hound can't smell shit unless she's wading in it.* "You should have kicked me out last night."

Sarah shook her head. "No. That wasn't it. Just before you got up here, I got a call from . . . well, from Deke, not that it matters now that our grand scheme's all gone to hell. They've found Hawk's body." She stared at her hands. "He went to them. The Brotherhood. He had our plans, the notes he'd taken, he even had a photo of Bri— Of the goddess, in my back room. Everything. He must have been trying to cut a deal with them."

"Jesus." I hadn't liked him, but no one deserved the kind of death the Fiana gave to double-crossers . . . Except, possibly, Boru. And Connor if I could get my hands on him. I didn't let myself think of Brendan. "Was he your friend?" I finally asked, not knowing what else to say.

Sarah shook her head. "Colleague, maybe. Not a friend. He was a jerk sometimes, and his ideas on the supremacy of Cernunnos in the insular Celtic pantheon were totally off base . . ." Her voice broke, and she scraped her bandaged hands over her eyes. "Goddammit, I can't believe he'd sell us out like that. I can't believe he's dead."

I wanted to let her grieve—God knows I'd caused too much of it—but I had to know more. "Was the kidnapping his idea?"

She shook her head, sniffling. "No. Mine. It wasn't the original plan; we'd just wanted to break her chain stones, since we could conceivably get to those without exposing ourselves. But when you told me you'd found a woman who carried the same scent—" She shrugged. "I trusted your nose, and I knew if you said she had the scent, it couldn't be just coincidence. It was a chance we couldn't pass up."

A week ago I might have called her on that, pointed out that you can pass up any chance if the price is too high, but now I thought of the promises I'd made, the things I couldn't turn down.

She looked down at her palms. "I thought . . . I thought, there's enough static in my back room to hide her, and if we wind her about with enough organic material, then she'll be safe from most scrying."

Hellebore and witches' ivy, I thought.

"The only thing I was worried about was you, and even then I had all that incense lying around. It was easy enough to hide her presence for a little while, and we figured we'd have her freed by the next new moon."

"Why go to all the trouble?"

"Why? Deke wanted to do something to cripple the Brotherhood. He'd heard they were coming back, and he's old enough to remember the old days, even if he wasn't openly practicing then. No magic that wasn't their magic, nothing without their say-so, and the Brotherhood playing all the other little gangs against each other like chessmen. He was terrified that it'd turn into that."

Don't trust anyone, because trust will bite you. Deke had tried to warn me, even after I'd met Brendan and their first attempt with Leon had failed. But like any magician who'd been in the undercurrent too long, he couldn't talk straight, couldn't tell me right out what was going on. Secrecy could be addictive too.

Sarah wiped her cheeks dry. "Hawk had these dreams of glory, and I, I thought that I was doing something right. Something that'd mean I'd done more with my life than just hedge-magic . . ." She wiped her nose. "I can be a world-class idiot sometimes."

"You've got competition for that title," I said. That won a fraction of a smile. "Sarah, about Mrs. Crowe—"

"Brigid."

"No. She isn't." I folded the edge of the hospital blanket between my fingers, then made myself smooth it out. "Boru—the head guy—he said she was the Morrigan. And I know you said he had no reason to tell me the truth, but Sarah, I think he's right. I mean, would the Brotherhood really expend all that effort just for a saint?"

Sarah was silent for so long that I turned to look at her. "This morning," she said slowly, "when I did that bit of divination, I . . . bumped up against her, I think, and she felt . . . not what I'd expected a goddess to feel like. Bloodier. More . . . more *angry*."

Yes. I could agree with that.

"I think you're right. I don't like it, but—" She rubbed her hands together as if to scrub something from them, then shook them. "It makes a creepy kind of sense for them to have chosen the Morrigan. For one thing, they'd have had a greater power from her; it'd be like hooking up your car battery to the Hoover Dam. Any deaths from warfare would have been sacrifices to her, and then when the killing in Northern Ireland began to taper off, her power waned . . . and they started making loci out of people." She shuddered.

"Bastards don't know when to stop."

"But don't you see? It's the same thing." She held out her hands, palms up, as if pleading a case. "Brigid was a triple goddess, like Matrona and the three great queens of Britain, just like the Morrigan. The Morrigan had three aspects: Badb, Nemhain, and Macha, each representing a different—"

"Say those names again."

Sarah quirked an eyebrow at me. "Badb, Nemhain, and Macha. Is there a problem?"

I shook my head. "No." Not for her anyway.

"But you see my point, don't you? Syncretically speaking, they're the same." Seeing my blank look, she began to talk more quickly. "All aspects of the triple goddess are related, and the pantheons were so blurry even then that it's hard to distinguish between goddesses."

I shook my head. Mythological theory only went so far, and it stopped well short of the point where goddesses became incarnate. "You don't believe that, Sarah. You brushed up against her. You know what she is."

Sarah stopped mid-word, and she didn't quite manage to hide the shudder that ran through her. She knew. She just wouldn't admit it, not yet.

A nurse tapped on the doorframe, interrupting my thoughts. "Miss Wasserman? Miss, uh, Scelan?"

Katie darted past her. She caught me by the legs and hugged me tight, shivers running through her one by one.

The nurse smiled. "She's doing just fine," she said in the face of the evidence to the contrary. "Stop picking at those bandages," she added to Sarah, who guiltily put her hands down.

I disentangled myself from Katie as the nurse left. "You okay, Katie?"

"*I'm* okay," she said, looking up at me. "When are we going to get Nate back?"

I bit my lip. "I don't know." Soon. Soon.

"Holy Goddess. They took him, too?" Sarah bit her lip. "Oh, this isn't good."

I shook my head and went to the window. "I can't take you with me, Katie."

"I don't care! I just—" She ducked her head, not looking at me. "I just want my brother back."

Sarah thumped the bed to get my attention. "Evie," she said, "tell me you're not thinking about going back for him. You nearly got killed last night."

I unfolded the Ogham spiral and traced it again. Back to the beginning, back to the maze. "Sarah, you'll have to keep an eye on Katie till I come back. Katie, your brother put together some papers on who to contact in an emergency, but don't go home for them without help."

"You're going underground again?" Katie said.

"Yeah." Just affirming it was like the last piece of the puzzle sliding into place. I *would* go underground again. "Yeah, I am."

Katie yanked on my stained shirt to get my attention. "You'll see her again if you do."

Neither of us spoke for a long moment, remembering that long passage through the underground, the other walking on either side of us, the third to our mismatched two. "I know," I said at last, and knelt down beside her. "Keep this for me," I said, pressing the Ogham paper into her hand. "For luck."

Sarah threw up her hands. "You are out of your fucking gourd, you know that, Evie?"

"Language, Sarah," I said as I stood up. Katie unfolded the paper flat onto the bed, next to Sarah's leg. "And I thought you knew that already."

"I do; I just didn't think you were this bad." She scratched at the bandages again.

"You have a place to stay? They probably won't let you stay here without a letter from your HMO."

Sarah muttered something, then frowned, staring at the Ogham spiral. "What was that?" I asked.

"Hm? Oh. For how long? I'll have customers, and Liz barely knows enough to work the cash register."

"A day will be enough." More than a day, and it'd mean Nate and I were dead.

"Better be. I had so much going on that my emergency plans are only half-assed, and I'd need another day to get things in order." She nodded to the paper Katie held. "You're kidding about that thing, right? *That's* your good-luck token?"

"It's all I've got. Got a problem with it?"

"No, it's just a little weird to be giving someone a paper that says 'place of the curse' on it for luck."

"I don't mind!" Katie chirped, crumpling the paper back up.

"Well, I don't have time to stop by the hospital gift shop, so—" I stopped, replaying Sarah's words. "Say that again."

"What?"

"The Ogham. What does it say?"

Sarah traced it from edge to center, and shrugged. "'Place of the curse.' It's a little hard to read with the spiral, and someone else would probably translate it differently, but—"

"Jesus Christ." Right under my nose. Right next door, for crying out loud. "Sarah, don't tell me this means nothing to you."

"Nothing I can see. Plenty of cursed land to go around on this side of the Atlantic—"

"We are in *Boston. Curse. Boston.* How many goddamn years have you lived in this city?"

"Twelve, but—" Sarah paused and gave me a skeptical look. "Is this some sort of baseball thing?"

I swore so loudly that a passing nurse raised her eyebrows. "Thanks. I gotta go—I'll come back when I can."

Sarah smiled, shaking her head. "You'll come back soon. I'm not going to think of it any other way."

I smiled at her, kissed Katie on the top of her head, and headed out.

Some sort of baseball thing, my ass. Baseball wasn't the half of it. There was a reason I had an office in the Fenway, after all. Magic-tainted stuff like the contents of Sarah's back room throws off static, and living matter will hide something from scrying, but there's no better cloak than human emotion. And if you have a place where a lot of people are all together, all caught in the grip of that emotion, it'll cover up even a full resurrection ritual. Crypts below cathedrals, the passages beneath the Coliseum— but here in America, the best place to hide something was under a stadium.

I cut through the parking lot, dodged an ambulance that was backing up, and took off toward Kenmore. The skyline from here was hidden by the closer buildings, hospitals and malls both.

Fenway had been built well after the Fiana had started up. The Morrigan must already have been here by then, triggering riots left and right even in her comatose state (and more, even? I remembered my mother telling me about a convent that had burned to the ground, but couldn't tease out the details). The Fiana must have found a fresh place to hide her where the emotional traffic would keep her hidden. And a few years after that, when the Curse of the Bambino settled in (or later, when people actually started believing in it), they'd have even more static hiding her signal. It didn't even matter if the curse was real or not; the way magic works, the belief in it was as powerful as the real thing, if not more so.

And then over the years, rogue adepts with a love of the Sox would try to undo the curse, chanting outside the gates with Sarah's brand of hedge-magic or summoning ghosts into the stands . . . when had Mrs. Crowe arrived at Crofter House, for that matter? Did the curse go when she did, or did the broken curse mean that she had to go too? Did the curse even matter, when you had the Morrigan's diluted influence stealing out through the grounds, triggering the fist-fights and scuffles that were all that was left of her power, when the chant of "Yankees Suck!" came out every game no matter who was playing?

Was this rivalry all that was left of her?

I dodged traffic and ran on, over the thin trickle of water that was all that was left of the Muddy River. Doughy scalpers waving envelopes of tickets muttered their sales pitches as if to themselves, ignoring anyone who didn't approach them.

Yacoubian had said his contact in the Fiana, the Sox fan who'd passed on the Ogham note, had a weird sense of humor, but he'd never said *how* weird. And I'd been so snarled in the undercurrent that I couldn't even hear the words properly till Sarah said them. Frank had even talked about it—the old woman under the curse, only I'd taken it the wrong way. She wasn't subject to a curse. She was literally beneath one.

The game wasn't scheduled to start till evening, but vendors packed Yawkey Way already, bringing with them the greasy delicious scents of fried dough and schnitzel and sausage sandwiches. I slowed to a stop as the crowds became too thick for even me to move freely, and the smells coming from the concession stands made it even harder to concentrate. I had to consciously remember not to drool.

I made my way around the park, eyeing the entrances and looking out for any hint of mildew scent. Nothing, and without a ticket, I couldn't just walk straight in.

I could try the scalpers . . . no. I would go in, but on my own terms. I was a descendant of the Hound of hounds; no *geis* or binding could hold me; and no measly security barrier could keep me from the hunt.

I walked around the park again, circling sunwise this time, my eyes half closed. Fenway began to resolve itself into one big knot of scents, a snarl of tendrils leading in and out and in again . . . the trails of those who'd been here yesterday and the day before and even beyond that, the patterns of the brick and wood itself, the soil it had come from, the hands that had made it . . . and I knew that if I wanted, I could trace any one of those back to its source, even the chalk on the baselines.

It was as if I stood at the edge of a pit into which I could tumble and happily fall forever. I caught blindly at the scent of mildew and jerked back into myself, forcing the patterns away. One particular trail, old and unused but present, spiraled widdershins around the park, tighter and tighter until it reached the wall . . . a trail that stank of blood and damp rot.

I grinned, and when I opened my eyes a moppet in a baseball cap was staring at me from the other side of the fence. "Get inside, kid," I told him. "You don't want to miss the game."

He turned red and ran, his souvenir bat banging along

the wire fence. I ran a hand over my face, tried not to look
as scary, and turned back to the wall.

The Fiana's door was here, somewhere between the
green maintenance fence and the cordoned-off general entrance. I tried pressing various bricks to see if there was a
secret catch. Of course not. I tapped the wall thoughtfully,
then tried a line of Latin that Sarah had once assured me
was a prayer to Janus, guardian of doors. No luck. I tried
closing my eyes and walking straight ahead. The only result
of that was a skinned nose and someone snickering behind
me. I rubbed my nose and stepped back.

Spirals. The track ran spiral around the park, the Ogham
had been in a spiral, spirals marked my skin . . . I took my
jacket off, tied it around my waist, and looked at the place
where I'd been scratched. The skin of my forearm looked
healthy to the touch, but it was a lie, as a swift prod proved;
it still hurt, and hurt worse than it had when I'd first been
wounded.

My keychain had a pocketknife, small and dull enough
to be a poor threat, but good steel at the heart. It would
serve. I flipped it open, looked the other way, and dragged
it down my arm. A thin line of blood oozed out, clotted and
painful. I closed the knife, smudged the blood on my left
forefinger, and reached out to touch the bricks.

I smeared the blood in a line, drawing a spiral about
as wide as my hand. The mark remained dark against the
bricks even though the blood was soon gone from my fin-
gertip. I jerked my hand away as soon as I'd finished the
spiral, but the lines continued to spread without my help,
branching into a triple spiral like the one I'd drawn for Nate
without thinking, each spiral connected to the other but
none touching me . . .

Sound disappeared so abruptly I thought I'd gone deaf.
I glanced over my shoulder to see the crowds going by,
kids shouting to their parents, vendors hawking their sou-
venirs—but all without sound, as if someone had hit a co-
lossal mute button. The fireworks scent of magic scorched

my nose for a moment, then receded as the ward here—not so unlike Brendan's wards—reached out to include me in its compass. This was a heavy aversion ward, keeping me from hearing the passersby as it kept them from paying attention to me. But I could still smell them, and that told me they were still real—and that I was still real too.

I turned back as the triple spiral sank into the bricks, warping them in its wake, the mortar twisting and peeling back like a sketch on melting plastic. The wall receded into a crude arch, and I passed through.

Here, the bustle was even more eerie; the silence remained, but twice as many people walked past me, none giving me a second glance. *Gives a new meaning to "alone in a crowd,"* I thought, trying and failing to make it seem jolly. A dim glow on the floor marked several paths, one leading down past the darkness of the stands.

I wound my way past the seats, past the dugouts, through maintenance tunnels that only the rats saw on a regular basis, past the stink of sweat and leather and chewing tobacco, past a second spiral carved into the floor. Had I just been walking past in normal space, I'd have missed it, but as I approached now it began to glow—a dim, sickly light that flared with blue at its edges, like a candle flame in unhealthy air. I stepped over it, hands raised to ward.

Blackness swallowed me. My eyes ached with the sudden loss of light, and only the reek of mildew leading out ahead convinced me that this was no oubliette, no trap to catch the unwary.

A jarring pain shot up my arm, and ghostlight outlined my fingertips. *You'll see her again if you go underground,* Katie had said.

Right now, I could use all the allies at hand. No matter what they were.

"Hello, Macha," I said, and the light wrapped closer around me, like my mother's hug after a long day at school. It sank into my skin, further into my bones, and was gone, leaving only afterimages.

No. More than that. The trail of mildew still led out of this pit, but now it was enhanced, full of the scents it led to. A heavy, whiskery reek: that would be Boru. Mildew and chemicals: Connor. Clean skin and linen—

I shook my head. It shouldn't matter if Brendan was there. Other scents dragged at my attention as well, one of stone and blood and iron, one warm and familiar, like smooth wood and firelight—

I stepped forward, trusting in the light around me and the trail leading me on. After a few minutes of blue-shot darkness, a gleam of yellow-white light appeared ahead, a gleam blocked and revealed as someone paced in front of it.

"I don't like it," said a voice. Connor. I grinned and quickened my pace. "Why not just let her hit the sleep ward again? We can bring her down here with no trouble."

"For once I agree with him," said Brendan's voice. "Perhaps if you let us in on your plan, we might see where you were headed."

"We're not headed anywhere—" complained Connor, and I brought my laced fists down on the back of his neck.

He crumpled under the blow, and I kicked him aside, all plans forgotten. The Morrigan's thunder raced through my veins, rising within me like a fire whipped by a whirlwind. I was here for slaughter, for red blood and iron.

At the end of this blocky room, Brendan spun around. His eyes widened as he saw me, and he reached out a hand but did not come closer. Between us stood Boru, who watched me over his shoulder. "I told you she'd come," he said, and turned in place, forcing the man he was holding to turn, the man at whose neck he held a crude, smoke-blackened blade.

Nate raised his head to look at me, blood trickling down to the torn front of his shirt. Boru pressed the tip of the knife harder against his throat. "Welcome home, Sceolang Sceolang's-child."

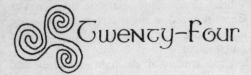

Twenty-Four

"E vie—" Nate croaked.

"Quiet, sheep." Boru twisted the knife, and Nate made a sound between a grunt and a curse.

Brendan started forward, hands open and empty. "Genevieve, what are you doing here?"

"Get back, Corrigan, before I decide killing you really is worth the effort." Boru grinned.

I bared my teeth and tried to reach for Nate—but my muscles wouldn't move. Boru crooked his finger, and I stepped over the groaning Connor, hands at my sides. Boru smiled in acknowledgment and moved the knife a hair's breadth away from Nate's throat. Nate, dazed and bleeding, didn't even seem to notice, his eyes rolling back into his head.

Brendan crossed his arms. "Boru, I fail to see—"

"Of course you fail. Knowing you, you probably don't even know why I summoned her. Lateral thinking, Corrigan. It's like I'm always telling you."

"You didn't summon me," I managed to say, and even those words were like sandpaper against my throat. "Let him go, and I might not kill you."

Boru laughed. "You really think you came here of your own free will, don't you? I love it." He lifted the hand that had held Nate's shoulder to show what else it held: a long coil of black hair, wound about with a gold chain.

Boru traced a line on the chain, and my legs twitched in response. I gritted my teeth until my jaws ached, but to no effect; my feet lifted and shuffled a step closer to him. "Gotta love sympathetic magic, Sceolang's child. It's great for working mischief from afar, it makes it easier to track someone down—but if you don't have time for all that, it's just perfect for drawing someone to you. Even if her entrance is a little unexpected. I'd had a whole setup ready for you down by the sleep wards in the Back Bay, and I suppose all that will go to nothing now. But that's free will for you. A real bitch sometimes. Not unlike you, I expect."

Brendan shook his head. "Goddammit, Boru. This is not how it was supposed to go. This is not how you treat her—"

"For the last time, Corrigan, get back before I send you into the darkness as the bait for our next locus." Boru's smile never wavered. Brendan glanced from him to me and put his hands down, but didn't move.

"What—" I heard a familiar snap behind me: Connor, switching off the safety on his gun. *My* goddamn gun. "What the fuck is she doing here?" he said, staggering to his feet.

"She's supposed to be here. Just as much as the lady we liberated this morning." Boru nodded to a door to his left, a locked and barred door.

I knew what lay beyond that door. White walls. A hospital bed. And someone who was not my mother. And slowly I realized that the locks and bars were all on this side, against whatever lay within.

Boru tugged Nate's head to the side. "Put the gun away, Connor; we have work to do. Or rather, she has work to do, for us."

Connor shook his head. "I don't get it. If you could call her down here any time you like, then what did we bring this sorry sack of shit down here for?" He circled me, still holding the gun, and kicked Nate in the leg. Nate jerked but didn't make a sound. His head nodded forward till I could no longer see his face.

"I'm at a loss too, Boru," Brendan said, though he didn't take his eyes off me. "There's no point in torturing her, especially if we want her to join us. We don't need to bring this man into it."

Boru laughed. "That's rich, coming from you. You're the one who targeted this poor sap for the kidnapping just because you were getting a little jealous. Couldn't stand anyone horning in on your territory, so you thought you'd take him out of the picture, too."

I struggled to look at Brendan. He turned red and glanced away from me.

"Poor possessive Corrigan, poor shortsighted Corrigan, poor bastard chafing at the bit just because you had to be second place to a dropout like me . . ." Boru's voice turned almost caressing, thick with malice. "You know, for all your college education and all your fancy-ass degrees, all your uptown airs like you're not part of the same Southie shit, I bet I'm still smarter than you."

Brendan's jaw twitched, but he didn't take the bait.

"I bet, for all your books, that there's still one word I know that you don't. And that's why I am who I am, and you are working for me." Boru's gaze shifted to me, and he smiled even wider. "Avatar."

All pretense of control dropped from Brendan's face. He stared at Boru, then at me, shaking his head. I couldn't move, not even to deny it . . . and having called her into myself, I could not deny it.

"You'd have seen it from the start, if you'd had half the brains you claim. I saw it the moment I found the chains empty, and I would have seen it earlier if I'd been there from the start. There are only so many entities for whom a sheela-na-gig would betray me, and most of them, well, most of them we have locked up in their own prisons of flesh, hm?"

Carefully, almost gently, Boru took Nate by the hair

and pulled it back so that his throat was fully exposed. My braid, still encircled by the chain of Bran, slithered across Nate's neck like a rope. "Nemhain, Badb, Macha, triple queen and source of our strength, I will not pretend to know how you found your way to this host. I will only say that you chose well." His hand tightened on my braid, and it was as if gold links pressed into my skin. "And I give you this."

He held out the knife, the blade balanced on the palm of his hand, hilt toward me.

I reached for it.

Connor gasped, then laughed, a high-pitched noise that abraded the ears. "Are you insane?" Brendan snapped. "We've always made sure the sacrifices were at a distance—across the water, none of our doing. Nothing direct. Do you know what could happen if—"

"She's just beyond that door, Brendan," Boru said, his eyes never leaving mine. "A sacrifice to her from this close—and not just *to* her, but through her avatar, blood shed by her own hands—yes, I know exactly what could happen. You look at her and see just a hound. I look at her and see power. I remember how it was when the Morrigan was strong with sacrifices, and that was fine, but this could be so much more. We could have a goddess at our beck and call, not sleeping but alert, alert and *ours*. Blame the hippies if you want, for giving me the idea; but can you imagine the power the Morrigan would give us once again if she were to wake? Can you imagine how strong the Fiana would be? The blood would flow in rivers, and it would flow as we directed." He tipped Nate's head back further. "Through *her*."

I heard their voices from a distance, as if they spoke underwater. All I could see was the bright iron of the blade, and Nate's exposed throat. A sacrifice, as they used to give to her, *to me in the days of strength, in the days when I was unfettered, when those I marked for death died screaming . . .*

I shook my head. No. This was Nate. This was my friend *a breathing man given to me, given in my name my legitimate prey . . .*

I clutched at my wrist, trying to drag my hand away from the knife. The desire burned like poison up my arms and down my spine, ice and hot iron and the sweet pain of sharpened bronze. *It had been so long—*

Nate raised his head. He didn't recognize me. I didn't recognize me.

And Boru held the chain and smiled.

"No," I said, and it was Sceolang's child speaking, Evie Scelan, daughter of Eileen and descendant of kings. *No chain may hold me. No geis may bind me. A gold chain is nothing to the Morrigan and the Fiana's bonds are nothing to the Hound.*

And I'll be damned if I let this bastard choose my prey for me.

My lips parted in a grin to match his, and I had the briefest glimpse of Boru's smile faltering before ghostlight exploded up my arms. I backhanded the knife out of his grip so hard it struck the wall. Nate ducked forward, tearing free from Boru, and as he did so I leapt over him, going for Boru's throat.

One of his fists landed against my ribs, but I felt it as no more than a momentary shock. It didn't matter; I was now close enough to score his face with my fingers. My other hand shot to his ear. I didn't even realize what I'd done until I dropped the scrap of flesh—I'd ripped his ear off like the tag on a sofa cushion.

Boru roared in pain, but I was already at his throat, one hand slick with his blood. We went down together, snarling and cursing in near unison. My hands locked around his throat, stretching their widest just to get hold of his massive neck, and I drove my hands against his gullet. Cartilage gave under that first blow, and it crinkled further beneath my grasp.

Somewhere beside me Connor was shouting something about getting a clear shot. A snarl almost as canine as my own answered him, and his voice cut off with a grunt as the gun skittered across the floor. Nate shouted again, yelling words I hadn't thought he knew, and the sound of blows striking flesh—*the sound of battle, of the heat and fury, my music*—flooded through me.

Boru couldn't speak to enspell me, but he still had his hands free, and those could do more than just hit. Lines of blood circled my wrists as he drew a pattern in the air, and the fine bones of my hands ground together, preparing for a break. Rather than let that happen—*I need my hands; I can do so many wonderful bloody things with them*—I let go of his neck and seized his sigil-drawing hands.

That was a mistake. He twisted one hand free and slammed it against my head so hard my ears shrilled with pain. I shook my head twice as if ridding it of a fly, then grinned, though it cost something to do even that. My teeth hurt, my face hurt, everything hurt, but all of the pain was somewhere else right now, somewhere that didn't matter at all. I returned his blow, and his head rocked back to knock against the floor. Blue light flickered where my hand struck, working its way into his wounds.

With the part of my brain that remained only Evie, I tried to look over my shoulder, see what had happened to Nate, when Brendan would attack. But Nate's incoherent shouts were clue enough, and as for Brendan—

He hadn't done anything. Not yet.

Boru choked and clawed at my back. I seized his head by the hair, slamming it against the floor until the slate tiles broke. His eyes rolled back, but he was in himself and alert again before I could do more.

Not the throat, I thought, and I didn't know which mind said it. *That's for establishing dominance, and there's no way dominance will hold with this one. For this one*—

With one hand I kept my grip on his windpipe, crushing it bit by bit. The other I drove up into his stomach, my fingers pointed together into a single claw, striking, pushing, rending—

The Morrigan's power screamed through me, and Boru's

pupils dilated as I dug into his flesh. What had been the doughy solidity of his stomach below the sternum gave way to something soft and warm, and I reached in, reached further—

"No," he choked through a throat full of blood. "Please." And with what mercy the Morrigan had, whatever bonds of the Fiana remained upon her and me, I granted him that at least. As he fumbled for the hole in his gut, I let go and took his head between my hands.

I don't remember what happened next. I know what must have happened, but my memory of it was washed out by the roar of triumph, of sacrifice and life, that thundered through me, like spring floods through a dry canal. What I do remember is that when the red mists lightened, Boru lay dead on the stone floor, blood on his shirt and his head twisted most of the way around. There were tooth marks on his throat, deep enough to cut but no more than that. My mouth tasted of iron.

I lurched away, revolted, but the Morrigan would have none of it. My head went up, and my hands clenched anew as I focused on Connor and Nate, who fought on, oblivious to everything else.

Not them, I begged, *not them—please, not Nate, don't make me—*

They fight, said a voice within me, and I knew that I was a fool to mistake any voice for hers. It was horribly like my own, like Sarah's and Rena's and Katie's and every woman I knew, any woman who'd had to fight for anything in her life. *They worship me through battle. They are mine already. Leave them.*

I shuddered or convulsed with relief. But there was one other in the room, and I turned to face my new prey.

As I turned, Brendan raised his hands and spoke three words. The air in the room grew heavy and oppressive, as if we'd just descended another hundred feet. I growled and leapt for him, but he dodged me just long enough to clap his hands. Dust spiraled around his feet, and I had enough time to close my eyes before the full force of a gale hit me and tossed me to one side. My head struck the floor by Boru's foot, and lights burst behind my eyes.

The blast hadn't been aimed at me. It lifted Nate and Connor both, dragged them apart, and slammed them against the wall. Nate slid to the floor; Connor's head left a long streak of blood on the stone.

"Genevieve," Brendan said.

I got unsteadily to my feet, glaring at him, panting with the urge to do to him as I had done to Boru. He was Fiana; he was the same as Boru; he deserved no less.

It's not the same, I tried to say. *He's not the same.*

"Genevieve, listen to me," he said. "This isn't you. This is the Morrigan, corrupting your mind. You don't want to kill me. You are Genevieve, not the Morrigan. Remember."

I remembered. Oh, I remembered. I remembered how he had smiled at me, never mind that it had been a lie. I remembered the smell of his skin, the way he had made it okay to speak about magic without fear for me or him. I remembered his voice leading me out of nightmare, remembered the bitter regret as he pleaded with me to believe he wasn't the bad guy. He had lied, but that didn't make how I'd felt any less real.

"Please. Try to remember who you are."

He betrayed you. He lied to you.

"It doesn't fucking matter!" I screamed.

"It does," said Brendan, who must have thought I was speaking to him. "If you let her, she'll take you over, rule you as surely as the vessel spirits rule their hosts' bodies. There'll be nothing left." His glasses reflected blue light as the lines on my skin surged in time to my heartbeat. "You're not meant for that—you've got to stay the Hound."

I could shut him out, if I stopped thinking, if I let her rage through me again. But that would mean handing myself over to her, giving up what little autonomy I'd had, whatever shred had kept her from accepting the sacrifice Boru had prepared.

Enough! I shrieked, driving everything out of my head, sinking to my knees, retching with the force of it. *Get out! No one tells me what I must do, and that includes you!*

The presence within me backed away, growling like a cat cheated of its malice. The fires of my skin dwindled, fading with each pulse. I drew a shuddering breath. "Oh, Jesus." I clawed at the floor, loathing the feel of Boru's blood on my hands, and turned to look for Nate. Connor's eyes stared sightlessly at my left foot. I didn't think there was any hope for him—but Nate was blinking and groaning, his left hand cradled against his chest. Two of his fingers stood out at painful angles to the rest. "Oh, God. We need an ambulance—"

Something cold and hard whipped around my throat. I clutched at it too late, and scraped my fingers against gold links. "I'm really very sorry about this, Evie," Brendan murmured in my ear, pulling the chain tight till it was a noose, a leash. "I hope you understand that. But I can't let it be any other way." I clawed at my throat. "Please understand," he said regretfully, "that there's nothing personal about this."

And that's supposed to make it better? I flailed at him, but he was out of reach. He didn't even need to dodge.

"We can't thrive while the hound runs free," Brendan said. "I believed Oghmios then, I believe him now. I have to do this." He touched the back of my head gently, almost a caress. "You asked me a long time ago what you could do to repay your debt to me. Consider this my answer. It won't be a hard servitude, I promise you."

And with that he put a hand against my bruised temple and spoke words that made my skin crawl. I screamed as his magic sank into me, reaching into my mind, groping for the part of my blood that wasn't quite human.

I could follow him always. Utterly loyal. Secure in my duty to him. I would never have to agonize over decisions again; they would be made for me, and by a much wiser person than I could ever hope to be. I would have no cares.

Only the security of loyalty. No responsibilities. Only commands. No guilt. Never guilt. The simplicity of it was its own siren song.

Brendan's magic reached further into my mind, searching, scouring, laying bare my secrets. I was a hound, bound to serve. I was the Morrigan, bound to the Fiana. I was a woman, beloved of this man, and love conquered all, love forgave all, love withstood all.

And then I heard a voice in my head, though where it came from I'll never know. It sounded a little like the Morrigan, but more like my mother, and an awful lot like the times I'd heard my own voice on a recording, the way it sounded from outside my head.

For him?

No. Not for him. Not for anyone.

Brendan frowned and pulled the chain tighter, paying more attention to the magical tempest in my head than to the thin prison of the chain. But I had enough strength left to hold the magical incursion off. We were at a standstill, and could have stayed that way till Judgment.

The trouble was that while I could hold my own on the metaphysical plane, I was at a distinct disadvantage on the material one. I couldn't dislodge the chain, and Brendan, whether he meant to or not, was slowly strangling me. I hadn't wanted to die, but what scared me more—what drove my fingers to claw at the links over and over—was the thought that just before passing out, I might weaken. I would never wake up as Evie again.

My skin parted as the edges of the chain cut deeper, and streams of blood trickled down to my collarbone. Through the haze of pain and asphyxiation I saw Nate rise to his knees, groping for something against the wall. When he straightened, he held in his broken hand a twisted shard of metal: the knife Boru had offered me. In the other he held my gun—*the wrong way*, I thought dimly, *not if he wants to shoot someone.*

"Evie!" he shouted, and hurled gun and knife at me.

My hand shot up to catch the gun. But Nate's broken hand fouled his throw; the knife was just out of my reach, grazing Brendan's arm. Brendan cursed, letting go of the chain—

I spun on my knees, wrapping the chain further around me, and fired into the soft space below his jaw.

His hands jerked the chain tight in a last convulsion, and I fell with him. One end of the chain came free, and in the concussion of sound following the gunshot all I could hear was a phantom chime as its links dragged over stone, a ringing that would not go away even after all was still.

I lay there panting. Nate was at my side, undoing the chain and saying something. "I'm all right," I croaked, though I couldn't hear myself speak. "Dammit, I'm all right."

After a moment, I gingerly felt at my throat. The chain had only dug in at a couple of places, but I'd have bruises for a long time, and my ribs had the hot and disassembled feeling that meant some of them had broken. It was easier to concentrate on such small hurts rather than the broken body at my back or the blood still sticky on my hands or the way my own skin wanted to crawl off my bones.

I dragged myself to my feet, blinked a few times, and managed to focus on the ground in front of me. The spreading pool of Brendan's blood just barely touched my feet. I put my head down again and took several deep, slow breaths. No, I wasn't really all right.

Nate held on to the wall to steady himself as he got to his feet, and his expression slowly changed as he saw first Connor, then the ruin of Boru's body. His horrified gaze shifted to me, and I looked away before I could see him make the connection. Instead I looked down at my hands, slick with blood. I fumbled at the safety on my gun and tucked it into my jeans, then scrubbed uselessly at my hands.

If the gunshot hadn't deafened me, I'd have heard the footsteps before I smelled him. But my sense of smell was alert, and this was a scent I knew, though not a comforting one. Stone and ink, age and dried skin, the heavy scent of magic let free.

I raised my head to see ranks of them, dozens of them, filling the passage that led away from here, to the Back Bay and the ward traps. Woman and man once but no longer, watching me with blank, intense eyes. A thick collar of ink circled each throat, thorned with Ogham that no doubt proclaimed their identity to any who could read it.

Finn walked ahead of them, carrying a basin. Water splashed over the side with each step. He glanced at the bodies, then set the basin down and dipped his hands in it.

Nate moved to put himself between Finn and me, but I shook my head and waved him away. Finn got to his feet and extended his cupped hands to me. "Drink," he mouthed.

I bowed my head and managed to drink a sip, then sighed and rested my forehead on his wrists. It was plain water, fresh from the Quabbin Reservoir and tasting faintly of sulfur, but at the moment it was better than any wine.

My ears tingled, then popped. I straightened up, frowning, and thin streams of something wet ran from both of my ears down my neck. I smudged my fingers in it and held them up: water, I realized, then realized further that I could hear again. My ribs no longer had that crackling feeling where Boru had hit me, and the dull ache of my bruises receded.

Finn smiled up at me as he knelt to the basin again. "It was said of me," he said, "that I could heal any wound, did I but give a man to drink from my hands. There is truth in it, though I was taught it too late, and was too bitter to save the one who taught it me." He offered his hands to Nate, who glanced at me. I nodded, and he drank too.

"Thanks," I croaked. My voice was still harsh, the bruises still present, though muted. "I—I killed them."

"The Morrigan takes her sacrifice," Finn said. "This one was a long time coming."

I shook my head. "The Morrigan takes whatever she wants, seems like."

Finn shrugged as if to say he'd seen worse.

"Ah." Nate rubbed at his ears and looked at his fingertips as I had. "Thank you."

Finn nodded in acknowledgment, then gave my clothes a glance, clucked, and upended the basin over my head before I could move. One of the vessels laughed a hollow, dead laugh. I spluttered, but the blood washed away, leaving me soaked but no longer soiled.

"Morrigan," Nate said. "What they said—about the Morrigan—Evie, what—"

"What am I?" I asked for him. "I don't know, Nate. I really don't know." I looked at my hands, still dripping pink water.

"The Morrigan takes her sacrifice," Finn repeated. "And she is not yet gone from this place." He pointed to the locked door. I glanced at it, and when I looked back, he held Boru's knife. "Her power holds us, cousin's child. Free us."

"Hell with you," I spat. "I can't just kill an old woman."

"Her power was used to bind us. And through her avatar she has killed," he added, gesturing with the knife at Boru's body. "She will be strong, and the usurpers will rise from their leader's corpse like maggots. And we will never be able to break free and end this servitude, not as long as she draws breath."

"Quite a way with words you've got." I yanked the ends of my shirt free and wiped at my hands.

"Will you leave your kinsman chained, then, and with him those who were likewise betrayed?" Finn asked, gesturing to the ranks of vessels who filled the tunnel behind him. "You have the strength to chase her from you now. Will you always? Will you when she is rich with blood?"

"I came down here for one thing. He's safe. Now I'm leaving."

"So you said before."

"Stuff it up your—"

"Evie." Nate caught my arm, and I felt a shudder run through him at the touch. But he didn't let go. "I won't pretend I understand anything of what's just happened. But I said I'd believe whatever you told me, and I believe you're here for a reason. And I don't think I'm the only reason."

I met his eyes. *Goodbye, Nate*, I thought. The man who had dragged me away from the bar was still here, but damaged by what he'd been through. We'd never be able to see each other the same way again. "Damn you both," I muttered, and took the knife from Finn. "I'm not agreeing to anything until I see her."

"The Morrigan must not wake," Finn said.

"You've made that point already." I lifted the bar off the door; the thing was slender, but solid iron, and my back would be aching in the morning for it.

I opened the door and went in, holding the knife against my leg so she wouldn't see it. No need to scare her. But after two steps, I realized there was no point.

I had been here before.

She was awake.

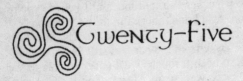 Twenty-Five

This room was as decrepit as the one I'd just left, crumbling brick and spiderwebs in every corner, but I kept seeing it as white-walled and sterile, the second image overlaid on the first like a painting on thin cloth. Though it was colder than the other room, the air had that melting-ice tang of a spring thaw, and it would not stay cold long.

There was no hospital monitor, but if I closed my eyes for more than a second I heard its steady, maddening beep. And while the bed was barely more than a cot, rotting wood with a few blankets, if I looked away it resolved into a hospital bed, all metal rails and antiseptic-bleached sheets.

The woman in it remained the same, no matter how reality flickered around her. She was old, older than I remembered, and no longer physically resembled my mother. But her eyes were open, and they were the same bright shade of blue as mine, as my mother's had been.

Would Sarah see those eyes as brown, I wondered, would Katie see them as gray?

I shifted my grip on the knife and walked the last few feet to the bed. "Sweet," she breathed, her voice full of dust, and then, "Jenny. My Jenny."

Only my mother had ever called me Jenny. Only her.

"You're not my mother," I said, but my voice quavered.

She sighed so deeply the bed seemed to crumple around her, then closed her eyes and nodded. "I am not," she said. "But it was a way to reach you, and I needed to reach you . . . as you needed her."

I shook my head, but it was true. Some part of me had needed her, or needed the woman to whom I'd made those promises so long ago. She had stepped into that gap . . . but need deforms the undercurrent, and it must have changed her too. Otherwise I wouldn't be able to stand here beside her, upright and sane.

She raised one hand as if to plead or bless, but dropped it again to the sheets, too feeble even for that little movement. "You . . . You stand at the center of the spirals, untouched by any, the axis they turn on . . . neither maiden nor mother nor crone, you were a channel for all, you could hold every aspect of me . . ."

"I can't be unique in that," I said. "Girls don't stay maidens for long these days."

She smiled. One of her bottom teeth was missing, and there was a wide gap between her two front teeth. "Do you think there were many when I walked the earth? Hardly. But few stand in the center of the spiral as you do, looking out onto all three and taking no part of any. You were . . . Had I been in truth alive, I would have sought you out, blessed you with my gifts, instead of giving you curse and gift together. It was accident that brought me to you, that put me in your blood, but I would not have harmed you had I the choice."

"I forgive you," I said, and surprised myself by meaning it. Sickened as I was by what I'd done to Boru, if it hadn't been for her I would have had no chance at all. Without her, I would still be chained beneath the Back Bay, and I might even have agreed to Boru's proposition. Katie, Sarah, maybe even Nate and Rena—all dead. The Morrigan takes her sacrifices, and though the blood of them might be on my hands, I couldn't hate her for it. "It's okay," I said.

She sighed and turned her face away, still smiling.

Without thinking, I took her hand, expecting the soft, frail hands I'd felt in the dream. The shock of it was like grabbing lightning. What I knew of magic was the debased, paltry work on the fringe of reality, and though I'd experienced a taste through Finn's gift of himself as locus, that was nothing to the Morrigan. She was raw magic, so powerful it burned through her even in her weakened state.

Images flickered around me, faster even than the blurring of the room: a green land sighted from the prow of a ship; the bloody plain of a battlefield and a stream of blood flowing between my feet; kings and Fiana making obeisance to me; ravens and men in black robes and the quiet under the *sidhe* mounds; then the pounding heat of blood in my ears and chains on my ankles, stones holding me down, men bending over me as I lay on a cot, men like Boru and Brendan, their faces different but the expressions the same; the same flat stone above me, the days drawing out into grayness . . .

I clutched the edge of the bed, expecting my hand to char and burn against hers, but my skin didn't so much as flicker. "It wasn't right," I croaked. "What they did to you wasn't right."

"Jenny—" She coughed, a racking cough that shook the bed. Blood flecked her teeth.

I held on more tightly, as much to anchor myself as to comfort her, and she returned the grip with a frail squeeze. Her hair was matted and twisted into clumps, and involuntarily I remembered how the nurses had brushed my mother's hair, before most of it had fallen out from the chemo. "You're not— You're sick, aren't you? You can't be—I just, I was just you, Boru's dead—"

She shook her head. "Let me tell you a story."

I almost laughed. "Go ahead. It's been a week for stories."

She smiled again, but did not open her eyes. "This is not a tale of my home, but it is close to me . . .

"There was a queen called Branwen, the White Raven,

the Holy Raven queen, and she wedded a man of my land. When he mistreated her, as she knew he would, she taught a sparrow speech, and it flew to her brother Bendigeidfran, who came to free her. There is more to the tale, but it matters not . . ."

Her eyes opened. It burned to return that blue gaze. "In the speech of that land, Bendigeidfran means Blessed Raven, Holy Raven. So it was not only her brother that she called, but herself, a piece of herself long gone . . ." Another coughing fit shuddered through her, and her free hand clawed the blankets. "Do you see? Do you see, Jenny? I gave you a part of myself, so I could call you, so I could be free."

She tried to breathe again, coughing as the air reached her ruined lungs. "And now I must ask you to fulfill your *geis*."

"I don't have a *geis* on me. Finn—my cousin told me that nothing can hold me except for that chain—"

She shook her head. "Mac Cool is wise in many ways, but he would have to eat seven salmon of wisdom to see the truth that lies before him sometimes. No, Jenny, you know this as well as I. No *geis* is harder than the ones we lay upon ourselves."

I looked down at our linked hands and thought of Nate, of the strictures he'd put on himself as a substitute parent for Katie, the way he'd bound himself into his role even as it strangled him. Of Rena, who had lived the police life so thoroughly that she couldn't see who she was without the badge. Of Sarah and her fear that all she would accomplish in her life was hedge-magic. Of Brendan, who'd convinced himself that he couldn't break the Fiana's rules, though he schemed his way through them.

And me? I'd said it before, though I'd never truly seen it for what it was. There were some things I couldn't turn down. Cases I couldn't refuse. Promises I couldn't break.

"What do you want me to do?" I asked.

The Morrigan sighed, and a gust of wind circled the room as if in answer. "Kill me."

I let go of her hand, and the room steadied around me, becoming once more its doubled self instead of an island in the sea of her memories. "No. Please, no," I said, backing away, holding up my hands as if to fend her off. "Not again."

"I cannot continue like this," she said. "I am sick of this incarnation, sick of these chains. Will you do this for me?"

"I *can't.*"

"Remember your *geis*, daughter." Her eyes were full of pain. "If you do not, who will?"

I closed my eyes and cursed, cursed my mother and myself and Finn and Boru and whoever had first bound the Morrigan.

She turned her face away. "Peace up to heaven," she murmured, as if reciting, "heaven down to earth, earth beneath heaven, strength in each . . ."

I shifted my grip on the knife. It burned like iron in January. "Damn you," I said, and each word was a blade in my mouth.

The Morrigan sighed, then pushed herself up to a sitting position. Her arms were thin as sticks, and her thin white shift revealed how skeletal the rest of her had become. "Take hold of my hair," she said as she turned away from me, and combed it back from her face with her fingers. "Don't let go."

I grasped the coil of her hair in one hand, as if I were going to put it up for her, as my own mother had done for me years and years ago. "I don't know how to do this."

She tilted her head back, exposing her throat. "Strike here," she said, touching the notch of her collarbone. "Once, from above."

I heaved a dry sob, raised the knife, and brought it down with the inevitability of gravity.

Blood splashed over my hand, burning hot, and the Morrigan blurred in my grip. Again my vision merged with hers, and I saw the *each uisce*'s pool, evaporating into a cloud of laughing steam; the sheela-na-gig, scarred and smiling as she sank into the wall; collars of Ogham around the necks of the vessels outside, blazing once and fading—and more, places and things I didn't recognize, set free. A dozen swans bursting from the surface of one of the fountains in the Public Garden, white wings scattering old soiled feathers; a tiny hummock of earth in the Fens collapsing in on itself; something slipping free under the water of the harbor and gliding out to sea.

I screamed, or she did, and the ground twitched in sympathy. Above, there would be broken pavement, shattered china, and arguments over whether it was seismic activity or just the water-saturated ground of the Fens settling. Below, there was only me and the Morrigan. The apparition I held blurred again, this time into dust, until I held nothing but the stained knife.

A roar echoed through the room, as if a whole hunting pack of hounds had been unleashed. I dropped to my knees, tasting saltwater as the scent of old blood and iron receded far away, further than I could ever hope to track.

My right arm burned, and I clutched at it. A thin sliver of stone, chain stone, birthed itself from the fresh cut in my forearm, smoke rising from it. The glow on my arms faded as it emerged, burning away into black flakes that drifted to the floor like the inverse of snow. The stone crumbled into sand, and with it the last echo of the Morrigan's voice in me died.

I hurled the knife away from me, covered my face, and cried until my lungs were as raw as my throat.

I don't know how long I huddled there in the dark. I didn't even notice when the door behind me opened and Nate entered. He didn't speak, only took me by the arm and helped me up.

We fumbled our way along the wall in the darkness, stepping over the bodies of Boru and Connor and Brendan. There were no vessels waiting now, and the only sign of them was the basin Finn had brought, now bone-dry and dusty.

The Fiana's path through Fenway was waning already as their power evaporated, rolling up behind us like a carpet. If we paused, the sound of the crowd seemed to catch up to us, growing as the magic faded. Nate's eyes were wide but weary; after what had happened, he had no room for miracles.

We passed through the marked wall just as the noise swelled around us, and as we emerged, the outside world resolved itself into full reality. And as in any fairy mound, time had gone more quickly outside. Sunlight had been traded for grainy neon, and the night was warm and muggy.

I shrugged off Nate's arm and leaned against the wall, taking in the rich smells of the park, hearing the crack of a bat and the answering cheer from thousands of fans, all here, all alive, all real.

Home.

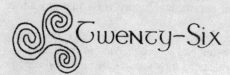

Twenty-Six

I had most of an Orange Line car to myself the next morning and was grateful for it. The marks on my neck hadn't faded; no matter how I tried to cover them, the bruises showed, and I'd eventually given up. I set my flowers down on the seat beside me and put my head in my hands as we pulled away from the station.

Nate had seen me home, or at least to my front door. I'd told him where Sarah and Katie were, but hadn't offered to go along for the reunion. He hadn't argued—whether because he saw how weary I was or because he wanted to get away from me, I didn't know. I told myself it didn't matter.

My office didn't appear to have been touched. Some papers might have been moved, or maybe I'd left them that way to begin with. Brendan's wards were gone with his death, the only trace of them a smudge of salt on the windowsill. I got a bucket of water from the kitchen and washed them away first thing.

I put the gun back in my desk drawer and locked it, then went around the apartment straightening pictures, picking up discarded coffee mugs and putting them down again on the next available surface.

A chunk of driftwood took up most of the top shelf of one bookcase, and I found myself running my fingers over the stones caught in it. I had been out on Revere Beach with a few friends when I found that. What I liked about it was that the wood had grown over the stones in a few places, so at least one of them had been there before the tree died. It was beautiful, but not magical in any sense that any adept would recognize.

I thought of the little sculpture at Brendan's apartment, the stones in wire that had served as one of the anchors for his warding magic. Funny how you can live in one place for years, with the same surroundings and same possessions, and then a few hours with someone can make it all different.

The whole place smelled of trapped air and dust, full of scents that I hadn't ever noticed before. I should have—even if I'd misunderstood what it told me, my nose had always told me the truth. But it was as if a picture had shifted into 3-D, as if a whole new dimension had been added to my sense of smell, and it worried me.

I collapsed onto the bed and stared at the ceiling until my eyes closed. By some unearned blessing, I had no dreams. Twice I woke up, each time thinking that someone was sitting in the chair by the window, but not even a shadow touched it.

Rena called while I was in the shower, then again as I was getting dressed. "You all right?" she asked before I could even say hello.

"Yeah. Mostly."

"You had me scared yesterday."

"*I* had me scared yesterday. It's over now. I don't think you want me to tell you any details."

"No." She drew a long breath, and over her silence I could hear the rumble of traffic. "No, I guess I don't."

"It's all okay now. I don't think anyone else is likely to turn up like Frank." If the vessels had been freed, then their bodies would have—well, if the original inhabitants had worn away as Brendan said, they'd have died. Or maybe they'd have come back to themselves, as I had after killing the Morrigan. If they had, the rest of the Brotherhood would have a fresh problem: a lot of malcontents who'd been let out of their own internal prisons. I didn't think we'd be seeing anything from the Brotherhood for a while, especially now that their center of power was dead, and if Sarah was right about the asocial nature of adepts, they'd fall apart quickly.

And Will? Well, I hadn't seen anyone outside my door this morning. I'd have to check on him, make sure the splintered *geis* hadn't done any permanent damage. If I could do it without him seeing me, so much the better.

Rena sighed. "The guy who killed Yacoubian? His boss?"

"Dead. Both of them."

"Good." She was silent again, and I could almost hear the question before she voiced it. "Did you kill them?"

I could say yes, I realized. I could tell her everything that had happened, even tell her about the Morrigan if I wanted, and she would just nod and let it pass. There wasn't any evidence, there wouldn't even be any bodies to ID. If it even made it into the paperwork it would be as a cold case. She'd let me off with a nod.

And one more Boston police officer would have let another killing go by. One more murder would be overlooked.

"No," I lied. I could take the stain of a lie on top of all the rest. "Internal problems, I gathered."

"Internal problems," she repeated. "Well. As long as it's over."

"It is."

We were both silent for a moment. "You free Saturday?"

"As long as you don't do the karaoke thing again."

"You're no fun, Evie. I'll see you, then."

I finished getting dressed and called Tania with the intent of negotiating myself back into her good graces. "Honey, didn't you get my call?" she said. "We had another schedule change. You're off till Monday afternoon."

"You're sure?"

"Positive. We just now got the system working properly, and I've got you down as having the next few days free."

I told her I'd be there Monday, hung up before she could change her mind, and went out to do what I had to.

I woke up with a start as the train pulled into Forest Hills. A gaggle of teenage girls had gotten on at some point; they glanced at me as I got up and gathered my flowers, then returned to their whispering.

I squinted as I got out into the sunlight. Even for midsummer, it seemed unnaturally bright. Or perhaps that was the result of too much time spent underground.

It's not too far a walk from the T station to Forest Hills Cemetery, but the cemetery itself is big enough that it can take a good twenty minutes to get where you want to go. I rearranged my grip on the flowers and set off across the grounds.

One funeral was just concluding, and a long line of cars made its way to the entrance as I passed. A couple of times when I'd come down here, I'd stopped at one of the funerals and listened; rarely any eulogies here, only a prayer and the final goodbyes. Though they aren't final, of course. Anyone who's come back to a grave knows that the goodbyes can go on for years.

Mom's headstone was off in a far corner, set apart from the huge family plots to either side. I brushed the dirt off; winter and a very muddy spring had left a thin film of detritus on most of the headstones. "Hi," I said. "Sorry I missed your birthday. I was a little busy."

I tugged the cellophane off the flowers and laid them at the bottom of the headstone, obscuring the dates. "I broke my promise, Mom. I wasn't careful. It all worked out, though; at least I think it did." The end of my nose prickled. "I owe you a lot. I didn't realize how much, but I know now. I owe you a lot."

Across the green lawns, one funeral procession stopped and another one started up. The flowers blurred, cleared, and blurred again.

I scented ink and age before I saw him, but didn't turn

around. Finn reached past me to put a single iris on Mom's headstone. "She was a good woman," he said. "I was proud to share her blood."

"She knew a lot," I said, and couldn't manage any more. For a moment neither of us spoke.

"I met her once." I glanced at him, and he read the suspicion before I'd even formed it. "Not as you think, foolish child. Your father's still your father." My cheeks flamed, and he continued. "But I did dream myself here once, before the usurpers caught me. I may not always remember my family, but I do like to know they are well, and I was well pleased with what I saw in her. I—" He paused, then chuckled. "I offered her a chance to learn my magic. She turned it down without a second thought. I never understood why."

"She never did anything without a reason," I said. "Even if it wasn't a reason other people would consider."

He nodded and was silent again. I scuffed one sneaker in the dirt. Finally Finn cleared his throat. "She is not the only one you mourn."

I flinched. "Why?" I managed. "She didn't have to— She didn't—"

"She did, cousin's child. I had not expected it of her, but she did what we could not. What is a victory for the Morrigan may not be a victory for her allies, and the reverse is true as well. She'd grown well aware of the chains of the Fiana and of her limitations. And she isn't quite gone, I'd imagine."

I wiped my nose again and gave him a wary look.

He continued to gaze at Mom's headstone. "I know death well, cousin's child. She exists, in some form or another, free from the raven stones and the usurper's grasp. You may see her again; after all, you carried her mark."

"I wish that were more consolation." I turned my arm over to show the thin white line that zigzagged over it.

"The Morrigan is no more gone than is Eileen Scelan—and, no, I'm not allowed to tell you about that."

He smiled, but there was a bitter quirk to the line of his

lips. I remembered that he had died too, that the Finn Mac Cool of the legends was as dead as Arthur, waiting for a time to return. This resurrection was incomplete, and would be so till he was called again. I had no envy for the gods then, and knew I never would again.

"I can't—" I said, and then stopped. "I can't seem to switch off my talent anymore. It's like it's always on, always scenting. I don't know whether it's what Brendan did or something else, but—"

"When blood wakes, it rarely goes back to sleep." He blew on his fingers as if to warm them, though we stood in full sunlight. "My hounds were the greatest in all of Eriu, and in many lands beyond. Adhnuall alone could run three times round Ireland without stopping, and he was not the greatest of them. My cousins were. I think there may be other talents in your blood that you will come to know, now that you are awake."

"That's not exactly comforting."

"It was not meant to be." He smiled. "There is a story of a land not far from mine, though it was bound to ours in many ways . . . I think the Morrigan may have told you some of it, of the White Raven queen and her brother."

"How did you know that?"

The smile turned wry. "Stories echo, cousin's child. Stories echo." He crouched and touched the flowers I'd brought. "There is a part to that story that she did not tell you, of when the raven queen's brother brought his armies to retrieve her, how his enemies burnt the bridge that they might not cross. So he laid himself down across the river so that his armies could cross over his body, for as he said, 'He who would be a leader must be a bridge.'"

"I don't want to be a leader."

"Maybe. You are a bridge, though."

I shook my head. "What about the—well, the man I'm speaking to now? And the other vessels?"

He stood. "Most of my kin have fled or sleep once more, and the bodies they spoke through begin to remember themselves. This man . . ." He held out his hands and turned them over, as if they were entirely new to him. "I . . . I think his name is Sam. He allowed me to stay, to say farewell to you. He says . . . he had a daughter, and would have liked to say goodbye, and gives me the courtesy he was denied."

"That's kind of him," I said, but my eyes prickled. A selfish part of me had wanted him to stay, tell me what to do, what I was becoming. But I couldn't ask him to stay. All of my supports seemed to have given way in the Fiana's wake.

"Cousin's child, be at ease. I have told you that no *geis* can hold you."

"Save the ones we place on ourselves," I murmured.

He shrugged. "Even those, should you claim them. Guilt is a *geis*, and it would chain you as surely as any other. Carry the deaths that the Morrigan asked of you—but do not make a chain of them." A gull flew overhead, crying mournfully, and he watched its flight. "You are always welcome in my halls, cousin's child. You should know that. Only get lost near the Hill of Allen, in County Kildare, and my doors will open to you."

"The Hill of Allen, in County Kildare," I repeated numbly.

"You may find me dreaming there." He reached out and turned my face to him. "I have spent time in the halls under the hills. I know what it is to stand between the gods and men, and what it is to be neither. I prefer being only man, and I know your ancestor did."

I closed my eyes and nodded. Couldn't argue with that, especially after all I'd done to stay human. "Take care, cousin."

"And you, cousin's child." He tapped the side of my face once, then turned and walked away.

I stayed where I was long enough for the shadows to change direction, thinking and remembering. The heat searing my shoulders told me that I'd suffer a sunburn for it, but at the moment that didn't matter.

My cell phone rang twice as I trudged back across the

cemetery: once from Will, once from Sarah. I let it ring, though I would eventually need to talk to both of them. I'd need to take care of a lot of things, not least the rumor control in the undercurrent; the last thing I wanted was to get a name for this sort of thing. Though I might enjoy the extra work; it would help me keep my mind off certain problems.

One problem, though, was waiting for me at the main gate. I cursed quietly, but it was too late to run. Nate looked up from his study of the cemetery rules, and his face lit up when he saw me.

"What are you doing here?" I said.

"Thought you might come here." He glanced over my shoulder. "My mom's buried here too."

I closed my mouth on my next retort. "I didn't know that," I said after a minute.

He shrugged. "No reason you should have." We were both silent a moment, neither of us looking directly at the other. "You all right?"

"Yeah. How's your hand?"

"Better. It looked worse than it was." *Which was bad enough*, I thought. "Katie asked about you. I told her you were fine."

I wasn't fine, and he knew it. His eyes met mine, and I looked away from what I saw there. "Evie, I've been thinking about a lot of things, about you and what happened, and I was wondering if—well, maybe it's better if I show you . . ."

Show me? I started to protest, but he was digging in his messenger bag, dislodging several notebooks and papers. I looked at his hands and ached. I wouldn't be seeing him again; the divide between undercurrent and real life was too deep, and I couldn't ask him to take any part of it . . .

Whatever he was looking for he couldn't quite find. "They're not much," he said, rifling through the bag again, "but I figured something might help you get your mind off, well, and anyway I had to sell my soul to get them . . ." I must have flinched, because he looked up, and the corners of his eyes crinkled in a smile. "Not like that. Not anything like that. No, I just promised one of the TAs I'd check his proofs and cat-sit for a month, and I just know if Katie gets even one week with a cat she'll want one for real." He yanked a slim envelope from a side pocket, looked at it, and smiled.

"Nate," I said, exasperated at last, "what are you talking about?"

He took two familiar pasteboard strips from the envelope. "Dinner and a Sox game?"

What the hell. Some things you just can't turn down.

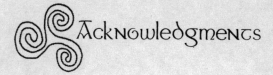

Acknowledgments

I'd like to be able to point to a particular moment and say that this is where *Spiral Hunt* started. But the book came from an awful lot of sources, and untangling them now is like trying to find where a knot begins. Professor Patrick K. Ford's class on Celtic Paganism provided a lot of material for my imagination, and if the tradition comes across as distorted, the fault lies in my approach and not in the source. A few of the Morrigan's lines are paraphrased from Elizabeth A. Gray's translation of *Cath Maige Tuired* (Irish Texts Society, 1982), which I first read in Ford's class.

Thanks to the faculty, staff, and students of the 2004 Viable Paradise workshop, particularly Jim Macdonald and Debra Doyle, who took the book apart and put it back together so that it worked. The Boston writers' group BRAWL critiqued a later draft and smoothed out all the new problems I'd introduced. Thanks also to Shana Cohen for taking a chance on representing my work, and to Kate Nintzel for her enthusiasm and meticulous editing.

This book wouldn't have even gotten started without the help of friends and family, among them Allegra Martin, who gave me the idea for a story that eventually mutated into Evie Scelan's first appearance. My parents, Jack and Connie Ronald, brought me up in a tradition of reading and telling stories, my sister Sally put up with me blathering

ACKNOWLEDGMENTS

about plot twists, and my twin, Emily, has been my harshest and best critic for as long as I've been writing.

And a world of thanks to Joshua Lawton, whose patience and unwavering support kept both book and author from coming undone.